The Albino's Secret

Also by Michael Moorcock

THE ELRIC SAGA

Elric of Melniboné, volume 1
  comprising—
  Elric of Melniboné
  The Fortress of the Pearl
  The Sailor on the Seas of Fire
  The Weird of the White Wolf

Stormbringer, volume 2
  comprising—
  The Vanishing Tower
  The Revenge of the Rose
  The Bane of the Black Sword
  Stormbringer

White Wolf, volume 3
  comprising—
  The Dreamthief's Daughter
  The Skrayling Tree
  The White Wolf's Son

The Citadel of Forgotten Myths

Von Bek: The Eternal Champion
  comprising—
  The Warhound and the World's Pain
  The City in the Autumn Stars

CORUM

Corum: The Prince in the Scarlet Robe
  comprising—
  The Knight of the Swords
  The Queen of the Swords
  The King of the Swords

Corum: The Prince with the Silver Hand
  comprising—
  The Bull and the Spear
  The Oak and the Ram
  The Sword and the Stallion

HAWKMOON

Hawkmoon: The History of the Runestaff
  comprising—
  The Jewel in the Skull
  The Mad God's Amulet
  The Sword of the Dawn
  The Runestaff

Hawkmoon: Count Brass
  comprising—
  Count Brass
  The Champion of Garathorm
  The Quest for Tanelorn

JERRY CORNELIUS

The Cornelius Quartet
  comprising—
  The Final Programme
  A Cure for Cancer
  The English Assassin
  The Condition of Muzak

Jerry Cornelius: His Lives and His Times (short-fiction collection)

A Cornelius Calendar
  comprising—
  The Adventures of Una Persson and Catherine Cornelius in the Twentieth Century
  The Entropy Tango
  The Great Rock 'n' Roll Swindle
  The Alchemist's Question
  Firing the Cathedral / Modem Times 2.0

The Eternal Champion
  comprising—
  The Eternal Champion
  Phoenix in Obsidian
  The Dragon in the Sword

The Dancers at the
End of Time
  comprising—
  An Alien Heat
  The Hollow Lands
  The End of all Songs

Kane of Old Mars
  comprising—
  Warriors of Mars
  Blades of Mars
  Barbarians of Mars

Moorcock's Multiverse
  comprising—
  The Sundered Worlds
  The Winds of Limbo
  The Shores of Death

The Nomad of Time
  comprising—
  The Warlord of the Air
  The Land Leviathan
  The Steel Tsar

Travelling to Utopia
  comprising—
  The Wrecks of Time
  The Ice Schooner
  The Black Corridor

The War Amongst the Angels
  comprising—
  Blood: A Southern Fantasy
  Fabulous Harbours
  The War Amongst the Angels

Tales from the End of Time
  comprising—
  Legends from the End of Time
  Constant Fire
  Elric at the End of Time

OTHER NOVELS
  Behold the Man
  Gloriana: or, The Unfulfill'd Queen
  Mother London

SHORT FICTION
My Experiences in the Third World War and Other Stories: The Best Short Fiction of Michael Moorcock, volume 1

The Brothel in Rosenstrasse and Other Stories: The Best Short Fiction of Michael Moorcock, volume 2

Breakfast in the Ruins and Other Stories: The Best Short Fiction of Michael Moorcock, volume 3

Also by Mark Hodder

BURTON & SWINBURNE NOVELS
  The Strange Affair of Spring Heeled Jack
  The Curious Case of the Clockwork Man
  Expedition to the Mountains of the Moon
  The Secret of Abdu El Yezdi
  The Return of the Discontinued Man
  The Rise of the Automated Aristocrats

OTHER NOVELS
  A Red Sun Also Rises
  The Silent Thunder Caper

NOVELS IN COLLABORATION WITH MICHAEL MOORCOCK
  Caribbean Crisis & Voodoo Island

The Albino's Secret

The Metatemporal Detectives

MICHAEL MOORCOCK
& MARK HODDER

First published in Great Britain in 2025 by Gollancz
an imprint of The Orion Publishing Group Ltd
Carmelite House, 50 Victoria Embankment
London EC4Y 0DZ

An Hachette UK Company

The authorised representative in the EEA is Hachette Ireland,
8 Castlecourt Centre, Castleknock Road, Castleknock, Dublin 15, D15 XTP3,
Republic of Ireland (email: info@hbgi.ie)

1 3 5 7 9 10 8 6 4 2

Copyright © Multiverse, Inc. and Mark Hodder 2025

The moral right of Michael Moorcock and Mark Hodder to be identified
as the authors of this work has been asserted in accordance with the
Copyright, Designs and Patents Act of 1988.

All rights reserved. No part of this publication may be reproduced,
stored in a retrieval system, or transmitted in any form or by any means,
electronic, mechanical, photocopying, recording, or otherwise, without
the prior permission of both the copyright owner and
the above publisher of this book.

All the characters in this book are fictitious, and any resemblance
to actual persons, living or dead, is purely coincidental.

A CIP catalogue record for this book is
available from the British Library.

ISBN (Hardback) 978 1 399 62744 3
ISBN (eBook) 978 1 339 62746 7
ISBN (Audio) 978 1 399 63513 4

Typeset by Input Data Services Ltd, Bridgwater, Somerset

Printed in Great Britain by Clays Ltd, Elcograf S.p.A

www.gollancz.co.uk

To the memory of Anthony Skene,
author of *Monsieur Zenith the Albino*
(London, Sampson Low, 1936)

CHAPTER 1
A Strangling Interrupted

The purpling sky of Istanbul made her crowded minarets and towers glow like enormous jewels. As the raw red orb of the sun spread its dwindling rays, the muezzins chanted the evening summons to prayer. Their musical clamour resonated across time-worn rooftops. Muslims streamed to their mosques, while Orthodox Christians departed their churches.

The last admonishing notes of the *ṣalāt al-maġrib* echoed into the distance, leaving behind a moment of seeming silence.

Several curious people noted a figure passing through the narrow lanes and shadowed alleyways. Tall and slim, the individual wore a smart black suit with a fedora angled low over the face.

They strode quickly and purposefully, with eyes fixed unswervingly ahead, for one could not afford to cast a sidelong glance when stalking the hulking yet slippery brute known as Suleyman the Strangler!

Tenaciously the follower stuck close to the killer, through the old neighbourhood, with its crooked and decrepit tenements leaning against each other as if exhausted by age. Were one to collapse, the others would fall like dominoes.

Stars salted the sky, but between the precarious dwellings the gloom only deepened. Candlelight and oil lamps provided illumination here and there, slanting from gaps in drawn blinds and closed shutters, briefly flickering as the hunted and the hunter went by.

Candlelight! This part of the city had been without a gas supply for nine days. Now the electricity had failed. Again, as so frequently happened, the infrastructure had faltered under the strain of hauling an ancient metropolis into the twentieth century.

Only the Strangler and his pursuer welcomed the darkness.

Intent, they pushed on through the Old Quarter. The follower, in thin rubber-soled shoes, found it hard going over the worn cobblestones but never fell behind, never lost sight of the lumbering creature as he skirted a manufacturing district where dyers and tanners proliferated, the air saturated with their rancid stench. Mint sellers offered sprigs to alleviate it. Suleyman and his shadow paid them no heed.

Nor did they notice, as they entered that busier zone of shops and residences, the half-veiled temptresses enticing them from murky doorways, the beggars wheedling for baksheesh, or the inebriated men shouting invitations to drink. They did not hear the distorted, cheap French jazz record jangling from an upper window, or the throbbing tom-toms that accompanied a zither in some hidden square nearby.

An old man kicked a whimpering dog and laughed. A woman sobbed hysterically. Something heavy dropped with a splintering crash. In the distance a cursing lad tried to start a stubborn motorcycle.

All this was ignored.

The pair progressed northward, stepping suddenly from foul air into pungent and delicious fragrances, as if a tangible border existed between the atmosphere of the tanneries and that of the spice market ahead.

The murmured prayers of those devout Muslims who remained in their mosques were barely detectible beneath the sounds of the yelling merchants and their customers.

Suleyman shoved through them all, like a silverback gorilla casually crashing through thick jungle. He came to the famous Galata Bridge. On the other side, the docks, offices, banks, agencies, embassies, and other buildings of mercantile Galata boasted power with their twinkling lights. Electricity there.

Also wicked, premeditated murder!

Passions and tempers ran high on this sultry and breathless April night. Arguing Turks and Armenians thronged the bridge; Greeks and Jews, Western Europeans and Arabs, exiles from a once-imperial Russia, even Chinese, all getting in each other's way, all unrestrained in their opinions of one another.

No one, however, dared to object as Suleyman elbowed them aside, especially when the power supply abruptly snapped back on in the Old Quarter, the lights lining the bridge blazing into incandescent life, revealing him in all his awful immensity.

Suleyman the Strangler was a solid mass of meat and bone, small-headed and slope-browed, with bristling black hair, beady eyes, and an apishly wide mouth. His legs were short, his shoulders vast, his arms thick, and the hands knotted, sinewy and lethal. He had once been a *pehlivan*—an oil wrestler—notorious for killing two opponents and breaking the bones of many others. Since then, less sporting forms of violence had added to his infamy.

He was a brute who plainly struggled to form a coherent

thought, but whose loyalty to his owner—of a certainty, he was more an owned beast than a free man—was absolute.

Who could command blind devotion from such a subhuman monster?

Some in Istanbul could answer the question in two words, whispered but never spoken, and only ever uttered where they could not possibly be overheard.

Suleyman's master was

The Red King!

For three years, from the very day Constantinople was reborn as Istanbul, the Red King, the mysterious master assassin, had terrorised the city. He and his gang were ruthless. His victims were many, his methods terrible and cruel, his motives a mystery. He confined himself to no single nationality, race, or religion. Most of his victims were men, but he had killed women, too, and even, once, a child.

Turks said he was a Latvian Jew. Others claimed him to be an Arabian sheikh and leader of a bandit tribe. In a British Secret Service file he was identified as a half Greek, half Kurd who had served with the *Okhrana*, the Guard Department—the Russian secret police—before the Petrograd uprising of 1917. Beneath this latter assertion, the word "Unconfirmed" was stamped, and under that, someone had scrawled, *Red King—red herring*.

In truth, the assassin was a mystery that, due to the unique nature of "the City of the World's Desire," spanned two continents.

But—

"If I have anything to do with it," the one who followed Suleyman vowed, "the Red King's henchman will commit no murder tonight!"

The silent pursuit continued.

At the end of the bridge, Suleyman swung left and ploughed

through a group of dockhands, upsetting their backgammon boards. With cigarettes between their calloused fingers and acrid smoke billowing from their mouths, they gesticulated furiously and cursed him for his bad manners . . . but only after he was well beyond them. They had quickly taken his dimensions into account.

He made his way toward Kasimpasa, one of the oldest residential districts, a sprawl of cheap, single-storey dwellings mostly occupied by sailors and harbour workers.

The crowds were soon left behind, and now that there were fewer people and more streetlamps, it might be noticed that Suleyman the Strangler, in addition to being hunted, was hunting.

His follower knew that some distance ahead, strode a Frenchman named Apollinaire de Villiers. He was a married gentleman of fifty-five who had allowed himself to be seduced by a woman two decades his junior. She called herself Mademoiselle Béatrice Lefevre. It was an alias, but had de Villiers known, he would not have cared. She was extraordinarily lovely, very charming, and so obviously wealthy that he had no qualms concerning her motives. She desired him, not his money.

Like Suleyman, Béatrice Lefevre was a member of the Red King gang.

Three, not two, then, were making their way to an assignment with death. The adulterer, the monster, and the slender figure in black.

They bypassed the commercial centre and ventured into the suburbs crammed onto Galata's slopes.

Suddenly, again, the power cut out, as if Suleyman's unholy presence somehow eclipsed all light.

From a house on the other side of the road, male voices raised an ironic cheer.

Someone yelled, *"Yaşasın Kemal ve beceriksiz hükümeti!"*

Long live Kemal and his incompetent government!

The Strangler did not pause. He lurched past a café, lit by a single candle, and filled with bearded men in greasy trilbies, peaked caps, and turbans. They were smoking flavoured tobacco from hookahs, and drinking minted teas and sugar-laden, sludge-bottomed coffee. And, in jabbering clamour, they enthusiastically heaped insults upon the president's decade-old republic, with its tidal wave of reforms and modernisations, and its absolute inability to keep the gas or electricity flowing. Yesterday, they had praised him. Now, they cursed him. Tomorrow, they would erect statues to celebrate him.

The streets grew narrower, quieter, darker still.

The black-suited pursuer saw, for the first time, de Villiers, far ahead, passing through the glow of an abandoned food vendor's brazier, its owner doubtless in a nearby bar. The Frenchman strode on with confidence. He obviously knew the area and did not fear for his safety, sure that he could talk, or, if necessary, bribe his way out of any potential difficulty.

More cautious now, Suleyman, some fifty yards behind, crossed the road and slipped from doorway to doorway, gradually closing the distance.

To the rear, and doing the same, came the follower.

One after the other, they reached a wide alley sloping up in long, shallow, cobbled steps. A brief spring shower earlier in the day had left the ground puddled with fresh rainwater. The acrid odour of vinegar from a hundred-year-old pickling shop cut the muggy air. Scavenger dogs yipped around piled garbage, slinking away as the three approached. From the Golden Horn came the mournful bawl of a departing ship.

De Villiers disappeared.

The last of the trio drew a snub-nosed S&W .38 police special.

The Frenchman had turned into a narrow passage, expecting to find a door at the end of it; the entrance to an apartment, in which he imagined Béatrice Lefevre waited in an enticing state of *déshabillé*. She would claim, no doubt, that it was to accommodate the night's warmth.

De Villiers had considered it an unlikely district in which to arrange an illicit assignation, but she had quickly persuaded him of the advantages. This would be the last place her husband suspected, should he wonder where she was. Moreover, property here was cheap. She was able to rent the little "bolt-hole" without Monsieur Lefevre noticing the expense.

That, at least, is what she had told her lover.

However, as he now discovered, his petite Béatrice was not in the apartment. There was no apartment. The passage was a cul-de-sac.

"Mon Dieu! Ai-je fait une erreur? N'est-ce pas la bonne adresse?" he muttered.

He turned.

Thick fingers clamped around his neck.

Suddenly, he could not breathe. A mountainous form loomed over him. He pulled desperately at meaty wrists. They were as immovable as rock. He was lifted off his feet, the strain on his neck agonising. His ears rang. His last breath squeaked with dissonant terror.

A husky command rang out. "Put him down, Suleyman, or I'll shoot you through the head!"

The giant wheeled, swinging de Villiers. The Frenchman's vertebrae crunched, almost breaking.

The Strangler snarled like a dog. "Huh?"

"Don't pretend to be dumber than you are. I know you understand English. Drop him and put up your hands. I shall count to three; then I'll shoot."

Through blurring eyes, de Villiers saw a tall, slim figure outlined in the mouth of the passageway.

"One!"

The Red King's man grunted and barked, "Suleyman!"

"I know who you are, stupid! Two!"

"I kill."

"Trust me," said the other, "I'll kill you first. Three!" A moment of stillness and silence, then, "I warned you!"

Crack!

A shot echoed down the passage.

De Villiers, abruptly released, crumpled to his knees. He sucked air desperately through his bruised windpipe.

"Put 'em up, Suleyman! Now!"

The Frenchman scrambled frantically across the ground toward his saviour.

"Get out of here," the shooter snapped at him. "Run! And don't see the Lefevre woman again. This was her doing, you dupe!"

De Villiers pushed himself up, slipped past his rescuer, and took to his heels. He left the passage, raced across the cobbled street, plunged into another black opening on the opposite side, and became nothing more than fading footsteps.

"Your attention, Suleyman! I just took off your right ear. That's how good a shot I am. You're now going to tell me the name of your master, and if you refuse, I'm going to put bullets through your hands, so you can never use them again. Understood? So, tell me: Who is the Red King?"

The beast took one shuffling pace forward, keeping his hands raised.

"Red King," he rumbled, "is Red King."

"Enough of that! Stay still!"

Suleyman growled deep in his throat. He advanced another half step and said, "Mr. Milk."

"I won't tell you again! Stay still. One more move and you'll lose fingers."

The brute grinned, his slablike teeth white in the darkness.

He took another step.

A flash, a report, and he howled as his left middle finger disappeared. He clutched at the wounded hand.

"Raise them!" the shooter commanded, voice pitched higher. "If you hold them like that, my next shot will go right through them and into your heart. *Levez les mains, vite!*"

With gore flowing and spattering onto the ground, Suleyman complied.

"Mr. Milk?" demanded the figure in black. "You say the Red King's name is Mr. Milk?"

"No," the killer rasped, "you work for Mr. Milk."

"I do not. I have never heard of him."

"Then—who sent you?"

"It is me interrogating you, my friend, not the other way around. I want everything you know about the Red King. And while you're at it, you can tell me about your Milk man, too."

"Huh!" Suleyman swayed and moaned in pain.

Gesturing with the pistol, the other said, "You had better start—"

The ex-wrestler pounced.

For such a big man, he was shockingly light on his feet. That great bulk moved as rapidly as a cobra. One second, he was standing unsteadily, the next, he had flung himself forward and barrelled into his opponent like an avalanche.

They careened out into the cobbled street. The gun went clattering away. Powerful fingers reached for a slender throat, but the blood made them slippery and the intended victim twisted, ducked, and jumped clear, losing the fedora in doing so.

Dark, bobbed hair flopped free of confinement.

"What?" Suleyman exclaimed. "A woman?"

It was no ordinary woman.

She slammed her fist into the side of his jaw. It hit with a resounding *clack*! His head snapped to one side, spittle spraying from his mouth.

Striking Suleyman, however, was akin to striking granite, particularly when his head was the target.

By the time she had regained her balance, his hands were again around her neck.

Now she was helpless.

Her fists thudded over and over into his ribs, her boots smashed against his shins, her knee went into his groin, but he was inexorable, and in a matter of moments, the strength drained out of her.

And he squeezed . . . and squeezed . . .

CHAPTER 2

An Old Friend Encountered

A dense cloud of steam billowed from the *Orient Express* as it squealed and hissed to a halt in Stamboul's busy railway terminus. Departing Paris three days ago, it had travelled through Munich and Vienna, Budapest and Bucharest, and was due in Turkey's ancient capital at eleven thirty that April morning.

The doors banged open. Weary and grim-faced passengers disembarked, glancing irritably at the station clock.

It showed a few minutes past nine in the evening.

The delay had occurred in Munich. A little over a week ago, the recently elected National Socialist German Workers' Party had dramatically purged Jewish and Leftist workers from the German Civil Service. Many bureaucratic duties, including the checking of travel documents, were now assigned to semiliterate *Sturmabteilung*. These brusque and aggressive Brownshirts offered no apology for the time taken to examine and stamp the passengers' papers. They simply returned them, with contemptuous disregard, by flinging them onto the floor of the guard's van. Then, while responding to indignant objections by drawing their pistols, they dragged a man, a woman, and a wailing child from the train before grudgingly permitting it to leave.

Now, nearly ten hours behind schedule, the metatemporal detective, Sir Seaton Begg, and his friend, Doctor "Taffy" Sinclair, stepped down from their carriage to the crowded platform. Begg was tall, rangy in build, with hawkish features and glittering blue-grey eyes. Sinclair was big, bluff, and balding.

They handed heavy suitcases to the most insistent porters. Begg gave brief instructions in Turkish.

"Phew! Poli at last!" Sinclair raised his voice above the station's hubbub.

"Istanbul in this period, old man!" Begg almost shouted. "Though, you are not alone in sticking to 'Constantinople.' *Alti Ok* is shaking everything up, and about time, too, but I daresay it will take a few years for everyone to adjust."

"Who?" the Welshman responded. "Isn't Kemal the president?"

"He is. *Alti Ok* is a what, not a who. The Six Arrows of new Turkey! You've seen them on the flag, surely? Republicanism, populism, nationalism—oof!" A badly manoeuvred suitcase had caught him in the ribs. "—laicism, statism, and reformism," he finished as the offending porter mumbled an apology and was swallowed into the hustle and bustle.

"It's a little hedonism I'm after just now, Begg," Sinclair yelled. "A generous supper, a long bath, and a comfortable bed!"

Begg chuckled. "*Üc Ok*, the Three Arrows of Contentment."

Jostled and elbowed from all sides, refusing the touts and followed by their porters, they pushed their way through to the customs office. There, they waited for their luggage and papers to be scrutinised before exiting into a heaving mass of carriage drivers, hollering street urchins, whining mendicants, and smart dragomans with the names of various hotels on their caps.

They crossed to where an old-fashioned horse-drawn hansom waited. The porters heaved their cases up onto the roof, and accepted a generous tip. The duo clambered aboard, settled onto the worn seats, and sighed, finally feeling the relief of arrival. With their next breath, they drew in the magical romance of a city that had been, for centuries, the exotic setting for mysterious cloak-and-dagger intrigue, a part of the Great Game between empires. Though the world surged forcefully around it, Byzantium persisted, under new names and in various forms, a gateway between the continents, and—though few were aware of it—between the infinite planes of the multiverse.

"Here we are," Begg declared, and rubbed his hands together.

With a despondent snort, the cab's sleepy old horse gathered herself and set off at a lackadaisical trot, inserting the vehicle into a gap in the traffic.

The sun had set. The dense, humid evening air blurred the lights, which glowed amber and saffron from cafés and shops, bars and residential buildings. Neither Begg nor Sinclair were aware that those lights had only recently returned after the most recent of the frequent power failures.

They passed down streets thronged with people and vehicles, then crossed the Galata Bridge. *Not a single tarboosh in sight,* observed Begg as the hansom turned onto a northward-bound road flanking the docks. That style of hat, a symbol of the Ottoman Empire, was now banned. Its absence, he thought, dramatically altered the appearance of the ancient city. He had been in Constantinople when Mustafa Kemal Pasha made Turkey a republic. He had seen for himself the shock of rapid modernisation, the bewilderment of a population forcibly yanked from a fantasy of the past into the reality of the present. As difficult as it may be, it was, in his opinion, all for the good. Time cannot be halted, and only adaptation and progress can enable the human species to safely navigate its vicissitudes and opportunities. Stasis can only lead to stagnation and—

Bang!

A violent halt! The squealing horse reared back in the hansom's struts. The two passengers, thrown forward then backward, banged their heads against the cabin's rear board.

"Great heavens!" Sinclair cried out.

Begg knocked on the little roof hatch. "I say! Driver! Was that a gunshot?"

No response. The detective slid the hatch open and peered up. No driver!

"Trouble?" asked Sinclair.

"Possibly."

Sliding down the window glass and reaching cautiously out and up, Begg groped for their cases, dragged them down and inside, and passed them to his companion. Sinclair unlocked one and took from it a couple of faux-Dresden figurines. He threw them to the floor and stamped on them. What he had told the customs officers were presents for Begg's housekeeper, Mrs. Curry, shattered, revealing a pair of serviceable short-barrelled revolvers.

Begg pointed ahead to where a tram had just slid to a stop.

"Our next ride," he said. "Keep your weapon concealed, use your suitcase as a shield, and don't dawdle."

He opened the cab door. They jumped down and—after Begg had briefly looked back at the hansom—crouched low and hurried to the half-full tram. Its passengers, all talking excitedly and gesticulating toward a group at the dockside, ignored them as they came aboard and found seats.

Begg scrutinised the street and saw every kind of man-drawn, donkey-drawn, horse-drawn, and motorised carriage, but none that appeared to be making a getaway.

"We were shot at," he murmured to Sinclair as the tram creaked into motion. "The bullet hit the front corner of the hansom. I suppose it put the wind up the driver, and he made off."

"Shot at from the docks?" queried Sinclair, indicating their fellow passengers. "Is that why they are so excited?"

Begg listened for a moment. "Ah! Someone got pushed into the water and was swept away."

"The gunman, I hope. Did he recognise us on the train and follow us from the station? Surely, our cover isn't blown already?"

"I saw nothing to suggest it." Begg fingered his chin. "But I can't imagine why anyone would want to shoot at a couple of visiting engineers, which, ostensibly, is what we are." He shrugged. "Well, whoever it was and whatever their motive, I suppose they did us a favour. Now we know to be more careful."

The tram clanked, groaned, and increased speed. Galata, with its famous tower and dirigible mast, humped up tier upon tier to the right, a dark mound sprinkled with sparkling points of illumination. As the tram clattered on, all those lights vanished, blocked by dock-facing warehouses. On the left, the Golden Horn reflected the spires and domes of the ancient city, giving the impression that, just beneath its rippling surface, the ghost of glorious Byzantium lurked.

Four times the tram stopped to allow people off and on, then it swung inland and rattled into the Kasimpasa quarter, beyond which it would steer right to ascend the hill into Pera.

Sinclair yawned. "How far to go? I'm growing a little weary, I must say."

"Buck up, Taffy, old man. Haven't you aways expressed a liking for the early years of the twentieth century? If I recall correctly, the Pera Palas Hotel is at her peak and just six stops farther on."

A moment later, as the tram emitted a sigh and ground to a halt, he added, "We may have to foot it." He nodded toward the conductor, who was repeatedly pressing the starter button on the small control panel. "Looks like a power cut. They aren't uncommon in this time and place."

The conductor turned miserably to address his passengers in French.

"Mesdames and messieurs, I apologise. The electricity has failed and we cannot continue. If you have far to go, you may want to wait until the repairmen resolve the problem. I cannot tell you when that will be. Not too long, I hope. Otherwise, it might be better to walk." He gave an exaggerated shrug. *"Je suis désolé."*

Begg turned to his friend. "It's shank's pony for us."

"Humph!" As they disembarked, Sinclair patted his pocket to be sure of his pistol, then tested the weight of his suitcase. "Those Munich Brownshirts must have shoved a few bricks into my bag. I'm positive it wasn't this heavy when I packed it. Perhaps we should have taken the R103 after all."

"Airships have weight restrictions," Begg observed. He eyed Sinclair's waistline.

They crossed the street, walked to a junction, and turned right.

"We'll cut through the residential district," the detective said. "It's not the most agreeable of areas, but if we were to follow the tramline it would take three times as long."

They started up the gently sloping road and exchanged no

words for the next ten minutes or so. Both were bone-tired and eager for the comforts of the hotel.

What few cafés they had passed were now far behind them. There was very little light. They picked their way carefully past puddles, tried—not always successfully—to avoid tripping on the widely spaced shallow steps, and occasionally swapped their suitcases from one hand to the other.

"Aren't there urchins one can hire for lugging one's bags?" grumbled Sinclair.

A gunshot echoed from a neighbouring street.

They stopped and exchanged a glance.

"Perhaps we have stepped into a war," said Sinclair. "There have been two shots since our arrival."

Begg, who had made a study of pistol and rifle acoustics, said, "It wasn't military. Police? It was certainly a revolver. Standard issue, I'm pretty certain. Great heavens! It could have been one of our own!"

Sinclair checked his pocket. "But I haven't lost my—" Then he realised what Begg meant. "A British Temporal Service agent?"

Abruptly someone burst from a side alley and cannoned straight into them, sending the pathologist to his knees. Begg grabbed the newcomer by the elbow, stopping him dead.

"What is it? What has happened?"

"The Strangler!" the man cried out in French-accented English. "Let me go! He tried to kill me! I have to get away!"

"You shot him?"

"No!" The man pulled his arm free. "But, of course not." He pointed into the side alley. "It was the other."

"There's someone else? Where are—?"

Another report cracked. The same gun.

The Frenchman yelped, jumped clear, and continued his wild flight down the hill.

"Come on, Taffy," Begg snapped. "Someone's in trouble."

They set off at a run along the narrow alleyway, barely able to see, guided only by the very dim outline of the opening at the other end. This gave onto another street, rising parallel to the one they had already traversed. It was empty. They dashed across it into another alley.

Then they were out, almost colliding with a bullet-headed mountain of muscle in whose throttling grip hung a dark-haired woman, her face blue in the starlight.

Begg reacted without thought. Not stopping to draw his gun, he swung his heavy suitcase, all his momentum behind it, and thudded it into the assailant's head.

The man rocked to the left—straight into Sinclair's case, which was coming at him from that direction.

The double impact struck with such force that the vicious grip at once fell away from the woman's neck. She folded to the cobbles.

Begg, still in motion, assessed the man's immense proportions, dug in his heels, and swept his case back up in a near vertical line, slamming it to the point of the other's chin.

The brute's head jerked backward with a horrible clack. He keeled over, but was immediately on his feet again. His dark, demonic face turned to Begg, teeth exposed in an animalistic snarl, but when he saw the detective drawing a pistol, he gave a bellow, launched himself into the darkness, and was gone, down the hill and out of sight.

"Taffy?" asked Begg, indicating the fallen woman.

Sinclair squatted beside her, and feeling for a pulse, noticed a small tattoo on her inner left wrist. "A red rose, Begg! She belongs to the Sisterhood of Solitude."

"Ah, not an agent of the Temporal Service, then," the detective responded. "Much more!"

A mysterious monastic community, the Sisterhood of Solitude was dedicated to contemplation of the eternally unfolding patterns of the multiverse, and occasionally interceded where and whenever an imbalance occurred. Such engagements, being rare, were always significant.

Begg crouched, placed his hand on the woman's head, and turned it to reveal the face.

"Good Lord! It's our old friend and foe, Violet Damm!"

Sinclair gave a grunt of surprise. "She, of all people, has taken the vows?"

"It appears so. How is she?"

"Bruised around the throat, but I think she'll be all right. I wonder what she's doing in Istanbul? If the Sisterhood—"

"Quite so, old fellow," said Begg. "We may be in deeper waters than anticipated."

He slid his right arm beneath the unconscious woman's shoulders, the left under her knees, and tall as she was, hoisted her up as if she were a child.

"Fetch the suitcases, please, Taffy. Let's get her to the hotel."

It took them twenty minutes to navigate out of Kasimpasa, into Pera, and to the Pera Palas Hotel.

Halfway there, the electricity supply returned.

Violet Damm regained her wits just as the lights of the big hotel came into sight.

"Oh, hello!" she exclaimed, in a voice that more resembled a croak. "How marvellous!"

Begg set her down. She leaned on his arm and allowed him to assist her the rest of the way, through the hotel's grand entrance, and into its lounge.

Begg left her with Sinclair and went to the reception desk. He and his friend had booked in advance. He asked for an additional room. No doubt Miss Damm had lodgings somewhere in Istanbul, but tonight she would stay here.

Then he returned to the magnificent lounge.

Palatially Franco-Moorish, awash with blazing tile and glass, plush and gold, the magnificent hotel had housed kings and queens, millionaires and exiled despots, diplomats and arms dealers. Now, three British agents had been added to its guest list.

His companions were at a corner table. Partially concealed behind a large potted palm, Damm sat with her back to the chamber.

"I take it you would rather not be seen, Miss Damm," the detective said with a smile as he joined them. "Are you on the run?"

With a white cravat and what little makeup she carried in her jacket pocket, she had expertly concealed all signs of her close encounter with the afterlife. Her chestnut hair, previously in disarray, was now restored into a tidy pageboy bob. Even in male attire, she looked wonderfully attractive, if a little wide at the shoulder and slim at the hip.

"Now, now, Sir Seaton, you know very well I've been on the straight and narrow these past few years." Her voice was so seriously hoarse, she sounded like a hard-smoking man. She had ordered brandy and soda, and now emptied her glass with a single gulp.

He reached forward and tapped the tattoo on her wrist. "And this?"

She grinned, revealing the wide gap between her upper front teeth. "The Sisterhood offers thrills aplenty, and such wonderful period fashions."

"Reformed, hey?"

"For the time being. What on earth are you two doing here, aside from saving my life?"

"We were summoned by Six A," Begg responded.

Six A: the head of the Secret Service, Turkish Bureau.

"Ah," she said. "Sir Vivian Clarke. My boss."

Begg raised an eyebrow. "Boss? You've been posted here?"

"Yes, in the guise of a temporal agent, for the past eighteen months." She pushed her fingers through her hair. "Sir Seaton, of the Sisterhood's involvement, I can tell you nothing. Certain events must—for you—unfold in their proper order, else a dangerous anachronism affecting multiple realms and chronologies will proliferate beyond any hope of correction."

Begg frowned, discomforted by the revelation that he was unknowingly involved in a matter of such enormous import.

"What *can* you tell me?" he asked, unable to conceal his impatience.

Violet Damm lowered her hand and placed it over his in a show of sympathy. "Only that, dear friend, for now, you should focus solely on affairs here in Istanbul. Sir Vivian will commission you to locate a certain person."

"Who?"

She tapped a thumb to her chest. "Me."

After a pause, Begg said, "You?"

"He gave me a similar assignment. I was to find somebody. I didn't succeed—but my quarry found me." She put a hand to her throat and grimaced, obviously in considerable discomfort. Her voice was fast becoming a gravelly whisper. "They spoke with me for some considerable time. In consequence, I reported my mission a failure. I also vowed to take no further orders from Sir Vivian."

The detective's eyebrows rose. "Now you have me thoroughly intrigued, and I would very much like to know more, particularly why you were tonight attacked by what appeared to be a gorilla." He stood and offered his hand. "But I can see that you're all done in, and I doubt you feel like conversation after the throttling you've received. Why don't we reconvene in the morning? We can then go through it properly. I've sorted a room out for you. Will you join us for breakfast, at eight o'clock, say?"

She nodded gratefully, took his hand, and allowed him to assist her to her feet.

They made their way to the elevators, Begg and Doctor Sinclair instinctively keeping Damm between them, sheltering her from any inquisitive gaze.

"Thank you again," she rasped when they reached the door to her room. "I'll see you tomorrow."

"Sleep well, Miss Damm," said Begg.

Of course, in the morning, she was gone.

CHAPTER 3
Two Missing Agents

Gelecek Engineering, the Turkish branch of the well-known Scottish company Reliable Futures Ltd., was located on the northwestern fringe of Istanbul. If crossing the Bosphorus took one from Europe to Asia, then travelling from the old city to the industrial complex took one quite literally from past into future.

This future was ugly!

A seemingly chaotic conglomeration of chimney stacks, vats, gantries, girders, office blocks, storage bays, workshops, furnaces, cranes, rails, pipes, and factories, it roared, glared heat, belched smoke, and resembled Hell.

Yet here were the materials and components currently building, beating, and bending the twentieth century into its ever-evolving form. The cogs, wheels, bands, and hammers made President Mustafa Kemal's vision for Turkey a reality.

Conducting the incessant cacophony with unfathomable but consummate skill, were the maestro-engineers to whose ranks Sir Seaton Begg and Doctor I. J. Sinclair were about to be welcomed.

Above the dirty fumes, the morning was clear and bright.

Below them, it was dark and sweltering. Sheened with gritty sweat, the two metatemporal agents entered the office of George Philips, director of Gelecek, to be greeted with unqualified enthusiasm.

"My dear Sir Seaton!" Philips gushed. "How utterly splendid to see you! My goodness, how long has it been? Seven years since that dreadful extortion case, I think? By the Lord Harry!" He stepped back to look at them. "I shall thank you again. If you hadn't got me out of that awful pickle, my reputation would be—" He lunged forward and gripped Begg's hand.

The detective smiled, extracted himself before Philips pumped his arm from his shoulder, and raised his palm in a pacifying gesture.

"Please, let's not have any of that. I'm no more inclined to dwell on my successes than on my failures. May I introduce Doctor Sinclair? He will be assisting me in this matter."

"Hello and welcome, Doctor. Please, come sit."

Philips ushered them to comfortable chairs.

"You look very well, Philips, I must say," Begg declared. "Turkey suits you?"

"Oh, tremendously!" The director offered cigars, cigarettes, and coffee, and as the social lubricants were prepared, told them how he had overseen many of the country's most ambitious construction projects.

"Railways. Bridges. Tunnels. Sewage systems. The list is endless. What a fantastic challenge Kemalism has given us. Why, I've never been busier. Nor happier. I've always admired Johnny Turk. Tough as they come, and now, with a vision. And what a vision, Sir Seaton!"

In his mid-forties, Philips had a long, droll, wide-eyed, and horsey face, ugly but not without charm. At rest, his features took on a mournful aspect, quite at odds with his ebullient character. However, as he described his company's various endeavours, his face became ever more animated, and he infected them both with his joyful pride in his job. His enthusiasm was enormous. Begg and Sinclair hung on to his words, celebrating with him.

"And the task you've assigned to us?" the metatemporal detective eventually asked, steering the conversation naturally to the reason for their presence. "Will it be a genuine contribution?"

"Why, yes, it certainly can be," Philips responded. "If it doesn't inconvenience you. I know you possess all manner of remarkable skills. How about assessing a bridge for metal fatigue?"

Begg drew on his cigar and nodded. "Yes, I have the requisite knowledge. I would rather we performed a real job. It makes for a more convincing cover."

"Quite so," Philips agreed. "Excuse me one moment."

He stood, crossed to the door, leaned out, and said to his secretary, "Miss Reid, please ask Mr. Voskanyan to bring the paperwork for the Galata Bridge survey, would you?"

He returned to his chair. "You are aware that the Galata is a pontoon bridge?"

Begg confirmed with a nod.

"It was never designed for the density of traffic that now crosses it, and with boats and small ships mooring against it, I fear the tides are causing considerable torque, straining the pivot points. I want you to examine them."

"Very well. We'll go over every inch," said Begg.

Philips smiled. "No need to turn it into full-time employment. You obviously have more important things to do. Just be there when you feel you need to be, and if you happen across anything of concern, let me know."

There came a knock, the door opened, and a slim, black-eyed man entered, his face bony and full of shadows.

"This is Mr. Vazken Voskanyan," said Philips as his guests rose for the introduction. Begg recognised the name as Armenian. "He is the Turkish government representative charged with monitoring the activities of foreign companies in the city. Mr. Voskanyan, may I introduce Mr. Septimus Blane—" Philips nodded first toward Begg then at Sinclair. "—and Mr. Edward Coulter? They are the new engineers sent over from our British headquarters."

"Call me 'Topper.' Everyone does," Sinclair murmured, barely suppressing his amusement. The pseudonyms had been his idea. They were taken from the fictionalised accounts of Begg's many cases, which were published each week in the Wayflete Publications story papers *Red, White, and Blue* and *The Septimus Blane Library*.

Voskanyan gave a sharp bow and click of the heels. "I am most pleased to meet you."

His English was good but heavily accented.

He handed an envelope to Philips. "You requested these, Mr. Philips?"

"Ah, thank you. The authorisations and permits. Are they in order?"

The Armenian inclined his head. "They are, and I have put my signature to them." He turned to Begg. "I will need to make a note of where you are staying."

"We are at the Pera Palas Hotel," said Begg.

"Ah, good. You will be comfortable there."

Voskanyan offered another polite bow, said, "If there is nothing else?" and departed.

"He's a little stiff in manner," said Philips, "but he doesn't much bother us, which is a great virtue for a man in his position. I have found, to my cost, that government officials are more often pompous and obstructive."

After the director had outlined their task in a little more detail and given directions to the office from which they could pick up safety harnesses and other items of equipment, the conversation turned to news from home. He was eager to hear Begg's opinions and insights, especially concerning the alarming developments in Germany. Once his curiosity was satisfied, the meeting ended.

They took their leave, two new additions to the great fraternity of foreign engineers labouring for the Republic of Turkey.

With their cover story properly established, they travelled by motor cab back to the hotel and enjoyed an early lunch.

"Time now," commented Begg when they had refreshed themselves and changed clothes, "to discover exactly why we are summoned."

The British embassy was five minutes' walk away, on the same broad, palm-fringed avenue as the Pera Palas. They entered it, approached the desk clerk, muttered a few words, showed a certain document, and were given two small keys. After passing through a door marked STAFF ONLY, they descended to the basement. Begg located a steel door, unlocked it, and led the way into a tunnel. It took them under six neighbouring buildings and ended at an identical door. He employed the second key. They stepped into another basement.

A man levelled a pistol at them, and said, "Byzantium endures."

"As Augusta Antonina," Begg replied. "As Nova Roma. As Constantinople. As Istanbul."

"And what do you amount to?"

"Eleven," said Begg.

"Twelve," said Sinclair.

The man smiled and lowered his gun. "Phew! It's been a while since anyone came through that door. You made me jump out of my skin. Welcome, Number Eleven, Number Twelve. Who are you here to see?"

"Six A," said Begg.

"He's on the second floor."

Begg nodded. "Much obliged."

He and Sinclair crossed to the foot of a stairwell and went up.

When they reached Sir Vivian Clarke's office, the detective rapped on its ornate wooden door. A muffled voice called, "Come!"

They entered a large, luxuriously furnished chamber, high-ceilinged and reminiscent of the rooms found in London's most exclusive clubs. Well-filled bookshelves covered the wall to their left. Begg perceived among them a cleverly fitted section that was undoubtedly a door to an adjacent apartment. Filing cabinets stood against the opposite wall, together with a radio apparatus and a big leather sofa, above which was hung a framed map of Central Europe. A heavy desk, positioned in the middle of the room, faced the door. Beyond it, two tall, narrow windows let in plenty of light. Overhead, a spinning fan stirred the clammy air.

A man stepped around the desk, hand extended.

"Sir Seaton, Doctor Sinclair, good to see you. I understand you were held up in Munich?"

"We were," said Begg, accepting the handshake. "I should have planned for it. The German authorities regard everyone with suspicion these days. They employ ignorant thugs who appear to be obsessively concerned with one's racial origins above all else."

The section head uttered a disapproving snort. "You were questioned?"

The detective gestured an affirmative. "But only perfunctorily. Real spies come and go as they please, it seems, yet a perfectly innocent travelling tailor along with a nanny and her ward were dragged weeping and terrified off the train. Why? Because they practiced a particular branch of our universal Judaic religion, or voted in a certain way, or were a shade darker than I. By heaven, I fear the worst for Germany."

"We all do. Please sit, make yourselves comfortable."

Begg and Sinclair settled into seats facing the desk, while their host took up his customary position behind it.

Sir Vivian Clarke was of medium build, but with hands and feet disproportionately large for his size. He had grey-flecked black hair, unfashionably parted in the middle, and a long, very asymmetrical face, his green eyes set on a slant in one direction while his thin-lipped mouth skewed in the other. His nose was big, bony, and bent. His teeth, being false, were perfect.

He pushed a box of cigarettes toward Sinclair, then took up a Peterson and a pouch of M&E tobacco, offering the latter to Begg. The detective politely declined with an "If I may," and slipped from his jacket pocket one of the four expensive Cuban cigars George Philips had thrust upon him as a parting gift.

Clarke set about tamping down tobacco. "I know you prefer to operate independently, Begg, and the Service doesn't often call you to duty like this, but your talent for getting to the bottom of matters is much needed. This is one of those occasions wherein an experienced metatemporal investigator is more suited to the job than an espionage agent."

The room began to fill with an aromatic fog of mixed tobacco fumes.

"I'm happy to place myself at your disposal, Sir Vivian. What is the nature of the problem?"

Clarke grimaced. "As to the exact nature of it, that's rather difficult to say. London headquarters instructed me to avail myself of your talents, but the directors are being very cagey about the whole affair."

He opened a drawer and pulled out a file, which he slid over to Begg. "It concerns this man, one of our most talented operatives. A career chap destined for a top position in the Service, I should say ... providing, that is, that he hasn't gone double."

Begg raised an eyebrow. "You think he might have?"

"I would be uncommonly surprised, but the possibility can't be discounted. It rather depends on what he's got and who wants it."

"What he's got?"

Clarke jabbed his pipe stem toward the file. "Cast your eyes over that first. It's the latest from London. There's not much to it, but sufficient that I'm reluctant to stamp it."

The detective picked up the file. Its card cover bore the words TOP SECRET. It was a convention that Begg had often, with good humour, derided. If an enemy ever infiltrated the Secret Service, he needed only to search for those words to find all the juiciest information. It would, Begg thought, have been far wiser to mark such documents with OFFICE STATIONERY REQUIREMENTS 1932/33.

"Stamp it with what?"

Clarke sucked at his crackling pipe, sending a spark into the air, then said, "Defected."

Begg opened the file and found two sheets of typewritten foolscap within.

```
JOHN NYE
    Born: 25 December 1890 (see note 1)
    Current age: 43 (see note 1)
    Family: REDACTED and son, Leonard, born 30 July
1913. (but see: Captain Nye. Ref: M77645329)
    Active service commenced: 10 June 1910 (see
note 2)
    Designation: 4 (see note 3)
    Rank: Major



SERVICE SUMMARY TO DATE:
    1922: Smuggled REDACTED to REDACTED during
the Russian Revolution and falsified information
to suggest that REDACTED had been executed. That
information now established as incontrovertible
truth. Ref: F60075443.
    1923: Convinced Howard Carter that REDACTED
should be secretly removed from the Tutankhamun
burial chamber before the discovery of the chamber
was made public. Resealed tomb and arranged for
Carter to fake entry in the presence of Lord
Carnarvon. REDACTED currently stored in REDACTED.
Ref: H88775429. (See note 4).
    1924: Assassination of REDACTED and REDACTED and
REDACTED and REDACTED and REDACTED during the Turkish
War of Independence. Ref: S77239255. (See note 5).
```

1925: REDACTED

1926: REDACTED

1927: Egypt REDACTED

1928: Egypt REDACTED

1929: REDACTED

1930: The REDACTED resulted in his current assignment to Turkish affairs. Operational throughout Eastern Europe.

1931: Active in Turkey, Egypt, Roumania, Austria, Switzerland, Wäldenstein, Germany.

1932: As a consequence of REDACTED, was able to identify the probable location of the SENSITIVE COMPARTMENTED INFORMATION // *SALUT CHRISTI* // SPECIAL ACCESS PROGRAMME ONLY (Ref: Y99992544) ABOVE TOP SECRET which was thought to have been REDACTED REDACTED REDACTED. Assigned to its recovery and delivery to REDACTED in Istanbul. Gained possession from the REDACTED family after locating REDACTED. Ref: Y99992687 (1922).

REDACTED

REDACTED

REDACTED

REDACTED

REDACTED

Notes

Birth year is approximated. Nye is notoriously unforthcoming, and records are notable by their absence. See 2 (below)

This date is frequently and mistakenly given

```
as Nye's birthdate. Though it marks his official
recruitment to the Secret Service, unverified
rumours suggest that he undertook missions for the
Service during the Great War. The late Sir Falstaff
Eddington (Ref: J77645663), director of the Service
during that period, was steadfast in his refusal to
discuss John Nye.
    Nye has been most frequently assigned "4" but
his numerical designation is the most-oft altered
of any agent.
    The Carter affair is ongoing. Ref: H88775429.
    1924 saw the commencement of Nye's involvement
in Turkish affairs. He is currently our most
experienced agent in this area.



SPECIAL OBSERVATIONS: John Nye is a senior-ranked
operative in the British Secret Service and has
also undertaken missions for REDACTED. His acute
insight, ability as a strategist, and talent
for manipulation and deception, have earned him
unwarranted freedom of action. He can be trusted
and should be permitted leeway when requested.
```

Sir Seaton Begg muttered, "Hmm!" and scrutinised the photographic portrait at the top of the page. Nye appeared to be very much older than his stated forty-three years, a stringy-looking fellow with a scrubby, greying moustache and pale eyes that, even in a photograph, made him appear introspective and somewhat disconnected.

"Rather a slim file for a man of significance," Begg noted.

"It's the redactions," Clarke said. "Without them, I'm told, it would have the weight of a set of encyclopaedias."

Begg passed the file to Taffy Sinclair, who donned a pair of spectacles and set about reading.

The metatemporal detective leaned back, his eyes glittering through his cigar smoke as he fixed a steady gaze upon the man seated opposite. "You are not especially forthcoming, sir."

"That's true," Clarke admitted. "The fact of the matter is that I simply have nothing to tell. All I know is that Nye's mission was to retrieve something called the *Salut Christi*, bring it to Istanbul, and hand it over to an unidentified authority. A month ago, I received a note from him stating that he'd arrived and would report to me the next morning. He did not, and has been neither seen nor heard from since."

Begg threw up a hand, his patience tested. "*Salut Christi?* What is it?"

"I haven't the foggiest."

"You've asked?"

"Naturally. Until I'm blue in the face. London is completely unforthcoming. 'What is it?' 'You don't have the clearance.' 'Where's it from?' 'You don't have the clearance.' 'What does it do?' 'You don't have the clearance.' 'Who needs it?' 'You don't have the clearance.' I might as well be the office cleaner for all they've told me."

Again, he reached into the drawer, and this time withdrew an envelope, which he tossed to Begg. "Your only clue, such as it is. I know you've solved cases with less." He looked at Sinclair and gave a lopsided grin. "Maybe, with that, he will have tracked him down by suppertime, eh, Taffy?"

Sinclair peered over his spectacles. "Entirely possible." And, because he didn't much like the liberty taken with his nickname, he thickened his Welsh lilt and added, "Boyo."

Begg, suppressing a smile, opened the envelope and extracted a sheet of vellum. The letter had been sent from the Hotel Bosphorus in Stamboul. Begg took note of the address, aware that there were at least eight establishments of that name in the city.

He frowned, put the paper to his nose, and sniffed.

"What do you make of that?" He passed the letter to his friend.

Sinclair placed the paper against his nostrils and inhaled slowly, keeping his mouth slightly open and the tip of his tongue against the roof of his mouth, as the detective had taught him.

"Floral," he said. "Some sort of tobacco? Nasty!"

He handed it back.

"Yes," Begg agreed. "And the fact that we're all smoking yet can still detect it suggests a particularly strong brand. I don't think it's Turkish. More likely Egyptian."

"By suppertime, be damned!" Clarke exclaimed. "More likely by afternoon tea."

The note was brief, written in acutely right-leaning copperplate:

10 MARCH 1933

SIR VIVIAN,

ARRIVED THIS AFTERNOON.

OBJECT SECURE.

WILL CALL ON YOU AT 9 A.M.

"4"

"And he didn't keep the appointment?" Begg frowned.

"He did not. He appears to have vanished from the face of the earth."

Sinclair said, "Are we to treat this solely as a missing-person case? I mean to say, should we concern ourselves as well with this salute thingamajig?"

Clarke examined the bowl of his pipe and, as if the tobacco within was thoroughly unsatisfactory, turned it upside down and tapped it repeatedly into an ashtray.

"The problem, Doctor, is that if the whatchamacallit is classified where I'm concerned, then it certainly is where you're concerned. I'm not, therefore, in any position to commission you to recover it, if—as I suspect you are suggesting—Nye has been done away with and the item in question stolen."

"Or reclaimed," Begg put in.

"Indeed."

After a moment of consideration, Begg said, "In which circumstance, I can understand your requirement for an investigator rather than an agent. Yet, you initially put an agent on the case?"

Clarke made a sound of confirmation. "Miss Violet Damm, with whom I know you have a past association."

"Association? You almost make it sound romantic. It was not. She twice nearly killed me."

"Yet you recommended her to the Service."

"I redirected her talents. They were wasted in criminal endeavours. What did she discover?"

"I sent her to Nye's hotel. Suite fifteen. It was empty, no sign of occupation. The hotelier says it was booked by telephone on the first day of March and reserved for two months. Nye registered on the tenth, paid by cashier's draft, went straight out again, and was not seen to return. He took with him a single item of luggage."

"The suite is still empty?"

"Yes."

"Did the hotelier allow Miss Damm to inspect it?"

"No, but she climbed a drainpipe and broke the window latch."

"Then I suppose I shall have to go in the same way."

Begg handed the letter and envelope back to Clarke, who said, "There's a complication."

The detective knew what was coming.

"I hate to be the bearer of bad news, Begg, but since she reported, Miss Damm has vanished. I fear she might have been killed, or—"

Begg's expression remained noncommittal. "Or?"

"Or she has betrayed us, killed Nye, and made off with the item."

"Have you any evidence to suggest it?"

"No. I want you to find some. Or, better still, find her."

For the better part of a minute, Begg stared mutely at the glowing tip of his cigar, deep in contemplation. Sinclair, familiar with such silences, sat quietly at his side.

Clarke fidgeted with his pipe.

"Sir Vivian," said the detective, "the British newspapers have reported that, since this city changed its name, there has been a campaign of murder by someone who styles himself the 'Red King.' Does it, do you think, have any bearing on the matter?"

Clarke put a hand to the back of his neck and massaged it. "God in Heaven!" he exclaimed. "I hope not. How could it? The killings are seemingly without motive, the actions of a homicidal maniac. It's a police matter. Besides, while it's true that Major Nye is the principal Secret Service agent in Turkey, he takes his orders from London, not from me, and spends most of his time beyond this country's borders. He has not been present during the Red King's murder spree."

Taffy Sinclair leaned forward. "Pardon me, sir, but I don't understand. How can Nye be the primary Turkish agent without being here? Without being under your command?"

"Because," Clarke responded, "he operates on what he calls an ontological scale; global; the big, almost-allegorical ideas of empires and statehood. You know what Kipling's so-called Great Game does to a certain kind of romantic imagination. Murder only fits his remit if it's of the en masse variety, à la Flanders Fields or the Russian Civil War."

Begg got to his feet and pressed his cigar into an ashtray. "Anything else, Sir Vivian?"

"Your cover," said Clarke, also rising. "Is it established?"

"Yes, sir. Pretty thoroughly."

"Then it remains only for me to wish you luck. I fear I've condemned you to a wild goose chase."

"Let us see, shall we? I'll report—if and when I have something to report."

They shook hands again, and as Begg and Sinclair moved to the door, Clarke reminded them that they had their pick of vehicles from the agency carpool.

A clerk led them to an underground garage and assigned to them an Invicta four-and-a-half Litre Sports "Scout," a low-slung two-seater perfect for manoeuvring through the city traffic. Sinclair, with much glee, took the wheel, steered up a ramp, and out onto the street.

"So, Begg, Miss Damm was searching for this Nye fellow. He, however, found her first and told her something that has sent her so far undercover that even her boss doesn't know what she's up to."

"That's the long and short of it. What on earth could have unnerved that young lady?"

The detective's eyes narrowed. His metatemporal senses tingled.

"Taffy," he murmured. "I don't know why, but I feel as if, where this case is concerned, the fate of worlds is at stake!"

CHAPTER 4
A Bosphorus Inferno

The Hotel Bosphorus was a square, unornamented, three-storey edifice on a hectic, traffic-clogged street. Opposite it, a film theatre was showing *Révolte dans la prison*, starring Charles Boyer and Mona Goya, with Laurel and Hardy's *Laughing Gravy* as a supporting feature.

"I hope I can find the time," said Taffy Sinclair. "Will they give me half price if I enjoy the starter, then skip the main?" He adored the comedy duo.

"We're not on holiday," Begg reminded him. He indicated the mouth of a narrow alleyway. "Through here."

"It's the one with the dog."

"Eh?"

"Stan and Ollie are hiding a dog from their landlord."

"You've already seen it?"

"Yes."

"No need to see it again, then."

Sinclair clicked his tongue. "Sometimes, old man, I despair of you."

The clamour of the street fell behind as they proceeded along the passage, kicking aside litter and stepping carefully over a mangled and abandoned bicycle. A rat scuttled away.

Sinclair persisted. "I mean to say, don't you know how to enjoy yourself?"

"I'm enjoying myself now."

"You're hunting for a missing spy!"

"Precisely."

They came to a junction with an alley running along the rear of the street-facing buildings, bisecting the block. It reeked of decaying food. To get to the back of the hotel, they had to squeeze past heaps of broken furniture and large containers of rubbish.

"We'll know which drainpipe to climb," said Sinclair, "because Miss Damm shinned up it."

"Quite so. As good as she is, there will be signs."

There were: small flakes of paint scraped from the pipe, and scuff marks on the brickwork.

"Second storey, I'll wager," said Begg. "I'll go up first. Can you manage? It looks strong enough to hold you."

"This is all muscle, not fat," said Sinclair, indicating his own considerable bulk.

Begg raised his eyebrows dubiously.

"Go!" The Welshman glowered.

The detective started up, climbing with remarkable agility. He possessed a notably hard, well-developed, and rangy musculature, which served him excellently when faced with such challenges.

He ascended hand over hand, feet braced against the wall, and did not stop until he was level with the window. Its sash was already wide open. Supposing that a maid had left it that way to air the room, he reached in and gripped the sill.

Suddenly, he caught a subtle whiff of Guerlain.

A cheerful voice came from within. "Can I assist?"

He smiled to himself.

"No, thank you, Miss Damm. I can manage."

As he clambered inside, the detective glanced back at a closed and curtained window in the opposite building. The alley wasn't wide, and had both the windows been open, a conversation in one room might easily carry across to the other.

"Hello," he said, straightening and brushing himself down.

Violet Damm was sitting on a wooden chair beside an unused bed. The chamber was rectangular and plainly furnished, with a wardrobe, a dresser, and a small occasional table—a typical low-cost hotel room as found in any city. Only a cheap framed print of the Hagia Sophia, hung slightly askew over the bedhead, gave a hint of location.

She greeted him with a charming smile and indicated the closed door. "It's locked. There's a sitting room on the other side. We can talk without being heard by anyone in the corridor beyond."

"I'm eager to discover the subject of conversation," Begg said. "But let's wait for Taffy. How's your neck?"

"Black and blue."

She was wearing a beret and a stylish three-piece suit. Her shirt collar was open. She pulled it aside and raised her chin to display her bruises.

Puffing and panting, Doctor Sinclair heaved himself over the sill.

"Piece of cake!" he exclaimed breathlessly. He closed the window, drew the curtains, then moved to the bed and plonked down onto it. A spring twanged. "What's the story, Miss Damm?"

"I have a few chapters, Taffy, but unfortunately not the whole novel." She turned to Begg. "I knew you'd come here. This was my first port of call when I set out to find Major Nye. Sir Vivian told you about him, of course?"

The metatemporal detective leaned against the wall beside the window and crossed his arms over his chest. "What little he could. You, no doubt, can tell me rather more."

"Oh, I wish it were true. No, I cannot say much about the mysterious Nye. However, were you to ask me about Sir Vivian . . ."

She jumped to her feet, paced the length of the room, then wheeled around in front of the door. "I've been investigating him, Sir Seaton. I don't trust him at all."

"Why not?"

She leaned back, shook her head ruefully, and chuckled. "Because after I made my first visit to this room, I descended the drainpipe and dropped straight into the arms of a little old lady. She had a lot to say. She stated emphatically that events taking shape in Istanbul may dictate the fate of nations. Even of empires! And Sir Vivian Clarke, despicable turncoat that he is, has cast in his lot with the other side. He is working against British interests."

"That's a serious allegation, Miss Damm. Sir Vivian is a high-ranking officer in the British Secret Service. His leadership in this region has been exemplary. Who was this old woman? What evidence did she possess?"

"I don't know who she was. She wouldn't say. She did, however, show me certain papers. I have verified what they hinted at. For his whole life, Sir Vivian has concealed a compromising secret."

"Which is?"

"Gammon."

"I beg your pardon?"

"It was five years ago, if I remember rightly?"

"I'm at a complete loss to know what—"

Sinclair cleared his throat.

Begg stopped. He blinked. "Ah! Ah yes! It was! But in what way does—?"

Violet Damm raised her palm, then turned to the detective's friend. "You were the principal player, Taffy, were you not? Would you refresh our memories?"

A little bemused, Sinclair nodded. "Very well. Although I can't see how—"

"Humour me, dear fellow."

The big Welshman shifted. The bedspring twanged again.

"Geoffrey Bacon," he said. "At varsity, they called him Gammon because of the rubbish he spouted. He was bursting with lunatic notions. He tried to incite a new Jacobite rebellion, was rusticated, and ultimately expelled for all his rabble-rousing. In 1926 he founded the Imperial League."

Sinclair ran his tongue around his mouth, as if to clear a bad taste.

"The league touted a thoroughly poisonous brand of pop-eyed nationalism based on Bacon's theories concerning race and eugenics. He whipped his blockheaded followers into a frenzy. They dressed like overgrown Cub Scouts and goose-stepped up and down local high streets, belting out patent balderdash at the top of their voices."

"Much like the Nazis," Damm muttered.

"Yes," Sinclair replied. "And we all thought the Nazis were utterly ludicrous until this year, didn't we? Perhaps Bacon could have pipped Hitler to the post were it not for a stroke of luck."

"Were it not for you," Sir Seaton Begg supplied firmly.

"Well, I doubt that I can claim—"

"What happened?" Damm prompted.

Sinclair scratched his balding head. "Luck, as I said. In the summer of twenty-eight, I spotted a crook with whom we'd had previous dealings. I was at a loose end, and he was looking shifty, so out of curiosity, I followed him. He unwittingly led me to a secret meeting of the Imperial League. I spied on it and overheard a dozen or so of its members reporting to Gammon. 'Entrapment and Bribery' was the name of the game. Their claws were in countless important people. I watched Geoffrey Bacon receive thousands in cash and distribute a portion of it in payment to his henchmen. He gave a lunatic speech about how the profits would finance a fascist revolution. Then he announced the time and place for the next get-together, at which further illicit gains would be collected. I, of course, immediately passed the information to Scotland Yard, and at that next meeting, the police swooped. We went along to lend a hand, and were happy to see the Imperial League get its just deserts."

"All except Gammon," Begg muttered.

"It wasn't your fault!" Sinclair exclaimed. He turned to Damm. "The cunning old fox had a little glass sphere of knockout gas in his pocket."

"And I woke up forty minutes later with an awful headache," Begg scowled. "Bacon fled the country and dropped out of sight. There are unconfirmed reports that he joined the Foreign Legion, was invalided out three years ago, and has since become a nominal French citizen living in Cairo."

"Do you know anything about his lineage?" Damm asked.

The detective gazed at her, intrigued. "Only that he was adopted, and the family who took him in received a generous annual stipend from an anonymous source. Why do you ask?"

"Because, thanks to the peculiar old woman, I was able to discover rather more. He was given up for adoption at eight years old. His madness was already apparent even at that tender age, and his parents feared him—and feared what others might think of him. They were wealthy, respectable, and he tainted their reputation. So, they faked his death by drowning and gave him away. His father, mother, and twin brother never spoke of him again. He became the skeleton in their closet."

"Twin brother?" Begg's eyes widened as he made the connection.

"Yes. Geoffrey Bacon was born Geoffrey Clarke."

Taffy Sinclair whistled. "Great Scott! Sir Vivian's twin?"

Absently, Violet Damm put her fingers to her collar and tugged at it. "Nonidentical."

Begg's expression darkened. "Are you suggesting they are in contact?"

"Yes, I'm suggesting that . . . and very much more," said Damm. "I'm suggesting that Sir Vivian shares his sibling's foul political ideology. He is a Nazi."

Begg pursed his lips. "This is a very sticky wicket."

"It is," she responded. "Even more so because Sir Vivian must not, under any circumstances, be allowed to get his hands on the object that Major Nye brought to Istanbul."

The detective took a packet of cigarettes from his pocket. "The *Salut Christi*. Why? What is it?"

She was silent.

He uttered an exasperated snort. "Surely, you asked the old woman? She is obviously Nye's go-between."

Damm gave a wide, expressive shrug. "She was very cagey. She didn't tell me what it is, only that the shape and form of empires depends upon it and that it must be protected at any cost. Nye has gone into hiding with it and cannot emerge until we make it safe."

"Safe from Sir Vivian?" Sinclair asked.

"Safe from Sir Vivian's hired assassin."

"The Red King?"

She nodded.

Begg unfolded his arms and considered his fists. "Then there is a connection between the assassinations and the *Salut Christi*?"

"I must presume so."

"Does Sir Vivian choose the targets?"

"Yes. Last night, one of the master assassin's gang, Suleyman the Strangler, was sent to kill a Frenchman named Apollinaire de Villiers. I interfered. You saw with what result."

"How did you know it was intended?"

"The old woman has been leaving me—"

With a tremendous crash, the window shattered. A bullet thudded into the doorframe, inches from Violet Damm's face. Instantly she dropped to the floor, heedless of the broken glass, rolling until sheltered by the wall.

Begg, on the left of the window, drew his gun.

Sinclair flung himself over the bed and knelt behind it, his pistol at the ready.

"Your enemies or mine?" Begg muttered.

"You don't think they're one and the same?" Damm grinned, as ever, enthralled to be in the thick of it.

Another shot. A bullet hit the wall beside the door. Sinclair started to say something, but a hail of lead came crashing in, shredding the curtains, gouging chunks out of the window frame, and filling the room with a cloud of splinters and plaster dust. The racket was deafening, the reports echoing up and down the alleyway. They found it impossible to estimate how many weapons were in play.

Unable to return fire. Begg, Sinclair, and Damm hunkered down to weather the storm, which seemed to last for minutes. In reality, it was over in thirty seconds.

Silence.

Begg quickly fished a small hand mirror from his jacket pocket and angled it past the ruined frame in such a way as to see the opposite window reflected. It was open, and the curtains pulled aside, but the room was dark.

"Careful," he muttered. "I can't see anyone, but they might still be there waiting for us to show ourselves."

Damm looked at him curiously. "You have enemies in Istanbul?"

"Apparently. Within minutes of our arrival, someone took a potshot at us."

"Who knew you were coming?"

"An old and trustworthy friend at Gelecek Engineering." He gave a wry shrug. "And, of course, Sir Vivian Clarke."

"Ah," she said. "You see!"

A small object sailed through the window and bounced onto the floor. Before Begg even recognised it as a hand grenade, Damm had flung herself at it, snatched it up, and pitched it back out.

The bomb exploded in the air, midway between the two buildings. Begg was protected by the wall, and Sinclair by the bed, but the blast hit Violet Damm square on, and slammed her against the door. She folded to the floor, unconscious.

Begg's ears filled with a frantic whining. He had tunnel vision. He couldn't think. It was not until long afterward that he was able to piece together his subsequent actions. They were all instinct.

He aimed at the door's lock, shot it to shrapnel, took three long strides, and hurled himself over Damm and at the bullet-riddled portal. He crashed through, thudded to the floor, rolled, and staggered upright.

Sinclair, his hands beneath Damm's shoulders, dragged her after him. The pathologist's mouth moved, but Begg's ears hadn't yet cleared.

The detective went to the main door, turned the key, and pulled it open. Hot air blasted against his face. A dense cloud of black, choking smoke rolled in.

The hotel was on fire! A two-pronged attack! While they were being shot at from across the alley, one or more of the enemy had set fire to the floor below.

Begg turned to Sinclair as more shots rang out. His friend was running back into the bedroom, shooting at the opposite window. No bullets came in response. The grenade blast had incapacitated the enemy, or they had fled.

Sinclair leaned from the window, then rapidly returned to the sitting room.

"The drainpipe! Blown off the wall!"

His voice sounded muffled and distant, but Begg's hearing was, at least, returning.

"Only one way out," he shouted.

Through the burning hotel. But which way?

He snapped an order. "Taffy, scout!"

Sinclair nodded and plunged into the corridor.

Begg quickly examined Violet Damm. She was out cold, her nose bleeding, her face badly scratched, but he could find no serious injury. He raised her in a fireman's lift.

Half a minute later, Sinclair returned. "Follow me, old chap." Taking hold of Begg's free hand, he led him into a passage, into great roils of smoke.

They turned left. As they moved, they heard shouting, shrieks of fear, the thumping of panicked footsteps.

They came to a junction with a wider hallway. Five people rushed past, radiating terror. They were fleeing to Begg's right, and it was in this direction that Sinclair led, until they came to the head of the stairs.

A wave of intense heat gusted up with suffocating volumes of smoke and showers of blinding sparks.

"Wait here," Sinclair yelled. He plunged down, and though they had been through peril after peril together, Begg feared the courageous Welshman would never return.

His senses were by now swimming, the stifling atmosphere filling his lungs, poisoning his blood. He blinked repeatedly, eyes dry, gritty, and smarting.

The minutes passed, every second a horrifying torment.

A figure came up the stairs.

Sinclair! His face red and scorched, his jacket blackened down one side.

"I don't know, Begg," shouted the doctor hoarsely. "There's just a chance!"

Wordlessly, Begg briefly clasped the other's hand. A goodbye, perhaps. If there was a chance, they would take it, but it might be the finish!

He followed the doctor down the stairs, with Violet Damm growing heavier and heavier on his shoulder. The blazing hotel was spinning around him. His legs shook, threatening to buckle.

At last! The ground floor.

Coughing, choking, fighting for breath, they used the left wall, with its blistering paper, for support. They pushed on, every step a massive effort. Begg's teeth clamped tight.

A hellish orange light glared through the smoke. The roar of the deadly inferno was all around them now, and with it the crashing of exploding glass, the screams of trapped men and women, the bang and clatter of collapsing masonry.

A great ball of flame came whirling from the right, enveloped them, then rolled past. Begg stumbled, his limbs like lead, trying to run but hardly able to stand, his clothes singed and smoking, the side of his face seared and excruciating.

He would have sunk to the floor in a swoon at that moment, would have dropped his burden and lost his senses, but fingers dug into his elbow. He was faintly aware of a door opening, was hauled through, heard it bang shut behind him.

The gripping hand pulled him down to the floor. He lost his balance and collapsed, toppling to his side with a thud, dropping the young woman.

A breath of fresher air. He gulped at it. His eyes cleared a little.

The black smoke formed a billowing ceiling about four feet above the floor. Below it, a thick haze, through which he saw the legs of tables and chairs. The hotel's dining room.

Beside him, Sinclair croaked, "Across there, Begg. The windows. I've got her."

On his hands and knees, the metatemporal detective forced himself on. Next to him, Sinclair dragged their friend. She was heavy, limp, and loose, like a broken doll, but Sinclair, Begg knew, possessed tremendous strength, and would choose to die beside her rather than leave her behind.

Closer now to the other side of the room, and to his ears came the clanging alarm of the municipal fire carts.

He saw a windowsill, reached it, and with numb fingers fumbled at the catch. To the rear, the dining room door suddenly cracked with a terrific report and fell inward. The smoke writhed like a living, carnivorous entity, and ravenous flames snatched at their backs.

The window went up. The fire leaped at it. But at the same moment they were through, dragging Violet Damm with them, flopping onto the pavement.

A Turkish fireman shouted and fleetingly turned his hose on them.

Soaked, half-cooked, but alive, they were pulled to safety.

Begg dropped into darkness.

When he next opened his eyes he was lying on a trolley and being wheeled beneath a blue sky, buildings to either side. The cacophony of the fire was all around, shouts and bells, hissing hoses and crackling flames, the horns and shouted protests of blocked traffic.

An old crone tottered beside the trolley, supporting herself with a cane, clutching his arm with her free, clawlike hand. She was dressed in traditional Turkish robes and diaphanous veils. He could discern nothing of her face.

She patted his arm, wheezing in accented English, "You won't want to be smoking after that, will you, m'sieu? You make sure you take those cigarettes out of your pocket, do you understand me, m'sieu? Take them out!"

Then she was gone.

CHAPTER 5
An Invitation

Two days later, in the middle of the afternoon, Sir Seaton Begg and Doctor Taffy Sinclair discharged themselves from the Surp Pirgiç Hospital, that famous medical centre located in the Fatih district. Their burns were not as serious as initially thought. Doctor Matossian, a German-trained, English-speaking Armenian of international repute, nevertheless protested vociferously. He was concerned about possible lung damage.

"I'm a qualified GP," Sinclair told him, "and I'm confident that, aside from our sore throats and, as you can hear, hoarse voices, there's nothing much to worry about."

"Oh, how I hate treating doctors," Matossian grumbled. "You're nothing but trouble. You all think you know better. Don't you realise how much smoke you inhaled?"

Sinclair considered for a moment. "Well," he said, "I don't resort to my pipe as often as I used to, but if I take that occasional indulgence into account, along with all the cigars and cigarettes, then I suppose about three weeks' worth."

Matossian clapped his hand to his brow and groaned in vexation.

Begg widened his eyes. "Good Lord!" The conversation had caused a disjointed memory to pop into his mind. "Would you mind fetching my jacket over, Doctor?"

The item, taken from a hook on the back of the room's door, was passed to him. He slipped a hand into one of its pockets and drew from it a packet of cigarettes.

"For goodness' sake, no!" Matossian protested. "Certainly not! I absolutely forbid it!"

"These aren't mine," the detective murmured thoughtfully.

"Makes no difference. If you light one, I'll force such a dose of sedatives into you that you'll be out for a week. Hand them over, at once."

There were, however, no cigarettes in the packet, just a small cardboard invitation:

You are herewith cordially invited to attend
On Sunday, April 23, at nine o'clock in the evening
A GRAND FANCY DRESS BALL
In the Balmumcu Pavilion.
Admission will be granted only to those in full fancy dress,
court dress, or uniform.

On the reverse side, in a trembling script such as might be expected from an elderly hand, was written,

Your costumes will be delivered to your hotel. To gain entry, announce yourselves as Mr. Flanagan and Mr. Allen, registered as guests of the Greek musician Cosmo Maropoulos. Immediately locate Hon. Henry Petherick. He will be attending as a harlequin. The Red King will attempt to assassinate him. Prevent it.

The ball was tomorrow evening.

There was now nothing Matossian could say to prevent Begg and Sinclair from leaving the hospital.

They departed.

Violet Damm remained behind. In addition to cuts, abrasions, burns, and smoke inhalation, she had suffered a bad concussion and was still unconscious. Matossian was adamant that she must remain until she was out of danger. On that point, he and Sinclair found agreement.

The metatemporal detective and his friend took a motor cab back to the half-destroyed Bosphorus Hotel. A police barrier blocked access to the alley at its rear, but Begg was able to make a fair estimation of which building the shooters had employed as a gun emplacement. It came down to a bank or, next door to it, a camera shop, and since it was highly unlikely that anyone could successfully make use of a bank for such a purpose, he and Sinclair entered the shop. It was unoccupied but for a tall, dignified-looking Turk, standing behind the counter. Grey-haired and wearing smart Western clothes, he greeted them in impeccable French.

"*Comment puis-je vous aider, messieurs?*"

"How many gunmen came in on the day of the fire?" Begg demanded without preamble. The huskiness of his voice made it menacing. "Three? Four?"

"M'sieu?" A glint of fear appeared in the man's eyes.

"Come on! You know what I'm talking about!"

"Ouf!" The shopkeeper glared. "Are you here to repair the damage?"

Begg changed tactic. He held up pacifying hands. "I am here to see it and to ask what happened."

The other raised his chin defiantly. "And if I refuse, what then? Will you hold a gun to my head? Threaten my family?"

"Nothing of the sort. I am, m'sieu, a British detective. I mean to identify the gunmen and present them to the police."

For a moment, the man said nothing; then his rigid posture suddenly relaxed. "In that case, Monsieur Begg, will you please lock the door and turn the sign?"

Begg complied, and with the shop now CLOSED, he and Sinclair followed its owner to the back of it, and up a creaking staircase.

"There were four of them. They burst in and, while three came up these stairs, the other stayed below and held me at gunpoint. I heard shooting. There was a very loud bang. Then they came rushing down, their clothes in tatters, their faces bloodied. They left—*Alhamdulillah!*—they left, and fled in a car. The hotel burned."

They reached a landing, and he led them to a door. "They used this storeroom."

He ushered them into a scene of devastation. The room looked as if a hurricane had torn through it. Its floor was strewn with fragmented glass and splintered pieces of window frame. Shredded packages of photographic paper, and twisted and dented items of darkroom equipment, lay against the walls.

Begg crossed to the window. Across the narrow alley, the back of the hotel was blackened but the fire had not reached the room that Major Nye had booked, and in which the detective, Sinclair, and Violet Damm had met.

Turning back to the room, he meticulously sorted through the debris, inspecting every inch of the floor, while the shopkeeper watched in bewilderment.

"What is he looking for?" the man asked Sinclair.

"He won't know until he finds it."

Five minutes later, Begg revealed the fruits of his labour. Two cigarette butts. He put them to his nose, then clicked his tongue in annoyance. The fire had robbed him of his sense of smell.

"What brand do you smoke?" he asked the Turk.

"Lucky Strikes, m'sieu."

"I can't be certain, but these are, I think, Murattis."

The shopkeeper put his fingertips to his forehead and groaned. "Won't you tell me why this happened, and why to me?"

Begg gave a grim smile. "It didn't happen to you. It happened to us. We were in the hotel opposite. Your intruders were trying to kill us."

"*Mon Dieu!* Do not involve me in gang warfare. This is Istanbul. A civilised city. Not Chicago."

"We're not gangsters. You can rest easy. There's no reason why you should be disturbed again." Begg took a couple of banknotes from his wallet, handed them to the Turk without comment, and turned to Sinclair. "Nothing more to see here, old chap. Let's retrieve our car."

They had left the Invicta Scout in a nearby garage and were asked to pay for the space it had occupied for the past three days. Begg handed over the money in good grace and added a tip, for the car had been well looked after, even cleaned and polished in their absence.

Sinclair slid into the driving seat, and they set off toward Pera.

"The Red King's assassination squad was at work three years in advance of Nye's arrival," Begg mused. "So many murders! It shouldn't prove difficult to find some common factor linking the victims. If we can identify it, perhaps it will give some clue pertaining to the *Salut Christi*." He paused, and added, "I think I know how to go about it."

"Let me guess—" began Sinclair.

"I would rather you employed the art of deduction, Taffy, else your time in my company has been ill spent."

Sinclair steered the car onto the Hayratiye Bridge, north of the more famous Galata.

"Right-ho. I deduce that we must first prevent this Petherick chap from being killed. We must also locate the Frenchman saved by Miss Damm from Suleyman the Strangler. Then, we'll put the two of 'em together and find out what they share. How's that?"

"Bravo! Apollinaire de Villiers was his name."

"I hope you'll bear in mind," said Sinclair, "that we must also avoid being assassinated ourselves. Sir Vivian may have set the Red King onto us. He knows our movements."

"It certainly looks that way."

Beneath a glaring blue sky, they crossed the Golden Horn, weaved through the cars, carts, and carriages, and made their way up the hill into Galata.

At the Pera Palas Hotel, before anything else, they soothed their raw throats with a chilled drink at the bar. Then they went to their suite to wash, change their clothes, and rest before dinner.

The evening passed pleasantly, and they took to their beds early.

Sir Seaton Begg dreamed of smoke, fire, screams, and death. The newspapers had reported five fatalities and eight serious injuries in the conflagration. It was plain that the Red King would stop at nothing so long as he hit his target.

In the morning, over breakfast, Begg ordered Sinclair to remain in the suite and under no circumstances to leave the hotel.

"Sorry, old son, I know you're champing at the bit, but it's Sunday, day of rest, for you. I have some errands to run, and I intend to do them alone and disguised. Sir Vivian knows we're in this hotel, which means the Red King probably does, too. I want you to lie low and keep your guard up while I'm out."

Sinclair, with a slice of spicy *sucuk* sausage poised inches from his mouth, asked, "Errands?"

"Do you recall William Duck?"

The *sucuk* disappeared into Sinclair's mouth. He chewed, a vertical line appearing between his eyebrows as he searched his memory.

"Ah," he said. "Dirty Duck, the extortionist."

"Yes, a man whose crimes inevitably caught up with him. Also, a man full of useful information concerning the illegal activities of certain luminaries in the political sphere. He turned King's Evidence in return for amnesty. After the trial and subsequent convictions, I arranged for him to move here, hopefully to find gainful employment among the many Europeans helping with the modernisation project. I believe he worked as a carpenter for a little while, but I heard some months ago that he landed a rather good posting as a gentleman's factotum."

"What has that to do with the price of beans in Byzantium, Begg?"

"Only that, no matter how respectable his job might be, he is not entirely reformed. He has occasionally lapsed, and hired himself out as an 'adviser' to local gangs. With his contacts in the Turkish underworld, he may be able to tell me something about the Red King."

Sinclair sliced into an egg. "I'll tell you what, I'm glad to be out of it. Duck is a disgusting creature. I recall the stench of him better than his face."

"He must surely have learned to bathe, Taffy. No gentleman would hire him otherwise."

Begg sipped at his tea. His blistered face and hands were healing nicely, and his throat was sounding much better this morning. His eyebrows would doubtlessly grow back in due course, and until they did, his disguise kit provided adequate, if somewhat satanically angled, replacements.

"I also," he said, "intend to reconnoitre the Balmumcu Pavilion."

Sinclair grunted. "Our costumes hadn't arrived last time I asked. I'll check again later. I wonder who we'll be?"

Hours later, he had his answer.

With other arriving guests, he and the metatemporal detective strode along a tulip-bordered path across the top of a hill to the entrance of the grand pavilion. It was a balmy evening and the moon was a thin sliver over the Bosphorus, which glimmered romantically below.

Sir Seaton Begg was rigged out as Hayreddin Barbarossa, the Ottoman corsair. He had on a white turban with a jewelled brooch at its front and a little crown atop. A thick, flaming-red beard half concealed his face. A patterned doublet, white pantaloons, leather boots, and a scabbarded scimitar completed the costume. He looked dashing and dangerous. Concealed in the scarlet sash around his waist, a loaded Luger P08.

Sinclair had come as Jack Ward, also known as Yusuf Raïs, another of the Barbary pirates. He was similarly attired, but with curling mustachios instead of a beard, a long black jacket instead of a doublet, and a Walther PP instead of a Luger.

The pavilion was magnificent, commissioned in 1825, and built to house Ottoman sultans during their hunting excursions. It was a two-storey edifice in the neobaroque style, the ground floor consisting of a long narrow room with arches on one side opening onto a river-facing veranda, and arches on the other providing access to the massive ballroom. The basement contained a kitchen, larders, and servants' quarters; the top floor, bedrooms, a divan room, and a long dining room. Extensive and beautifully designed flower gardens surrounded the pavilion, filling the air with heady perfumes. Lawns sloped gently down to the river where, in the high wall around the estate, an arched gateway opened onto a long wharf. Some guests, arriving by boat, were walking up from that direction.

Begg and Sinclair, among a small crowd, came to the pavilion's entrance, where servants dressed as characters from *Alice's Adventures in Wonderland* stood greeting the guests. They waited their turn; then Begg announced, "Flanagan and Allen." He ignored Sinclair's muttered, "Underneath the arches," and added, "We are with Cosmo Maropoulos."

The King of Hearts checked his list and allowed them through.

The ballroom was dazzling, all Italian marble and Hereke drapes, plush furniture and gold-leafed mirrors. Bohemian crystal chandeliers glittered overhead like delicate diamond nebulae.

"Keep your eyes peeled," Begg advised as they strode in. "We're looking for a . . . oh . . . oh dear."

They were looking for a harlequin.

From where they stood, they could see at least fifteen of them.

CHAPTER 6
Corsairs Versus Harlequins

A horde of harlequins! Whichever way Sir Seaton Begg and Taffy Sinclair turned, there they were. Harlequin with Harun al-Rashid, harlequin with Buffalo Bill, harlequin with Marie Antoinette, harlequin with Sherlock Holmes, harlequin with Napoleon, harlequin with Dick Turpin, harlequin with harlequin! Tall harlequins, short harlequins, rotund harlequins, skinny harlequins!

"What the blazes are we going to do?" shouted Sinclair in despair. It was necessary to raise his voice because the orchestra had started up, blasting out a fast and furious foxtrot at a near-deafening volume. "It's impossible! How are we supposed to find Petherick among that lot?"

Begg also shouted. "Look on the bright side, old chap. The Red King faces the same problem. And we have an advantage."

He took a *flûte à Champagne* from a tray carried by a passing Frog Footman.

"We do?" asked Sinclair.

"Of course! We're searching for Petherick, but also for an assassin who's doing the same. Cuts the odds. If you see someone meeting harlequin after harlequin, and it's not I, the fearsome Barbarossa, don't let him out of your sight. Let's get to work."

With that, Begg plunged into the colourful crowd.

It occurred to Sinclair that if he bellowed, "Message for Henry Petherick!" between the dance numbers, he would not have to find the man, the man would find him. However, he realised that if the Red King were already present, as Begg had suggested he was, such an action would effectively throw the chicken to the fox.

He gave a weary sigh, muttered "Here goes!" and set about introducing himself to the closest of the innumerable harlequins.

This proved to be Bay Hasad Öztürk, the secretary of foreign affairs, who, though the ball had only just commenced, was drinking with methodical intent. Next Sinclair met Mohammad Ibrahim Al Habbai, director of a sugar beet export enterprise and a chronically dull man who talked interminably until Sinclair abandoned his manners and simply wandered away. Then, in quick succession, Mr. "Bingo" Ramsey, who happened to be an engineer employed by George Philips at Gelecek; Bay Murat Gülen, a senior diplomat; Bingo Ramsey again; an author; an admiral; an economist; a religious leader; Bingo Ramsey; an actor; an historian; and Bingo Ramsey.

"By golly!" the young engineer exclaimed cheerfully when Sinclair cornered him for the fourth time. "Call me Septimus Blane, but I'd bet my bottom dollar you're looking for someone. You're only talking to harlequins!"

"I plead guilty," smiled Sinclair, tickled by the reference to Begg's fictional counterpart. "One of you is the Right Honourable Henry Petherick, but I don't know which. I hope you won't take offence, Mr. Ramsey, but I do wish you had a distinguishing feature, like knock-knees or a big nose, then I'd know not to bother you again."

"I daresay I'd be more bothered by those than I am by you. A friend of yours, is he?"

"No, I've never laid eyes on him. But I need to give him some important information."

Ramsey, whose face was half-concealed by a black domino, gave a wide guileless grin. "I think I can narrow it down for you. He's one of the little plump harlequins, and he has a gammy foot, so he probably isn't on the dance floor."

"You know him?"

The latest foxtrot suddenly ended, and the orchestra paused to retune its instruments. Sinclair felt relieved to lower his voice. His smoke-scorched throat wasn't up to all the yelling.

"Yes, I know him," said Ramsey. "That is to say, I'm acquainted with him. We've been introduced a couple of times at shindigs like this. Let's see now—" He turned this way and that, casting his eyes over the colourful throng. "No, definitely not that one—you see, with Al Capone? He shares the general dimensions, but doesn't have the posture. And the roly-poly harlequin over there, chatting with the moustachioed Queen Victoria, is far too spherical. Tell you what, how about we circle the perimeter, so to speak? I'm positive I can point him out if he's here."

"Thank you, that would be a big help," said Sinclair, and as they set off, he asked, by way of conversation, "Have you been in Istanbul for long?"

"For its entire existence, the full three years. A gang of us graduates from Imperial College in London came over when the reforms were announced and Gelecek started hiring. We thought there'd be a lot of work for us here—and we were right." He stopped and stared, then shook his head. "Nope, that one is a little too curtailed in the leg department. See? His feet barely reach the ground."

"You have a good eye," Sinclair noted.

"Oh, the human body is a fascinating feat of engineering if you regard it as nothing but rods, hinges, oil, and—Hallo! There's our fellow! Over there with Charlie Chaplin. Come on, I'll introduce you."

They threaded their way through the mass of partygoers, the hubbub of chitchat and laughter all around them, the clink of glasses, a distant ripple of applause at some announcement made, until they drew alongside a tall, broad in the beam, female Chaplin, and a diminutive, but remarkably stout, harlequin.

"Well I never!" Ramsey exclaimed. "It's Mr. Petherick, isn't it?"

The little harlequin peered in bafflement at the bigger one. "It is," he confirmed, "but I'm not sure I—"

"Bingo Ramsey. We met briefly at—let's see now, where was it?—the Greek ambassador's reception? The French ambassador's? Good gracious! What a social whirlwind dear old Poli presents! To be honest, I don't recall where it was, but our paths have crossed at least twice, I'm sure of it."

"Well, if you say so, Mr.—um—but I'm afraid I don't—"

"Ma'am," said Ramsey, turning to Chaplin. "Pray forgive my intrusion and bad manners. Bingo is the name, an engineer, tunnels, and other what-have-yous, and this is Mr. Allen, he's a—er—"

"Corsair," said Sinclair.

They all chuckled, the ice broken.

Ramsey looked expectantly at Petherick, who after a slight hesitation obliged: "May I introduce Baroness Blittersdorf of Bavaria?"

"Ah! A baroness, no less. I say! Delighted to meet you. My goodness, you've got Charlie off to an absolute T."

"Herzlichen Dank," the baroness responded with a clumsy bob, her voice deep and stentorian. "It is most fortunate that Herr

Chaplin and I are of a similar build, *nein*? It makes the costume, I think, a little more convincing. *Unt* you make a very handsome *harlekin*, Herr Bingo." She put her knuckles to her mouth and giggled. It sounded like a small avalanche.

Sinclair turned to Petherick. "Sir, if I might—"

The orchestra started up again, the new foxtrot a frantic window rattler.

"Oh! How remiss, we are all dry, what!" exclaimed Ramsey loudly. "We must remedy that immediately." He snapped his fingers at a nearby March Hare, who approached bearing a tray of brimming flutes. Ramsey replaced their empty glasses with filled ones.

"Good health, one and all," he declared.

They imbibed.

"Tunnels, Herr Bingo?" boomed the baroness, her voice carrying easily over the music. "You have heard of the *schratzlloch*, *nein*? There are very many in Bavaria. More than seven hundred, and still no one knows what they were used for. It is a great mystery. When I was a little girl—"

While she thundered on, Sinclair stepped closer to the smaller of the two harlequins, put his mouth close to the man's ear, and said, "Mr. Petherick, would you come out onto the veranda with me? I need to tell you something. It's of vital importance. Actually, a matter of life and death."

"—that they were used by dwarfs. Of course, I don't believe—" Ramsey was saying.

The orchestra's latest went into a percussive break.

Banga banga tat, banga banga tat, banga banga tat—

"Sir, please, if you would?" Sinclair persisted.

"Ack!" Petherick replied.

He clawed at his neck.

"Mr. Petherick?"

"Ack! Ack! Ack!"

"Petherick!" Sinclair cried out.

Banga banga tat, banga banga tat, banga banga tat—

Behind his harlequin domino, the little man's eyes rolled up. He dropped to his knees.

Baroness Blittersdorf issued a scream of phenomenal volume. Sinclair would later claim that it made the chandeliers jingle.

Ramsey shouted, "What the deuce?" and backed away until he bumped up against an ebony-skinned Saracen warrior.

Petherick gave a last "Ack!" and slumped to his side. He shuddered, kicked his legs, and became still.

All of a sudden, Barbarossa—Sir Seaton Begg—was kneeling beside the fallen man and putting fingers to his neck. The detective looked up at Sinclair and gave a slight shake of his head.

Sinclair gaped at him. "But how?" He turned to Bingo Ramsey. "Did you see—?"

Ramsey said, "Ack!" and crumpled to the floor.

The baroness let loose a second, even more terrific screech.

The *banga banga tat* missed a *banga*, faltered, and stopped. The ballroom became preternaturally silent.

Begg moved to Ramsey, beneath whom blood was pooling. The hilt of a dagger protruded from the engineer's left side, just beneath the armpit. Ramsey coughed and gore splattered around his mouth.

"Is—is he dead?" he whispered through ghastly bubbles.

"Petherick?" said Begg. "Yes, I'm afraid so."

Ramsey responded with a sick smile. "Good. I drop . . . dropped curare into . . . into his glass. The Red King . . . scores again!"

"You?" Begg exclaimed, astonished.

Ramsey moaned and grimaced. Blood trickled across his face and into his ear.

"You are the Red King?" asked Begg.

"No . . . no . . . just one of his . . . his supporters."

The word struck a chord.

"Supporters? Are you a member of the Imperial League? Is the Red King Geoffrey Bacon?"

"Who? I don't . . . I don't know what you are . . . talking . . . about."

Begg leaned away as the dying man went into a fit of violent coughing. Blood sprayed. Women shrieked. At the periphery of his vision, he saw a debutante faint.

After a few moments Ramsey quietened, and his convulsing body sagged back. His respiration slowed and rattled.

"Who stabbed you?" Begg demanded.

Ramsey's face froze in a horrible rictus grin.

"You need ask?" he rasped. "Why, it was . . . it was . . . Mr. Milk, of course. If . . . if . . . if he—"

He died.

"Begg," said Sinclair, his tone tense. "The Saracen. Ramsey fell against a Saracen. He was right here—and now he's not."

"Outside!" Begg snapped, jumping up.

They bolted to the nearest exit, yelling, "Move aside! Move aside!"

With the crowd parting before them, they charged into the sultry night, peering urgently this way and that. They saw couples and small groups standing in the grounds under the starry sky, all gazing with curiosity at the pavilion from which the baroness's tremendous screams had echoed.

Running hard, the two men pitched around a corner.

"There!" Sinclair pointed at a white-robed figure strolling nonchalantly down the slope toward the wharf. They dashed after it, and Begg, with his long legs and athletic prowess, quickly outpaced his lumbering assistant.

He did not draw his Luger. Though he was an exceptional shot, there were other guests around the wharf, and he would not risk harming them.

He managed only a short distance before feeling the damage done to his lungs by the hotel fire. He began to wheeze like an old pair of bellows, and pain stabbed into his ribs.

He kept going.

The Saracen reached the arched gate and paused to light a cigarette. He did not once glance back. Having successfully murdered his man and departed the scene without hinderance, he apparently considered himself safe. His audacious attitude was remarkable.

He sauntered through the arch toward the wharf.

The wall now blocked Begg's view of him.

The metatemporal detective slowed, panting, holding his side. Doctor Matossian was right, he had been unwise to discharge himself so precipitously from the hospital. Yet had he not done so, he would not be here, and if he was not here, the killer would get away.

The killer was not going to get away!

The Saracen was making his escape by boat. It would take him a few moments to reach it, untie its moorings, and start its motor.

There was still time.

Begg, limping, passed among the partygoers gathered around the entrance to the wharf. Snatches of conversation reached his ears, but no mention of the deaths in the pavilion. In a few minutes, they would be talking of nothing else.

A faint, pungent odour touched his nostrils. It was maddeningly familiar, but his sense of smell was so impaired that he was unable to identify it. Strangely, it put him on his guard, made him suddenly far more wary of his quarry.

He heard Sinclair's thudding footsteps behind, the pathologist breathless, similarly hampered by the rawness of his lungs. Then the guttural bark of an engine cut the air. Begg ignored his pain, barged forward through seven young Dutch cavaliers, and sprinted along the wooden planks of the wharf.

The Saracen was at the wheel of a motorboat, steering it into the Bosphorus.

Begg launched himself out over the water, crashed onto the deck, and rolled. As he scrambled up and grabbed for his pistol, the Saracen turned, whipped a scimitar from its scabbard, and whacked the flat of it into Begg's rising hand. The Luger went spinning overboard.

The detective gained his feet, and with numbed fingers, slid his own blade from its scabbard.

Swaying unsteadily, he faced the murderer.

The boat was by now chugging toward the middle of the strait. Without turning, the Saracen reached back and switched off its motor.

He gazed in amusement at Begg.

His eyes were a startling pink.

"It can't be!" Begg gasped, suddenly realising the odour he had detected was that of an opium-laden cigarette.

"Yet, certainly, it is," the Saracen responded, his baritone voice rich, deep, and mellow. He bowed with a sardonic movement of his hand. "And your pretend beard entirely fails to disguise you, Sir Seaton Begg!"

CHAPTER 7
The Duel

Black as oil, the Bosphorus swelled beneath the boat. The reflected lights suggested a different reality down there, inverted and mysterious. Were a person to fall headfirst into the strait, perhaps it would be to stand on the other side of the surface, in another place—maybe eternal Byzantium—with the tense, unstable, threatening 1930s upside down and shimmering beneath the feet.

The truth of Begg's opponent, if there were any solid truth at all to such a mercurial and elusive man, also lay beneath a film of oily black, for he wore theatrical paint. It concealed bone-white skin, just as the turban hid hair equally as colourless. Only his sad ruby eyes gave him away.

An albino!

He and Begg now crossed swords. It was not for the first time. They had done so metaphorically and literally over and over these past fourteen years. Yet after repeated encounters, the detective still knew little of his opponent. He was capricious, unpredictable, and audacious, that much was certain, but also strangely intangible. No solid fact about him could be established. Not even his name. Sometimes he was Monsieur Zenith, sometimes Count Zodiac, sometimes White Wolf.

What, Begg wondered, could be the reason for their perpetual *affaires d'honneur*?

His gaze locked with that of his volatile, unfathomable, dangerous opponent.

"So," he breathed. "You are the mysterious Mr. Milk."

Their scimitars touched, the blades scraping.

"That is what the carrion I am doing away with choose to call me," said the albino.

Begg's blue-grey eyes grew harder. "But what, I wonder, do you currently call yourself?"

A slight shrug. "I am Zenith."

"Do you expect, Zenith," said Begg, "that I will stand by and do nothing while you murder with impunity? The man you just stabbed—"

"Was known as Ramsey," Zenith interrupted, "but his real name was Gregory Monteith, referred to by the criminal fraternity as 'the Chemist.' He poisoned a dozen innocent men and women. By disposing of him, I have done the world a service."

"It is for the courts to decide whether—"

"This game is mine, Begg!" Zenith snapped. "Oblige me by staying out of it. I do not threaten England or her interests!"

He suddenly twisted and slashed his blade sideways, cutting at the base of Begg's weapon to knock it out of his hand. The detective, wise to such tricks, lifted it, allowed the steel to sweep harmlessly beneath, then swiped hard at the top edge of the scimitar as it passed. A clang echoed over the water.

Zenith staggered, unbalanced.

Begg stepped forward and jabbed his left fist into the other's head, above the ear.

The side of Zenith's turban softened the blow, but still he tottered, and his blade, slicing back, was robbed of force. Begg blocked it easily, his sword held vertically, point down.

The master crook's riposte was instantaneous, a savage left hook that caught Begg on the side of the jaw and sent him reeling backward, almost falling.

The boat rocked beneath them as it drifted rapidly southward out toward the middle of the strait, spinning, born along on notorious currents, which all mariners knew to be powerful, contrary, and without mercy.

"You're in bad condition, Sir Seaton!" Zenith exclaimed. "I've never seen you breathing so hard. And what has happened to your face? A fire?"

"Hotel Bosphorus," Begg panted.

"Ah, that! You were the target, no doubt." Zenith poised his blade, ready to make—or respond to—the next move. "The Red King is crude, brutal, but very effective in his methods."

The detective again touched the leading edge of his weapon to the albino's. Once more, there came that preliminary metallic scrape.

"You accuse the Red King?" he rasped. "Why?"

"Because it was I who prevented his first shot at you four days ago."

Zenith feinted.

With icy restraint, Begg made no move.

The albino resumed the *en garde*.

"I had not been in the city long, but already my contacts in the underworld had given me a lead. I was following a man suspected of being in the Red King's gang, hoping he might lead me to his master. Instead, he led me to the train terminal. You can imagine my great pleasure when you, of all people, stepped out of it. Pleasure, but also, I confess, considerable annoyance, for I realised I would be inconvenienced, as I always am when you choose to concern yourself with my affairs." He laughed, a deep and sorrowful sound. "Ah, Sir Seaton, my good friend, my implacable enemy, how contrary is our connection. You, unable to bring me to heel; me, unable to kill you; as if some supernatural force holds us in abeyance, bound together in an eternal dance."

"Monsieur Zenith," said Begg. "Lay down your weapon and let this be the end of it."

The command went unheeded.

"Outside the terminal, you boarded a hansom. The Red King's man followed it, and I followed him. When he raised a pistol and shot at you, I pushed him off the docks. He was swept away and drowned." He mockingly raised a hand. "I refuse to let you thank me. I did it only because I cannot allow another the honour of killing you. That is my right, and mine alone. I must continue to attempt it until I succeed and this impasse that holds us is broken."

His scimitar flashed. Begg parried, swiped, and his edge was in turn deflected.

Back and forth they fought under the brightening stars. Their steel rang like bells. It blurred and sparked. The boat rocked and whirled ever southward, while Barbarossa and Saladin duelled, as if the city had transformed herself to old Constantinople and recreated her heroes of yore.

Slash—block—counter—dodge—

No restraint! It was to the death!

Then, out of nowhere, a resounding gunshot! With a noise like a hammer striking a cracked gong, Zenith's blade flew out of his hand and went point over hilt into the water.

Without pausing for thought, the albino jumped to the wheel, hit the starter switch, and yanked the throttle. The motorboat leaped ahead. Begg's fingers were just closing on the albino's shoulder. He was rocked backward.

Zenith twisted and swung a left to the edge of the detective's jaw. Begg's teeth clacked. Completely off-balance, he stumbled backward and toppled over the side, splashing into the cold embrace of the fast-flowing strait.

With a roar, the motorboat was away.

"Au revoir!" Zenith called. "Until we meet again!"

The current snatched Begg, dragging him along, straining to pull him under. The greedy Bosphorus was eager for another soul.

Yet there might still be a chance!

A boat snarled to a fast, frothing stop beside him and a familiar voice called, "Begg!"

Strong hands hauled him aboard.

Having commandeered a small vessel from the wharf, Taffy Sinclair had fired the shot! "All aboard, old fellow."

"Let her rip!" Begg ordered, hoarsely, falling to the deck. "Don't let him escape. It's Zenith."

The astonishment Sinclair felt would have paralysed most men. The pathologist, however, had experienced many adventures with the metatemporal detective. He knew not to pause. He grabbed the wheel and sent the boat streaking after the other.

There were, as always, many craft traversing that vital waterway, which divides Europe from Asia and connects the Black Sea to the Sea of Marmara and, by extension, the Aegean, the Mediterranean, and the distant Atlantic. Every size and shape of vessel was represented, from small pleasure cruisers to giant cargo tankers, and weaving recklessly between them, bouncing precariously over their wakes, Zenith sped toward the mouth of the Golden Horn.

Begg and Sinclair, in a smaller, faster motorboat, closed the distance behind.

Sinclair raised his Walther PP, emptying its clip, aiming to hit not the man but the engine. With the distance and rocking and jumping of both craft, all the shots went wide.

Begg caught his breath and sat up as the Golden Horn opened up on the right, with the lights of the Galata Bridge strung across it, and the shore of Stamboul looming just ahead.

He recalled how William "Dirty" Duck had revealed to him that, recently, the city's criminal underworld had been excited by rumours of warfare between the Red King and an equally ruthless rival gang. The assassin had so far lost four of his followers.

Now the detective knew that it was not a rival gang at all. It was simply Zenith.

Why, though? Why was the albino in Istanbul? Why had he set himself against the master assassin?

"Look," Sinclair shouted, pointing. "He's heading for that gap between the docks. Do you see it? Where the dirt road comes down to the water?"

"I see it," said Begg, his expression hard and eager.

Zenith barely slowed. At the exact moment that his vessel collided with the land, he sprang from it, hitting the muddy end of the road and rolling over and over, with the motorboat sliding to a stop on the slope beside him. Then he was on his feet and away, his slime-stained white robes flapping around him.

Seconds later, Sinclair brought their boat to a scarcely less precipitous stop. They hit solid ground running, and despite their scorched lungs, immediately gained on their quarry.

Zenith was limping. That imprudent leap had cost him a wrenched knee.

He hobbled up the slope, across an empty road and a railway line, over a narrow stretch of wasteland, and alongside a tall tenement building.

Doggedly, Begg and Sinclair followed. They were back in the Fatih quarter, where the hospital was located, though it was some distance to the west. This part of the district was all tenements, workshops, and patches of open land. They ran, struggling for breath, past a woodyard and a brickmaker's. They were at the albino's heels when he came to an eight-foot-high wall and scrambled over it.

"Zenith!" Begg rasped as the albino slipped out of sight. "Give it up! You'll not get away this time!"

Only an amused laugh came in reply.

They launched themselves at the wall, swung their legs over, and dropped—

—in Sinclair's case, straight into a solid uppercut!

The Welshman rocked back against the wall and slid to the ground, out for the count.

Begg flung himself at Zenith, crashing into him, intent on disabling his foe with a barrage of unrestrained, ferocious punches. He was met in kind. For the next minutes, the only sounds were the shuffling of their feet as they vied for dominance, the heavy thump of knuckles against flesh and bone, and the wheezing gasps of two men, tired, injured, and desperate for air.

Begg's costume beard was long gone. Now they lost their turbans. Zenith's white hair stood out starkly in the darkness, with pink orbs blazing beneath, his face still hidden by the theatrical paint.

The nature of the combat momentarily changed from a no-holds-barred brawl into a more scientific fight. Adjusting his stance, Begg noted that his opponent was favouring his right foot.

Zenith watched the detective's eyes.

They circled, ducked and weaved, feinted and blocked.

Then Begg shifted and delivered a long left, intending to follow it with a right hook, and if occasion offered, a rapid left-right-left. Zenith anticipated the attack and caught the left with an open hand, thrusting it aside with such force that Begg was thrown off his balance. He flinched, pressing his elbow against his side, expecting a fist to land there, and instead received steely knuckles to the side of the uncovered jaw.

Though he was reeling, looking through a tunnel, its mouth receding farther and farther away, Begg forced himself back into close quarters.

The two men were hardly aware of their surroundings. Supremely fit, they pounded their fists repeatedly into rock-hard muscle. They were fighting in a yard of some sort, thick with shadows, the only illumination an orange glow from some unidentified source. It wasn't until a haphazard blow caught Begg on the ear and sent him back against a big stone block that he realised, dimly, they were in a smithy. The block was a furnace, its bricks searing through the back of his doublet, the glow emanating from its coals.

Another hard swipe caught his chin, and now he was stalling off and hunching his shoulders against a pummelling, which his blurring eyes would not allow him to measure, or his languid muscles to respond.

He was close to insensible when, entirely unaware of a presented opportunity, his body took it anyway, and his right fist lashed out just as Zenith, succumbing to exhaustion, dropped his guard.

That punch was a sleeping draught, with Begg's full weight behind it.

Zenith's head snapped back. He retreated three steps. Then,

with a sigh, his legs folded, and he sat down, head drooping forward, bleeding hands limp at his sides. A moment later, he emitted a faint snore.

The mighty albino was completely unconscious.

"Now," mumbled Begg, stepping forward. "You'll—"

He pitched to the ground, lights out.

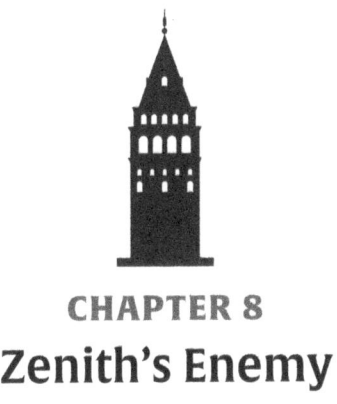

CHAPTER 8
Zenith's Enemy

Doctor Sinclair was the first to regain his wits. When he shook Sir Seaton Begg's shoulder, his friend moaned, blinked, sat up, and put fingertips to his tender jaw.

Zenith was nowhere to be seen.

"I could almost give credit to his notion," the metatemporal detective mumbled through split, bleeding lips.

"Notion?"

Begg took hold of Sinclair's extended arm and allowed himself to be hoisted to his feet. "Zenith suggested that some manner of occult force prevents us from ever resolving our feud."

"Poppycock! You'll have him where he belongs soon enough."

Begg, a little unsteadily, brushed himself down and straightened his corsair's costume. "Where is that, Taffy?"

"Why, behind bars, of course! Need you ask?"

Begg gave an uncertain grunt. "According to every law in our land—and in this one—yes, he has earned a long rest in a small cell. I can't help but wonder, though . . ."

His eyes lost focus, as if looking inward.

"Begg?"

"Why has he come to Istanbul to set himself against the Red King? There's some secret about him, old fellow. Something we have never learned. I'm sure of it. We've long thought him to be from the Balkans, but where in the Balkans, exactly? Roumania, our best guess, is a country of shifting borders which, in recent history, has incorporated many other lands."

He rubbed a hand across his eyes and looked around.

Sinclair pointed to a door in the encircling wall.

They moved toward it.

"I would very much like to identify Zenith's homeland," Begg went on, "and discover his status in that place."

"You've tried before," Sinclair murmured.

"And it is, in itself, intriguing that I failed."

They found the door firmly locked, so they went as they had come—over the wall. Circling to the front of the building, they saw from a sign above the entrance that it was a silversmith's.

They walked away from it, following a quiet, unlit road westward.

It was nearing midnight. The moon, which would be new tomorrow, provided no illumination, but the stars were legion and metallic bright, as if fashioned in the workshop they had just left.

From all around sounded the drawn-out whistles and high-pitched *hoot-hoot-hoot-hoot*s of scops owls.

"They are singing four beats to the bar," Sinclair noted. "When I update our records, I shall refer to this as 'the Night of the Foxtrot.'"

He realised he had advanced a few steps ahead of Begg, and turned back. The detective was standing motionless, his mouth open.

"What is it, Begg?"

"I just remembered a detail from Major Nye's file. He was recently active in Roumania."

"A connection between him and Zenith?"

"It is possible."

Rather than heading into the heart of the old district, where they could have found a cab and returned to their hotel, they hiked to the Surp Pirgiç Hospital. The establishment was a fine example of Turkey's modernisation, being large and clean, with well-equipped wards and an almost luxurious nursing home attached.

The medics, having established the superficiality of Begg and Sinclair's wounds, succumbed to hilarity incited by their patients' torn, muddy, and blood-stained pirate costumes.

"Plainly," said one in French, as she tended to Begg's cuts, "you are thoroughly incompetent corsairs. I suppose your galley is at the bottom of the Bosphorus."

Another, dabbing alcohol onto Sinclair's face, asked whether their enemy had made them walk the plank.

The two men took the ribbing with good grace and when asked to clarify what had really happened, gave an explanation entirely in keeping with their reception. They had been fighting a Saracen!

Having been to some extent repaired, they were making their departure when they encountered Doctor Matossian in the corridor. He was in a suit rather than hospital whites, and was clearly finishing a long shift.

He eyed them up and down. "Well," he said dryly, "I'm glad to see that you are looking after yourselves."

"Sailing the seven seas," quipped Sinclair. "It's a perilous life."

"Evidently."

Smiling grimly, Begg asked, "How is Miss Damm, Doctor?"

"I was just with her. She's a little groggy but awake. I'll keep her under observation until I'm satisfied the bruising to her brain has had no lasting effect." He looked at his wristwatch. "It's far past the visiting hour, but we can make an exception if you want to see her."

"Yes, please."

"Ten minutes, no more. She needs her sleep. So do I. Good night to you. I expect when I see you next, you shall have broken bones or internal injuries."

He signalled for a nurse to assist them, then departed.

They were escorted to Violet Damm's room and left to speak with her alone.

"How perfectly jolly to see you," she exclaimed weakly. "You both look ghastly."

She was hardly any better herself. She was pale, with bruised eyes and scabbed-over scratches marring her face.

"How do you feel?" asked Begg, perching on the edge of her bed and laying a hand over hers.

"My head aches abominably, but aside from that, I'm as fit as a battered old fiddle. What happened? I've been trying to remember."

"What happened is that you did something terribly brave and saved our lives."

Sinclair said, "They tossed a hand grenade into the hotel room, and you chucked it right out again. I've never seen anyone move so fast. You should bowl for England, Miss Damm."

"Ah," she said. "And I suppose it went off and knocked me for six?"

"Yes," Begg answered. "Then the Red King set fire to the hotel. It was a close call. We only just made it out."

Her eyes widened. "Carrying me?"

"Needless to say."

He went on to describe everything that had occurred: how they'd spent a couple of days in this hospital, how the old woman had directed them to the fancy dress ball, how one of the Red King's gang had murdered a man, and how Monsieur Zenith had then killed the assassin.

"Zenith!" She gasped in surprise. "Well, there's a complication. How is he involved in this?"

"I have no idea. I intend to find out."

Damm addressed Sinclair. "Would you go fetch a pen and paper, Taffy? I don't recall the names of all the Red King's victims, but I can certainly list a few."

Sinclair nodded and left the room.

"If I were you," she said to Begg, "that is where I would begin. Sir Vivian, if he is directing the Red King, must have a reason for killing these people. Doubtless, they have something in common."

Begg gave a grunt of agreement. "I had already reached that conclusion. I intend to interview the Frenchman you saved."

"Apollinaire de Villiers. I have his address."

"What does he do?"

"I never found out. The old woman gave only his name. There was no time to—"

"How?" Begg interrupted. "How does she pass information to you?"

"I was told that if I ever heard this tune whistled, I was to check a certain post box in a particular office." She whistled four bars of a simple refrain, while taking from the bedside table a small purse, which had been retrieved from the pocket of her shredded and scorched jacket. Withdrawing from it a small key, she passed it over. "You should go and check it. She told me it would, from time to time, contain a note identifying the Red King's next target, and where and when the assassination would be attempted. De Villiers was the first to be named in this way. I tried to prevent his murder, and—you know the rest."

"I wonder," mused Begg, "how the old woman learns who is to be killed?"

"I imagine that Major Nye is somehow intercepting communications between Sir Vivian and the assassin. He then passes what he learns to her, and she to me."

"Hmm." In his mind's eye, the metatemporal detective pictured the radio transmitter he had seen in the Secret Service director's office.

Sinclair returned and passed to her a notepad and pen. She wrote an address and number. "This is where you'll find the box. And this"—another address—"is where de Villiers lives. It's not far from your hotel." She thought for a moment then listed eight names, paused, her brow creasing with concentration, and added three more. "Those are the victims, the names I remember. Perhaps some misspellings."

She lay back on her pillows and her eyes fluttered with tiredness.

"My apologies," Begg murmured. "We should let you rest. It has been—"

"Wait!" she said. "There's a 'scarlet woman.' De Villiers fell under the spell of Mademoiselle Béatrice Lefevre. It was she who sent him to his intended doom. If you can . . ." Her voice grew faint. " . . . if you can find her, she might lead you to . . . to the Red . . ."

She was asleep.

Begg tore the page from the notebook, and also the blank one beneath it—a precaution, for the pressure of the pencil had made indentations—and pocketed them.

He and Sinclair left the room, made their way out of the hospital, and secured a calash, always to be found waiting near hotels and public institutions.

They journeyed back to the Pera Palas in silence, Sinclair nodding off and Begg immersed in thought.

When they finally took to their beds, they slept long and soundly.

The next morning, their sixth day in Istanbul, they arose late and consumed a large breakfast.

"That's quite a shiner," Sinclair observed, scrutinising Begg's aquiline face.

"If anyone asks, I'll tell them I was thrown from a horse."

"Before being run over by the stampeding herd."

Sinclair was much more presentable, having only a bruise on his chin, which was easily concealed with makeup from the theatrical kit they had brought with them.

An hour later, in the guise of a messenger, the pathologist knocked on Monsieur de Villiers's door. The Frenchman's home, located five blocks from the hotel, was a large, many-roomed, top-floor apartment.

Begg waited along the corridor.

A servant answered and stiffly declared that his master had gone to work. He gave the office address. Sinclair started to thank him, but the door slammed in his face.

The isolated two-storey office building was not far away, on the Galata side of the Golden Horn, overlooking the water. Its ground-floor rooms were empty and available to rent. The Frenchman occupied the two upper rooms, both opening onto a landing and connected by an internal door.

De Villiers received them with puzzlement, trying to place their vaguely familiar faces, looking askance at Begg's swollen eye.

"British detectives, you say?" he asked, ushering them into a stylishly furnished room and to chairs facing his desk. He settled behind it and offered cigars and cigarettes, which they politely declined. "I can't imagine how I might be of any assistance to you. What is it you are investigating?"

"Your attempted murder, m'sieu," said Begg.

The man blanched. "I . . . I do not understand. I have not . . . there has been no—"

"Five nights ago, a brute named Suleyman attacked you. When you fled from him, you collided with us. Do you recollect?"

De Villiers moistened his lips with his tongue. He coughed, picked up a pen and put it down again. "*Je m'excuse. Je ne sais pas* . . . I do not know to what you refer. What you say happened, never—"

"Can you explain to me how you acquired those bruises around your neck?" Begg interjected.

De Villiers put a hand to his collar. "I . . . I cannot—"

"Also," murmured Begg, "there is the matter of Mademoiselle Lefevre."

The Frenchman gaped.

Taffy Sinclair murmured, "Perhaps a brandy, m'sieu?"

De Villiers gulped and nodded.

Sinclair stood and crossed to a bureau, on which stood a decanter and glasses. He brought them to the desk and served de Villiers a large measure.

Their host, with a trembling hand, put the liquor to his lips and tossed it back.

"Suleyman is a member of the Red King gang," Begg told him.

"*Mon Dieu!*" de Villiers groaned. "That demon! What have I done to him? I am . . . I am just a—"

"As a matter of fact, it is what you are that interests me. I saw the title 'consultant' on your doorplate. A consultant in what field?"

De Villiers took up the decanter and hastily poured more brandy.

"I . . . um . . . I advise Turkish governmental organisations and various religious bodies regarding the practice of *laïcité*—the constitutional principle of secularism. As you must surely understand, the separation of the church from the state in a land as ancient as this is a very tricky business."

"I imagine so," said Begg. "For how long have you acted in this capacity?"

"I was commissioned by the Turkish government shortly after the founding of the republic."

"Have you ever received threats?"

"*Bien sûr!* But only of the fleeting, indignant sort. As a part of my role, I am perceived to deprive certain people of their influence, and as you might suppose, they are not happy about it. I have been a victim of anger and insults, but I have never truly felt myself to be in danger."

"What of the Red King? Do you know anything of him? Has he ever approached you or communicated with you?"

"I know only what I have read in the newspapers. If I have ever had any contact with him, I was not aware of it."

Begg was quiet for a moment, then said, "That is not strictly the truth, is it, m'sieu?"

De Villiers frowned. "What do you mean?"

"I mean that you were lured into Suleyman's hands by Béatrice Lefevre, who appears to be a member of the Red King gang."

The Frenchman groaned and lowered his face into his hands. "I am an imbecile. A complete fool."

"How did you meet her? Under what circumstance?"

Without looking up, he answered, "It was one evening some weeks ago—seven, eight, I do not remember—and I had just finished a long dinner meeting with a member of the foreign office. We finished at the restaurant and went across the road to a bar. Béatrice was in there with two female friends. I later learned that it is a place they frequent most evenings. It was there that she first spoke to me and . . . and . . ." His voice faltered.

"Where is this bar?"

"It is on the Siraselviler road. It is called the Sultan's Palace."

"And if she is there, how would we recognise her?"

"Her two friends are tall and black skinned. Béatrice, she is the most beautiful woman who ever lived."

The detective was silent for half a minute, then said, "Do you have any connection with Roumania?"

"Roumania? No, none whatever."

"Do you know what a *Salut Christi* is?"

"No."

With a nod to mark the end of the interview, Sir Seaton Begg got to his feet. Sinclair followed his example.

"That will do for now," said the detective. "If anything occurs to you that might be useful to us, we are staying at the Pera Palas."

"*Attendez!*" de Villiers cried out. "You are going? But . . . but . . . am I still in danger?"

Begg shrugged. "I do not know. If you have family back in France, perhaps this would be a good time to visit them."

They took their departure.

"Where to now?" Sinclair asked as they stepped into the street.

"We're going to check the post office then spend a few hours in the Köprülü Library," Begg replied. "It is by no means the largest in the city, but it is certainly the most ancient. It will have the best selection of old maps. You will collect together those that chart the Balkans, dating back as many years as possible, and identify and list every province, kingdom, principality, and nation state that has ever existed in that region. While you are doing that, I shall seek information concerning the *Salut Christi*."

The post box was empty.

By sunset, they knew a great deal about the Balkans, but very little about the mysterious object thought to be in Major Nye's possession. Begg had found but a single reference to it, which stated that a silversmith had crafted the *Salut Christi* in Constantinople over a thousand years ago. It was among many treasures given by Irene of Athens, empress of the Eastern Roman Empire, to Pope Leo III, as symbolic rapprochement between East and West.

This told Begg that the object was ancient, but maddeningly, aside from it being made from silver, it failed to reveal exactly what it was.

As evening drew in, he and Sinclair took a cab to Siraselviler and had a long dinner in the restaurant opposite the Sultan's Palace.

At nine o'clock, they crossed to the bar and settled in a shadowy corner table, each nursing a glass of raki.

Mademoiselle Béatrice Lefevre entered at eleven. As expected, she was accompanied by her two tall friends. The trio ordered drinks and occupied a table near the window.

She was a small, dainty woman, probably in her thirties, with a profusion of black hair and the kind of face that could be beautiful or ugly, depending on her mood.

Begg's eyes widened.

"Do you see who it is, Taffy?"

"By George, yes!" answered Sinclair. "She has aged a little, but it is unmistakably the criminal Madame Vera Pym."

"Yes," said Begg. "La Pym . . . who, the last time we encountered her, attempted to kill Monsieur Zenith!"

CHAPTER 9

The *Sigiliul Tutorelui*

"Pym and Zenith have—or had—a complex relationship," Begg went on, "for their deadly rivalry, which I believe began in Petrograd during the February Revolution, later, in Paris, transformed into a romantic affair. They were together for nearly a year, until she mysteriously vanished. It was rumoured they had quarrelled, even that he had done away with her. She has been neither seen nor heard from since 1921."

His friend gave a low whistle. "So are they in Istanbul as friends or foes?"

The metatemporal detective shrugged. "I rely on you to find out. We are going to divide our forces. You'll stick to her like glue, while I attempt to pierce the veil obscuring the object at the heart of all this."

Doctor Sinclair sipped his drink and looked over its brim at Vera Pym. He could only catch glimpses of her now. The bar was getting lively. She was chatting and smiling.

"But don't take any unnecessary risks," Begg warned. "She can be tricky."

Keeping his face averted from the women's table, he rose. "I shall see you when I see you. I daresay you're in for an all-nighter. When you've finished that raki, fill yourself with coffee."

Begg took a circuitous route out of the bar, careful not to be noticed.

Striding up the hill toward the hotel, he pulled from his pocket a packet of cigarettes. Then, remembering his lungs, he muttered an imprecation, and was returning it when an old beggar approached and reached out with a whining plea.

Begg passed the packet over.

The act of generosity was a signal to every other mendicant on the street.

"I haven't eaten for two days," whimpered a ragged youth.

"I have nowhere to sleep," claimed a one-armed man.

"Baksheesh, baksheesh," moaned a withered Arab.

"I can't feed my family," wept an obese woman.

"Give generously," creaked an ancient hag. "And, for pity's sake, keep moving."

Begg pressed a coin into each extended hand. When he walked away, it was with a folded note in his fingers.

Major Nye's agent!

As much as he desired to stop and question her, the directive had been clear, and Begg was too well trained to allow his curiosity to get the better of him. He strode on, leaving behind all the answers she undoubtedly held.

How extensive was Nye's network of operatives? Begg was obviously being watched, his movements reported.

Rounding a corner, he increased his pace, slipped into a side street, and sheltered in a dark doorway. Ten minutes later, he concluded that he was not being followed.

He angled the note to catch a glimmer from a nearby window and read the crabbed handwriting.

Time bomb in your room.
The Red King's third attempt!

The detective resumed his journey.

Tomorrow, he would seek new accommodation—and keep the address from Sir Vivian Clarke.

At the Pera Palas, he went straight to his suite and looked under the bed. Nothing there. He began a systematic search, straining his ears for the faintest ticking. Where was it? For what time was it set?

He pulled furniture away from the wall, felt under it, yanked out drawers and emptied them, opened cupboards and the wardrobe, discovered nothing. Under the mattress. Behind the curtains. The suitcases. The chamber pot.

He rolled the rug and examined the floorboards.

He tapped every inch of every wall.

When he could not think of anywhere else to look, he glanced at his wristwatch. His painstaking search had taken more than an hour. It was quarter past one in the morning.

The bomb, he supposed, would be set to explode when he was most likely to be in bed.

"Could be any time now," he said, peering around the room. "If it's not in the furniture, or under the floor, or in the walls, it can only be—"

He looked up.

Then, he was through the door and sprinting for the stairs. He went down three at a time, shot across the lobby, and barked, "Night manager!" at the desk clerk.

"M'sieu? Might I enquire—?"

A door behind the clerk opened and a smartly suited Turk emerged. "Can I assist?"

"I'm in twenty-two. Which suite is directly above?"

Responding to the detective's urgency of tone, the man answered, "Thirty-two."

"Anyone in it?"

"It was booked early this morning but the man, who arrived this afternoon, only stayed for half an hour before claiming the hotel to be unsatisfactory. He was a rather bad-tempered—"

"It's empty?"

"Yes, m'sieu. Do you wish to—?"

"Give me the key. There's a bomb in there."

The Turk blanched. "A . . . a bomb?"

"The key!"

Begg's authority was overwhelming. The night manager jerked the key from the wall rack and handed it over. Begg snatched it and was up the stairs in a blur of motion.

Suite 32 matched exactly the dimensions of the rooms below. He careened into the bed chamber, heaved the bed aside, and tore up the rug.

A floorboard had been cut through, a small section removed, then replaced. He squatted, lifted it out, and exposed—

Four sticks of gelignite! Sufficient to blow out the side of the hotel!

The detonator and timing mechanism consisted of a cap, probably containing fulminate of mercury, a large battery, and a ticking alarm clock. A metal box, bolted around one end of the battery, concealed its terminals. From it, a bundle of red wires emerged. He knew that only two of them were connected, but there was no way of telling which. Nor could he see where they attached to the cap, for that was similarly protected, and also thick with decoy wires. Furthermore, wires wrapped the entire contrivance to hold it together. It was impossible to see to what, if anything, they were connected.

Cutting a wrong wire could set off the bomb.

The alarm was set for one-thirty.

It was already twenty-eight minutes past.

No time to get it out of the hotel.

Begg pulled his pipe tool from his pocket—a tamper with various foldable blades, rods, and scrapers. He selected the biggest blade and placed it against a wire.

He paused.

The seconds swept by.

Then he hissed through his teeth. There was no time for finesse, and he was not a gambler. Brute force was required!

He moved the point of the blade to the edge of the alarm clock, dug it in, cracked open the glass front, levered it off, and threw it aside. He tapped the exposed clock face. It was tin. Again, he jammed in the knife, next to the number three, and pried up the side of the disc. He bent it, then used his fingers to bend it more.

A minute remaining.

A metal plate, attached by three tiny screws, shielded the clock's mechanism.

He selected a small flat-ended blade from his tool and put it to use.

Fifty-five seconds.

The first screw came loose.

He started on the next.

Forty seconds.

A bead of perspiration dripped from his forehead.

Done. Now, the last.

Thirty-five seconds.

The final screw came away and, with fifteen seconds remaining, Begg pulled away the plate. He snapped the blade back into the tool and unfolded a thin rod meant for cleaning the stem of a pipe.

He jammed it into the clock's cogs, squeezed his eyes shut and held his breath.

Three. Two. One.

Silence.

Begg expelled air and opened one eye.

The clock had stopped two seconds before the alarm.

After assuring himself that the tool was wedged securely, Begg fell back, sat on the floor, and waited for his heart to stop pounding.

Only then did he become aware of a commotion in the corridor.

He stood and left the suite, locking the door behind him.

The hotel's night staff was busy rousing the guests.

"Fire alarm, m'sieu," a maid told him as she passed. "You must vacate the premises, please."

Begg went downstairs and located the night manager.

"It is all right. I have deactivated it. The guests can return to their rooms. It is perfectly safe." He passed over the key. "In the morning, I will arrange for someone from Gelecek Engineering to come and remove the device. Until that person arrives, do not enter the suite or allow anyone else to do so."

The Turk was plainly frightened. "I do not understand. Why would anyone—?"

"They were trying to kill me. I am sorry. Tomorrow, I shall check out. There will be no further incidents, I assure you."

As he returned to his room, Begg muttered to himself, "None at the Pera Palas, anyway."

He undressed, washed, went to bed and slept soundly.

The next morning, there was no sign of Taffy Sinclair. Begg was not unduly concerned. His friend knew how to handle himself.

After breakfast, he put through a call to George Philips and told him about the time bomb. The engineer agreed to send a man to fetch it.

"I must apologise," said Begg. "There has been no opportunity to survey the bridge. I'm not even certain the cover story is of any use now. It feels as if all the principal players in the affair are already aware of who I am—and also of my every move."

"Not to worry, old chap," said Philips. "About the bridge, I mean."

They talked for a few minutes more. Begg asked about Bingo Ramsey, who had worked at Gelecek.

"Just another of my many engineers," Philips said. "Tunnels, I think. I had little personal contact with him. I'll ask old Voskanyan next time I see him."

"Why him particularly?" Begg enquired.

"Oh, I once or twice saw them knocking around together, that's all."

The call ended with Philips offering whatever further assistance Begg might require.

The detective spent the rest of the morning visiting embassies. At the British, he arranged for a message to be transmitted to Secret Service headquarters in London. Though written in code and accompanied by numbers and certain phrases that established the bona fides of its sender, the substance of it was,

```
URGENT. Send any and all information by which
connections might be established between Monsieur
Zenith and artefacts of historical interest.
```

Begg didn't expect the reply to be anything more than a list of antiques the albino had stolen or attempted to steal—but it was worth a try.

Next, he cross-checked Violet Damm's list of assassinated men against the embassy's register of British citizens. There were three matches. Their occupations were listed as architect, economist, and professor of history. The Hon. Henry Petherick, who could now be added to the list, was registered as a curator of art.

At the Dutch embassy, he found one match, a retired minister of agriculture.

The remaining seven victims were French: a railway engineer, two political theorists, another economist, and two who, like Apollinaire de Villiers, bore the somewhat vague title of "consultant."

At midday, Begg secured new quarters for himself and Sinclair: the top-floor suite in a much smaller hotel—the Shangri-La—over the bridge in the Fatih quarter. He returned to the Pera Palas, packed his and Sinclair's suitcases, and checked out. He left two notes with the desk clerk: one for the pathologist and the other for Violet Damm. Both were written in code and gave the address of the Shangri-La.

Leaving the Invicta two-seater for Sinclair to bring later, he sent his luggage ahead by one cab and travelled himself in another. He instructed the driver to take a circuitous route, disembarked half a mile distant from his destination, and proceeded the rest of the way in such a slippery fashion that anyone who might be following would certainly be lost.

The noise, frenetic commotion, and heady odours of Istanbul enfolded him but hardly registered on his senses. He was absorbed, his intellect so engaged in speculation that, though he was intent on losing any shadow that might be following, he moved mechanically, guided by sheer experience.

He entered the hotel, quickly arranged the luggage and hung up the clothes, then went out again and lunched in a nearby restaurant.

Begg ruminated on what he had learned. He was beginning to form a theory. He had a tentative idea of what linked the assassinated men.

With hunger satisfied, and unexpected rain now falling, he returned to the British embassy. The reply was waiting. It was precisely what he had expected: a list of burglaries, each incident accompanied by a reference number. Begg was familiar with all the cases but one. It was listed as "The Battle for the *Sigiliul Tutorelui*."

"I need to commandeer your telegraph office," he told the clerk.

"Will you require an operator, sir?"

"No, thank you, but it's a Secret Service matter, so I'll require privacy. It shouldn't take long."

"It's quite all right, sir, take as much time as you need—but wouldn't it be more secure to—?" He glanced at the door marked STAFF ONLY, as if to ask, *Why send from here and not the Secret Service HQ?*

Begg, with an acknowledging nod, said, "Under normal circumstances, yes, but—well—I can't speak about it. You understand, of course."

"Ah! I do, sir, I do." the clerk exclaimed, though he plainly did not. He tapped the side of his nose, and said, with a conspiratorial smile, "This way, please—"

Minutes later, in a locked and windowless room, Begg signalled London and requested particulars concerning the item of interest.

The response came in code. He thanked the sender, signed off, then settled to decipher the jumble.

Status: Top Secret.

Information gleaned from the deathbed confession of Thomas "Trolleyman" Batson to Detective-Inspector William Harcourt on 27 February 1930. Reported to Secret Service by Chief Commissioner of Scotland Yard Sir Henry Fairfax.

Winter 1922. Gun battle at Woodbine Hall, Scotland. Multiple fatalities. Three factions fighting for possession of a ring known as *Sigiliul Tutorelui*, "The Guardian's Seal."

Factions led by:
1) Colonel Simeon Vassilionu, Roumanian, ex-military. Criminal.
2) Sir Edmund James Woodbine, with General Josef Gojkovic, a mercenary.
3) The albino (Zodiac/Zenith/White Wolf) and his gang (the League of the Last).

Details are vague. Vassilionu is understood to have gained possession of the ring circa 1918 while raiding and pillaging provincial territories in what is now northern Roumania. Sir Edmund commissioned Gojkovic to recover it. At Woodbine Hall, all parties engaged in battle. Only the albino and his criminal gang survived. Sir Edmund's fate is unknown (presumed dead). His identity has since been questioned. The albino took possession of the ring, but is understood to have later lost it.

The *Sigiliul Tutorelui* is described as a large black opal on a gold setting. The gemstone is inscribed with eight arrows radiating from a

```
central point. While extensive research has been
undertaken by the department, few historical
references have been found. From those discovered,
it can be understood that the ring was once
considered a powerful symbol in the land of its
origin (unidentified) and was said to confer
Dreptul de Tutelă (the Right of Guardianship).
Guardianship over what is not known.
```

Sir Seaton Begg sat and pondered for a few minutes, then slipped the transcription into his pocket and left the embassy. He was eager to now spend time with the sketches Taffy had made in the Köprülü Library: his summaries of all the unstable borders and ever-shifting—and vanishing—territories of the Balkan peninsular.

He returned to the Shangri-La.

The sketches resembled scribbles, but there was a method to them. They were a palimpsest of place names, many of them unfamiliar, others recognisable but with their spelling contorted, all surrounded by—and in numerous instances bisected by—multiple intertwining lines, which marked their ever-changing borders.

Thracia, Thema, Dyrrhachium, Serblia, Pokuttya, Bukovina, Hertza, Chrobatia, Dalmatiae, Tara de Sus, Dobruja, Valachia, Maramureș, Bessarabia—and so many more.

Now, a process of elimination.

Zenith had begun his criminal career in London fourteen years ago, in 1919, at the age of twenty or thereabouts, though Begg knew this detail to be meaningless, for the albino was, like himself, a metatemporal, with a tendency to appear the same age at all times, his life nonsequential. Nevertheless—1919! It was only a year after Colonel Vassilionu had looted the *Sigiliul Tutorelui* from the northern Balkans!

It was on that region that the detective now focused, considering only those provinces or principalities existing around the turn of the century, when the albino was supposedly born.

He narrowed it down to five territories and memorised their names: Tara Norilor; Tara Fierarilor; Lamaneagra; Muntibolnavi; and Morminte de Munte. All tiny. All gone.

He decided to revisit the library. As he stood up and reached for his hat, he glanced at the mantelpiece clock. The day had slipped away.

The sun was setting. The muezzins were summoning the faithful.

The library would be closed.

Where was Taffy Sinclair?

CHAPTER 10
Sinclair on the Trail

Begg did not learn until many hours later what had become of his friend.

After the metatemporal detective had left the Sultan's Palace bar, Madame Vera Pym and her two friends remained until past midnight. They then paid their bill and departed, with Taffy Sinclair following cautiously behind. Kissing cheeks, the women went their separate ways, the tall women in a calash turning west, La Pym in a hansom heading north.

A spring shower had just begun, and for the first time since Begg and Sinclair's arrival, the air felt cool and fresh.

Restaurants and bars lined this stretch of the Siraselviler road, all now closing. People, many of them drunk and rowdy, were spilling onto the street—hailing, arguing over, and occupying carriages as soon as the vehicles appeared.

Sinclair had no time to join the fray, so he set after Pym on foot. He hurried through the thinning crowd of carousers, trying to keep his considerable bulk out of sight should she happen to look over her shoulder.

Just as the traffic cleared a little and the hansom started to outpace him, a Ford Model A passed. He raced after it, surreptitiously jumped onto its back, and clung to the spare tyre, crouching as low as he could. The driver surely felt the weight of him, yet did not stop to investigate. Sinclair covered almost a mile that way, the rain soaking him through, the hansom not far ahead.

They travelled alongside the Bosphorus. The road soon opened out and the car accelerated to overtake the hansom. Sinclair hopped off, staggered, caught his balance, and sprinted. He kept it up for another half mile, his quarry drawing steadily ahead, before his chest tightened and his breath began to whistle and rasp.

Determined as he was, he had to stop, just for a moment, and bent over with his hands gripping his knees, panting hard.

He heard an approaching engine. Thank heavens, another Ford! It was a stroke of good fortune—there were relatively few cars in Istanbul, let alone at this time of night—but not altogether surprising. Eight years ago, the American motorcar company had established a manufacturing plant in the Tophane district, which he had just passed, and many of its car-owning executives lived in the richer quarters that Vera Pym was now entering.

The Model A clattered by, belching smoke and obviously in dire need of attention from a garage mechanic. Sinclair bolted after it and repeated his trick of making himself an uninvited and unseen passenger. The fumes stung his eyes, his lungs protested at yet more punishment, and the spare tyre was slippery with rain, but with muscles burning, he clung on for all he was worth.

Ahead, the hansom rolled steadily onward.

A mile in this fashion, then they were in the Beşiktaş neighbourhood, where the venue for the ill-fated fancy dress ball was located, its surrounding walls now to the right.

The motorcar turned inland and Sinclair hopped off. The road was empty, and he had no choice but to resort again to what little athletic ability he still possessed, compromised as it was by the awful hotel fire.

He jogged alongside the pavilion grounds, saw the grand old building on the hilltop, the Bosphorus behind it, and over the water, the black valley slopes of the Scutari quarter on the Anatolian shore. There were only a few twinkling lights there, like fallen stars.

To his left, the land sloped up, all trees and houses and darkness.

The shower abruptly stopped.

He slowed, hobbled on, wheezing, determined but hurting, the lamps of the distant hansom only just visible.

Stay with it! he told himself. *If she doesn't lead you to the Red King, perhaps she'll lead you to Zenith!*

Five minutes later, he knew himself defeated. His quarry was out of sight, and he was out of breath.

He stumbled on and on, limping past manor houses, none lit, until he eventually came to one that was.

On its perimeter wall, either side of a big wooden double gate, there were two paraffin lamps. Both were glowing, which suggested to Sinclair that someone was expected home late.

A small door was inset into the right-hand gate. He tried the handle. Locked. In the damp ground, he saw fresh prints of a woman's shoes. He followed them backward. They disappeared at the side of the road beside the fresh-looking indentations made by wheels and hoofs.

The signs were clear as day. The hansom had stopped here, Vera Pym had disembarked and gone in through the door, and the vehicle had departed.

Walking alongside the wall, the doctor circled the manor until he came to a flowering horse chestnut tree, clothed in its "candles." In daylight, it must have looked spectacular, but at that particular moment, to Sinclair, who eyed the branches overhanging the wall, it was worth consideration for one reason only. It was his way in.

He jumped, grabbed hold of a low bough, heaved his considerable bulk up, and found a comfortable position in which to rest and wait. Through the foliage, he could see the manor's various lit windows. All were curtained. He would wait for the lights to go out—and for some time after that—before entering the grounds.

He shivered. His clothes were damp and the air, while not cold, was nothing like as humid and clammy as it had been over the past week.

"Poor old Begg," he told himself. "Asleep in a comfortable bed while I'm having all the fun."

Had he only known it, Sir Seaton Begg was at that moment applying a blade to a time bomb!

An hour later, one after the other, the windows went dark, until only two, both on the ground floor, remained illuminated. The front door opened and people emerged. He heard men's voices. He couldn't make out what they were saying, they were too far away, but he recognised Turkish and French. There was a third language, which was unfamiliar.

He watched as two Buicks and a large van drove from the rear of the premises to the front. Six men and one woman—not La Pym—then set about transporting boxes and items of luggage from the house to the van. The woman started to sing "Goodnight Vienna" and her voice carried on the still night air and was one of the loveliest Sinclair had ever heard.

But for a single fact, he could have imagined himself mistaken:

that the signora had not entered this property; that it belonged to a famous songstress who, like most performers, kept atypical hours and was now preparing to travel to another city, there to thrill new audiences.

However, there was that single fact—

One of her companions was Suleyman the Strangler! His immense form was unmistakable.

This manor, Sinclair thought, *must be the headquarters of the Red King.* Except, not for much longer, for certainly the gang was on the move.

He would not be able to follow when the vehicles departed. It had been difficult enough tailing a hansom at midnight. Chasing two Buicks and a van at this hour—impossible! Nor could he creep closer in the hope of overhearing a clue to their destination. There was no cover. The grounds were just flat lawns and shallow flower beds. The only option was to wait until they departed, then break into the house and search it.

He sat, hoping for one of them to step into what little light emanated from the two windows, and while he waited, he listened with pure enjoyment to the woman's marvellous voice. Now she was singing "April in Paris."

Her hair was platinum white and styled after Jean Harlow's, but aside from that he could discern frustratingly little. Of the men, only their suited and hatted shapes were clear. Suleyman was gigantic, another was dwarfish—and bawled an occasional Americanism, such as "Gee whiz!" and "Waddya say?"—but the remaining four were thoroughly average in build with no feature that stood out in the gloom.

It took them forty minutes to load the van. Then one of the men strode along the driveway and opened the double gates. The rest got into the vehicles, apart from one who remained in the house, and for whom they waited. When he emerged, having extinguished the last lamp, he was laughing—a particularly cruel laugh that made Sinclair shudder.

The man closed the front door, crossed to the van, and climbed into the cabin.

Engines started. The vehicles moved out onto the road. One of the Buicks stopped while the person by the gates closed and locked them. Then he was aboard and it was off. The sound of motors faded into the distance.

Sinclair waited for ten minutes, then shinned out along a branch and, in a shower of leaves, dropped into the garden. He dashed to the house and pressed himself beside a window. He tried it and, as expected, found it secured. The next was also locked. Treading carefully, rounding a corner to the back of the house, he tested two more with the same result. Then he came to a back door, which, at his touch, opened inward on well-oiled hinges.

From somewhere below, he heard the jangle of bells, and looking up, saw a wire stretching from the top of the door. He had set off an alarm.

Cursing himself for an amateurish dolt, Sinclair drew his Walter PP and sidled into the passage.

Outside, the stars were still obscured by the passing rain clouds. Inside, all the curtains were drawn and no light shone. Sinclair could hardly see a thing. Except—

A little way along the passage, a line of illumination marked the bottom of a door. Since, seen from outside, all the rooms were in darkness, this either opened onto an inner chamber or, more likely, given the common layout of manor houses such as this, to the top of the stairs to the cellar.

The bells had clanged then stopped. There was now absolute silence.

Sinclair, with his ears straining for the slightest sound, cautiously moved forward. He came to the door, slowly wrapped his fingers around its handle, and very gently and slowly turned it. He paused, listened, then pulled the door open just an inch. The hinges gave an enormous shriek. He jumped out of his skin and, shocked, froze, his finger whitening on his pistol's trigger.

Light radiated from below. There came a thump followed by a muffled, panic-filled female voice.

"Hmmmph!"

Sinclair threw caution to the wind. He yanked open the door and hurtled down the stairs into a well-lit cellar. There, he stumbled to a halt, eyes widening, mouth dropping open, confronted by a sight so fiendishly horrible he would never be able to forget it.

The details would only come to him much later, seen in nightmares, for the most part.

The chamber was large and high, the ceiling crossed by wooden beams. The flagstone floor was strewn with lengths of rope of varying thicknesses, many of them tied at one end, seemingly without rhyme or reason, to diverse objects: a chair, a flat iron, a bicycle wheel, a small anvil, a sack of potatoes, a three-legged stool, and a rack of fire tongs.

A rubber hose, attached to a tap at a sink in one corner, snaked across the floor then rose to a ceiling beam, to which it had been affixed. From it, a thin stream of water trickled into a large bucket of the sort employed on building sites. This was suspended from the same beam and was very gradually lowering as it filled. The rope holding it ran through a fixed pulley bolted into the beam, across the ceiling below the next three beams, then through another fixed pulley attached to the fourth. From this, it ran down to where the counterweight was held in a noose.

The counterweight was Madame Vera Pym!

Her face was turning blue, her eyes were wide with terror, her hands were tied behind her, and she was standing on the very tips of her toes. In a matter of seconds, the weight of the water would drag her up. Death by hanging!

CHAPTER 11
The Missing Chapter

The Köprülü Library was a small, square, and rather unattractive structure located in the Eminönü district, across the street from the tomb of Sultan Mahmut II.

After a restorative sleep, Sir Seaton Begg travelled there in a horse-drawn cab. It had rained during the night and looked as if it might rain again. The streets were puddled, and the air was deliciously cool and fresh. He filled his lungs and felt them much recovered.

Where was Taffy?

Begg fretted.

He crossed the library's well-kept gardens and, upon entering the building, immediately perceived that something was wrong. The three librarians, their voices low but their gesticulations wild, were conversing with a fourth man. He was attempting to placate them. They were plainly angry about something.

Begg approached, maintaining a casual air, as if on his way to the maps section that he and Sinclair had visited yesterday.

His Turkish was adequate for most occasions, but the four

men were conversing too rapidly for him to follow. He heard only snatches of conversation:

"—to commit an act of vandalism like this in our—"

"—knowledge that can be found nowhere else! Nowhere, I tell you! This is a crime against—"

"—as I already told you. He was white, everywhere white, except for his eyes, which were a ghastly red, and he was—"

"Pardon me," Begg said, altering course and stepping to the table around which they were gathered. "Did I hear correctly? You referred to an albino?"

"Yes!" chorused the librarians.

The other man turned and glowered. "This is an official matter, sir. If you would please go about your business—"

He was an extraordinarily unprepossessing fellow. A twisted spine pushed his left shoulder up and forward. One eye was wide and bulging, the other small and squinting; his nose crooked and mashed flat; his snaggled teeth too big for his mouth; and his ears misshapen lumps of gristle. There was not a single strand of hair on his head but, in compensation, a curly, jet-black beard tangled down to his chest.

Begg murmured, "If I might speak to you for a moment—*Polis Memuru?*"

The man responded with a derisive snort. "I am not a police officer. My name is Sabahattin Sans-Serif—"

The metatemporal detective felt a twinge of amusement. In a library of ancient manuscripts, this man was surely the only sans serif present! And no doubt Sinclair, when told, would note the name of a common typeface of that variety: *"Grotesque."* Singularly appropriate!

"—I am a special agent of the MAH."

"Ah," said Begg.

Millî Emniyet Hizmeti, the National Security Service, named MAH by the Turkish government to keep the unauthorised guessing what the misleading acronym might mean.

"I am Sir Seaton Begg, a private detective, currently on assignment for the British Secret Service."

Sans-Serif made a noise like a locomotive releasing pent-up steam.

"A moment, gentlemen," he said to the librarians, then grasped Begg by the forearm and dragged him forcibly across to one of the small reading rooms. It was empty. The agent kicked the door shut behind them.

"So!" he said, releasing his grip. "Yet another comes crawling from under his rock. By God, will you foreign devils never give up? We have just shaken off an empire, and already others seek to swallow us up again. No, Mr. English Spy! This country will not be owned by your country! I said the same to your German counterpart yesterday, and if I ever locate the Bolshevik spy—because I don't doubt there's one here, too—I shall tell him as well. We are not Ottomans, we are not English, we are not Germans, we are not Russians." He slapped his chest. "We are Turks! Turks! Turks!"

"Quite so," Begg agreed amicably. "I am here to hunt a man who is assassinating men and women of all those nationalities, as well as your own."

Officially, he was here to locate Major Nye, but to say so might complicate matters.

"You mean the Red King?"

"I do, and I have reason to believe that an albino is in some way involved. May I ask what happened here?"

Sans-Serif's bulging eye narrowed. He gazed at Begg dubiously.

"I don't like you," he growled. "You awful English with your weak milky tea and your how-do-you-dos. Do you play cricket?"

"Yes," said Begg.

"Cricket is an abomination. Golf?"

"Yes."

"A game for simpletons and children. Uff!" He paused and exhaled noisily. "The albino was the first customer to arrive this morning. He took from the shelves a bound volume entitled *Al'amakin Wal'ashya' Almuqadasat Li-rumilya*. That's Arabic."

"The Sacred Places and Objects of Rumelia," Begg translated.

"He ripped out an entire chapter," Sans-Serif went on, "then ran down the stairs into the vault and vanished into thin air."

"How is that possible?"

The Turk shrugged his right shoulder. "Foreign trickery of some sort. You are all the same. Satan makes you artful." Reaching into his pocket, he pulled out a pistol. "Anyway, it's time for me to shoot you. Where would you prefer, in the arm or the leg?"

"Shoot me?" said Begg. "Why?"

"Because I have an aversion to spies. Also, I've told you what I know, and in return, I have heard nothing."

"He calls himself Zenith. Sometimes Zodiac. Other names, too. In America, they know him as White Wolf."

"Zenith? Zodiac? White Wolf? What kind of idiotic names are they? They are as ridiculous as Sir Seaton! There are no such names." He stepped back and raised his weapon, holding it close to his face and squinting his already-squinty eye along its sights, aiming at Begg's legs.

"I believe he's Roumanian," the detective added.

"What? Oh ho! Well then! Yes, I can believe Zenith or Zodiac or Wolf of a Roumanian. I'll believe almost anything of them." He lowered the gun and sighed. "Roumania was once a part of Rumelia. Do you know that?"

"I do."

"Rumelia. The Ottoman Empire's name for the Balkans. But now, the Roumanians are Roumanians and the Turks are Turks."

"It may be," suggested Begg, "that there are parts of Roumania where the people don't consider themselves Roumanian at all. I suspect that Zenith is from one such place."

"And what? The book contained damning information about that place? About its people? Ah, that's what it is. They are not people at all. He is a vampyr! The Carpathians are teeming with the accursed creatures. Zenith or Zodiac removed the chapter which told how he might be destroyed. Then he disappeared from the vault by turning into smoke. You see, Mr. English Spy? It's all making sense now."

"I am not inclined to believe in the supernatural," Begg objected, rather disingenuously. "I'll not be convinced he vanished into thin air until I've examined the vault and discounted any other possibility."

"Then come and see it," said Sans-Serif, pocketing his pistol. He led the way back into the main library.

"A moment," Begg murmured, and crossed to the desk where the librarians remained gathered around the vandalised book, mourning as if it were a dead child.

"Which was the chapter removed?" he asked.

One of them, elderly and stooped with long grey hair and pebble-lensed spectacles, answered. "The eighth. It concerned an ancient necropolis located somewhere in the north of Roumania."

"What province?"

"I have never read the chapter in detail, sir. I don't know." He looked at his companions. They shook their heads. He continued, "There was . . . yes . . . I think, a legend . . . concerning the guardians of a holy relic."

At the word "guardians," Begg quirked an eyebrow, recalling the affair at Woodbine Hall. "And a symbol composed of eight arrows?"

"I don't recall a symbol," said the librarian, "but the chapter's title was '*Thamaniat siham wasayf wahid*,' which means, *Eight Arrows and a Single Sword*."

Sabahattin Sans-Serif called, "English spy! Must I stand here waiting? My God! Chat, chat, chat! Typical of your people."

Begg gave the librarian an apologetic smile, made to move away, then stopped. "One last question. Agent Sans-Serif told me the albino was your first customer. Was he waiting outside when—"

One of the three interrupted. "No, he misheard. I didn't say the man was the first customer—"

"Begg!" Sans-Serif called again, his tone impatient.

"—I said he was the first in the library. We came earlier than usual today, as we need to make space for a delivery of manuscripts from Damascus. He was already here when we arrived. We caught him in his act of destruction."

"He broke in?"

"There is no sign of it."

With a nod of thanks, Begg left them and joined the special agent.

"I already told you everything you need to know," Sans-Serif said. "There's no cause to go bothering people unnecessarily. This way. These stairs lead down to the vault. Be careful, they are steep. If you fall and kill yourself, you will rob me."

"Of what?"

"Of the pleasure of shooting you."

They started down the spiralling stone stairwell.

Begg's voice echoed. "Zenith was already inside when the librarians arrived. His means of entry and exit were probably the same. Let's see if we can locate it."

Sans-Serif stopped, wheeled, and looked up at Begg. "You can give orders in your own horrible country, not here. Don't annoy me, foreigner. My trigger finger is restless today."

They continued down.

With wry amusement, Begg asked, "Did you shoot the German agent?"

"I came close, but he's only here to find a missing person, another of you pestilent Englishmen, and one with a name as silly as yours. 'Sir Seaton.' What was your mother thinking? Was she drunk?"

They entered the vault, which was lit by electric lights and crowded with freestanding bookshelves and document cabinets.

"What is this missing Englishman's name?" Begg asked.

"Nye."

The detective's jaw muscles flexed. "And the German agent?"

"Ulric von Bek. A good Nazi name, eh?"

Begg blinked. The name sounded familiar but he could not place it.

"He's a Nazi?"

"Aren't they all?"

Begg cast his eyes around the vault, taking in every detail automatically. "If there's a Nazi searching for an Englishman in Istanbul, the British embassy should have been informed."

"Pah! What do I care what you foreigners do to each other? Just stay out of Turkish affairs. If you don't—" Sans-Serif patted his gun pocket.

The special agent paced forward into the middle of the chamber and swung around, his arms wide. They were mismatched in length.

"Books, books, and more books," he declared. "Dusty old scrolls and decomposing parchment. Where's your albino hiding, Begg? Has he tucked himself away between the crumbling pages?"

To the metatemporal detective, who possessed the sharpest of eyes, the solution to Zenith's disappearance was so obvious it might as well have been signposted.

"Look at these shelves," he said. "You see how they extend out from the wall into the room and are on rails, so they can be slid sideways? It maximises the storage space."

"Marvellous. Ingenious. What of it?"

"Given what's stored here, dust is unavoidable. Despite daily cleaning, a thin layer inevitably settles during the night. Therefore, should any of these shelves have moved in the past few hours, we would know it by the displacement of dust on the rails." He pointed. "Such as you see over there."

"Hmm," said Sans-Serif. He walked to the indicated shelf unit, took a hold of it, and slid it to one side. "Moves easily. No weight at all."

On the newly revealed section of wall, there was a three-foot-square wooden panel.

"For the electric cables," the Turk observed, indicating the four that emerged from its upper frame and climbed the wall to the ceiling.

Begg made a noise of agreement. "Do you see the flakes of parchment at the base of it? Unquestionably, that's how our man got in and out. Let's see—"

He moved to the panel, squatted, and pushed a bottom corner. The entire square tipped out into his hands. He put it aside.

"Do you have a torch? There's a tunnel."

Sans-Serif produced one from inside his long jacket. "You call yourself a spy, yet you don't even carry basic equipment?"

"I don't call myself a spy. Lead the way. I'll follow."

The MAH man handed him the torch. "I prefer to keep you where I can shoot you."

Smiling, Begg crawled into the tunnel and moved along on his hands and knees while shining the light ahead. It illuminated an opening about twenty feet distant. When he reached it, he clambered out into a much larger brick-built tunnel, ten feet high, with cables drooping along the length of its arched ceiling.

"Oh ho!" exclaimed Sans-Serif as he emerged. "We are in the old catacombs."

"I wasn't aware there were any," Begg commented.

"Ha! You see, you foreigners think you know everything, but you don't. The incredible catacombs of old Byzantium! Well, service tunnels, to be accurate. They run between the ancient cisterns. My ancestors had supplied the city with water when your people were sitting in wooden huts and picking lice from their hair."

"As a matter of fact, we were building cathedrals," Begg corrected. "Look at this."

He directed the torchlight at the muddy ground.

"Footprints," Sans-Serif observed.

"Coming and going, and for certain Zenith's. I recognise his size of shoe and the length of his stride."

"You know him well, then?" asked the Turk. In the shadows cast by the orange torchlight, he looked horrific, like Victor Hugo's Quasimodo.

Begg started forward, feet squelching, following the trail.

"I've been trying to send him to gaol since 1919."

This was not strictly accurate, but had he quoted an earlier date, questions might have been asked about his age and his understanding of the calendar.

Sans-Serif whistled. "All these years with no success. You must be Britain's worst detective."

"I suppose so," agreed Begg, in a droll tone.

They moved along the tunnel, instinctively falling silent, the footprints guiding them to the right when they came to a junction, and on for what Begg judged to be a mile. Then the two men emerged into a vast, echoing space, the darkness of which proved resistant to the torchlight.

It was one of the cisterns, its dimensions impossible to judge, its ceiling supported by hundreds of mismatched marble, limestone, and even carved timber pillars. When these fell within the beam of light, they looked to have been recycled from across the Ottoman Empire and beyond. The blocks on which they stood were placed sideways or upside down. Images that once held profound religious or political significance now possessed none—carvings from ancient Rome, ancient Greece, ancient Egypt. Here, never to be seen, beneath the city and, when the cistern was functional, submerged.

A graveyard of empires.

The footprints led them through this strange, dark forest to a flight of steps, then up into the mouth of another tunnel. As they entered it, Begg, with his eyes on the ground, walked straight into a chest-high steel wire extending from wall to wall. It stretched as he inadvertently pressed against it, then twanged taut when he backed up.

"We're in trouble," he whispered. "I just tripped an alarm."

CHAPTER 12
The Nazi Agent

The day before Sir Seaton Begg's visit to the library, while he was still examining citizen registers at the various embassies, his friend Doctor Sinclair knocked on a bedroom door and received an invitation to enter. The pathologist turned the key, pushed open the portal, and stepped in with an apologetic shrug. "Good morning, madame. I apologise. I hope you understand."

Vera Pym was sitting, fully dressed, on the bed.

"Oh, I do. You locked me in because you do not trust me. Is that not so?"

Sinclair spread his hands. "You have been working for the Red King. You lured Apollinaire de Villiers into the hands of Suleyman the Strangler."

She recoiled from him, shocked.

"No! No! You have it all wrong! My association with de Villiers is not at all what you think. I tried to protect him. I knew the Red King would assassinate him. I did all I could to stay close to him, so that when the fatal hour came—" Abruptly, she stopped and frowned. "What are you doing here, Doctor? Is Sir Seaton with you?"

"In Istanbul, yes. As to what we are doing, that is not for you to know."

She coloured a little. "You still think me a criminal? It was more than a decade ago that I was leader of Les Vampyres in Paris; more still since I did what I did in Petrograd. Matters with me are different now. You must not judge against me, for there is much you do not understand, information you do not possess. This attack on de Villiers, I give you my word, was not my doing. I am entirely reformed since last you and Sir Seaton saw me."

It was a lot to swallow, but Sinclair nodded as if accepting her explanation. The more he could keep her talking, the more he might learn. He opened the door a little wider that she might precede him through it.

"They left a pot of coffee in the kitchen," he said. "Also cheese and crackers and some other bits and pieces. Will you join me for a makeshift breakfast?"

She stood, smoothed her skirt, and led the way out onto the landing, down the stairs, and into the manor's dining room. What few comestibles Sinclair had found, he had laid out on the table.

They sat. For a moment, she blanched and gripped her neck, recalling the noose tightening around it.

Last night, upon finding her nearly hanged, Sinclair had acted without thinking. The weight of the bucket was about to pull her off her feet. Flinging himself across the room, he had braced his upper back against the bottom of it and heaved. A sheet of water crashed onto the floor and pooled around him. With the vessel more than half emptied, he then rushed to her side.

She was not seriously hurt, but the experience had left her too shocked to explain immediately how she came to be placed in such a monstrous predicament.

Sinclair, after searching the manor from top to bottom and finding it empty, had suggested that he and Pym, having been up all night and both exhausted, should take a bedroom each. Those who had abandoned the place were unlikely to return.

He had guided her to a room with a key in its lock.

Both slept deeply, for far longer than intended, and it was now late morning. They felt much refreshed.

"Perhaps," he said, passing her a plate of crackers, "you will now explain how you came to be in such a dreadful fix? Was it the man they call the Red King?"

"Yes, his gang, at any rate," she replied. "They were using this house as their headquarters."

"Do you know where they've gone?"

"No. They learned I was a spy—I don't know how—and you saw with what consequence. They have found somewhere new."

Delicately, she cut a piece of cheese and popped it into her mouth. Sinclair sipped his coffee.

"A spy?" he asked.

La Pym sighed and pushed her plate away. "You may not be aware of this, Doctor, but though I pretend British nationality, I am half-Roumanian, half-French. I was born Constanța Elisabeta Anna Lacusta. We did not move to my father's native Paris until I was seven years old, and I did not return to Roumania until I had broken away from Les Vampyres, and from—"

She hesitated, and fidgeted.

"From?" Sinclair prompted.

"Monsieur Ze—the albino, with whom, I know, you are familiar. He and I were initially enemies, but we made amends and . . . and . . . well, there was *une affaire de coeur*. I was infatuated, but he was strange and unpredictable, and after a year, I fled from him.

I did so in possession of information that he considered personal. It concerned a former colonel of the Roumanian military, Simeon Vassilionu, whom the albino hated with ferocious passion."

Noting that she mentioned Zenith only in the past tense, Sinclair suppressed the impulse to mention the albino's presence in Istanbul. Better to wait for her to reveal whether she knew of it or not.

"Hated him for what reason?" he asked.

She shrugged. "I am not certain, and it does not matter, for Vassilionu is dead and time has moved on."

Sinclair frowned. "In which case, what has it to do—?"

"Only this," she said. "I took the information to the Roumanian authorities, who had an interest in Vassilionu, and I emphasised that I had obtained it by consorting with a very dangerous criminal at considerable risk to myself. I requested that they take this into account when I applied to join the Secția a II-a."

"What is that?" Sinclair's Roumanian was not as broad as Seaton Begg's.

"The Second Section. The Roumanian Intelligence Service. I am an agent—for ten years now."

Sinclair cut a slice of apple and chewed it contemplatively. He gazed past her at the window.

Should he trust this woman? Her beauty, he had detected, was mostly in her makeup, and there was an unsettling hardness in her eyes. He found it unnerving, and felt a little out of his depth.

"You are here to investigate the Red King?" he enquired.

"That is my mission. The Second Section knows very little about him. He is thought a native of Transylvania, where he may have occupied a position of importance—perhaps a *voivode*—until Roumania incorporated that land. Since then, he has worked against Roumanian interests. I was ordered to infiltrate his gang, establish his exact identity, and discover what he and his people are doing in Istanbul."

"No small job," noted Sinclair. "You have your answers?"

"No. When he meets with his gang, he is always in red robes, with a golden mask hiding his face."

"His voice?"

"He converses only in French or English and uses a stage whisper to disguise its true tone."

Sinclair considered for a moment. "I counted seven people here aside from yourself. None in costume."

"He was gone by the time I arrived. They had already received their orders." She shuddered.

"That was the whole gang?"

Pym took a packet of cigarettes from her jacket pocket and offered it. He declined, but after she had taken one for herself, he struck a match and offered its flame.

"It is now, Mr. Sinclair. They have just lost another member." She exhaled blue smoke. "Monteith the Chemist met his demise while on a mission."

"You know all their names?"

"Yes."

"In that case," said Sinclair, "I had better take you to Sir Seaton Begg. Finish your breakfast, madame, then we will see whether we can flag down a vehicle."

She looked uneasy. "Will he listen to me? He and I have not been—"

"Begg believes in second chances. He will listen."

After a more detailed search of the premises, during which Sinclair collected a handful of cigarette butts, they went outside. At this time of day, the road was well serviced by a variety of vehicles, from donkey carts to Rolls-Royces. They secured an old-fashioned phaeton. The driver took them straight to the Pera Palas Hotel. There, Sinclair learned that Begg had moved to the Shangri-La.

The Invicta Scout had been left for him, so with Pym in the passenger seat, he drove to the Old Quarter.

While he was parking the car, the call of the muezzins started to echo across the rooftops:

"Ash'hadu an laa ilaaha illallaah! Ash'hadu an laa ilaaha illallaah!"

Sinclair and the woman entered the hotel. The clerk took his name, checked the book, nodded, and handed over a key. "Suite five, m'sieu." He glanced at Pym. "Um?"

"A brief visit," Sinclair explained.

The clerk made a sound, if not of approval, then at least of permission.

They went to the rooms. The doctor's sketched maps were strewn across the floor. Begg was absent. He had not left a note advising of his whereabouts.

"Northern Roumania," Pym commented, after scrutinising the maps. "But this is the country I represent. Why is Sir Seaton studying it?"

"I have no idea," Sinclair lied. "I'm sure he will provide an answer when we catch up with him."

Back in the lobby, the clerk revealed, "The gentleman stepped out just a few minutes before you arrived. He did not say where he was going."

Sinclair considered for a moment, then made a decision. While he was inclined to believe La Pym, it might be wise to put her statement concerning Apollinaire de Villiers to the test.

"I want you to come with me to the Surp Pirgiç Hospital," he told her. "There is a British Secret Service agent there who has been investigating the Red King. An exchange of information might prove useful to you both."

"Very well," she responded. "But if the Red King has him under surveillance—"

"Her," Sinclair corrected.

"If he has her under surveillance, and I am noticed, it will be dangerous for us all."

Sinclair gave her his scrutiny. She looked, whatever her background, unmistakably European. He murmured, "Perhaps if we—"

The hotel was on a shop-lined street. Only a few paces from its front entrance, he was able to purchase for her a cape with a deep hood. Because it was now raining, he also paid for two umbrellas. It was sufficient to shield them from casual curiosity.

Had Sinclair looked through the window of the restaurant adjacent to the shop, he would have seen Sir Seaton Begg eating his lunch before his return to the British embassy, but Fate did not favour him that day.

They took a cab to the hospital.

As they made their way to Violet Damm's room, Pym kept her hood up, her face in shadow.

"Good Lord!"

The exclamation came from Doctor Matossian, who had spotted Sinclair approaching along the corridor. Pym turned her face away as he paced over.

"Not again!" Matossian cried out in mock horror. "Though I'm glad to see you in normal togs. And you look fine. The scratches and bruises are healing nicely. What is it now, then? Internal injuries? You drank poison? Swallowed a spanner?"

Sinclair grinned. "Visiting your patient, that's all."

"So is the other gentleman," said Matossian. "You can take her home. She's in the clear. Don't come back. I'll be giving several foreign dignitaries the grand tour in a couple of days, and I don't want it interrupted by you hobbling in dressed as the Genie of the Lamp and dripping the red stuff."

He strode off.

"Other gentleman?" Pym murmured.

"Begg, thank goodness," Sinclair responded. "And you don't need to hide from old Matossian. If he worked for the Red King, I'd be dead by now. He's a bit of a—"

He broke off as they passed into Damm's room to find her not with Begg, but in earnest conversation with a tall, slim, blond stranger who straightened politely at their entry.

Damm was wearing a plain grey dress supplied by the hospital, her clothes having been reduced to rags by the grenade.

"Taffy, my dear!" she exclaimed. "I was about to come hunting for you." She gestured toward her companion. "This gentleman is Herr Ulric von Bek, an exiled German anti-Nazi anarcho-syndicalist. He—"

She stopped and gaped at Sinclair's companion. "Vera Pym!"

Pym pulled back her hood, then raised her palms. "Don't jump to conclusions, Violet. I am not who I used to be."

"I should hope not," said Damm.

"Don't pretend you didn't enjoy every minute of our old criminal partnership," Pym countered. "It is, however, all in the past. I am now reformed, an agent with the Roumanian Second Section, and I have no quarrel with you. You can easily check my credentials through your agency."

Damm turned to von Bek. "I cannot confidently vouch for Madame Pym, Herr Bek, but this gentleman is Doctor Sinclair, Sir

Seaton Begg's right-hand man." She addressed Sinclair. "Herr von Bek has vital information for Major Nye's ears only, but like ourselves has been unable to find him."

Vera Pym stepped forward. "No, Violet, you have made a very grave error. Herr von Bek is not with the anarcho-syndicalists. I know him well. He is gestapo. A killer of anarchists—and their women and children!"

Sinclair cried out, "What?"

Abruptly, in a blur of motion, von Bek jumped behind Damm, wrapped an arm around her neck, and put a silenced Luger to her head.

"Hands up, both of you! Kick the door shut, Sinclair, or I swear, I'll shoot her."

Sinclair obeyed.

"Madame Pym, I have no idea who you are, or why you think it is necessary to spout foul untruths, but it will make no difference. I have a job to do, and I will do it whether I'm mistaken for a Nazi or not. Get onto the bed. Face down. Come on! Move!"

Pym's nostrils flared. "You'll pay for this, you traitor," she hissed, and with fury in her eyes, did as he had ordered.

Sinclair noted the insult and wondered how it applied. Von Bek—a traitor to whom or where? To Germany?

Von Bek nodded toward some dressing gowns folded on a chair. "Use the belt cords from those to bind her hands and ankles, Sinclair. Gag her, too. Make it tight." He pressed the silencer into the side of Violet Damm's head. "If you don't, I'll put a bullet in her first, then one in you."

Sinclair obeyed, while von Bek retreated to the door, pulling his captive with him. "I'm taking your friend with me. I need to find Nye. She knows him and will assist."

"I will not," Damm declared.

He ignored her. "I will then release her, unharmed. Do not interfere unless you want it otherwise."

"What business do you have with him?" Sinclair asked. "He is Secret Service. So are we. Why not tell us?"

"My business is none of your concern." Von Bek paused, then went on, "But understand this: It is too significant a matter to be handled by operatives of the various undercover agencies. There are families—dynasties—that have prepared through centuries to deal with it."

"You belong to one of them?"

"I do."

Sinclair secured Vera Pym's bonds.

Von Bek said, "All right. Turn around and back slowly toward me."

Knowing what was coming, Sinclair did as he was told, intending to spin at the last moment to kick the gun from the German's hand.

Von Bek anticipated the move. He took two paces forward and slammed the butt of his pistol into the side of Sinclair's head.

CHAPTER 13
In the Cistern

Sinclair was unconscious all night. Sir Seaton Begg was entirely unaware of what had happened to his friend. During the morning, while the doctor was slowly regaining his wits, the metatemporal detective, with Special Agent Sabahattin Sans-Serif, stumbled and slipped another mile through the filth-smeared tunnels below the city, expecting to be attacked at any moment.

Nothing happened.

Begg now doubted he had triggered an alarm at all.

He and Sans-Serif turned at three junctions—left, right, left—doggedly following Zenith's footprints.

"The albino must have a map of these tunnels," the Turk mused.

"Obviously!" responded Begg irritably. "He didn't guess his way into the library."

"I do not like it. These are Turkish tunnels. They should not be infested with foreigners."

Begg snorted. "Well, foreigners doubtless helped build them. Slave labour! And, regarding your enthusiasm for all things

Turkish, I'm curious. I recognise Sabahattin and Serif as Turkish names—but Sans?"

"Spanish. My mother was from Barcelona."

The detective chuckled. "So, you're as purely Turkish as these tunnels, then."

Sans-Serif gave his torch a shake. "These batteries won't last forever."

They trudged on. Ten minutes passed in silence, save for the dripping and splashing of distant water.

Sans-Serif's beam now picked out an arched opening in the right-hand wall. The footprints led into it. They saw six feet of floor then an edge beyond which was nothing but utter blackness.

"Maybe descending steps?" Begg suggested.

"Or a sheer drop," his companion countered. "You go first."

Begg thought it odd that their voices did not echo.

Cautiously, they moved forward.

With a tremendous clang, steel bars slammed down, sending them reeling backward—against more bars! Begg threw up his arm to ward off a sudden blinding light. A cage had dropped around them. There had been no darkness. Instead, a big, heavy, black velvet curtain, spanning ceiling to floor and wall to wall, had concealed the greater part of a well-lit chamber. Not a single chink of light had penetrated it. Now, as it swept aside, a small, clean Byzantium cistern was revealed. Two mismatched pillars supported its low vaulted ceiling. More velvet curtains draped the walls. Plush black rugs covered the stone floor. Lanterns provided illumination.

Minimally furnished in ebony and ivory, the room contained a cocktail cabinet; a display case of pistols; a rack of épées, foils, and sabres; and, in the middle of the room, a black divan, upon which stretched a languid figure of white marble.

Zenith, the master crook.

In a white shirt and black trousers, his crisp white hair brushed back from his colourless face, and with his crimson eyes half closed, he looked startlingly perfect, like a Michelangelo brought to life.

His fingers were loose around a yen-hok. The air was pungent with opium.

Begg recognised an attending Japanese servant, who, having finished tying back the curtain, approached the cage and bowed politely.

"Your weapons, please, honourable guests."

"Hello, Oyani," said Begg. "I am unarmed. My friend has a pistol in his lower right pocket. He will give it to you now."

"I don't think so," Sans-Serif objected.

"You will be shot if you refuse again," Begg warned.

"The honourable Mr. Begg is most wise," Oyani commented.

"You'd better hand over the torch, too," the detective advised. "It could be used as a club."

"I knew it," Sans-Serif muttered as he was relieved of the items. "You devils are all in it together. What now for my poor country? Are we to be part of your British Empire? Or must we all become Japanese?" He looked curiously at Zenith. "Or perhaps made vampyres and incorporated into the ghost realms?"

Begg folded his arms and gazed at his old enemy.

"I recommend utmost caution, Sans-Serif. If you show bad manners or insult our host, he is liable to snuff you out with a snap of the fingers. For all that he appears harmless in his current state, he has a hair trigger and is entirely unpredictable."

Frank Oyani, Zenith's longest serving and most loyal retainer, said, "His Excellency is resting. I will provide rugs upon which you can sit while you await his pleasure." He indicated the drinks cabinet. "Will the honourable gentlemen take refreshment?"

"If I'm not mistaken," said Begg, "I see a rare Armagnac. If I may?"

"Certainly, Sir Seaton," said Oyani with a bow.

"Ugh!" Sans-Serif exclaimed. "You condescend to drink in company with foreign criminals? You have no standards. The liquor is surely stolen from some honest Turk." He turned to Oyani. "You have mint tea, of course?"

"I am afraid not, honourable sir."

"Coffee?"

"Regretfully, no."

"Raki?"

"No, sir."

"Aryan?"

"Please, forgive my intolerable ignorance and failure to know what that is, sir."

"Salep? Boza? Tursu suyu? Şalgam?"

Oyani shook his head. "My education is sorely lacking. In travelling with my master, I have had little occasion to visit your magnificent nation."

Sans-Serif clapped a hand to his brow. "Barbarians! You leave me no choice. I am forced to accept a large glass of your very finest Bordeaux."

A few minutes later, the English detective and the Turkish special agent settled onto soft rugs, drinks in hand.

"I have it in mind—" Sans-Serif muttered.

Begg was hardly listening. While he had the chance, he studied the albino's handsome features. He had never seen him so motionless, and for the first time since their initial encounter, a decade and a half ago, he perceived a hint that his antagonist's opium addiction was finally having a deleterious effect. Zenith's face appeared a little longer and thinner, the cheekbones sharper. His eyes had somehow acquired the vaguest hint of a slant. His hair, worn longer than in their previous encounters, gave him a more Bohemian appearance.

"—that we are beneath a hammam."

Begg turned to his companion. "A public steam bath? What makes you think that?"

"Can you not feel the heat and humidity?"

"No more than usual."

"No more than usual for a sunny spring day in Istanbul, Seaton Begg. But it is raining outside and cooler than it has been for weeks."

"Ah! I had overlooked that."

Begg sampled his Armagnac. He arched an eyebrow in appreciation.

"Besides," added Sans-Serif, "cisterns of this size and shape are nowhere except beneath hammams."

"I see."

"Next door to this chamber, there will be a furnace room, still used, with steps up to the bathhouse. That will be our means of exit when I save you and lead our escape." The Turk pointed to two thick pipes, which emerged from behind the top of the curtains on the opposite wall and disappeared into the ceiling. "Those pipes carry the steam. They run from the boiler over the furnace and divert through this chamber to rise through the old well holes. To judge from their position, the door to the furnace room is behind the curtain to the right of us." He sipped and grimaced. "Yuck! This foreign abomination is sour. It needs some honey."

"Useful to know," said Begg.

"Yes. In Turkey, we always add it to improve the flavour. Of course, we have our own wonderful vineyards now. Soon, their produce will dominate Europe. Then, you will know what good wine is."

"I meant about the door."

Oyani returned from his master's side. "His Excellency is waking, honourable sirs." He crossed back to the cabinet, filled a tumbler with the same Armagnac served to Begg, and took it to Zenith.

Assisting the albino into a sitting position, Oyani gently put the glass to his master's lips. Zenith drank it down swiftly, then murmured, "More."

Begg and Sans-Serif got to their feet.

Zenith blinked, his ruby eyes unfocussed.

"I conversed with a dragon, Oyani," he whispered.

"Yes, Excellency."

"Our minds were as one." He leaned forward, elbows on knees, head drooping. Hoarsely, he added, "Always the same dream. The insistent notion that I belong elsewhere. But where? I forget. I always forget."

Oyani warned, "We have guests, Excellency."

The albino appeared not to hear him. He accepted the replenished glass, drained it, and passed it back. "Another."

He covered his face with his hands. His voice, though muffled, was savagely despondent. "Only one thing do I recall. Always, I am obliged to take up the black sword."

Unconsciously, Begg clutched his companion's arm to quash any intended utterance.

"Ah, to be born under the accursed Eight Arrows is worse than—"

"Excellency!"

The word cracked like a whip.

Zenith's head came up, his eyes open. He regarded Oyani, then followed his gesture to the cage.

The crimson orbs rested on Sir Seaton Begg.

The detective saw in them first a flicker of fear, then flames of intense rage, then the usual cold glint of mockery.

Zenith drank the third tumbler of brandy. He had consumed half a bottle in just a few minutes. Rather than befuddle him, the spirit apparently sharpened his senses.

Without averting his gaze, he returned the empty glass to his servant, took a cigarette from a platinum case on the small table beside the divan, and with an ebony and silver Calibri, applied a flame to it.

He spoke through a billowing cloud. His voice had lost its rough edge and was now deep and mellifluous.

"My dear friend, Sir Seaton Begg. What the devil have you done to poor Doctor Sinclair? He looks positively monstrous. Is he training to ring the bells of Notre Dame?"

Sans-Serif began to rumble.

With restrained amusement, Begg spoke before the Turk could explode. "As I think you know, monsieur, this is not Sinclair. May I introduce Mr. Yilmaz? He is an electrician. I encountered him laying cables in the tunnels, and he was kind enough to offer assistance as a guide. A harmless fellow"—he tapped the side of his head—"not all there, unfortunately, and dependent for work on a local charity. I am positive his silence will be easily purchased, and he can be sent safely on his way."

Sans-Serif added, "I see three unopened bottles of Bordeaux in your cabinet, Mr. Vampyr. Let me take them, and I'll walk out of here not having ever seen you."

Begg rolled his eyes and sighed despairingly.

"Mr. Yilmaz has a discerning palate," drawled Zenith, "and speaks excellent English." He drew on his cigarette and exhaled a plume. "For a simple electrician."

Oyani murmured, "He was carrying a pistol, Excellency."

"Because the tunnels attract vermin," Sans-Serif remarked pointedly.

Zenith's gaze, all the while fixed on Begg, now turned to the Turk.

"And vermin must be exterminated, is that not so, Mr.—?"

Sans-Serif straightened as far as his twisted spine allowed. He stuck out his chest. "I am Special Agent Sabahattin Sans-Serif. I am a Turk, and I am not fond of spies."

With an insouciant flick of the hand, Zenith dismissed him, a slight irritant, a worthless distraction.

He stood and brushed down his clothes.

"You have inconvenienced me, Sir Seaton. I only recently made this rathole comfortable, and already you force me to abandon it."

Oyani, behind him, raised a black jacket, into which Zenith slid his arms. As he buttoned it, Begg noted that the master crook had abandoned his usual flamboyant evening wear in favour of this expensively tailored but subdued suit. In Istanbul his preferred attire would attract even more attention than it did in London, which would have meant nothing to Zenith under normal circumstances—

—which suggested that these were not normal circumstances.

Oyani knotted and straightened the albino's bow tie. He presented a mirror.

"I shall do the rest," Zenith advised him. "Round up a few of the men. Make it snappy. I want everything removed."

The Japanese servant bowed, crossed to the curtain to Begg's right, and disappeared behind it.

"See?" Sans-Serif whispered. "Furnace room."

Begg turned to him. "Do you understand the Roumanian language, Sans-Serif?"

Zenith, overhearing the question, raised a quizzical eyebrow.

"What has that to do with it?" the Turk responded with a puzzled frown.

"Answer me."

"Well, for a certainty, Turkish is the superior language, but we special agents must be proficient in others. I speak fluent English, French, Spanish, and German. Of Roumanian, regretfully, I have no—"

Begg cut him off.

"Domnule Zenit," he said rapidly, *"aceasta poate fi singura noastră oportunitate de a vorbi singuri."*

Mr. Zenith, this may be our only opportunity to speak alone.

"Hey!" Sans-Serif objected. "None of that! No conspiring!"

"Be quiet!" Begg barked.

The agent's bulging eye bulged harder, but his mouth closed.

"You are correct," Zenith responded in the Roumanian tongue. "My men will be here soon. Of what would you speak?"

"We are enemies," said Begg. "We have been enemies for a long time. Yet, we fight our war within the bounds of a certain code of conduct, would you agree?"

"Indeed, I would," Zenith crushed the remains of his cigarette into an ashtray. He picked up the platinum case and slid it into a pocket. "I have gone as far as to presume a form of friendship between us." He approached the cage, still limping slightly after jumping from his boat three nights ago.

Zenith took the now-empty brandy glass from the detective's hand and carried it to the cabinet. "We even share a taste in Armagnacs."

Sans-Serif, he ignored.

Begg's smile was thin. "In most things, save who serves the law and who prefers a chaotic world, we have similar views. Also, we have a code of conduct that bonds us—one that, perhaps, is regarded as somewhat eccentric in a postwar world."

"Do you now intend to call upon it?"

"I do."

Zenith returned, handed Begg the refreshed glass, and raised his own. "Then let us first toast the Game of Time."

"To the Game of Time," agreed Begg.

They imbibed.

"Very well," said Zenith. "State your move."

Begg regarded the albino. This past week he had learned more about his adversary than in the entirety of their conflict. He had evidence that Zenith carried a secret, and he felt he was close to tearing away the veil that concealed it.

When he made this clear, how would the albino react? The man was as unpredictable and as lethal as a Siberian tiger.

Begg did not hesitate.

"For the past three years, across Turkey but mainly in Istanbul, the man they call the Red King has been waging a campaign of assassination. His targets are foreigners, here to aid westernisation." He spoke rapidly, his Roumanian clear and precise. "You have recently set yourself against him. Why?"

In silence, Zenith gazed at his old adversary.

"Shortly before your arrival in this city," the detective continued, "a British Secret Service agent went into hiding. He has with him a certain object crafted in silver. I do not know what it is, but I do know what it is called."

Zenith became still as stone.

Begg said, "The *Salut Christi*."

At the periphery of his vision, he saw Sans-Serif back slowly away until he was pressed into the corner of the cage. The cistern had filled with palpable tension, and felt as if it were now the focus of all existence.

From the words I now speak, Begg thought, *endless realms of future history shall be born. Which path through them will we take?*

Relentlessly, he pressed on.

"In 1920, you gained—or perhaps I mean regained—possession of a ring known as the *Sigiliul Tutorelui*, the Guardian's Seal. Two years prior, a Roumanian, Colonel Simeon Vassilionu, had stolen it from a principality in what is now northern Roumania. You killed him. You later lost the ring. How?"

The glass in Zenith's hand shattered. Bloody fragments fell to the floor. Still, he did not move, his unwavering eyes on the detective.

Begg's mouth was dry but he nevertheless continued. "The *Sigiliul Tutorelui* was said to confer *Dreptul de Tutelă*, the Right of Guardianship, on its wearer. Guardianship of what? Of the *Salut Christi*, perhaps? Does that mysterious object, like the ring, and like you, come from Roumania? Do you all have your origins in a tiny vanished province named Lamaneagra, which translates to English as—*black blade*?"

Zenith abruptly swung around and paced to where his pistols were on display. Rather than releasing the catch and lifting the lid of the case, he punched straight through its glass and snatched up a weapon. He returned to the cage, his face contorted with fury, his eyes ablaze. He aimed at Begg's head. His bloodied hand was trembling violently, his trigger finger white.

"What is the *Salut Christi*?" Begg rapped out. "Tell me! I do not believe you are seeking it for profit. This is not another of your criminal escapades. What does it mean to you? As far as I know, you are not an outlaw in Turkey. We can find it together."

Zenith's face was almost unrecognizable with rage.

"What has it to do with the Red King?" Begg demanded. He heard Sans-Serif babbling beside him, incoherent with fear.

Suddenly, the Turk threw himself forward and, near hysterical, screamed, "I know what you are! I know what you are! Unholy fiend! Vampyr!"

With an inarticulate cry, the albino stepped back, jerked his gun toward Sans-Serif, and pulled the trigger. In the small cistern, the report was deafening. The bullet hit the cage, cracked a bar, and screamed away, embedding itself in the ceiling. He fired again, and again, and two more ricochets saved the shrieking Turk.

"Undead! Unclean! Vampyr!" Sans-Serif grabbed Begg and yelled, "Make the sign of the cross! Repel him, you Christian fool!"

Zenith stumbled backward, his expression transformed to deep shock. He folded onto the floor, his pink eyes staring disbelievingly into space.

Begg pushed Sans-Serif away, back to the corner of the cage, where the Turk cringed, panting, clutching at his pocket for the pistol that was not there.

The detective allowed a couple of minutes to pass while the albino sat slumped, lips working but no words coming forth.

When he judged that he could speak without being immediately shot dead, Begg said softly, "Monsieur Zenith?"

The pistol came straight back up.

"No," the albino rasped. "No. It is a transgression that can never be forgiven."

He pushed himself unsteadily to his feet, his face ghastly, his eyes glassy. He looked hollowed out and alien, as if some essentially human part of him had been removed.

"I never thought it would end." His melancholy baritone was profound and dreadful. "But our game is over."

The pistol dropped from his fingers.

With his head bowed, he limped to the divan. Lifting a violin case from beside it, he stumbled to the curtain concealing a door to the furnace room and disappeared through it.

He did not look back.

After a minute, Begg rasped, "Do you have a cigarette, Sans-Serif?"

Breathing heavily and unable to speak, the special agent offered one and took another for himself.

They smoked in silence.

Begg's fingers trembled.

Later, five masked men entered and removed the furniture.

The chamber was becoming uncomfortably hot. Sans-Serif's bald head beaded with perspiration.

One of the servants returned. Wearing thick gloves, he carried a mallet in one hand and a big chisel in the other. He crossed to the curtain concealing the pipes and ripped it down. Then he put the chisel to a pipe and set about it with the mallet—*Bang! Bang! Bang!*

The chisel suddenly flew from his hand and a jet of steam howled out, hurling him backward. He hit the floor, squirming, screeching in agony, his hands clutching his scalded face. Squealing like a pig in a slaughterhouse, he stumbled to his feet and reeled from the chamber.

The burning steam billowed into the cistern.

The temperature rocketed.

Begg and Sans-Serif looked at each other in horror. The Devil was dining in Hades! They were about to be cooked alive!

CHAPTER 14
Madam Melody

Sir Seaton Begg and Sabahattin Sans-Serif were to die by suffocating heat. To that end, Zenith's men had closed the furnace's safety valves. They had, however, misjudged how rapidly pressure in the boiler would build.

The unplanned but inevitable explosion was enormous. It pushed the street and hammam high into the air, to slump back as a pile of rubble and dust.

Beneath the city, the shockwave smacked into Taffy Sinclair and sent him tumbling back along the tunnel in a roiling cloud of brick fragments and blistering steam.

Recovering consciousness, he found that the strap of his electric torch remained around his wrist. The light was still shining. He directed the beam at his watch. He had been out for only a few minutes.

Through the clangour in his ears, he heard the thunder of falling masonry echoing along the passage.

He got to his feet and retraced his steps. When he passed the farthest-flung debris, he was able to follow the line of footprints back to the library.

Earlier that day, the pathologist, regaining his wits in Violet Damm's hospital room, found Doctor Matossian looking at him with eyebrows raised.

"All this fun," the Armenian had said, "is doing you no good at all."

"What happened?"

"A nurse found your cloaked and hooded lady friend bound and gagged on the bed. You were on the floor, senseless. There is an egg-sized bump on your head. No serious damage. You have a remarkable constitution. Perhaps, no brain and a cranium of solid bone. As a fellow doctor, would you mind if I subjected you to rigorous and invasive experiments?"

"Yes, I would, rather." Sitting up, Sinclair felt his bump. "Ouch! Where is Madame Pym?"

"Your companion? As soon as she was untied, she made off. To chase after a Nazi, I gather."

"Then I had better do the same."

"Huh! I don't think so, old boy."

Sinclair ignored the Armenian medico's protests, left the hospital, made his way back to the Shangri-La, and learned that Begg was revisiting the Köprülü Library.

The three librarians told him the rest.

Entering the tunnel, he set off in pursuit, only to be knocked for six by the explosion.

Taffy Sinclair now clambered back out through the electricity access panel. One of the librarians gave him a stern look. Mindful of the ancient manuscripts, Sinclair waited until he was in the library's garden before patting himself down. Dust clouded around him. His mouth and eyes were gritty. His head ached and his ears rang.

"Our next case," he promised himself, "will be somewhere mountainous and remote, so we can breathe pure, cold air. The Arctic, perhaps."

Because, for certain, there would be a next case.

Sir Seaton Begg was alive.

Not killed by that explosion.

Why? Because, while his line of business had exposed Sinclair to innumerable corpses, he could not, by any stretch, imagine his friend as one.

The rain had passed. The afternoon sunshine shone like burnished gold on the back of a dense reddish-brown cloud, about two miles distant, rolling slowly eastward over the city.

Sinclair, whose mind was not functioning normally, stood and contemplated it. "And what rough beast," he whispered sardonically, "slouches across Byzantium?"

He laughed, and a woman passing nearby stepped hastily away, alarmed by the despair in his strange cackle.

Unsteady, dazed, he started walking,

His pace increased.

Now, he was running.

Filthy and wild-eyed, he reeled through the crowd-filled streets, hearing snatches of conversation, his mind automatically translating as best it could—

"—bombing our city to regain control of the Bosphorus and—"

"—war so soon, but with Hitler advancing his agenda it seems—"

"—Bolsheviks and Nazis, and now even Italy has—"

And over and over, the words *"Kirmizi Kral."*

Turkish for the *Red King*.

The Red King!

So complete was the assassin's fearsome grip on the city that he was first to be blamed for this shocking blast.

Sinclair knew the truth. The white king, and not the red, was responsible. The metatemporal detective had followed Zenith down those subterranean service tunnels . . . straight into a trap.

It was the obvious explanation, and usually, the obvious was fact.

Sinclair ran, staggering, chest burning, a pain in his side. As he drew closer to the source of the hideous cloud, his whirlwind thoughts calmed and gradually settled. A coldness came over him. He quelled his churning emotions with pitiless force. It was not a British stiff upper lip. It was emotional paralysis.

Doctor Sinclair stopped feeling.

He shouldered past onlookers, his face set hard, his mouth a thin, grim line.

He entered the zone of destruction.

Chaos ruled here. Through a dirty haze, he saw a giant heap of rubble. A blanket of silence hung over the scene, as if manifest shock banished all noise. Shattered glass everywhere. The wounded were soaked in blood, some sitting, still bleeding, others giving aid to those worse off than themselves. A few lay ominously still.

A section of the road, rent along its length by a yawning crevasse, had collapsed into a tunnel below.

Uniformed policemen appeared close to panic, looking for leadership, and gestured frantically at the crowd to keep back. Many carried long canes and were not shy in using them. Occasionally, they reached for their holstered pistols to emphasise their authority.

Sinclair thrust forward, pushing people aside, picking his way over debris to an officer.

"What happened?" he asked in French.

The policeman, assuming from the Welshman's dishevelled appearance that he had been nearby when the hammam erupted, said, "The boiler exploded, m'sieu."

"Not a bomb?"

"No, don't listen to the gossip. The steam pressure dropped in the baths. A blockage of some sort. It was fortunate, in a way. God protected us. All the customers argued for their money back and stormed out. The owner went off to find his brother, who is responsible for servicing the machinery. As far as we know, there was only a single attendant left inside. Killed, of course. No doubt, we'll find what's left of him when we clear the wreckage."

Could it be true? That it was an accident, not a trap? If that was the case—

"Was a European seen anywhere about the place? Tall and slender. Well-dressed. Blue-grey eyes?"

The policeman shook his head. "As far as I know, it was just the usual clientele, all Turks, aside from Monsieur Milk."

Where Sinclair had been cold, he now became ice.

"Monsieur—?"

"Milk. It is English—*lait, non*? A white-skinned, white-haired fellow. He only recently began visiting the hammam. His Turkish is excellent, if a little old-fashioned. He is certainly not one of us. Pink eyes!"

"But, he wasn't in there when—?"

"No, he had a lucky escape. I think he was doing the owner a favour. Some men came, removed furniture from the place, and put it into a truck. When they finished, Milk came out, joined them, and they all drove off. It wasn't long after that—" The policeman grunted and rubbed his chin thoughtfully. "Hmm! Maybe in shifting the furniture, they dented a pipe or something." He frowned and looked Sinclair up and down. "Are you injured? We have a couple of doctors here if you—"

"No, I'm all right. But I'd like to find this Milk fellow. I think I know him, you see. Any idea where he's gone?"

"I'm afraid not."

"What did the truck look like?"

"It was a dark-blue Morris pantechnicon with *'Altin Boynuz Seramik'* written on the side. There are a few of that sort in the city. Golden Horn Ceramics is a big company. Milk works there, I suppose."

Sinclair nodded and moved away.

He walked without knowing where he was going.

He needed a clue. Something to occupy his attention. A suspect to follow or interview.

Instead, he had nothing but dead ends. Ulric von Bek had kidnapped Violet Damm. Vera Pym had apparently gone in pursuit. He had no idea where they might be.

He bit his lip in frustration. Major Nye in hiding. Sir Vivian Clarke, not to be trusted. Zenith and the Red King gone to ground. Certainly, the albino's men had stolen the truck, so that was not worth following up. And the mansion had yielded no clue.

Should he use the British embassy's radio transmitter to call London HQ?

Sir Seaton Begg is dead. Send help.

He could not face it.

He walked the streets with no destination in mind. At length, he dimly registered the setting sun casting a long shadow across a familiar doorway. Somehow, he had found his way back to the Shangri-La.

After requesting a basin of hot water, Sinclair made his way up to his room.

No notes. No messages.

Washed and in fresh clothes, he lit his first pipe since the hotel fire and sat on the bed, smoking and staring at the wall.

Minutes later, he was on his feet, pacing. He had an idea. A drowning man clutching at a straw, perhaps, but it was something.

Apollinaire de Villiers.

The Frenchman had known Vera Pym's favourite bar. How familiar was he with her two tall drinking companions? If they could be traced, they might direct him to her apartment. A place to which she dare not return! The Red King, if he knew she still lived, would certainly be watching it—but watching for a woman, not for a heavyset, balding man. Maybe Sinclair could break in and search it. He might find a clue to her current whereabouts or to the Red King's identity. That would be progress!

He would be satisfied, even, with anything that answered one simple question, was La Pym friend or foe?

Sinclair became diamond-hard focussed.

He checked his Walther PP, left the hotel, and took an old Austin motor cab, still bearing traces of military paint, to the Galata side of the Horn. If de Villiers had already left his office, Sinclair would go to the man's home.

Just as his taxi approached the bridge, the city fell into absolute darkness. Sinclair groaned. The driver cautioned him: These frequent blackouts often lasted for many hours and offered the city's criminals a window of opportunity. *"Fais attention!"* the man advised as Sinclair disembarked. *"Il y a des monstres dans ces ténèbres!"*

Sinclair knew full well that there were monsters in the darkness. He had been fighting them with Begg for years.

But tonight, he thought, *I could become one of them.*

Certainly, if it was necessary, he would subject de Villiers to what American cops called "the third degree."

Candlelight glowed in the Frenchman's office window.

At the front door, Sinclair ignored the bellpull and used a trick Begg had taught him to trip the lock. All remained deathly quiet. He entered silently, pulled out his torch, and ascended the stairs. Approaching the top, he heard voices.

De Villiers with—

A woman!

The transom windows revealed which of the two rooms they occupied—the same Sinclair and Begg had previously visited.

He stepped closer. De Villiers was speaking heavily accented English, which suggested he was not with his wife.

"—and the candlelight makes it much more romantic, no?" he murmured.

"It is lovely." A seductive female voice. "And with the stars so bright and reflecting on the water, so tranquil. I think I like the city better this way."

"And me?"

She laughed. "Do you ask whether you are more handsome in subdued light?"

"Ah, Madam Melody, you tease me!"

"And you have cast a spell on me, m'sieu. I came here to seek advice, not to be swept off my feet. We have known each other for only half a day, yet it feels like half a lifetime."

Sinclair clicked off his torch, crossed to the empty room, and crept in. The closed door to the adjacent chamber also had a transom, and the glimmer shining through it revealed he had entered a records office crammed with filing cabinets and chests of drawers.

"Your hair is like silver," said de Villiers, "and your eyes, I see infinity in them. When I gaze into their depths, I am lost. They mesmerise me."

Sinclair picked up a wooden chair, moved it to the connecting door, and climbed onto it. The fanlight consisted of differently coloured glass sections, with two completely clear. Through these, by standing on tiptoe, he was able to see de Villiers beside his desk with a woman in his arms.

She was small, with a perfect figure bent back a little in playful resistance. Her hair was as white as Zenith's, contrasting with her olive skin.

"Oh, I should resist you," she said. "I know I should."

It was the *chanteuse* from the Red King's mansion.

"Say my name the way only you can, *mon amour*," de Villiers murmured.

"Apollo," she trilled. "Oh, Apollo!"

Sinclair ran a hand over the pocket that held his pistol.

"Freni—Freni, my Persian princess. My Madam Melody."

"Listen to me," she purred. "There is something I must tell you, my love. If you are serious about leaving Istanbul, I know a secret place in London where we can be together. A magical place, known by only a few. Let me whisper its name."

De Villiers turned slightly, which brought the woman's face round, so that Sinclair could see it better. Her eyes, he observed, were large and almond shaped, of the deepest brown. Her lips, painted dark red, offered a tantalising half smile, the promise of a houri's kiss. She put them against de Villiers's right ear. Her hands stroked up over the sides of his head, until she was clutching it passionately, holding it immobile.

"The place, it is called—" She drew a breath, bringing him closer still.

She screamed.

At the fancy dress ball, Baroness Blittersdorf had produced a phenomenally loud shriek that rattled the candelabrum. It was a murmur by comparison. Madam Melody gave vent to a pure yet agonising note that hit like a steam hammer and pierced like a sword.

The glass in the fanlight shattered.

Sinclair clapped his hands to his already damaged ears and squeezed his eyes shut, but the scream could not be muted. It throbbed in his cranium, drilled into his brain, and went on and on—long, steady, and utterly excruciating. He doubled over and toppled from the chair, thudded onto the floor, and writhed in unutterable torment.

He had no idea when pain ceased. Deep inside his ears, it carried on, a single musical tone, like the undying echo of a gong, obscuring all other sounds.

The torture gradually subsided.

He rolled onto his side and vomited.

He lay still, knees drawn up, eyes watering, nose bleeding, unable to move, in the grip of stomach-churning vertigo.

Perhaps thirty minutes went by before, suddenly, the lights snapped on. The city's latest power failure had ended.

As Sinclair tried to get up, another wave of dizziness sent him back down. He groaned, took deep breaths, and tried again. He made three attempts before he was finally able to rise to his feet and steady himself against the wall. He waited until the room stopped spinning, then stumbled into the adjoining office.

Apollinaire de Villiers was dead on the floor, blood oozing from his ears.

Madam Melody had vanished.

Sinclair reeled to the bureau. The decanter and glasses had

fragmented. In the cabinet, he found an undamaged silver flask of brandy. The spirit settled him a little.

He went to kneel by the corpse, using his thumbs to close the man's eyelids. A mixture of grey matter and blood, forced from de Villiers' cranial orifices, had pooled on the boards beneath. What horrific sound could liquefy a man's brain? Some sort of amplified wave, perhaps, that a singer of peculiar and dreadful talent might harness? It was incredible. Ghastly! Sinclair tried to recall a legend, perhaps of a siren or harpy capable of such horror.

He straightened and surveyed the office, quickly searched the desk drawers, but found nothing of note. His head was pounding abominably. He wanted to sleep.

After snuffing the candles, he limped toward the landing and was just stepping out when something on the pig-bristled welcome mat caught his attention. He bent and picked out of it a small tuft of fibre, a fragment of hessian rope, half-covered by a sticky black substance. He put it to his nose. Though the hotel fire had damaged his sense of smell, he nevertheless detected oil and something else, reminiscent of the sea.

Carefully, Sinclair slipped the tuft into his shirt pocket.

Time to move. The scream cannot have gone unnoticed. The police might be on their way.

Yet another assassination for their list.

He went downstairs, found a back door, and slipped from the rear of the building unseen.

The journey back to the hotel was uneventful.

The tone in his ears was now reduced to a continual, frantic whispering. It would not stop. It felt like an urgent warning from swarming ghosts.

When he at last dragged himself into his room, desperate for his bed, he found that the connecting door was open. Light flooded in from the neighbouring suite. Pain and fatigue jumbled his thoughts. The maid, he concluded, was careless. He tottered across to close the door, his legs barely holding him.

Sir Seaton Begg was in the next-door room, sitting in an armchair, freshly bathed and wrapped in a hotel dressing gown. He was reading a newspaper and smoking a cigar. As Sinclair entered, he gave a broad smile, threw the paper aside, and with evident relief, jumped up to greet his colleague.

Taffy Sinclair's legs buckled. He dropped to his knees and swayed.

Begg leaped forward, took his friend by the shoulders, and spoke. Sinclair frowned, trying hard to listen.

Begg's lips moved more emphatically.

But there was no sound.

In the brief moment before Sinclair's senses departed, he realised that Madam Melody's scream had made him profoundly, and perhaps permanently, deaf.

CHAPTER 15
The Blind Egyptian

Sinclair woke between clean cotton sheets, well rested, his headache gone, and feeling very much better. A single musical note droned in his ears. He could hear nothing else. Even when he clapped his hands in front of his face, he heard not a sound.

He washed and dressed and joined Sir Seaton Begg for breakfast.

"If there is no improvement by lunchtime," the detective said, "we shall consult Doctor Matossian."

"What?" Sinclair yelled.

Begg flinched, waved him to a lower volume, then repeated himself more slowly, allowing his assistant to read his lips.

"Good Lord!" Sinclair exclaimed. "Spare me. He thinks we're collecting injuries for fun." He peered at a dark bruise in the middle of Begg's forehead. "Speaking of which, I am not alone in acquiring a fresh set. What happened?"

Utilising lip-reading, sign language, and shorthand in a notebook, they exchanged stories.

The detective told how he and Special Agent Sabahattin Sans-Serif were captured by Zenith. He wrote,

> *The albino flew into a rage and fired three bullets at the Turk. By sheer good luck, they hit the bars of the cage, cracking two of them. When we were left alone with scalding steam flooding into the chamber, we were able, with considerable effort, to bend those damaged bars aside and squeeze through the gap. The enormous heat coming from the furnace room precluded escape in that direction, so we found the mechanism to raise the cage and went out the way we had come in. In the tunnel, footprints went in both directions, ours and Zenith's to the distant library, many more the other way. Presuming a closer exit, we groped our way along in the latter direction. The explosion came a few minutes later. Flying debris knocked us unconscious. When we recovered, we found our way to the surface.*

He added,

> *Sans-Serif is now combing the city for Zenith.*

Sinclair, still speaking far too loudly, gave his account: the Red King gang leaving Vera Pym to die; her claim to be a Roumanian agent; Ulric von Bek abducting Violet Damm to help him locate Major Nye; Pym going after them; and Madam Melody's bizarre murder of de Villiers.

He handed over the cigarette butts from the manor and the tuft of hessian rope from de Villiers's office.

Begg, examining the latter, asked, "From Madam Melody's shoe?"

"It could have come from anyone's," Sinclair roared, "but it has a maritime flavour, and I can't associate dockhands or sailors with an expert on secularism."

Begg put it to his nose and nodded. Enunciating slowly, so his friend could follow his lips, he said, "Yes. Oil and seawater. You suggest, then, that Melody and the rest of the Red King gang have relocated to a ship or a dockyard property?"

"It's a tenuous connection, Begg. A guess."

"Indeed so. Is it not more likely that it came from the manor house cellar? You said there were lengths of rope, each tied to an object, all over the floor."

"Yes," Sinclair confirmed, and listed what he remembered: flat iron, bicycle wheel, anvil, sack of potatoes, and the rest.

Begg said, "But none were in any way attached to the bucket, pulleys, hose, or noose?"

"That's correct. They were just lying around. I don't recall seeing any oil, such as is on this fragment. That, and the whiff of salt water, is why I think it came from somewhere else."

"Hmm."

Begg turned his attention to the cigarette ends. He gave a cry of excitement, held one up, and spoke rapidly.

"Slow down, I don't understand," Sinclair pleaded.

Begg scribbled in the notebook:

Cardboard end instead of a filter. This is a new brand: Belomorkanal. Created last year to commemorate the construction of the White Sea-Baltic Canal. It is Russian. Exclusive to the Soviet Union. It cannot be purchased anywhere else.

"Then, one of the Red King gang is Russian?" Sinclair asked.

"More than one. The cardboard end functions as a holder. Some smokers flatten it. Others twist it. There are examples of both here, see? Two separate smokers."

"Bolshies!"

"It can't be discounted. The Soviet Union might easily gain the Bosphorus Strait if Turkey can be destabilised."

Sinclair slapped a hand to his high, shiny forehead and gave a low whistle.

"If the Red King is a Bolshevik," he shouted, unable to moderate his voice, "and Sir Vivian is a Nazi, and von Bek a Nazi agent, then this attempt to upset Turkey's westernisation is an international plot of stupendous proportions! But, how does the *Salut Christi* fit into the picture? Why is Zenith trying to conceal that it comes from his native land?" He frowned. "Might it be a weapon?"

"Crafted from silver? Unlikely, if we think of weapons in the traditional sense." Begg stroked his freshly shaven chin, grappling with the sense of a blocked memory; something experienced that, were he to recall it, might cause a metatemporal conflict. The year 1917 sprang to mind, but he could get no further than that. "However," he said, "when nations set themselves against one another, their armies carry more than weapons, don't they?"

"Begg?"

"Flags. Standards. Colours. It may be an object of purely symbolic power."

"Symbolic of what?"

"More than a thousand years ago, when it was gifted to Pope Leo III, it symbolised rapprochement between East and West."

"And now—great heavens!—surely not to signify an alliance between Nazi Germany and the Soviet Union?"

"I fear so."

"But—but doesn't that mean Zenith is working for the common good? Are we on the same side?"

"It's a distinct possibility, old man. Roumania is currently falling beneath the heel of the Gestapo-inspired Iron Guard. If Zenith has any love for his native country, he would certainly set himself against such an invidious meeting of political philosophies. I would certainly like to know, though, how he learned of the potential alliance, if there really is one."

"So, what now? Track him down? Propose a truce? Persuade him to fight with us against a common foe?"

Begg nodded. "Yes, if we can, though it will prove difficult. He is furious that I have delved into his past, and before we approach him, I must dig deeper. I want to see what else we can learn about the object at the heart of all this. I intend to revisit the silversmith's where we had our buccaneer boxing match with the albino. In ancient crafts, there are often oral histories independent of anything written. Perhaps this artefact, fashioned so long ago, is still spoken of by today's artisans."

"I want to come with you," said Sinclair, "but I feel useless without the old lug holes. You're not going to confine me to quarters again, are you?"

The detective smiled. "No. It's the donkeywork for you. Your ears are defective, but your eyes are fine. There are many other libraries besides the Köprülü in the city. You shall trudge from one to the other searching for whatever references you can find to the *Salut Christi*. I predict you will discover none; nor any to the land of Lamaneagra; or to the von Bek family; or—" Begg paused, a vertical crease appearing between his eyebrows. "—to Wäldenstein."

"Wäldenstein?"

"It was listed among the places recently visited by Major Nye. You and I are exceedingly well travelled, but I have never heard of it. Have you?"

Sinclair shook his head thoughtfully. "It rings a bell, though. Rather Anthony Hope, eh? Ruritania!"

"I find it thoroughly intriguing," said Begg. "Von Bek and Wäldenstein are names that I feel I should know—that I *do* know—but, grope as I might, they persistently elude me. I have the years 1917 and 1962 knocking around my cranial cavities, too. What do you think, Taffy? Might the Sisterhood of Solitude be pulling strings in this year and those, while enveloping you and me and Zenith—perhaps even La Pym—in a cloud of amnesia?"

"It would not be the first time we have been so inconvenienced."

"Indeed not, but—I don't know—what the blazes is at the heart of it?"

The conversation—if the gesticulations, scribbled shorthand, exaggerating mouthings, and Sinclair's bellowing could qualify as such—came to an end. The detective and his companion went their separate ways with no inkling that they would not see each other again for a considerable period—or, when reunited, that it would be under extraordinary circumstances and far from Istanbul!

Begg drove to the silversmith. The sky was now clear, the unusual spring heat and humidity returning with greater intensity. The bustling twentieth century city sprawled across seven hills, and as many layers of ruins, and tirelessly continued the business of entering the future.

The silversmith, Begg found, was a friendly and well-mannered Greek.

"It is Gulvenkian Ogg you want to see, m'sieu," he told Begg. "He is chairman of the Guild of Gold and Silver, and possibly the most talented artist this city has ever seen. An elderly gentleman. Two thousand years old, I should say, but he hasn't lost his touch."

Begg gave a quizzical tilt of the head.

The silversmith grinned. "His memory seems to go back that far, anyway. I've never heard of this *Salut Christi*, but if anyone has, it will be old Ogg. He has a taste for raki. If you take him a bottle, he will talk your ears off. He loves to talk, that man!"

He gave Begg the address of a clubhouse in the Mevlanakapi neighbourhood, near the ancient Theodosian Walls.

Begg thanked him and returned to his car. As he was climbing into it, he heard a whistled refrain. There were only a few people passing by. It was impossible to tell which of them had given Major Nye's signal.

"All right, then," Begg muttered to himself. "Change of plan."

He set course for the post office, close to the southern end of the Galata Bridge.

On arrival, he opened the box with the key Violet Damm had given him and found a note.

```
The Aram Bekir confectionery shop on Haydar Caddesi.
Take care that no one follows. Tell the proprietor
that you despise Turkish delight. To his response,
answer, "The Egyptian would argue malban."
```

Begg consulted his street map. Haydar Caddesi was half a mile to the west, a long street in a poor neighbourhood. He decided to walk there by a very circuitous route, veering suddenly into alleyways, doubling back on himself, and lurking for minutes at a time in doorways. Once he was certain that he had shaken loose any shadow, he exited a short passageway and moved southwest along

Haydar. The street was narrow. This part was residential. Wooden scaffolding shored up cheap, jerry-built tenements. People strolled, lounged, gossiped, and smoked. Idleness was an art here. Many of them eyed his well-pressed suit with predatory speculation. There were occasional cars, a few wagons, and a profusion of cats. Cats everywhere! Begg knew they were revered in Islam, as they had been by ancient Egyptians.

He passed a stretch of thousand-year-old wall, a semiderelict church, a recently built mosque, a tiny police station, and a gang of dangerous-looking youths. These wore their hair short at the sides but long at the top and back, an emulation of the Hunnic style sported by the factions of young men who had rioted through Constantinople fourteen hundred years ago.

One of them approached him and growled in French, "You have money? Give it to me."

Begg instead gave a certain look, and the youngster took sudden interest in a pigeon.

The detective strode on, past piled rubbish, through mephitic odours, an ivy-clad old edifice to his right, a graffitied new wall to his left: KEMAL BIR APTAL! *Kemal is a fool!* And beneath: KEMAL BIR TANRIDIR! *Kemal is God!*

He came to a tall house with an overhanging upper storey, and from there onward the residences gave way to shops, and the street became crowded and much noisier. From each store, a sign stuck out at right angles, declaring its name and wares. He glanced at each as he passed. There was a preponderance of tobacconists. He went into one.

"Do you sell Belomorkanal cigarettes?"

"I am sorry, m'sieu, I do not."

"Do you know where I might find them?"

"Moscow."

"Nowhere in Istanbul?"

"Nowhere in Turkey."

"Excellent!"

Begg gave a nod of satisfaction and returned to the street, leaving the shopkeeper bemused.

A little farther on, he came to the confectionary store, an open-fronted, ramshackle little place replete with discoloured jars on sticky shelves, powdered counters, and sugary perfumes.

To judge from his waistline, the owner was his own best customer.

"Bonjour," said Begg. "I despise Turkish delight."

"We do not call it Turkish delight," the man responded, folding his arms over his immense stomach. "Here, it is *lokum*."

"The Egyptian would argue *malban*," Begg responded.

"She probably would," the confectioner agreed. "You can ask her yourself. Through the back and up the stairs. The blue door. She is expecting you."

"Thank you."

Begg skirted the counter, squeezed past the owner, who didn't move to accommodate him, went through a curtained doorway, and mounted the stairs. They creaked in apparent agony.

Before he reached the top, he heard a key turn, and the blue door swung open to reveal a woman in Arab dress.

"I heard you coming," she said in English. "You are?"

"Sir Seaton Begg."

"Good. Come in, please, effendi."

He entered a small but tastefully and expensively furnished apartment, quite at odds with its location. A large radio receiver and transmitter dominated the main room.

"Aha!" he exclaimed. "Might I presume that you intercept Sir Vivian Clarke's transmissions from here?"

"That is correct, effendi. Will you take coffee with me?"

"Yes, thank you."

"It is prepared. Sit, please." She gestured to where cushions surrounded a low table.

Begg suddenly realised she was blind.

She was also, as suggested by the password phrase, Egyptian. In her mid-twenties, she was round-faced and rather plain in appearance aside from her skin, which was a beautifully smooth deep brown, without a single visible line or blemish.

"My name is Dalilah," she said as they lowered themselves. "I assist Major Nye."

"I need to find him," said Begg.

"It is doubtful that you will." She reached for the coffee pot and, by feel alone, poured two cups. "When he does not want to be found"—she slid a silver dish of sugar lumps across—"he is not found."

"I am here to help him. He is being hunted by the Red King, by a man named Ulric von Bek, and perhaps by Zenith, the albino."

"He knows this. The arrival of the albino and the man from Wäldenstein has complicated matters. When it was—"

"Wait!" Begg snapped. "Wäldenstein?"

"Von Bek's country."

"Oh! I had thought him German."

"Wäldenstein has been Germany. It has also been Austria and Bohemia. Its borders are very unstable. So, too, its name. Always it is different depending on who is asked. Even its capital, the city of Mirenberg, is given different names on different maps. The place itself is, I think, a living palimpsest, many ideas of nationhood layered over one another. Most often, you will see the whole region marked simply as Mittelmarch—the Middle Territory—claimed by all and none, formed by ancient, forgotten, but persistent dukedoms."

Begg, who considered his knowledge of Europe to be as comprehensive as possible, was astounded.

After taking a sip of coffee, she continued.

"When he was opposed only by the Red King, Major Nye was able to make use of the agent Miss Violet Damm. Now, he considers it too dangerous to let her continue with—"

Begg interrupted. "She has been abducted." He put two sugar lumps into his coffee and stirred. "By von Bek."

"That is unfortunate."

"You understand, perhaps, why it is of critical importance that I speak with Nye?"

"I do not know how to find him. I have not seen him for many days. We were communicating through a new post office box, but he has left nothing in it nor taken anything from it since Monday."

The day when Nye's other operative, the old woman, had warned him about the time bomb!

"In addition to you, Miss Dalilah, how many agents does he have in the city?"

"I know only of Violet Damm. I suspect there are more."

"An ancient crone in robes and veils?"

She shrugged.

His coffee was hot and strong. He added a third lump.

"Is his lack of communication the reason you summoned me?"

She gestured the affirmative. "Major Nye instructed me that, should I hear nothing from him for three days or more, I should give you the transcripts of all intercepted communications between

Sir Vivian Clarke and the Red King." Her fingers found a thick envelope Begg had already noticed on the table next to a thinner one. She lifted it and passed it to him.

"Damning evidence," the detective murmured.

She pulled a folded sheet of paper from her dress. "And this to add to it. It was transmitted from Clarke's office two hours ago."

Begg took it.

```
Surp Pirgiç Hospital, tomorrow, Friday, 28th.
3 p.m. Doctor Gaspar Matossian will give a tour to
foreign dignitaries. Kill him.
```

"Matossian!" Begg exclaimed. "And Nye hasn't seen this?"

"He has not."

Begg set his jaw, his muscles tensing. "By heaven, I'll prevent this assassination, even if I sacrifice my own life to do so!"

For a moment, there was silence. Had the Egyptian been able to see Begg's blazing eyes, she might have recoiled in fear. Instead, she simply sat, waiting until he was able to speak again.

Finally, he said, "That other envelope?"

"A document, effendi. You are to read it, then burn it. It is classed as above top secret."

"Its contents?"

"It is the story of the *Salut Christi*."

CHAPTER 16
A Gentleman's Gentleman

Begg parked the Invicta in the garage behind the securely locked building that disguised Secret Service HQ. Leaving the vehicle, he entered the passage to the street.

He possessed all the evidence. Sir Vivian Clarke's career was about to crash to an ignominious end. His best probable future was death by British firing squad.

The metatemporal detective, his anger simmering, intended to lay the transcribed messages before the branch director, and one by one, name every victim whose death the traitor had ordered. Clarke would then find himself subjected to unsparing interrogation. Nothing less than a full confession could satisfy. People. Places. Plans.

The Red King would be unmasked, captured, or killed. The potential alliance between Germany and the Soviet Union would not occur. The future of Turkey, under President Kemal, was secure.

Begg stepped into the street, then immediately ducked back into the passage, hugging its wall.

Clarke was just across the road in conversation with a man the detective recognised.

William "Dirty" Duck!

Begg had visited him a few days ago. The old lag had revealed that the Red King was at war with a rival gang—which turned out to be Zenith—but claimed no further knowledge.

I don't much mix with bad 'uns, no more, Sir Seaton. I'm workin' for a perfick gent, an' earnin' a decent crust. I've gone 'spectible. Ain't that a thing!

And here he was, dressed smartly, every inch a "gentleman's gentleman," and looking for all the world as if he were receiving instructions from his employer.

"Great Scott!" Begg whispered.

He watched as the two men finished their business and parted. Clarke made for the embassy and, presumably, the tunnel to HQ. Duck went in the other direction.

Begg made a quick decision. He followed the ex-crook. With luck, he was on his way to Clarke's private residence. The detective was curious to know where it was. He wanted to search it.

Duck mounted a tram. Begg hopped on behind him, keeping his distance. The detective was wearing his customary wide-brimmed slouch hat, and now pulled it low.

Down the hill, across the bridge, and into the Old Quarter. William Duck jumped off, pushed into the teeming market, and joined the vociferous haggling.

Begg watched as he purchased vegetables, eggs, and a rack of lamb, filling a large brown paper bag. Duck then extricated himself from the throng, boarded another tram, and travelled a mile and a half southwest to the outskirts of the Bakirköy district, a rather exclusive suburb of large houses and well-kept gardens. The vehicle clanked to a stop outside the ruination of the neighbourhood: the Yeşilköy Airport. Duck disembarked. Begg followed.

The din of a building site assaulted their ears—a new terminal was under construction—but faded behind as they walked away and turned right into a tree-lined avenue.

There were plenty of people about. Shadowing Duck was easy. The man didn't once glance back.

He turned into a side road, then passed through a gate. Begg loitered near it, watching as the man crossed a private garden compound and entered a large house through the servant's side door.

The detective walked the perimeter, and when he was certain no one was looking, grasped the iron spikes atop the fence and vaulted over. He sprinted across the lawn, put his back against the house, and waited. There was no outcry, no window or door thrown open, no dog let loose.

Crouching low, he moved to a window and peeked over the sill into an unoccupied study. A suit of armour stood in a corner, its white tabard marked with a red cross. A Knight Templar.

Begg quietly stepped to the next window, beside the door through which Duck had passed. It illuminated a small lobby, from which four doors gave access to other parts of the house. One was standing ajar, revealing a stairwell. Begg knew by his familiarity with houses of this sort that it descended to a kitchen and various utility rooms.

He tested the exterior door. Unlocked. Begg entered, crossed to the stairs, and carefully descended.

The basement lobby followed the pattern of the one above. Sounds of movement came from behind one half-opened door. Through the gap on the hinge side, Begg spied on Duck, in a kitchen preparing to cook lunch.

He stepped in and, in a nonchalant tone, said, "My dear William, you neglected to mention that Sir Vivian is your master."

Duck wheeled. A cast iron frying pan fell from his hand with a loud clang. He stepped back, shocked. "Begg!"

"We need to have a chat before he comes home," said the detective. "I'm afraid you have got yourself into—"

A buzz interrupted. Begg looked at the wall to his right and saw six bulbs on a wooden panel. One was glowing red, above it the words DRAWING ROOM.

"Ah! He has already—" he began, turning back to Duck.

A fist smashed into the angle of his jaw.

Duck was neither large nor strong but took Begg by complete surprise, and the detective went down.

He was, however, by no means stunned. He hit the floor, rolled, and kicked out, knocking Duck's legs from beneath him. The man fell heavily, and on the way, the back of his cranium made noisy contact with a table. The crook heaved himself up, swaying on his knees, groaning, eyes unfocussed.

Begg snatched up the dropped pan and got to his feet.

"Dirty—" he said.

"I'll kill you, you nosy parker!" Duck snarled, baring his tobacco-stained teeth. He reached for a bulge in his jacket.

Begg pounced forward and whacked him over the head with the frying pan. Duck toppled, hit the floor, and lay still.

The detective rubbed his jaw and muttered, "I should pay better attention."

Taking a carving knife from a cutlery drawer, he used it to slice the cable from an unplugged electric fan. With this, he bound the unconscious man's wrists behind his back. For good measure, he tied the shoelaces together, too.

Begg took possession of Duck's weapon, an automatic.

The buzzer sounded again.

"So, Sir Vivian must have driven home while Dirty Duck was doing the shopping. Why he's here at this time of day I cannot fathom. Whatever happened to office hours?"

He put the carving knife on the floor where Duck would be sure to see it.

Affixed to the wall near the door, there hung a small blackboard and little container of chalk. He wiped from it the words ONIONS and MINT and replaced them with LAST CHANCE, DIRTY! CLEAN UP AND KEEP STRAIGHT!

It would take the old lag at least an hour to free himself. If he had any sense, he would quietly return to his job as a carpenter.

The metatemporal detective checked the gun's clip. It was full. The weapon was a Turkish copy of a Remington 51. He could not be sure of its reliability. He clicked off the safety catch.

"Well, here goes."

He ascended the stairs.

Sir Vivian was in a study, sitting at a table, writing a letter, with his back to the open door.

Begg, after pausing to listen until he felt assured no other servants were present in the house, entered. The Secret Service director, hearing his footfall, murmured, "Bring me a pot of tea, would you, Ducky."

"Sorry," said Begg, moving to the other end of the table, gun raised. "You appear to have mistaken me for your—"

He stopped.

The mistake was his.

"Gammon!" he cried out. "By God!"

Sir Vivian's twin, Geoffrey Bacon, looked up from his letter, startled, then shocked, then furious. He leaped to his feet, his chair toppling back.

"Don't call me that," he yelled. "Don't call me that! What the devil? It's Begg! Sir Seaton Begg, you filthy—"

"Careful!" Begg barked. "Careful what you say. I could shoot you on the spot, and they'd give me a medal for it."

"Get out of my house! Ducky! Ducky! Come here, man!"

"Duck is inconvenienced. Pick up your chair. Sit down."

"I will not."

"How old are you, Gammon? Sixty? Don't make me force you."

Bacon snarled at the nickname but fear showed in his eyes. First and last he was a coward.

He turned, lifted his chair, and sat.

Begg also seated himself, facing the other, his features hard, implacable, grey eyes like steel.

"No gas pellet in your pocket this time," said the detective. "Just you, me, this automatic, and the death sentence hanging over your head."

"Go to blazes!"

"If I do, you shall certainly be there to greet me." Begg shook his head, amazed. "I had you down as a madman and a fascist swine—but Bolshevik?"

Bacon recoiled. "What?"

"Don't bother playing the innocent. I know all about it. You have been working to destabilise this country. Are you the Red King?"

A sudden shriek of laughter—tainted with insanity!

"What? Me? The Red King? Ha!"

"Then who is he?"

"I have no idea!"

"But you and your brother commissioned him to assassinate foreign workers. You—"

"My brother?" Bacon rasped. "You . . . you know?"

"That Sir Vivian Clarke is your twin? Yes, I know. And now that I know, I can see the family resemblance."

Bacon's mouth moved as if he were chewing. He glanced to the left and right, shifted in his chair. "I . . . I still don't . . . Bolshevik?"

"Don't try to hide it. I have evidence of Russian affiliations among the Red King gang."

In truth, Begg was fishing. His evidence—the Belomorkanal cigarette butts—was slight, his conclusion more inference than fact.

"I know nothing about his people," Bacon asserted. "Russians, Turks, Chinamen, or Aborigines, it makes no difference to me. The assassination gang is simply a tool. Voskan—" He stopped himself, gritted his teeth, then went on, "And . . . and they get the job done."

"Voskan?" A sudden inspiration. "Ah! Now I see it! Voskanyan! Vazken Voskanyan, the government inspector! I met him at Gelecek Engineering. So, he gives you information about foreign advisors, perhaps recommends targets?"

"I don't know who you mean. I don't know any—"

The detective's laugh was mirthless. Bacon had no control over his impulses. He was so helplessly mad, he wanted to brag!

Begg's piercing gaze was unwavering. "So, the gang gets the job done, you say? What is the job? What is your purpose?"

Bacon leaned forward and, with his right elbow on the table, raised his hand and clenched it until his knuckles turned white. His eyes blazed. His face held an expression of fanatical mania.

"Begg! Can't you understand? It is simple patriotism! We can't allow Kemal to modernise Turkey, least of all this city. If he succeeds, the Mussulmen will gain firsthand experience of Western achievements and living standards. They'll find 'em irresistible.

They'll swarm across the Bosphorus into Europe like locusts. In seeking our heights, they'll drag us down to their depths. It cannot be permitted! Westernisation must be seen to fail. It is imperative we show Constantinople to be a gate with a broken lock. Imperial powers must have one option only—sovereign rule. British rule! Nail the gate shut. Make the Bosphorus a hard barrier—the first bastion against invasion."

"Arrant nonsense," Begg objected. "Political actions cannot be predicated on fear."

"We are threatened. We must defend ourselves."

"We progress by educating ourselves, not by fighting others."

"We fight others because they hold us back. They are savages. Banish them—or better still, eliminate them!" Bacon's eyes were wide, the whites visible around the irises. Spittle flecked the corners of his mouth. He slammed his fist onto the table. "Do you know the motto of the Imperial League?" He jumped to his feet, gesticulating wildly, thumped his chest and extended his arm in a Nazi salute. "Keep them out and breed them out!"

"That's quite enough of that!" Begg snapped.

Bacon ignored him and paced across the room. "Arabs, Gypsies, Jews, imbeciles, cripples, ni—"

"Stop!" Begg leaped up and levelled his gun. A sharp crack. Bacon's head exploded in a shower of blood and brains. His corpse crumpled to the floor.

After a frozen moment, Begg expelled a breath. He checked his automatic. The safety was on. The chamber was full. He had not pulled the trigger.

He looked at the window. There was a hole, a web of cracks radiating from it.

Abruptly he was moving—out of the room, along the hall,

across the lobby, and through the external door. He careened into the garden just in time to see, beyond the fence, a dwarf, holding a rifle with a big sniper sight attached, clambering into a car.

The vehicle roared away.

Taffy Sinclair had reported a dwarf among the people at the manor.

Another Red King assassination!

Begg returned to the drawing room. After briefly examining Bacon's corpse, he set out to search the house, commencing with the study. However, his hand was on that room's door handle when something occurred to him.

He hurried down to the kitchen.

"Dirty?"

"Curse you, Begg! I'm goin' to—"

"Your master is dead. Shot through the head."

Duck, lying on his side, stopped struggling with his bonds. "What? You killed 'im?"

"No, don't be a fool. Tell me, how much do you know about his activities? I want the truth."

Begg retrieved the knife he had left on the floor.

Duck's eyes widened as the detective approached. "Don't!"

"I'm cutting your bonds. You are in out of your depth. Best you tell me what you know."

He sawed at the electric cable.

After a pause, Duck said, "I know he was wanted by the police back 'ome. An' I know he was about as nutty as a bloomin' fruit cake. But, if he was up to no good, he didn't tell me anythin' about it."

"All right," said Begg. "Now listen carefully. Do you want to get mixed up with the Red King?"

"God, no!"

"You already are. That's who just shot your employer. I can get you out of it, so you would be wise to keep your fists to yourself, understood?"

"Yes! Yes, all right."

The cable dropped from his wrists.

Begg straightened while Duck sat and applied his numb fingers to his shoelaces.

"What do you want me to do?"

"Did Bacon have a car?"

"Yes, parked out front. The Rover Pilot."

"Where are the keys?"

"In a drawer by the front door. I'll show you."

Duck led the way upstairs. As they passed the drawing room, he glanced in and cried out in horror. There was blood spattered over the wall and pooled across the floor.

"God almighty! This is not . . . I don't want—" he wailed.

"I know," said Begg. "The keys?"

Duck retrieved them and passed them over. "The gears are good . . . the clutch takes a bit o' gettin' used to."

"Then you drive," Begg responded, and handed the keys back.

Duck swallowed and nodded.

They left the house, made their way to the car, and set off.

"Pera," Begg instructed. "When we get there, you can go. I doubt the police will come looking for you. You don't figure in the affair. If they do, I will put in a word, but only if you give me yours."

"My word, Mr. Begg?"

"That you will go back to your wife, back to carpentry, and stay straight as a die."

"The word is given! By 'eavens, it is!"

When they were close to the Pera Plaza Hotel, Begg told Duck to stop the car.

"Off you go. Make sure I never see you again."

The former extortionist, and now ex–gentleman's gentleman, offered a nod of gratitude, then turned and vanished into crowded Istanbul.

Begg moved to the driver's seat and drove the short distance to the Secret Service HQ.

The Red King had killed one of his own sponsors.

Another remained: Sir Vivian Clarke.

CHAPTER 17

The Massacre

Major Nye's documents had revealed to Sir Seaton Begg what the *Salut Christi* was and what it represented, though Monsieur Zenith's connection with it remained a mystery. He understood why Gammon and Sir Vivian wanted it. If it fell into Bolshevik hands . . .

Stay hidden, Nye!

As the British embassy came into view, he veered the saloon to the curb, slammed on the brakes, and skidded to a precipitous stop. Turkish police were milling around in front of the building.

Jumping out of the vehicle, he hurried to the entrance.

"No entry!" an officer shouted. "There has been a crime here."

"I am—" Begg began, but was interrupted by Sabahattin Sans-Serif, who stepped from within.

"Ah, the English spy. I am sorry. It is bad."

"What has happened?"

"Come in."

Begg followed him inside. The clerk was slumped over his desk, a bullet hole in his forehead. A woman was dead on the floor.

"Fourteen of the eighteen staff members were present," said Sans-Serif. "These two, shot dead. Seven, in the main office, I don't know what happened to them. It looks as if they all had brain hemorrhages. In other rooms, three strangled, and two knifed in the heart. It is a massacre."

"The Red King," Begg said grimly. "One of his gang, Madam Freni Melody, caused the hemorrhages."

"How?"

"With her voice. She has abnormal vocal cords."

"Don't be ridiculous."

Begg shrugged. "Suleyman the Strangler was here, too. I don't know the identity of the shooter or knifeman. When did it happen?"

"Not much more than an hour ago. Earlier, a van drew up outside. Four people entered the embassy. About forty-five minutes later, they came out and drove off. Five minutes or so after that, a woman came to collect her replacement passport and found"—he gestured—"this."

Begg noticed that the door marked STAFF ONLY was half an inch open.

"Forty-five minutes?" he asked, feeling himself turn cold.

"Eh?"

"Before they returned to the van?"

"According to the witness—in the shop, over the road. He was sitting on his doorstep, saw them come, saw them go."

"Special Agent," Begg said. "Listen to me. This affair—it's big. International. You need to tell the police chief to keep it from the press. At least for now. Then, I want you to follow me."

Sans-Serif dragged his fingers through his black beard and glowered, angling his head, directing his bulging eye straight at Begg. "You give orders to a Turkish official in Turkey?"

"Legally, this embassy is considered British soil, and you are half Spanish. No time for games, my friend."

"Humph!"

Sans-Serif jerked his chin and strode over to a police officer. He spoke rapidly to him, then returned and said, "Well?"

"This way."

Begg walked across to the staff-only door, went through, and descended the stairs.

"Last time we visited a vault, it didn't end very well," the Turk observed.

"It won't this time, either," said Begg.

"Why not? What are you getting me into this time?"

"They didn't require three-quarters of an hour for that slaughter. There's more."

"I should round up all you foreigners and kick you out of the country," Sans-Serif muttered.

They reached the cellar. The door to the tunnel was open.

"A little while ago, I was speaking with a man who held a similar view of foreigners," said Begg as they passed beneath the neighbouring buildings. "Only he was rather more serious about it than you."

"Who says I'm not serious?"

"I'm a good judge of character. I see your heart, Sans-Serif."

The Turk made no reply.

They emerged into the basement of the Secret Service HQ. The guard was limp in a chair, shot in the head.

"Mother of God," said Sans-Serif. "It's war."

Begg closed the tunnel door and turned its key to prevent any curious policemen from coming through.

On the way to Sir Vivian's office, they passed five more corpses.

Begg called, "Hello? Anyone here? It's safe to come out!" but no one did.

They found Sir Vivian Clarke stretched out on his desk as if it were a sacrificial altar. The hilt of a knife was protruding from his chest, pinning a sheet of paper. The note was edge-to-edge soaked in blood, but its words remained visible.

"What language is it?" Sans-Serif enquired.

"Russian. It means 'Of no further use.'" The detective turned to his companion and gestured toward Clarke's radio transmitter. "I must alert London. Will you go through the building, see how many are dead?"

The Turk nodded and left the office.

Begg sat at the apparatus. He broadcast a code phrase that all British agents in the region would receive and understand. It meant "compromised" and required them to cease all operations and lie low until further notice.

Next, because Dalilah, intercepting the transmission, was not an official agent and might not recognise its significance, he sent,

```
She who cannot see must avoid being seen.
```

He hoped it was sufficient, that she would find somewhere to hide.

Begg then broadcast a long, detailed, and coded report on the frequency used by London HQ. He appended it with,

```
Request that you contact the Sectia a II-a,
Roumania. Verify that Madame Vera Pym is one of
their agents.
```

He received an immediate response.

```
Stand by.
```

Sans-Serif returned. "It is catastrophic. You have lost twenty-one of your people."

Begg scribbled down an address. "You will find another of the Red King's victims here. His name is—was—Geoffrey Bacon. He and his brother, this man"—he indicated Sir Vivian—"selected the victims and paid the Red King to assassinate them. A government inspector named Vazken Voskanyan advised them. He shouldn't be difficult to find."

Sans-Serif gazed at the dead body. "And this man, who was he?"

"The director of the British Secret Service, Turkish Branch. He was a traitor."

"Phew!" said the Turk. "You people!"

"Not just mine. We are in a deep game. Sir Vivian was a Nazi sympathiser. The Red King may be a Bolshevik agent. I suspect that Germany and the Soviet Union are making a play for the Bosphorus Strait."

"And the vampyr?"

"Zenith, as ever, is an enigma. How goes the hunt for him?"

Sans-Serif lifted his hunched shoulder in an uneven shrug. "I have men searching the city. I feel it unlikely that the albino would reestablish himself underground, so they are instead watching abandoned and isolated buildings. I remember he took a violin with him when he departed the cistern. They are looking for anyone who has recently heard such an instrument where none was played before."

"Excellent!" Begg exclaimed.

"I know how to do my job."

"I have never doubted it."

A light on the radio set blinked.

"A team will be sent from British HQ in Greece to clean up this mess," said Begg. "Will you deal with the police? Clarify that this is an agency matter and get them off the scene?"

Murmuring an affirmative, Sans-Serif again departed.

Begg obeyed the incoming message to close down the HQ and the embassy and lock all sensitive files in the strongbox hidden behind Sir Vivian's bookshelves. He had complete independence to proceed with the case in whatever manner he felt appropriate, and received access to unlimited funds. Only one local operative maintained authority over him: Major John Nye. The team from Greece was expected to arrive tomorrow. An addendum:

```
Vera Pym corroborated. She is Agent 35 with
Roumanian Second Section.
```

Begg was occupied for all the remaining daylight hours, sifting through files, securing sensitive information, working quietly and efficiently, alone in the houses of the dead.

Anger pulsed through his veins like molten lava. The murdered men and women had been administrators, not agents. They did no fieldwork and, aside from the guards, had minimal weapons training. They were killed only because they stood between the Red King and Sir Vivian.

Begg checked the armoury. Before securing it, he took a holdall and placed into it two Walther PPKs, two Browning 1911s, and two Mauser M32s. The latter, with magazine boxes holding twenty rounds, was the shortest machine gun in the world. He added a large quantity of ammunition.

The evening call ululated from the city minarets as he left HQ. The faithful summoned to prayer. The metatemporal detective—summoned to battle.

He drove under a darkening sky to the Shangri-La Hotel.

"M'sieu! It is intolerable!" the manager said in angry tones as Begg entered. "I must ask you to pack your luggage and check out immediately."

"I beg your pardon?"

"Parties are forbidden. Especially noisy ones that disturb the other guests. Had your friends not departed when they did, I would have called the police."

Suddenly, Begg was running. He pounded up the stairs, crashed through the door to his suite, and bowled into the aftermath of a terrific struggle. The room's furniture was broken, the window blind torn off, splashes of blood on the floor and walls.

Amid the wreckage, Vera Pym was struggling to get up, only half-conscious, a wound marring her forehead.

Begg dropped his holdall and went to her assistance.

"Is . . . is that you, Sir Seaton?" she croaked as he slid an arm around her shoulders and drew her into a sitting position.

"It is. Are you all right?"

"My . . . my head. They struck me. I'm . . . yes, I am fine. But what of Doctor Sinclair? Is he—?"

"You can support yourself?"

"Yes."

"One moment."

Begg quickly checked the other rooms, then returned. "Taffy is not here."

"They attacked him, Sir Seaton. The Red King's followers. Three of them. My goodness! What a fight he gave them!"

Begg's logic cut through turbulent emotions. If they had killed Sinclair, his body would be here. So—?

"They abducted him?"

"I don't know. I tried to help. Someone struck me. That is all I recall." She put a hand to her head. "Help me to my feet, would you? I can stand."

He assisted. She pulled herself up and brushed down her slate-grey suit while casting her eyes over the wreckage, searching the floor. "My gun was knocked out of my hand."

"Here," Begg strode to a broken chair and fished a little snub-nosed pistol from beneath it. "What were you doing here, madame?"

She slipped the weapon into a shoulder holster. "Looking for you. My goodness—hello, I'm glad to see you after all these years, especially on such improved terms. We were once—"

Impatiently, he flicked his hand, brushing the past aside.

She stopped, nodded an apology, and went on. "I have discovered where Ulric von Bek is holding Violet Damm captive. I came to seek your help in rescuing her."

"You have it. But tell me how—"

He was interrupted by frantic knocking at the door. He opened it and found the thunderous-looking manager on the threshold. The man stared past him at the state of the room. "Out! Get out! I have never seen such—"

Calmly, Begg drew out his wallet and extracted four large-denomination banknotes.

"It was not a party, m'sieu, it was a violent attack by thugs who walked in off the street apparently without a challenge. But I will not lodge any complaint concerning this hotel's security. I will simply pay for the damage, a little more for the inconvenience, and request that you make another suite available for me. I do not expect to occupy it for more than a few days."

He handed over the money.

The manager blinked at it. "I suppose—" he mumbled. "I suppose—"

Begg closed the door.

He turned to Pym. "Where are they?"

"In an old waterfront building in the Kuzguncuk district, on the Arab side of the Bosphorus. He is torturing her, Sir Seaton. We must go at once. I will kill him. I will have vengeance for the misery he has caused."

"Misery?"

"Ulric von Bek is an enemy of the Roumanian state. He raised funds for Corneliu Codreanu, the founder of the *Legiunea Arhanghelul Mihail*, the Legion of the Archangel Michael. They follow a radical version of Eastern Orthodox Christianity and, for the past six years, have promoted an ultranationalistic, anti-Semitic ideology. Three years ago, von Bek also helped establish a quasi-military branch of the Legion, the Iron Guard, which is allied to the Nazis. It is currently rampaging through my country, terrorising its people."

Begg crossed to the holdall and picked it up. "I leave it to you. Von Bek is not my concern. I desire only to rescue Miss Damm, and when that is done, locate and rescue Doctor Sinclair."

"Together, we will do that," she said. "Better than the old days, when we were enemies, I think."

"Much better," he responded.

However, as they left the Shangri-La and got into the car, he made the same decision as Taffy had done, and decided not to mention the presence in Istanbul of Zenith the albino.

He was not sure why.

CHAPTER 18

The Red King

Sir Seaton Begg and Vera Pym crossed on one of the many little ferries which day and night traversed the Bosphorus like needles threading together Europe and Asia.

Warm night air brought a thick salty fog rolling down the strait. Waters swirled beneath a heavy blanket of silence, broken only by the steady chugging of their engine and sporadic fog horns bellowing mournfully with supernatural force, like stranded sea beasts.

For the past twenty minutes, the French-Roumanian woman had spoken only when necessary.

Flinty-eyed and unapproachable, Begg was equally silent, wrapped in his thoughts.

He was revising his ideas.

From Secret Service HQ records, he had untangled a web of misdirections and false information spun by Sir Vivian to divert resources away from his planned assassinations. The director and his brother believed by this means they advanced their own treacherous agenda.

They were duped.

The Red King intended to destabilise Turkey, allowing an imperial foreign power to control the Bosphorus Strait. The English twins wanted Britain and her allies to declare a protectorate. They did not know their master assassin was a Bolshevik—that Russia was coiled like a snake about to strike at Turkey's heart.

German involvement was less certain. The Clarke twins were Nazi sympathisers, but Begg had found no evidence of contact between them and Hitler's new government or its agent, von Bek.

Yet—

"Madame," he said. "You told me that Ulric von Bek has been active in Roumania. Why is he now in Istanbul?"

The ferry rocked and she clutched his arm. The strait was choppy tonight, its currents formidable.

"I have been wondering the same, Sir Seaton." She released her grip. "Why did the Red King suddenly question my loyalty? How did he learn there was a spy in his midst? Clearly, I was recognised. Von Bek! He alerted the master assassin. There is no other explanation."

"He is a member of the gang?"

"Perhaps as a representative of Hitler. Von Bek brought Nazism to Roumania. Now, maybe, to Turkey."

It was a credible theory. The Red King and von Bek, the architects of a Soviet and Nazi alliance, both searching for Major Nye—for the *Salut Christi*. Taking Sir Vivian and Gammon out of the picture had changed nothing.

"Then we may be outnumbered," Begg said. "Von Bek might not be alone with Miss Damm."

The scrap of oil-stained rope from Madam Melody's shoe possibly came from the waterside property to which they headed. The whole gang could be there.

La Pym shook her head. "I spent much of the day watching the warehouse. I am convinced only von Bek and his prisoner are inside."

The ferry lurched in the wake of a cargo tanker.

A sonorous foghorn vibrated the air. Begg waited for the echoes to fade, then asked, "What led you to them?"

Taking a perfumed lace handkerchief from her pocket, she held it to her nose. The atmosphere was sodden with the stench of seaweed, oil, and city effluence.

"You will recollect the man with whom I once had an association," she said. "Where he and I were the first time you saw us together?"

Begg could not recall at all, and silently cursed the unpredictability of metatemporal memory.

She provided the answer. "The thieves' kitchen in London? In the year I was with him, I learned much about such places, where criminals socialise without fear of police intrusion. Every city has them. I know how to enter them, how to ask questions in the correct manner, how to get information, and how to employ the criminal network when a person must be found."

Begg understood. He had used such places himself. No doubt the Red King also had that resource. It was a testament to Major Nye that he nevertheless evaded the master assassin.

"It was a nobody, a little burglar," Pym continued, "who located von Bek. He was looking for somewhere to hide what he stole. The warehouse suited his purpose. It is isolated and derelict. He approached it and heard screams from inside. This, I learned, and the rest—" She gave a shrug.

Begg clenched his fists, nails digging into his palms. If Violet Damm—

"Ah, the wharf," Pym exclaimed. "Thank goodness! What a rough crossing. I was beginning to feel sick."

The ferry moored against a sagging plank jetty. Its few passengers disembarked.

"This way, Sir Seaton. The fog is good. It will conceal our approach."

From the wharf, Begg and Pym turned left and proceeded along an empty, half-rotted wooden quay, down uneven steps, and onto sand tufted with wiry grass. The fog glowed faintly, illuminated from the opposite shore and stars, but insufficiently to see by. Begg used his pocket torch, keeping the beam directed at the ground.

After minutes of silence, Pym murmured, "I did not miss him."

"Madame?"

"The albino. I had grown afraid of him."

"Why so?"

"He was too strange. When he took opium, he became another person. Hardly a man, but something more powerful, alien, and melancholy. He insisted that this world was a dream, and that his true self was elsewhere, in a different sort of world. Also, there was a man he—"

Begg gave a sharp hiss and grabbed her arm. He clicked off the torch. They froze. Movement in the fog.

To their left, the agitated strait was noisy against the shore. Beneath that arrhythmic din, the detective heard the approaching sound of—

"A stray," he observed, as a thin-ribbed mongrel yipped at them and panted away into the night.

Torch on, they moved ahead.

"Have we far to go?" he asked.

"A little way."

"You were saying—?"

"I was speaking of the albino."

She cannot say his name?

"Often, he would rant in his drugged sleep about a man named Vassilionu. He was hunting this person, seeking revenge for some past offence. It was an obsession! I believe he began his criminal career in your country only because Vassilionu had taken refuge among its crooks. I heard the albino finally caught up with him at a house in Scotland. A mysterious crime. Do you know anything of it? Perhaps the British Secret Service . . ."

"Agents are not privy to all the police records. I know nothing of the affair."

An outright lie. He knew it had been a battle for possession of the *Sigiliul Tutorelui*. He was also aware, thanks to the document left with the blind Egyptian by Major Nye, that the ring was currently hanging on a cord around that elusive agent's neck!

"Ah, a pity," Pym said. "I have for many years been curious about it."

Sir Seaton Begg was curious, too.

How could this woman be unaware that Zenith was in Istanbul? Why was she digging for information about the Woodbine Hall massacre?

"There." She stopped and pointed ahead.

A large structure loomed from the fog.

With the torch switched off and their pistols at the ready, they crept forward.

The warehouse was in a state of severe decay. Its upper storey extended out over the strait, allowing cargo to be lowered through a trapdoor onto a vessel's deck. Supported only by one thin pole, it was perilously close to collapse. Beneath were moored four motorboats. The building was surrounded by a platform, about three feet above ground level. A series of arches gave access to the lower floor. Inside, Begg could just about discern a multitude of stacked crates, presumably empty.

Dim light glowed from an upper window.

"Four boats," he noted.

Pym whispered, "They were here when the burglar heard the screams. Here all the time I was watching."

"Yet you are convinced that only von Bek and Miss Damm are inside?"

"Yes."

They came to a short flight of steps. Moving ahead, she signed unnecessarily to him to hug the left side to minimise creaking.

He went up, Mauser ready, eyes peeled.

Behind him, Pym ascended the right side. She was halfway up when a step caved in, the wood snapping with a report like a gunshot. She gave a yelp and sat heavily, her face contorted with pain.

Begg halted, alert to every sound and movement.

She groaned. "My ankle!"

He shifted back to her, looked down at the step, and his eyes narrowed.

"Twisted?"

"Broken. I am a fool!"

"Then we retreat. We shall have to—"

"No! There is a code among agents, is there not? We do not leave one of our own in enemy hands. Miss Damm cannot be condemned to further torture. You go ahead. I will drag myself into a position from which to provide rear-guard action if it becomes necessary."

He gave an abrupt nod and moved into the darkness between the crates. Moments later he was back.

"Sir Seaton?"

"Have you fired a Mauser before?" he whispered.

"No."

"Take it. If there is occasion to shoot, von Bek might think from its racket that we are more than two. Be careful, it kicks! Give me your Browning."

They swapped weapons.

He turned back to the warehouse and crept inside.

Concealed by the gloom, he grinned.

The ground floor was composed of two sections, the open space he was crossing, and a closed section containing one or more rooms. The light had come from upstairs, so he continued on until he came to the staircase. It was in much better condition than the weathered steps outside. He went up slowly and carefully in near-complete darkness. When he reached the top, he saw a faint line of light at the bottom of a door.

Treading gingerly, he crossed and groped for a doorknob. He twisted it with painstaking slowness, then eased the portal open just sufficiently to peek inside.

The room beyond was unlit but for a circle of orange candle-light, which revealed a small table and, beside it, a wooden chair. A woman sat slumped forward, wrapped in a cloak, a hood concealing her face. To judge from her gasps and sniffles, she was weeping and in pain.

There was no other sound.

Cautiously, Begg slipped in and moved toward her. He could sense the scale of the surrounding room. Probably, it occupied the entire upper floor.

He drew close to the woman and, so quietly that his voice was almost inaudible, said, "Miss Damm?"

She lifted her hands, turned her face, and drew back the hood.

Madam Melody.

He recognised her from Taffy Sinclair's description, and was not surprised. Damm was taller and unlikely to snivel, regardless of what tortures she had suffered.

"I have been eager to meet you, Sir Seaton Begg." She gave a dazzling smile. "Place your automatic on the floor, please, or I shall sing a little song to make your brain bleed."

"I could shoot you first."

"We are not alone."

He squatted, put down the Browning, and straightened.

"I have seen the appalling effect of your remarkable voice. How do you do it?"

She put a forefinger to her neck. "A deformation in here. It ruined my stage career. Now it curtails the careers of others." She shrugged, raised her hand, snapped her fingers, and called out, "Lights!"

From various points around the room, Begg heard matches striking, saw flames applied to oil lamps and figures revealed by the growing illumination.

A dwarf. Suleyman the Strangler. Three other men. All aiming guns at him.

"You retain a love of melodrama, I see," he commented.

Melody gave a throaty chuckle. "I do! I truly do!"

She stood and threw aside the cloak. She was wearing an inky-blue dress with white polka dots. Her platinum hair seemed almost phosphorescent. "Viktor, tie his hands behind his back, will you?"

One of the men, bulky and mean-faced, picked a coil of rope

from the floor and approached. In a thick Russian accent, he said, "It will go better for you if you cooperate."

"Oh, I doubt that!" Begg exclaimed. "But I won't spoil the party. It is far too interesting." He crossed his wrists over the small of his back—and over the slight bump caused by the second Browning in its special holster.

"I am familiar with Suleyman, of course," he said to Melody, "having last week thumped his head with a well-packed suitcase. But I do not believe I've had the pleasure of—?"

She gave an acknowledging bob and gestured toward her colleagues. "Then let me extend your life a little that I may introduce the Red King's circus. Viktor Mikaelovitch Bolotnikov, expert knifeman, currently tying a knot. He's from Leningrad. Pyotr Arturovitch Obolensky, with the pretty pale-grey eyes and dimpled chin, is a gunman from Moscow, ex-Section Six. The short fellow is 'Sureshot' Orville Thott, former stage performer, a sharpshooter, from New York. And the individual with the scarred face is Max Dragan, street brawler of Bucharest."

"Where are the others?" Begg asked.

"Others?"

"Four men attacked the Bosphorus Hotel. Three of them smoked Muratti cigarettes. Neither Bolotnikov nor Obolensky were present, for they prefer Belomorkanals. Thott wasn't there, either, else his size would have drawn comment. Same goes for Suleyman. That just leaves Dragan."

Begg stumbled back a step as Bolotnikov tugged at his bonds to check they were secure.

"You are correct," said Melody. "Max Dragan led the assault. Monteith the Chemist was with him. He was killed four days ago. The remaining two were women in male attire. They are not here."

"And Ulric von Bek? Where is he?"

A flicker of annoyance. "I do not know, but rest assured, he cannot evade us forever."

Begg showed no sign of the exhilaration that gripped him. If they were hunting for von Bek—there was no alliance!

"Now then, Sir Seaton," Melody said. "If you would be so kind as to walk over to that pole and put your back to it—" She pointed to where the pole supporting the overhanging part of the room came up through the floor and into the ceiling.

Begg obeyed. The floor squeaked, rocking beneath his feet, so rickety and rotten it could collapse at any moment.

Bolotnikov followed, and when the detective was in position, looped rope around his neck and tied him to the pole. "Loose enough now, *da*?" the Russian commented. "It is an arbor knot. If you strain away from the pole, the rope will tighten and throttle you."

"Right-ho."

Madam Melody turned to Dragan. "Max, inform the Red King that his guest is waiting."

Dragan nodded and departed.

Imperceptibly, Begg was already working to free himself. He had employed a simple trick. Rather than crossing his wrists flat against each other, he had rotated the right, placing its inner edge against the base of the left. Binding them in that position required almost an inch of extra rope—which now slackened when he turned the wrist flat. It was shockingly easy to then, little by little, squeeze one hand out of the bonds.

While he was thus occupied, the assassination gang opened a box, took out white tabards, and put them on. They were similar in design to the Knight Templar's in Geoffrey Bacon's study. However, rather than a red cross, they were decorated with eight black arrows radiating from a central point.

It confirmed what Begg had begun to suspect.

This was much more than a Bolshevik plot.

Though he gave no indication of it, his hands were loose when the door opened.

Max Dragan dragged in a large sack, tied at the top, in which someone was struggling.

"Your friend," he said to Begg, "did not put up much of a fight. Ankle busted. Good thing, too. That breaking step gave us plenty of warning." He laughed and hauled the sack into a corner. Then he put on a tabard and joined the others, who were forming a semicircle around Begg.

He had left the door open.

An extraordinary figure stepped through.

"Praise Arioch!" Madam Melody called out.

"Praise Arioch!" they repeated.

The figure passed through the semicircle and stood facing the metatemporal detective.

"I am the Red King, High Priest of Chaos, avatar of Lord Arioch."

The voice was a husky whisper.

It belonged to one who, though not tall, was made imposing by extravagant red robes. The black arrow symbol adorned the chest, and a cloth bag concealed the head, with a mask of gold affixed to the front and over the cranium. It depicted the face and curled hair of an extremely handsome youth, his lips slightly parted in a sardonic and cruel smile, holes where there should have been eyes.

"Are you, indeed?" Begg drawled.

"You stand in the way of the Great Plan, Sir Seaton Begg."

"Plenty have said as much. Most ended on the gallows."

"Not this time."

"Perhaps so. Hanging is far too good for some."

A moment of silence, then the Red King said, "I took this Mauser from the woman." He raised the weapon, taking aim at Begg's chest. "Tradition dictates that offerings to Lord Arioch must die by the black sword. Unfortunately, at this time, that is not possible. The gun must suffice."

"No explanations first?" Begg drawled. "My enemies usually brag before attempting my murder. Monomaniacs do so enjoy the sound of their own voices, don't they? They think they are clever and are compelled to show it. Are you clever? Not so much, I suspect."

The Mauser did not waver.

The masked figure intoned, "Ah, the overweening self-righteousness of the British. It is equal only to the misplaced self-confidence of the Americans."

A momentary pause, then, "And now, Sir Seaton Begg, I give thy blood and soul to Arioch. For standing in our path, I condemn thee to eternal torment—as a plaything of Chaos!"

The Red King pulled the trigger.

CHAPTER 19
Dire Strait

Click! Click! Click!

"I emptied the clip," said Begg. He reached into the back of his jacket, drew his Browning, and pointed it at the Red King. Loose bindings dangled from his wrist. "Attention! If any one of you moves a muscle, your leader will die!"

The Mauser dropped from the robed figure's limp fingers.

With his free hand, the detective worked at the knot roping his neck to the pole. Viktor Bolotnikov had identified it as an arbor. That knowledge made it easier to undo. It fell away in moments.

The detective gestured toward the wriggling sack. "Madam Melody, release your colleague, please. There is no need for her to suffer further discomfort."

Melody hesitated, then, at a slight nod from the Red King, crossed to the hessian bag and untied it.

Begg smiled at the golden-faced master assassin. "Even curled up as she is, I can see she's too tall to be you."

Vera Pym removed her golden headgear.

She looked ready to spit venom.

"You thought I would miss that the right side of the step outside was half cut through?" Begg asked, his pistol unwavering. At the periphery of his vision, he saw a tall woman step out of the sack and recognised her as one of the two who had met Pym in the Sultan's Palace Bar.

To her and Melody, he said, "Come stand with the rest. No sudden moves."

"Begg—" Pym began.

He interrupted.

"Those objects tied to ropes in the manor cellar were not as random as they appeared, were they? All there to divert attention from the one that had a purpose. The bag of potatoes, maybe? It rested on the hose and compressed it. When you heard Doctor Sinclair trip the alarm, you hauled on the rope, shifted the potatoes, the water started to flow, and—there you have it—poor Vera Pym in a fiendish fix."

His gaze hardened.

"You had Sinclair abducted and faked your injury at the scene. Where is he?"

She raised her chin. "No longer in Istanbul."

"Then where? Speak, or so help me, I'll shoot you in the leg."

"He is on his way to the Temple of Arioch."

"In Lamaneagra?"

Pym gasped and staggered back. "How can you know that?"

"I know a great deal more than you think. I know you need the *Salut Christi* and *Sigiliul Tutorelui*. I know you will not leave Istanbul without them."

Her jaw muscles worked, teeth clamped, eyes blazed. "They are holy to the Cult of Arioch. You cannot possibly comprehend their significance." Suddenly, she shrieked, "Give me Major Nye!"

He answered calmly. "I do not know where he is. You have set yourself against perhaps the greatest of our British agents. He is quite astonishing."

Viktor Bolotnikov suddenly flung his hand back over his shoulder, gripping a knife by its blade, poised for throwing. Begg swung his Browning a little to the left and shot him in the thigh. The Russian reeled to one side and went down, clutching his leg, moaning, his weapon clattering away.

Suleyman lurched forward.

"Stop!" Begg barked, aiming at the Strangler's low forehead.

The killer halted, snarling, twitching with pent-up rage.

"Simmer down," Begg advised, soothingly, as if addressing an animal.

The Turk quietened and Begg looked back at Pym.

"What is the Cult of Arioch?" he asked. "Why do you require the *Salut Christi*?"

Her answering smile was nasty. Then her eyes glazed over, and she crooned, as if in a trance, "Arioch, King of Chaos, Knight of the Swords, Earl of Entropy, Lord of the Seven Darks! From thy left hand cometh disorder, from thy right hand cometh destruction. For thee, all must fall that it may be renewed."

She blinked, refocussed, and in her usual voice continued, "As ever, insipid monotheism must appropriate an ancient symbol and reduce its meaning to a pathetic platitude for the grovelling masses. No more!" She pointed a finger at Begg. "Your colleague's blood shall fill the *Salut Christi*. His sacrifice will wash away the stain of the Meek One."

"That," said Begg, "is not going to happen."

He quickly aimed at Sureshot Thott, who had taken a pace forward.

The dwarf stepped back.

A still, silent moment, then Begg said, "Madame, you are Agent Thirty-Five of Roumania's Secția a II-a. Whatever this Arioch business is, I have it in mind that you are also a double agent pursuing a Bolshevik agenda."

She tipped her head back and laughed. "I am no Bolshevik! I hate Koba the bandit, who now calls himself Josef Stalin, almost as much as I hate you. Do you know, I sometimes imagine myself in the past, hunting him amid the madness of the February Revolution? That you are there with me in Leningrad—or Petrograd, as it was then? Imagine what the world would be now had we stopped him! Strange, is it not, to have so vivid a fantasy that it could almost be a memory but for the impossibility of it?"

"Just another symptom of your insanity," Begg responded. "So you are not a Bolshevik?"

"You are surprised? But neither am I a Roumanian operative, Sir Seaton. That was a little untruth for Doctor Sinclair's benefit. I do, however, have a disciple in the Second Section, who forged my credentials. A man named Klosterheim. He is everything I falsely attributed to the traitorous von Bek. It is Klosterheim the Nazi who funded the *Legiunea Arhanghelul Mihail*. Klosterheim who helped establish the Iron Guard." She spread her arms, her red robes draping from them. "And it is Klosterheim who has cut off the region once known as Lamaneagra, so that none but the Disciples of Arioch may enter. He is a vicious and violent man. I tell you this because, once Sinclair arrives at that place, none of your allies will ever reach him. There is no hope of rescue. It is impossible to get past Klosterheim."

"My allies won't have to," said Begg. "I shall do it myself."

"You will be dead." She smiled and murmured, "Suleyman, thy soul for Arioch."

Suleyman roared and shot forward, launching himself at Begg like a charging bull. Two bullets drilled through his shoulder before he slammed into the detective. Begg, lifted off his feet, crashed backward into the pole, the full weight of Suleyman upon him.

With dramatic consequence!

An immense rending and splintering! The floor sliding from under their feet! The entire overhanging side of the warehouse tearing away!

The pole toppled like a chopped tree and took a third of the upper storey with it. As the floor, walls, and ceiling arced out and down, they disintegrated, planks and fragments raining around Begg and Suleyman. The two men went spinning into the churning Bosphorus.

The Strangler's fingers somehow found Begg's neck, and though a massive weight of wood collapsed onto them, his brutal grip did not for an instant loosen. Whirled around, knocked half-senseless, they were forced to the slimy bottom of the strait. Mud sucked at their limbs, hampered movement.

Already, Begg was desperate for air.

He hit, kicked, gouged, and scratched, but that single hand was like a ring of steel bolted tight . . . and getting tighter. In the pitch darkness, he saw flashing lights—the visual alarms of a brain starved of oxygen.

A sliver of wood struck his thrashing right hand. Instinctively, he grasped it and stabbed. He had no idea it was pointed, no awareness that it sank a full six inches between Suleyman's ribs and punctured a lung. He knew only that he was suddenly free.

Frantically, he kicked for the surface, debris banging into him from every direction.

Air! He dragged in a desperate breath, filled his lungs, his senses jumbled, the fierce current buffeting him along. Through the fog, he momentarily saw lamplight shining from the remains of the warehouse; then it was left behind as he was swept away.

Dizzy, disoriented, he attempted to float on his back, face upward, to catch a breath and recover his senses. The strait, however, was in an angry mood, rolling him over, pulling him under, and throwing him about.

Hoping that a vague glow was the European side, he started away from it, swimming as best he could toward where he thought the closer shore must be.

Suleyman erupted out of the water beside him.

Begg grabbed and held a meaty wrist, preventing the fingers from reaching his throat, then punched his other hand repeatedly into the Turk's bullet wounds.

The Strangler opened his mouth to bellow. It filled with water. Begg drew up his legs and ploughed his heels into the other's face. The wrist slipped from his grip. Suleyman sank.

The detective resumed his efforts. He was fast losing strength. He was being drawn into what the Turk's call the *Seytan Akintisi*—the Devil's Current—which foams, whirls, and boils southward along the strait at more than three miles per hour. If Begg failed to reach land in the next few minutes, he would be swept out to sea.

A foghorn blasted nearby. He heard motorboats approaching at high speed. A hand closed round his ankle. He was yanked back and down.

Again, he kicked, hit out, and struggled, but once more, lethal fingers found his neck, and now he knew he was going to die.

Inches above his head, the hull of a vessel sped past, felt but not seen, for the fog was still thick, and the water muddy. He and Suleyman were turned over and over. For an instant, just as a second motorboat passed, almost hitting them, Begg's head broke the surface. In the dim illumination cast by the lights of a nearby oil tanker, he glimpsed a flash of white hair and recognised Madam Melody.

The boats belonging to Vera Pym and her gang had escaped destruction. The collapsed section of warehouse had evidently arced right over them.

Then he was beneath the surface again, almost unconscious, the crushing fingers blocking the flow of blood, his limbs losing motive power, a peculiar sense of peace embracing him.

He had no awareness of what happened next. He did not feel the underside of a third boat skim past so close that it parted his hair. Did not feel his hand come up under Suleyman's chin, shoving the man's head back. Did not even feel the tremendous shock that almost broke his arm as the boat's propeller smashed the Strangler's cranium to fragments. Nor did he feel the momentary warmth of blood and brains flowing over him before instantly dispersing.

Begg wasn't even aware that Suleyman was gone.

He floated, sometimes on the surface, sometimes beneath it, tumbling loosely, his mind adrift.

Above, the fog parted, and a crescent moon turned spume to silver and prompted a vision. A strangely glowing silver chalice, some eight inches across, the outer surface unadorned, the inner engraved with eight arrows radiating from the centre of the bowl to its brim. Inset in the middle, a fire opal, bloodred, with a dark patch—a "grain centre"—at its core, reputed to be a drop of blood taken from the Lance of Longinus.

The *Salut Christi*.

Begg swallowed water and vomited it back up. Seaweed

tangled around him. A bell clanged. A shout echoed. Driftwood bumped against him. He clung to it, and . . .

. . . was in his Sporting Club Square chambers, slippers on his feet, dressing gown wrapped around him, pipe in hand.

"The three silversmiths who fashioned the *Salut Christi* in AD 629 were also sorcerers of high repute," he told Doctor I. J. Sinclair. "They created the chalice to mark the end of the siege of Constantinople. In the artefact, Christian and Zoroastrian beliefs combined in a single message."

"What message?" asked Sinclair, pouring steaming coffee from a pot.

"God might have an unfathomable plan," Begg said as a wave splashed over his face and filled his nostrils, "and our sufferings are a part of it; or, God may be fickle and unpredictable, and we are victims of holy whim. Either way, it is our duty to love and support one another through whatever vicissitudes are inflicted upon us. The eight arrows extending from Christ's blood therefore represented human love radiating in all directions."

He put his pipe to his lips, but it tasted salty, and he spat, then noticed a ship within hailing distance. If he could only muster the strength to cry out!

But already it was gone.

He sighed, and turned back to Sinclair. "That is the Christian interpretation of the eight arrows. There is, however, another, which circulates among those who study the occult."

"Oh?"

"That the gemstone in the chalice was, in prehistory, brought out of the Arctic by a band of Norse raiders. It was at that time known as 'the Albino's Eye,' and it contains not the blood of Christ but rather the colours of an alien spectrum."

"And what, exactly, does that mean?"

Water filled his nose. A plank of wood banged into his head.

"I haven't a clue, but whatever the truth, the chalice was transported to Ctesiphon, the Persian capital, and hailed as a harbinger of stability. It brought about the resolution of the long war between the Sassanids and Byzantines. There was, at last, peace."

Sinclair shook his head. "There is never peace."

He was right, of course. Eight years later, the great, unstoppable tide of Islam had reached Ctesiphon's walls. Constantinople, fearing the chalice would fall into Muslim hands, sent a spy into the city to recover it. The mission was successful, and as the chalice returned to the city of its birth, the Sassanid Empire crumbled.

"From that moment on," said Begg, "the *Salut Christi* became associated with the fate of empires."

In a flash of realisation, he felt himself sinking. It was peaceful, everything easy, his saddleback armchair comfortable. The fire flickered in the grate. A delicious scent wafted up from the basement, where Mrs. Curry, his housekeeper, was cooking dinner.

Half-heartedly, he thrust for the surface.

"Did the chalice remain in Constantinople?" asked Sinclair.

"Until AD 800," Begg answered, "when it passed from Irene of Athens to the pope, and from the pope to Charlemagne. Of course, the Holy Roman Empire flourished, and after it, the Habsburg. This sustained success was attributed, in no small part, to the artefact's supernatural influence."

"Bunkum!" Sinclair opined.

The turbulent water shoved Begg into the air, wrenched him back, and hauled him down. The bubbles thundered past his ears.

"The Ottoman Empire eventually recognised the power of the *Salut Christi* and demanded it be returned to Constantinople. That demand became an element of the Battle of Mohács in 1526, which was won by the Ottomans. Full-scale war now threatened, two vast empires battling for a small silver bowl."

The Bosphorus tumbled Begg over and over. He wanted desperately to close his eyes and think no more, but felt he must finish the story.

"To prevent it," he persisted, "the two empires agreed to place the *Salut Christi* in the vaults of a necropolis in Lamaneagra. This was considered, from a geographical perspective, a point of balance between them. It was an isolated location from where the benefit of its influence could be received equally by both. Apparently, there was another reason—"

He yawned and water filled him.

"—but I don't know what it was."

He was not, as he thought, back at his temporal base, saved by some trick of the clock. Neither had he dreamed his Istanbul assignment, or the vaguely suspected affair in Petrograd of 1917, or the other in London, 1962; these three somehow weaving a complex orbit around one another. He had accepted the logic of the multiverse and its dangers, following the moonbeam roads between realities to his inevitable dissolution—for once he had embarked on a mission of this nature, its significance obscured and its vicissitudes half-forgotten or misremembered, he could do nothing but immerse himself in the contrary reality in which he found himself.

Immerse. Immerse.

The detective sank to the bottom of the ancient strait, down and down to where once the beautiful corpses of the Sultan's discarded houris waved like graceful dancers, their veils clouding around them amid the mud and the tangled weeds . . .

CHAPTER 20
Major Nye

When he opened his eyes, Sir Seaton Begg saw a shiny bald head, one bulging eye and one squinting, a crooked nose, big uneven teeth, and a glossy black beard.

He wondered what Sabahattin Sans-Serif was doing in his Sporting Club Square consulting room.

"Sans-Serif," he croaked.

"Doctor Matossian asked me to tell you that the burning hotel did not set fire to your lungs, so there was no need to fill them with water." The special agent smiled—not a pretty sight—and added, "I am also to inform you that last night, the doctor went to the cinema, and found the misfortunes suffered by *Sisman ve Zaif* to be less frequent, and less impressive, than those experienced by you and your colleague."

Sisman ve Zaif—the Turkish names for Laurel and Hardy.

Through immense lethargy, Begg looked around and saw that his Sporting Club Square chamber in every way resembled a hospital room.

"What is happening?" he asked, and felt shocked by the

feebleness of his voice. "Why are you—" He cleared his throat. "Why are you in London?"

The Turk stepped back in horror. "I assure you, I would never set foot in such a barbaric, unholy city. This is the Surp Pirgiç Hospital."

"The . . . the—?"

Memory fragments vied for dominance—for form and meaning. The Bosphorus seized him and dragged him back into its depths.

"Hey!" Sans-Serif cried out.

"Hmm?"

"Are you conscious?"

"I think—" murmured Begg. "Yes." He heaved in a deep breath. "How did I get here?"

"By a stroke of good fortune. The Devil looks after his own, hey? You recall that my people were searching for the albino in abandoned buildings? One thought Maiden's Tower might be worth a look. Do you know it?"

Begg nodded and immediately regretted doing so. The room somersaulted and darkened. He battled to bring the wayward world into order as it flexed and tilted around him.

Hold on! Don't sleep! Think!

Maiden's Tower. It was an eight-hundred-year-old lighthouse on a tiny islet in the southern mouth of the strait. Last used as a quarantine station, many years ago, it had since stood empty.

"Early this morning," Sans-Serif said, "my man went to examine the place. He discovered you jammed among the rocks on the shore. You were wearing a death shroud of seaweed. He slung your corpse over his shoulder, threw it into his boat, and took it to the nearest morgue. They refused to accept it. 'Take it to the hospital around the corner,' they insisted. So, that's what he did."

The special agent stroked his beard and angled a speculative eye at Begg. "I wonder what you English are made of?"

Begg reached a trembling hand to his bedside table and lifted a glass of water. He drank it all, desperately thirsty, feeling salt clogging his veins.

"That's it," Sans-Serif commented. "Put more of the stuff inside yourself. Are you so determined to drown?"

The Turk took the empty glass before the detective could drop it.

Begg said, "This is the Surp Pirgiç? It was not the closest hospital, surely?"

"Ah! But you see, though the papers in your pocket were half-disintegrated, sufficient remained to identify you as Mr. Septimus Blane of Gelecek Engineering. Of course, when I heard, I recalled you telling me that Blane was your cover. I therefore made certain that the corpse was yours, then had it moved here. I know it is your favourite place in all Istanbul."

Begg murmured, "Presumably, Zenith was not at the lighthouse?"

"He was not," Sans-Serif confirmed. "He is in the Perili Köşk."

Begg translated. "The haunted mansion?"

"Yes. Very suitable for a vampyr, no? And given your condition, perhaps you should take up residence there, too."

"I'm not dead, Sans-Serif."

"You certainly are. Wait until you see yourself in a mirror. Your skin is wormy blue."

"I have been . . . been in . . . worse—"

The room melted into—

Hair and veils wafted around her head, eyes blank and white, an enigmatic smile, arms loosely extended. She swayed with the tide, dappled with light from the surface, the sultan's intended bride, thrown into the strait after her betrayal, so beautiful, so dead. Her smile widened, revealing the gap between her upper front teeth.

"Hello?" said Sans-Serif, snapping his fingers in Begg's face.

"Whu—?"

"Ah, there you are."

"How . . . how long was I—?"

"Less than a minute. I think Seytan tugged at your ankle, eager to drag you to where foreign corpses belong."

Begg felt Suleyman the Strangler's fingers closing around his leg. He shuddered.

"I must deprive you of my delightful company," the special agent decided. "Matossian says you must stay in bed for a week. I say a coffin, permanently, would be more appropriate, but he has his own peculiar ideas."

Begg pressed the heels of his hands against his temples and squeezed his eyes shut. "No, stay. I need to know. The haunted mansion?"

"Built just twenty-two years ago by Yusuf Ziya Pasha, a member of the Ottoman government, but never properly finished and quickly abandoned. Constructed on cursed soil. It is rumoured to be haunted by his wife. Occasionally, ghostly piano music emanates from it. But last night, another of my men heard—a violin!"

With difficulty, Begg sat up. "We must go there at once."

Sans-Serif snorted. "You are in no condition to go anywhere excepting your overdue funeral. You have spent the past hours regurgitating the Bosphorus."

The detective fell back against his pillows.

"I'll rest until lunchtime," he murmured. "But then we must see Zenith. It is imperative. I need his help."

"Lunchtime?" the Turk exclaimed. "That has been and gone, my friend. It is past three."

"Past... What day?" Begg's eyes glinted. "What day, Sans-Serif?"

"Cuma."

Cuma—Friday!

"By heaven!" Begg threw back the bedsheets and heaved himself up. "Where is Matossian? Get me some clothes! Have you a spare weapon?"

Sans-Serif grabbed Begg's arm to steady him. "I have my own pistol, no other. I am not an armoury. You need one? Why?"

"The Red King! She intends to assassinate Matossian. Today! Now!"

"She?"

"Where is he?"

"The doctor is giving a tour." Sans-Serif released Begg, went to the room's wardrobe, and took from it a cheap set of clothes. "He has seven or eight foreigners with him."

"Where?"

The special agent shrugged his humped shoulder. "I have no idea. They could be anywhere by now. It is a big building."

"For pity's sake, find out! Hurry!"

Sans-Serif nodded and departed.

As rapidly as he could, stumbling and fumbling, Begg dressed himself in the hospital-provided underwear, shirt, and suit, all which were a size too small. His own shoes were at the side of the bed, still saturated. He slipped them on regardless.

"I'm told they are in the nursing home wing," Sans-Serif announced, returning.

"Lead the way."

"Shall I carry you? Perhaps I can find crutches or a wheelchair."

Not knowing whether he was serious, Begg waved him ahead. They left the room and made their way along a hospital corridor. The detective walked like a drunkard, unable to coordinate his limbs, using the wall for support, battling a bone-deep exhaustion that threatened at any moment to overwhelm him. Only his iron will kept him upright.

They came to the main foyer, crossed it, and followed a sign marked BAKIMEVI.

From the end of a long passage, a gunshot echoed. Then a second. Women screamed.

Sans-Serif started running, drawing his pistol. Begg lurched along, falling behind, reeling into a hospital trolley. He went to his knees, scrambled back up. He was unarmed.

Hospital staff had frozen at the loud report, their eyes wide, glancing at each other uncertainly. The two agents careened past them, one following the other, toward big double doors.

Another report. A man's voice yelled, *"Óchi! Parakaló! Min pyrovoleíte!"* The language was Greek. *No! Please! Do not shoot!*

Slamming through the portal, with Begg just behind him, Sans-Serif entered—pandemonium!

It was a large chamber, comfortably furnished, where the elderly residents gathered to socialise. There were armchairs, sofas, several tables, a piano, and well-stocked bookshelves. Some chairs had been upturned, with men and women sheltering behind, but most of the occupants were simply sitting, paralysed with shock, utterly helpless. Behind two tables, tipped onto their sides, men in suits crouched, Doctor Matossian among them.

Three motionless bodies sprawled on the floor.

To the right side of the room, French windows had been kicked open. Sureshot Orville Thott, Pyotr Obolensky, and Max Dragan had entered, automatics raised, and were spreading out, coming at the two tables from either side.

This scene, Sir Seaton Begg took in at first glance as he barged through the door behind Sans-Serif. Then he watched with bemused interest as the vista, in its entirety, slowed down and rolled sideways.

The floor thudded into him. His legs had given way. The exertion had been too much. He clung to consciousness by the slightest of threads, and watched, helpless, as one of Matossian's guests peeked around the side of a table and received a bullet through his head. The dwarf, Thott, smiled, pleased with his shot.

At the same moment, Dragan, his attention attracted by Sans-Serif's arrival, swung round and fired at the Turk. He missed. Sans-Serif threw himself onto a sofa, bounced from it onto the floor, and in an untidy tangle of gangly limbs, scrambled to shelter behind an armchair.

Dragan started toward it, putting two bullets into its upholstery as he approached.

Sans-Serif bobbed up and returned fire, clipping Dragan's ear, and, by doing so, alerted the other gunmen.

Thott and Obolensky emptied their weapons into the armchair. It shredded, disappearing into a cloud of fibre. Bullets ripped through the special agent's clothing, took off the end of a finger, gauged a furrow in his left biceps, yet—miraculously—failed to disable him.

Begg's prone form went unnoticed. Dazed, as if witness to someone else's dream, he watched as, behind the attackers, an elderly woman rose to her feet. Like many of the female residents, she was in old-fashioned veils, her form hidden by loose robes.

He recognised her immediately. Major Nye's agent. She had given him the invitation to the fancy dress ball, had warned him about the time bomb.

Sans-Serif cried out as a bullet knocked the automatic from his hand. He clutched his fingers, grimacing in pain, both hands now wounded.

The old woman drew a pistol from her clothing and, almost casually, put a bullet into Obolensky's back. The Russian gave an anguished scream, dropped his weapon, and keeled over.

Thott hurled himself to one side, swivelled, and shot the woman in the head. His projectile ricocheted from her skull with a clang and drilled into the piano.

She whirled, thrown backward, and as she went down, her headscarf snagged on the corner of a table and was torn free, exposing a brightly polished silver helmet. It rolled from her head as she hit the floor.

"Gee! Will ya look at that!" Thott cried out. His voice was high-pitched, like a young girl's. "Dragan! Is it what I think it is?"

Dragan backed away from San-Serif's position, keeping his eyes on the chair behind which the Turk still crouched.

Begg sighed and blinked sleepily.

Move. Get up. Do something.

He turned his eyes, focussed them on Matossian. The doctor, still concealed from the Red King's men by the table, was desperately trying to stem the blood pumping from the neck of one of the foreign dignitaries.

Then he sat back and shook his head, his expression grim.

"Dragan!" Thott repeated. "So help me, ain't this the chalice?" The dwarf stepped forward, and with his free hand—the other keeping his gun levelled—picked up the silver helmet. It shimmered in the room's light, seeming to glow, the metal incredibly bright and reflective. "For the love of . . . it is! It's the durned *Salut Christi*! Look, my bullet skimmed off the side of it. A small furrow, but it's okay."

He paced back to the fallen woman and looked down into her face.

"And—heck!—this ain't no old dame! It's him. Major Nye."

Dragan joined him, squatted beside the fallen "crone," and said, "Nye! You have—what is the English expression?—led us a happy dance. You are hiding here all along, yes? A little old lady all this time?"

Thott demanded, "The *Sigiliul Tutorelui*. Where is it?"

To Begg, the answering voice sounded like the rustle of a paper bag.

"If you think you're going to get anything out of me, think again."

The dwarf snarled, "I'll shoot innocent people in front of you until you spill the beans!"

"It's in Wäldenstein."

"Liar," said Dragan.

Thott pointed his gun at Nye's stomach. "Worst place to be shot," he noted. "Hurts real bad."

Begg somehow found a reserve of strength. While the assassins were distracted, and with every muscle protesting, he slowly dragged himself across the floor to where Sans-Serif's gun had fallen. The Turk signalled him, as if to say, "Throw it to me," but when the detective picked it up, he found the weapon useless. Obolensky's bullet had dented the end of its muzzle.

Thott suddenly wheeled and shot at the door. It had started to open, someone attempting to enter.

"Keep out!" he yelled. "People will die!"

Women in the room whimpered. One let out a wail.

"Shut up! No one move!"

"What's this?" Dragan suddenly exclaimed. He reached to Nye's neck and snapped away a leather thong. Begg saw something glitter at the end of it.

"Ha! Look!" the assassin cried out. "The ring. Simple, no?"

"Wäldenstein, my eye!" Thott glowered down at Nye. Without averting his gaze, he said to Dragan, "See to Pyotr."

"He's dead."

"Aw heck!"

The dwarf again directed his automatic at Nye's stomach.

"It's the end for you, Nye."

He pulled the trigger.

Dragan called, "Matossian! Show yourself! Or do we have to shoot every—"

"Forget him," Thott snapped. "Let's get out of here while the going is good. Nothing matters 'cept we deliver the ring and chalice to the Red King. Then, at last, we can leave this filthy city."

They backed toward the French windows. Thott had the silver bowl in his left hand. Dragan slipped the *Sigiliul Tutorelui* into a pocket. Then they were gone.

After a moment of stillness, Begg croaked, "Sans-Serif, are you injured?"

"Finger. I shall live."

"Can you help me up?"

Sans-Serif grunted, stood, and crossed to the detective.

"You weren't much use," he noted, offering an arm.

Begg grasped it and hauled himself upright. His knees buckled. The Turk caught him, stopped him falling.

"Get me to Nye," Begg rasped, "before I pass out."

Sans-Serif put his arm around Begg's waist and half carried, half dragged him to the stricken British agent, lowering him to his knees beside his countryman.

"Don't move me," Nye whispered. His face was ashen white with agony. "By James, Begg, you look awful."

Turning his head, Begg managed to get some strength into his voice. "Doctor Matossian? As soon as you are able, please. This man has taken a bullet in the stomach."

"Begg," said Nye faintly. "Get the *Salut Christi* back. The future of Turkey might depend . . . depend on it. The future of . . . of Europe. I sanction any action. Any! It is . . . it is all on you now, old chap."

Matossian stepped to Begg's side and crouched beside him. "The gunmen are gone?"

"Yes," said Begg.

Sans-Serif added, "I don't think they will come back, Doctor. You are safe."

"Me?" Matossian exclaimed. "What have I got to do with it? I am not concerned with—" He stopped, turned, and shouted, "Balut! Go and fetch help. Doctors. Nurses. Emergency equipment. We have casualties here!"

A man nodded and ran from the room.

Matossian put his fingers into Nye's blood-soaked robes and tore them wide open over the torso. He picked up the fallen headscarf, rolled it into a ball, and pressed it gently over the bullet hole.

"What are you doing out of your bed?" he asked Begg, in a stern tone. "My God, man, you are in no condition to—"

He was interrupted by the entry of his medical colleagues. They spread quickly around the room, quelling their horror, going straight to the injured. One of them got to work on San-Serif's hands.

Matossian hailed two men and a woman. They hurried over to help stabilise the now unconscious Nye before moving him to surgery.

"Prognosis?" Begg murmured.

"If we're quick, I think we can save him," said Matossian. "Why is he dressed as a woman?"

"Major Nye and I are—"

He didn't finish the sentence.

He was overwhelmed by the realisation that Vera Pym had just scored a huge victory.

She had the ring of Guardianship.

She had the *Salut Christi*.

She had Sinclair.

She had everything required for ritual sacrifice.

CHAPTER 21
A Truce Declared

The drawn-out strains of a mournful violin sobbed over the Bosphorus, slow and sultry, darkly passionate, profoundly contemplative.

The music issued from a nine-storey castellated mansion in the Sariyer district, overlooking the strait. The edifice was all red bricks and stained glass windows. Opposite it, Sir Seaton Begg and Sabahattin Sans-Serif lurked in the doorway of a semiderelict building.

"Such unbearable beauty," Sans-Serif moaned. "It is agony. It is mortality."

"It is Zenith," said Begg.

A day had passed since the hospital attack. Major Nye was unconscious after surgery, expected to survive but confined to a bed for six weeks or more.

Begg slept long and deep, his extraordinary constitution working its miracles. Two hours ago, Sans-Serif had prodded him awake.

"The Red King gang has broken cover. One of my men spotted the gang boarding a tramp steamer at an old dock on the Anatolian side."

Despite grave warnings from Doctor Matossian, the detective again discharged himself, fatigued and weak but at least functional.

The ship had already sailed, its destination registered as Constanța, the Roumanian Black Sea port. Sans-Serif telegraphed the Secția a II-a, requesting that it be intercepted and the assassins arrested.

Begg warned, "La Pym's ally Klosterheim has infiltrated the Second Section and will be on the alert for such a communiqué. He will see to it that the vessel makes harbour without interference. We have to get moving, Sans-Serif. We need the albino!"

It was now early evening.

Begg gestured for the Turk to follow, crossed the road, and mounted the four steps to the haunted mansion's entrance. He tried the door. It was unlocked.

"The reputation is security enough," Sans-Serif whispered. "No sane person would enter a place like this. Your insistence that we come unarmed is appalling."

"A grand gesture," said Begg. "Zenith must be made sufficiently curious that he will listen to us rather than kill us."

"All very well, but if it doesn't work, it won't matter to you, will it? You are already dead. But me? I prefer we kept our guns and tried to impress him with an extravagant cake."

"I don't think he eats cake, and with your hands bandaged as they are, I doubt you could even hold a gun."

"Ugh!" said Sans-Serif. "I am led into a vampyr's nest by a corpse."

Treading softly, they entered a gloomy hallway and crossed to the foot of a staircase. The music was coming from the second floor. They ascended slowly, alert for traps.

On the landing, Begg put his ear to a door, then opened it, and stepped into a small parquet-floored antechamber. A thin line of light from below a door opposite suggested an occupied room.

Brazenly, with Sans-Serif following reluctantly behind, he moved to the portal and knocked.

A single musical note quavered to silence, and a languid voice called, "Come in, von Bek."

Begg's eyebrows rose. He and Sans-Serif entered.

"A case of mistaken identity, I'm afraid, monsieur," the detective declared. "And an intriguing one." He raised his empty hands. Sans-Serif did the same. "We come under a flag of truce."

Zenith, standing beside a divan, lowered his violin and fixed his ruby eyes on Begg.

"I see no flag," he said, and turned away. "Oyani, would you be good enough to shoot these intruders?"

His Japanese servant emerged from a dark corner and raised a pistol.

"We must discuss the *Salut Christi*," Begg said.

Zenith bent over the divan and placed his instrument in its case, snapping the catches shut. He spoke with his back to his visitors, his words clipped, their tone frigid, lacking the customary mocking nonchalance.

"I have already condemned you to death for your unforgivable violation of my personal business."

"We are not armed. We pose no threat."

"Your theatrics mean nothing. Enough is enough. In the head, Oyani—do it now."

Begg rapped out, "La Pym!"

"Stop!" Zenith raised a forefinger.

The gun lowered.

The albino straightened and turned.

"Why do you declare her name?"

"Because she is the Red King. She has gained the *Salut Christi* and the Guardian's Seal. She is on her way to Lamaneagra."

A long, motionless silence.

Sans-Serif, still with his hands up, murmured, "My arms are aching, Lord Vampyr."

"Quieten your gargoyle, Begg. Oyani, check for weapons."

His Japanese retainer obeyed.

"Sir Seaton spoke the truth, Excellency. They carry none."

With a jerk of his chin, Zenith permitted the lowering of hands.

"Vera Pym," he said softly. "I have not seen her in thirteen years. Thirteen. That malignant number. Perhaps I should not be shocked to hear her name now, yet I confess that I am."

"No more surprised than I," said Begg. "Sufficient to find the two of you at the same time in this city, unaware of one another, but to then discover—"

"The Red King."

"Yes."

Zenith was again quiet for a stretch. He gestured to an armchair. "Very well, a temporary truce. Please sit and explain. Armagnac?"

Begg nodded. Frank Oyani got to work at a sideboard.

Ignored, Sans-Serif sighed and helped himself to a chair. Begg signalled to him to remain quiet. The detective's expression communicated sympathy and understanding. The Turk was being spurned and insulted. This, however, was not the moment to address that wrong.

Zenith settled on the divan. He lit a little brown opium-soaked cigarette, Begg a cigar.

Over the course of the next forty minutes, the detective gave a concise account of everything that had occurred since his arrival in

Istanbul. He then told all he knew concerning the *Salut Christi* and the *Sigiliul Tutorelui*.

Zenith listened and made no interruption. At the finish, he sat motionless, eyes unfocused.

After a minute, he said, "This entire affair, my dear Begg, concerns the appropriation of an ancient symbol, the alteration of its original—"

A knock at the door.

Oyani drew his pistol.

"Come," Zenith called.

The door opened and a tall, well-built, blond-haired man entered.

Zenith and Begg stood. Sans-Serif crossed his arms, scowled, and stayed put.

"Sir Seaton Begg," said Zenith, "allow me to introduce Ulric von Bek. He is a distant cousin of mine. No, don't reach for your automatic, von Bek. We have called truce."

The newcomer hesitated, then stepped forward and extended his hand. "Sir Seaton, it is my pleasure . . . I think."

Begg did not accept the offered grip.

"Where is Violet Damm?" he demanded.

Von Bek lowered his hand, clicked his heels, gave a slight bow, and smiled.

"She has gone ahead into Roumania. She will do what she can to stop the Red King reaching Laman—reaching his destination, should he succeed in—"

"The Red King is female, has already succeeded, and is presently en route to Lamaneagra."

Von Bek gasped.

"Cousin," said Zenith, "our detective friend has discovered

much, including that the assassin is none other than Madame Vera Pym."

"The . . . what?"

Zenith addressed his servant. "Oyani, an old-fashioned, I recall, for von Bek, and refresh our glasses, too."

"I think," murmured Begg, "that Mr. Sans-Serif would appreciate a glass of wine."

Zenith glanced at the Turk, then flicked his hand at Oyani in a negligent manner.

The Japanese man served the drinks. Sans-Serif gulped his down in a single swig and handed the glass back for a refill.

Begg failed to contain a smile. He turned back to von Bek.

"Miss Damm is unharmed?"

"As far as I am aware, Sir Seaton. Certainly, she experienced no mistreatment from me. She has willingly offered her services."

"To what end?"

Von Bek settled in a chair and acquiesced to Zenith, who answered the question.

"That will become clear momentarily. I was speaking, von Bek, of how the meaning of a symbol can be entirely altered." The albino considered the glowing tip of his cigarette. "Consider, if you will, the *croix pattée*. That particular design of cross, first introduced in England in the thirteenth century, decorated a coat of arms, with the motto 'By virtue not by force.' It is an interesting inversion."

"Inversion?" Begg asked.

"The *croix pattée* is more frequently associated with absolute power, whether virtuous or not. It appears on the crowns of monarchs. It was carried by the Teutonic Knights during the Crusades. As the tatzenkreuz, it symbolises the military might of Prussia, and more recently, of all Germany. At Gallipoli, I fought men driven to insane violence that they might be awarded the iron cross."

Sans-Serif stirred in his seat. "Lord Vampyr, my brother and I also fought at Gallipoli. He was bayonetted to death by such a man."

Zenith turned his face and appeared to see the Turk properly for the first time. He rose to his feet and bowed.

"I owe you an apology, m'sieu, and I give it with all my heart. I had regarded you as mere carrion, and have spoken harsh words to you. It was a misjudgment. Will you take another drink with me?"

"As a rule," countered the Turk, "I drink with neither foreigner nor any supernatural creature, but since we are brothers-in-arms, I will gladly make an exception. I suspect the wine your servant served me was of a lesser quality. Perhaps—?"

"Oyani," Zenith said, "the best Bordeaux for our honoured guest."

Sans-Serif turned his bulging eye to von Bek. "On which side did you fight, Herr German?"

"Strictly speaking," von Bek answered, "I am not German. Nor did I fight. I was at school."

"Humph!" the Turk responded.

Zenith returned his attention to Begg.

"What the *croix pattée* illustrates is that a symbol has no fixed meaning. It can be altered. Even made its opposite."

"This is significant because . . . ?" Begg asked.

"Because it is what happened to an emblem composed of eight outward-pointing arrows." Zenith paused. "Now, my dear friend, I must tell you about my distant branch of our extensive family, and a little of my personal history. I do so with considerable reluctance."

The detective raised a palm. "Wait. *Our?*"

The albino smiled. "Indeed. You and I are related, though in what manner I have so far failed to assert. Certainly, you are as much a cousin as is von Bek."

"I find that hard to believe."

Zenith shrugged. He crushed his cigarette into an ashtray and took another from his platinum case. The room was already potent with opium fumes.

Begg said, "What, then, is your true name?"

The enquiry received a raised, negating finger in response. "No, no, dear friend. A name revealed relinquishes a degree of power, and you shall not grip my reins in such a fashion. It would spoil the game."

Begg raised an eyebrow. "The game is to be resumed?"

"Perhaps in a more lethal form. If we survive what comes."

The detective raised his glass in a salute.

Zenith continued, "I was apparently born in the first seconds of this century, perhaps its first child, though how such a birthdate can be possible, I fail to understand, for I remember when—ah, no, I shall not digress. My place of birth was Lamaneagra, a tiny, isolated principality nestled amid the Carpathian Mountains. There, my family was an important one, our lineage stretching back for more than two thousand years. We are rightly considered Vlasi, but to be absolutely accurate, we are also Munćani, and . . . something else."

"Something else?" Begg echoed.

"Our mysterious progenitor was, it is believed, a fallen angel—or a risen demon—from whom we inherited our strain of albinism. Every few generations, our line produces a white-skinned male, sometimes twins, the occurrence said to foreshadow times of great upheaval in the world." Zenith's pink eyes glittered. "I am, my friend, the White Raven, the Pale Wolf, the embodiment of a bad omen."

He crossed to the window and gazed out at the shipping on the strait. To Begg, however, it seemed he was watching the ebb and flow of time itself, the variable past, and his unwritten future.

"I shall return to the subject of my family," said Zenith, keeping his back to the room. "But first, I must explain *Cele Opt Săgeți*—the Eight Arrows."

He again fell silent.

Sans-Serif made to speak, but Begg motioned him to hold his tongue. Zenith was under the sway of powerful emotions, though the white face, reflected in the window glass, betrayed no sign.

The detective's intercession did not go unnoticed.

Zenith wheeled around and gazed at the Turk.

"Are you a religious man, Monsieur Sans-Serif?"

The special agent, taken aback, stammered, "I . . . I was . . . I was born Coptic Orthodox." He shifted awkwardly in his seat, then frowned, exhaled, and put his right hand to his raised left shoulder. "But, look at me. If God is love, why am I made like this? And, I crave pardon, but why make you like that, Lord Vampyr?" The Turk slapped his hand down onto the arm of his chair. "I will tell you this: a tumour in the brain killed my neighbour's little girl when only ten years old. I have a colleague who was made an orphan when his parents were crushed by a collapsing building. He was just six. I know a woman who lost all five sons in that damnable war. There is misery everywhere. Pah! What little faith I ever had, it disappeared after Gallipoli. My mother pesters, 'Come to church! Come to church!' but I will not go. I do not pray. I do not believe. If there is a God, I feel only rage toward him. He is not love. He is cruelty and misery, terror and spite."

Sans-Serif stopped, panting, and peered at his companions, suddenly self-conscious. "Forgive me," he muttered. "That was not a good question to ask such as I."

Zenith left the window, approached him, and extended his right arm. Surprised, Sans-Serif accepted the handshake with bandaged fingers.

The albino said, "Truly, we are brothers."

He returned to his chair.

"You, Sans-Serif, have brought us to the crux of the matter. Once there were many gods, all capricious, unpredictable, and to be feared. Religion functioned not to worship but to placate. It was only with monotheism that we were subjected to the foul notion that God is unconditional love, yet also holds us in judgment; is the source of all, yet finds fault in his creation; is forgiveness, yet metes out harsh punishments."

Sans-Serif muttered, "God should condemn himself—for producing faulty goods!"

Begg interjected, "I fail to see how—"

"*Of course* you fail!" Zenith snapped, rounding on the detective. "You are an embodiment of law! You seek to eliminate any that unbalance the status quo. You believe that if the uncontrollable could be contained, then civilisation would be an earthly paradise—Utopia! You fail to realise that law unchallenged is stagnation. Only the uncontained can drive the human species forward. It is the lawbreakers, the destroyers, the transgressors, the outlaws, and wolf's-heads who provide the raw stuff of creation." He gave a single clap of the hands. "That is the meaning of the Eight Arrows! The symbol represents Chaos—the destruction of stale order that something new might arise—and the name of the terrible, fickle, untrustworthy, unstable god made manifest in that symbol is—"

"Arioch," Begg finished. "But, as you said, symbols change. The arrows of the *Salut Christi* also represent the dissemination of human love in the face of life's vicissitudes."

"One meaning obliterates the other," Zenith agreed. "The original *Opt Săgeți*, the Seal of Arioch, was the emblem of a widespread cult that once predated all current religions. By 1530, however, it had dwindled to a small community of warrior-priests in Lamaneagra. That year, they were approached by representatives of the Holy Roman and Ottoman Empires. The visitors, upon seeing the seal on a ring worn by the High Priest, noted that it matched the engraving in the bowl of the *Salut Christi*. They took this to be a sign from their god. The warrior-priests were first threatened, then reassured. They would be permitted to live undisturbed in secrecy and isolation only if they abandoned their pagan god to become protectors of the chalice. The ring, which supposedly belonged to our legendary progenitor, became the *Sigiliul Tutorelui*—the Guardian's Seal."

Ulric von Bek clicked his tongue disapprovingly. "Not all the cult agreed to this usurpation, Sir Seaton. My ancestors broke away to settle in Bek, in Saxony, taking with them Ravensbrand, one of the two black swords sacred to the Ariochians. Another group rebelled more violently. They laid claim to the sister blade, the name of which can never be spoken, and attempted an insurrection. They were defeated and exiled. We believe they settled somewhere in Russia. The unnameable sword remained in Lamaneagra."

Zenith lit yet another of his cigarettes. Begg was beginning to feel the effect of their fumes. The account, carried on the smoke, gained a visceral depth, the words holding more than their obvious meaning, as if reviving the *zeitgeist* of a distant era.

The albino resumed his account. "My family ruled Lamaneagra until 1918. By then, we, the *Salut Christi*, and the principality itself, were forgotten by the world. Only a very few highly placed people in various governments and intelligence agencies knew the chalice existed.

"Then came that great upheaval following the Bolshevik Revolution, when civil wars tore across half of Eastern Europe, and the whole world became a quaking morass of political and religious discontent. That is when Roumania seized her moment." Zenith's voice turned as brittle as ice. "Came the evil day! Colonel Simeon Vassilionu, commanding a small force composed of local militias, bandits, and tribeless Roma, attacked our province. My people had no experience of modern weaponry. They were mercilessly slaughtered. With their screams ringing in his ears, the High Priest managed to conceal the *Salut Christi* in the secret chamber of the black sword. He was only just in time. After he had resealed the room, without it being detected, Vassilionu pounced on him. The kulak brute bayoneted that wise and kindly old scholar in the chest, and ripped the *Sigiliul Tutorelui* from his finger. It was the only treasure the High Priest could not hide, for he was the appointed Guardian, and was bound by faith always to wear the emblem of his office."

An awful melancholy infused Zenith's wonderful voice.

"Begg, I must ask you to disclose nothing of this, or of what I shall now reveal. You, also, brother Sans-Serif. My family's identity must never be disclosed. You must swear to this on your honour."

"I swear," said Sans-Serif.

"You have my word," said Begg.

The albino lowered his face into his hands. For a full minute, he said nothing.

The detective waited.

Then, speaking hoarsely, Zenith said, "That wise High Priest, from whom Vassilionu stole the Guardian's Seal, that just old nobleman . . . his name was Sadric . . . and he was my father."

CHAPTER 22
Into Roumania

The *Miranda* sliced through the sea, sails straining, rigging thrumming in the wind, making excellent time. The sky was bright blue, and spotted with small white clouds, which skimmed rapidly across it. Constanța lay ahead, its famous Art Nouveau Casino already visible on the promontory, dazzling in the early morning sunshine.

The sleek, modern yacht had departed Istanbul at midnight. It was now eight o'clock. Its passengers had slept through most of those hours.

Sir Seaton Begg stood at the prow, enjoying the fresh, cool air. He felt almost himself again, though his neck was still tender, livid with finger-shaped bruises.

"You were right," came a voice from behind.

He turned and greeted Ulric von Bek. The man from Wäldenstein was unshaven, his skin darkened with walnut oil, attired like a labourer.

"We have followed a storm?" asked Begg, who was similarly disguised.

"A veritable tempest. The wireless man was just speaking with the dock authorities. Fortune has favoured us. Vera Pym's steamer floundered for three hours—and we are only three behind her." Von Bek grinned. "Miss Damm is also working for our advantage. A goods train is 'delayed' at the Constanţa terminal. It won't depart until we are aboard. It will take us a hundred miles west to Cálárasi, where further instructions await."

Begg snapped his fingers. "Excellent! While I cannot approve of the way you went about it, von Bek, your shanghaiing of Miss Damm has proven very useful."

"The credit is Zenith's. It was he who spotted her in Istanbul. He told me he recognised her from Petrograd but could not remember the circumstances of that former acquaintance. Rather odd, no?"

"Not so much as you might think," Begg muttered a little ruefully. "He told you to abduct her?"

"Recruit," von Bek corrected.

"Hardly the word," Begg commented. "But what's done is done."

They stood at the rail and watched the nearing port, the sunlight flaring from the glass atop the old Genoese Lighthouse.

Late yesterday evening, after revealing the high status of his father, and his position as that man's heir, Zenith had fallen into a silence that would not be broken. After two minutes of it, Sans-Serif put flame to a fuse.

"It occurs to me, my foreign friends, that we are wasting time better spent in pursuit. The Bebek wharf is a little south of here. Fine yachts moor there. I am going to commandeer one. Go and pack whatever you need and meet me there in two hours."

Thus, the *Miranda* set forth at an uncommon hour, its captain a happy man, for he was guaranteed generous remuneration from the National Security Service.

"It is busy," von Bek observed, as the yacht now glided past the industrial docks, on its way to the marina.

Begg made a sound of approval. "Two years ago, in this country, the price of wheat dropped below the cost of harvesting it. Thousands of Roumanians starved. Look at it now, von Bek. They are exporting to the world. A marvellous recovery!"

As the vessel swung into the marina and her crew set about furling her sails, Zenith and Sans-Serif stepped out onto the deck. Neither had altered their appearance. The Turk didn't need to, and would have found it difficult. But Zenith—

"You are liable to be recognised," Begg commented.

"I am as I am. I wear these dark glasses to protect my eyes. If they also serve as some little disguise, well and good."

"They don't, and I have no doubt that the Iron Guard will be on the lookout for us. Vera Pym has an ally in Roumania, a man named Klosterheim. He—"

"Klosterheim!" Ulric von Bek cried out, clutching the detective's arm. *"Gott im Himmel!"*

"You know him?"

"Yes, Sir Seaton, if it is the same man—and it surely must be—I certainly do. The Klosterheims have been enemies of the von Beks for the past three hundred years! The current incarnation, Johannes, is a high-ranking Nazi, and as morally and ethically destitute as a man can possibly be."

"Then, we must hope that Miss Damm can steer us past him."

"Nein! Nein!" The opposite! I am eager to meet and kill him!"

Zenith drawled, "If I am recognised, perhaps it will lead to the fulfilment of that ambition."

The *Miranda* moored, and after thanking the captain, the four men disembarked and made their way toward the railway station, within easy walking distance.

Constanţa was an attractive, cosmopolitan port, with low, picturesque apartment blocks and wide, tree-lined avenues. Every race found representation in its bustling streets. Church bells clanged, and a muezzin chanted from the minaret of the Grand Mosque. To Begg, it sounded as if Istanbul had not yet relinquished its hold on him.

The metatemporal detective walked, smoked, exchanged an occasional word with his companions, and fretted about Taffy Sinclair.

It occurred to him that he had seen only one of La Pym's two tall female friends. The other, he suspected, had charge of transporting the pathologist to Lamaneagra. Even were Sinclair drugged, it was unlikely she could do so alone. Therefore, the Red King gang involved more people than so far identified.

How many of them, he wondered, were currently in Roumania?

At the train terminal, von Bek spoke with the stationmaster, who guided them away from the passenger platforms and to the goods yard. Here, a locomotive was waiting with six covered freight wagons attached.

A man stepped from beside one and enquired, "Herr von Bek?"

"I am von Bek."

"All is arranged. If you will—?"

He slid open a wagon door. The group clambered up.

"Good Lord!" Seaton Begg exclaimed.

The inside was well furnished, with a large rug, armchairs, a low table, a box containing bottles and glasses, another with crockery and cutlery, and a third filled with bread rolls, cold meats, and various other foodstuffs.

"Miss Damm has excelled!"

"We'll depart as soon as the signal allows," the man said. "Two hours to Cálárasi. No windows, I'm afraid, but you won't miss much. It's all farmland."

He knuckled his forehead and hauled the door shut, leaving the interior illuminated only by slits along the top sides.

The four settled into the chairs. Sans-Serif lifted a large flask from the food box. He opened it and sniffed the contents. "Ah! Coffee, gentlemen? Not up to Turkish standards, but it will suffice."

He filled cups and distributed them.

"Monsieur Zenith," Begg said. "Since we have some time to spare, perhaps you would resume your account? Colonel Vassilionu murdered your father—?"

Zenith sipped his coffee and sighed. "You seek to torment me?"

"I desire only such information as may be useful."

"Very well," Zenith responded. "My father, unlike his predecessors, had ventured into the world and knew something of it. Perhaps, in some manner, he foresaw that our long isolation could not last. I was the first—and, as it turned out, the last—of us to be sent away from Lamaneagra. I was educated at the Lycée Louis-le-Grand in Paris, and accepted for the Paris Sorbonne, but I never attended. The world had gone to war, and I felt it my duty to fight. Like so many other foolish young men, I lied about my age and was sent to the slaughter." He turned to Sans-Serif. "Gallipoli was my first experience of battle."

"And mine," said the Turk. "I received a bullet in the side. The wound wasn't serious, but the doctor took one look at me and declared that the army should never have conscripted me in the first place. That was the end of it for me."

"For me, no," said Zenith. "My assigned bullet did not arrive until the Somme. I was invalided out, wounded in the leg, and after a spell in Petrograd, returned to my homeland. That was early in 1918. By evil coincidence, I arrived on the very day of its destruction. I found Vassilionu and his troops encamped in the valley. Castle Arioch, my home, was burning. Nevertheless, I surreptitiously made my way into it, found my father, and held him in my arms. With his dying breath, he told me where the *Salut Christi* was hidden. I retrieved it, escaped undetected, took it to Wäldenstein, and gave it into the care of the von Beks."

"The chalice but not the sacred sword?" asked Begg.

"You imagine I could carry a large black broadsword across war-torn Europe? A silver chalice was difficult enough."

The detective turned to von Bek. "When did your people depart Saxony?"

"My ancestor, Graf Ulrich, relocated us to the Mittelmarch during the Thirty Years War," von Bek replied.

Begg decided that one day soon, he must visit that oddly elusive pocket of Europe.

They grabbed their chair arms as, with a squeal of metal, the train lurched into motion.

Zenith continued his story.

"Colonel Vassilionu was later arrested for his actions. His superiors, not having sanctioned the massacre, condemned him as a war criminal. Before he was tried, he fled to London and plunged himself into its underworld. I followed and did the same. I was searching for him. I wanted the *Sigiliul Tutorelui*, and I wanted revenge."

"That, then, is how you began your criminal career?" Begg murmured.

"Perhaps. I was not wholly compos mentis. I had taken a bullet, was discharged with shell shock, and got caught up in Russia's February Revolution, of which I recall barely a thing. I then stumbled upon the massacre of my people, my entire family. I daresay I've not been in my right mind since that black day. If it has made me an agent of Chaos, it is a suitable fate."

"It is never too late to reform."

The albino shook his head. "A man cannot live a normal life when he belongs nowhere, when all that he ever knew is gone."

The train settled into a regular rhythm, reaching its optimum speed.

A ray of daylight, slanting in, caught Zenith's face, and his eyes suddenly glittered, crimson and deadly. Begg felt the hairs on his neck bristle.

"In 1922, I finally caught up with Vassilionu. I killed him and recovered the Guardian's Seal. I could not bear to wear it, though it was my right and duty to do so. Instead, I gave it to a young member of the von Bek family to deliver to Wäldenstein, where it could be kept with the *Salut Christi*."

"A bad mistake," von Bek put in. "I was a callow youth, Sir Seaton, secretly addicted to gambling and in considerable debt. I lost the ring in an infamous poker game. You may have heard of it. They called it the Cracking of Crabbe."

Begg raised his eyebrows. "Ah, that! Lord Carmichael-Crabbe lost his entire estate in a single hand, if I recall."

"Sir Randolph Gulley didn't fare much better," von Bek added. "John Jones, a humble waiter, ordered to join the game to make up the numbers, walked away a stupendously rich man. Such drama, including Carmichael-Crabbe's subsequent suicide, served to obscure the names of the remaining four players. I was one of them, and I lost the ring to another." Von Bek exhaled forcibly, almost a whistle, and pressed the heel of his hand to the side of his head. "Monsieur Zenith may think otherwise, but I know you are right,

Sir Seaton—it is never too late to reform. I am no longer that idiotic youth, and I have since dedicated myself to the recovery of the *Sigiliul Tutorelui*—and now, too, of the *Salut Christi*. They belong together. The chalice, without a Guardian, is a problem."

"A problem? How so?"

"Our cousin here"—von Bek indicated Zenith—"did well to get the *Salut Christi* out of Roumania, but its removal has already caused imbalance. Just four years after it was removed from the temple, the Treaty of Lausanne came into force, and the Ottoman Empire was no more."

Begg frowned. "You cite that as a sign of imbalance yet ignore the Great War that precipitated it? A war that occurred, I remind you, while the ring and the chalice were still in Lamaneagra."

"The *Salut Christi* was there from 1530," said von Bek. "How many wars have torn through Europe since then? The *Salut Christi* doesn't prevent conflict. What it does—or supposedly does—is channel the influence of Chaos to good effect. Wars occur, but what comes after is better than what went before. That the chalice possesses real supernatural power may be a fallacy. However, so long as governments believed it was real, and situated where its influence affected the principal powers equally, there was a sense of slow though sometimes painful progress toward a brighter future."

"And after it was removed?" asked the detective.

"Has it occurred to you that, since the Great War, events in Germany have made no sense? It was defeated. It should be humbled and eager to make amends, yet here we are with Hitler elected and hell-bent on empire building."

Begg regarded him askance. "The presence of the *Salut Christi* in Wäldenstein has been favourable to Germany?"

"I don't say that," von Bek responded, "but news of the Lamaneagra genocide must have caused certain people to wonder what had become of the chalice. When they saw the rise of the National Socialist German Workers' Party, they may have attributed it to the presence of the *Salut Christi* somewhere in that region of Europe."

"And," added Zenith, "those people sent an agent to locate it."

"Major John Nye," said Begg.

Von Bek nodded. "That is correct. He met with little success until, by sheer chance, he one day overheard in a London club a discussion concerning the Cracking of Crabbe. The *Sigiliul Tutorelui* was mentioned and described. It put Nye on the scent. His enquiries eventually led him to an Alexandrian market, where he found and purchased the ring. He then traced me to Mirenburg, the capital of Wäldenstein. When he showed my father the ring, Nye was able to claim possession of the *Salut Christi*, for that is the Guardian's indisputable right."

"And he who wears the ring is the Guardian," said Begg.

"Precisely. Of course, we von Beks weren't happy about it. My father ordered me to follow Nye. It was not easily done. I lost his trail many times. Finally, we both arrived in Istanbul. Nye went to ground. I alerted—" He indicated Zenith.

The albino drew his platinum case from his pocket. "It is unclear to me why Nye took the chalice to its birthplace. You know it was supposedly created in Constantinople?"

Begg nodded.

Zenith said, "But when I learned that it and the *Sigiliul Tutorelui* had been reunited, I decided I must reclaim both. I am the last true custodian. I have an obligation."

"Nye brought it to Istanbul," Begg revealed, "to purchase Turkey's allegiance, so that if Hitler sparks a war, he will be forced to fight on an eastern front, as well as a western."

"Ah," Zenith murmured.

"A gross misuse," von Bek objected. "If the *Salut Christi* has true power, such an arrangement would simply throw off the balance in a different direction. Turkey would find itself facing many powerful enemies."

"It already has one," Begg said. "Vera Pym is a Bolshevik agent, though she vehemently denies it. She was sent to interfere with the country's efforts to westernise. When Sir Vivian Clarke instructed her—in her guise of the Red King—to find Nye and seize the chalice, he must have spoken of its reputed power."

"No," said Zenith. "He didn't need to. She was already aware."

"How so?"

"I know her true nature." The albino's expression hardened. "As I think you are aware, for almost a year—most of 1920—I loved her. But we were not long together before I became suspicious. She too readily encouraged my vices, sat with me when I dreamed, asked too many questions when I was most prone to carelessly answer. She was after something."

"The *Salut Christi*," said Begg.

Zenith gave a single nod. "I was much relieved when our romance ended and she fled from England."

"I always wondered where she went."

"Now, it is obvious?"

"Russia."

Zenith drew on his cigarette, and expelled smoke. "From whence she had also come. She claims a Roumanian mother and a French father but I am certain it is a lie. I believe she was born a Russian among those of my people who, due to their fanaticism, were long ago exiled to a remote region of that vast country. Vera Pym, Sir Seaton, is a High Priestess of the forbidden Cult of Arioch!"

CHAPTER 23

Prophecy

The railwayman who had closed the door to their wagon now opened it. His face, hands, and overalls were grimy with soot. Clearly, he was one of the locomotive's footplate crew.

"Cálárasi, messieurs."

As they climbed down, he pointed to a uniformed individual, who was inspecting the wheels of a neighbouring locomotive. "The yard manager. I understand he has a letter for you."

"Instructions," the detective announced, after receiving and reading the missive. "We are to find our way to the Mihai Voda Monastery on the northern border of the city. A Gypsy caravan is waiting in its grounds. We will travel with it in a northwesterly direction. The Red King gang is apparently on the Danube, going by boat to Galati. That's about a hundred miles. They will be faster, but it is indirect. By the time they start their land journey, they might even be a little behind us. I should think they will have motor transport, but the roads in that part of the country are bad." He clicked his tongue. "It will be a close race."

"Should we not travel by motor car?" asked Ulric von Bek.

Begg shook his head. "The farther north we go, the more liable we are to run into the Iron Guard. For certain, once we get into Transylvania, the roads will be watched and there will be many checkpoints. It is better that we depend on Gypsy guile to get us through. Their knowledge of this land is unparalleled."

The yard manager touched the peak of his cap. "Transport waiting outside the station for you, gentlemen."

Begg thanked him and led his colleagues in the indicated direction, past carriages loaded with logs and sawn planks, then onto a platform and out through the terminal. The driver of a horse-drawn calash signalled them to climb aboard.

The journey to the monastery was short and without incident. Cálárasi chiefly existed as an industrial centre for lumber and paper. The calash trundled along its ill-kept streets, and the group breathed the scent of sawdust. Stray dogs chased their vehicle past low apartment blocks, small houses, and a preoccupied-looking population. Sir Seaton Begg thought it reminiscent of a Lancashire manufacturing town.

The buildings abruptly fell away behind and a vast expanse of absolutely flat land stretched before the travellers. Fields of spring wheat rippled like water all the way to the distant horizon, here and there cut by tributaries to the Danube, smooth and mirror-bright.

Turning left, the carriage followed the town's perimeter road for a little way. The old monastery came into view. It was a blocky, unromantic pile that captured their attention for only a moment before their eyes turned to the foot of its forbidding walls. Here, beside a swift stream cresting through little rocky outcrops, were parked seven wooden, gaudily painted caravans. Loaded with baskets and tinware, these *vardo*—as the Gypsies called them—were large, big-wheeled vehicles, requiring dray horses to pull their considerable weight. The animals, with eight smaller mares, were tethered nearby, cropping contentedly at sweet young herbage. All appeared well-kept and were adorned with ribbons. One was standing apart from the others, with a young man brushing her glossy black coat.

"I will stop here, messieurs," the driver murmured. "I do not like to get too close to the *Tziganes*. They are unpredictable. They are thieves and sorcerers." He crossed himself.

"A corpse and a vampyr," muttered Sans-Serif as they disembarked, "and now sorcerers. Maybe my mother's warnings were true. What have I ever done to deserve this?"

They set off toward the encampment.

Drawing closer, they noted more details. Around small tents of sacking, children capered, performed acrobatics, and uttered savage cries while play-fighting. A log fire crackled and snapped; a cauldron suspended over it from a tripod of sticks. Men and women crouched, sprawled, or moved around it. An occasional boisterous laugh carried through the air.

The men were all alike in appearance, tight-waisted, long-limbed, bearded, with bluish-black hair tangling down to their collarbones, and skin as swarthy as Moors. They bore a striking similarity to images of Christ, making the scene oddly biblical, though this was tempered by the women, who looked anything but holy. The younger females wore bright dresses, with large embroidered scarlet flowers giving the predominant colour. They were adorned with beads, ribbons, and poppies. In even the most casual of movements, they radiated a seductive wildness that, to Sir Seaton Begg—and even from a distance—was both attractive and intimidating.

The older women resembled fairy tale witches, noses sharp, their eyes black beads, darting sharp glances, missing nothing.

"Ho!" a man called, separating himself from the rest. He came forward to meet them, walking with a staff. His attire consisted of a wide-brimmed Gabor hat, a grubby untucked white shirt, purple neckerchief, colourfully embroidered waistcoat, knickerbockers, and knee-high boots.

"Lachi tiri divés!" He switched to French. "Good day to you. The English princess paid us generously. You will be well looked after, honoured guests. We are Caldararii—honest tinkers. You need not fear that—"

He saw Zenith, stopped, gaped, then dropped to one knee and bowed his head.

"Excellency! Forgive me, I was not aware that you were travelling with these *gadje*."

Sir Seaton Begg, who had spent time with Gypsies before the war, knew that *gadje* meant "house-dwelling barbarians."

Zenith, his voice low, employed the Gypsy's own language to ask his name. *"So'i tjiro nav?"*

"I am Gideon Lakatos, my lord. I am *vodja*."

"Chieftain of what?"

"Of the *familia* to which this group belongs. But I do not lead today. We have the *rom baro* with us."

"Ah, the king! I shall be honoured to travel in his company. His name?"

"Arcan Maljodi, Excellency. He is excited to meet the famous Sir Seaton Begg."

Zenith froze, stared at the man, then tipped his head back and uttered his rich, baritone laugh. "Even here, my dear Begg. Even among these itinerants. Your reputation is universal!"

The detective said nothing, merely indicated the kneeling man.

"Opre!" Zenith commanded. *Arise!*

Lakatos obeyed. He nodded respectfully at Begg, at von Bek, and—

"Oh, Excellency, you have brought your *drabarno*."

"What did you call me?" demanded Sans-Serif.

Begg muttered an answer. "A seer. A teller of fortunes."

"Plainly, you have the eye," Lakatos explained. "The *dook*—the second sight."

Sans-Serif glowered.

"Our own *drabarni*, Ancient Lilith, is powerful. Perhaps the two of you combined could—"

The Turk crossed his arms over his chest and straightened his crooked back as best he could. "I shall not be combining with ancient anybody."

"Vodja Lakatos," said Zenith. "My companions—O raj Begg, O raj Sans-Serif, and O raj von Bek—will be accorded the same respect as I. That is understood?"

"Perfectly, Excellency. We were informed that you must travel north as rapidly as possible." He gestured for them to follow and started back toward the camp. "There must first be a *pachiv*—a ceremonial celebration to honour our special guests, and to thank the land for hosting us."

Begg said, "We respect the importance of your traditions, Vodja, but the urgency of our mission—"

"The Iron Guard has passed close by in the direction we must go, O raj Begg. One of our people is watching them. He will report back to us when they are out of the way, and it is safe for us to proceed."

That cast a different light on the matter.

"We shall eat now, though it is early," said Lakatos. "We will be on the move by early afternoon."

They entered the camp and were greeted courteously and with curiosity on all sides, with many bowing to Zenith.

"How do these people know you?" Begg asked.

"The Tziganes were once the supply chain between Lamaneagra and the outer world," the albino answered. "Only they know the secret route through the mountains that surround the province. My people traded silver from the mines for food and other essentials."

"Only they knew? Then how was it that Colonel Vassilionu—?"

"We were betrayed."

Lakatos, overhearing, turned his head and spat onto the ground. "By that pig, Black Djordji. He was of the Familia Laetzi. The Laetzi are not like the Caldararii. They are thieves, liars, and stealers of children. He was the worst of them. No Tzigane has ever suffered a death as long and excruciating as that of Black Djordji. We made him pay in full for what he did. Before he died, he watched us slit the throats of his entire family, that his line be extinguished forever."

Begg, appalled, changed the subject.

"There are mines? Roumania has appropriated them?"

Zenith shook his head. "Vassilionu never reported them. He intended to exploit them for himself. He died before he could. The Carpathians have a tendency to retain their secrets."

Sans-Serif murmured, "But not their vampyres."

On blanket-covered boxes, Begg and the others settled around the campfire. From the cauldron came the delicious odour of rabbit stew. Gypsy women distributed flagons of ale and filled their plates. Young men took up accordion, fiddle, and drum; a woman shook a tambourine; and supported by much tongue-clicking and hand-clapping, they provided a merry accompaniment to the meal.

To the civilised world, the Tziganes were outlaws, impelled

by their own will from place to place, sustained by opportunism, trickery, and deceit, and entirely unconcerned with the lives of the *gadjes*. Begg and his companions were therefore surprised at the keen interest shown by their hosts in the politics of Europe, especially those of Germany. Their hosts knew the Great Depression had tilted Roumania in a dangerous direction. Furthermore, they were aware that the Nazis were funding the Iron Guard, eager to put a flame to smouldering discontent.

"The *gadje* once relied on us for their pots, pans, tools, and baskets," Lakatos said. "Now, these are produced cheaply by factories. We used to sharpen their knives. Now they just throw the blunt ones away and buy new. We entertained them with music. Now they have the wireless and gramophone. We are no longer needed, and they want us gone. Today, when we enter a town or village, they ask for what reason. We are accused of many wrongs. The Iron Guard and their supporters spread foul rumours about us. They avoid being hated themselves by provoking hatred toward us."

"It has happened the same way in Germany," said von Bek. "There, your people are rounded up, and placed into camps where they are starved and maltreated. The German people don't object. They believe Hitler's lies."

Lakatos muttered, "One madman makes many madmen, and many madmen make national madness."

The albino put aside his emptied dish and rose to his feet. "I shall speak with the *rom baro* now, Vodja Lakatos."

The Tzigane chieftain stood. "Very well, Your Excellency. I will take you to his *vardo*."

They walked from the fire. Sir Seaton Begg watched them go. What, he wondered, did Zenith have to discuss with the Gypsy king?

A skeletal hand gripped his shoulder. He turned and looked into the toothless face of a wizened hag. From deep sockets surrounded by uncountable wrinkles, eyes of penetrating darkness held him with mesmeric intensity.

"C'est l'heure!" the crone declared, her voice a dry croak.

Dancing Tabitha, a young woman to Begg's left, said, "Ancient Lilith is a hundred and three years old, m'sieu. She has lived through much of the past and has a clear view of the future."

"I am pleased to meet you, ma'am," he told the old woman. "It is time for—?"

"The cards," she responded.

Dancing Tabitha said, "We must prepare to leave. There are some little ceremonies to perform. You go, O raj Begg. She will tell your fortune while we are busy."

"I am not sure that I want—"

Long fingernails dug into him. "It is time," Ancient Lilith repeated. "Follow."

Begg glanced at Sans-Serif. The Turk had become intent on his bandaged hands. Von Bek said to a neighbouring Gypsy, "I will help you to load the caravans."

Begg, resigned, trailed after the *drabarni* to where a small foldable wooden table and two chairs stood a little apart from the camp in the shade of a tree. The detective pulled one chair out and held it while Ancient Lilith creaked into it, her joints popping. He then sat opposite.

Closing her eyes, she extended a hand, palm up.

He knew what was required. He drew coins from his pocket, selected a silver one, and placed it amid the creases and sticklike fingers.

Sighing, as if relieved of a great burden, she slipped the payment into the folds of her shapeless robes. When withdrawn, the hand held something else, a small package, wrapped in purple satin. She placed it on the table, unfolded the material, spread it flat, and revealed a pack of faded, well-worn tarot cards. Picking them up, she shuffled them slowly.

Ancient Lilith looked directly at Begg—more, he felt, into him.

In an accented voice and a rhythmic tone, she chanted.

"Dost thou create thy past, O man? Or art thou created by it? Be it fixed and done, O man? Or a past each day reimagined? Feel thee the present, O man? Dost thou sail time's currents, or art thou swept along by them? Dost thou make thy future, O man? Or be it dreamt for thee and despite thee?"

Begg offered no answers, for this was ritual and the questions rhetorical.

"That which moves thee—" She drew a card and placed it face up. "The One Cup."

A second card. "That which forms thee—" She lay it down beside and to the right of the first. "Five Coins."

A third card. "That which awaits thee—One Sword."

She offered the pack to him. "Draw now, O man, that which tests thee."

Selecting a card at random, Begg passed it to her. She put it down, a little apart from the others.

"Six Coins."

Ancient Lilith gazed at the cards as if transfixed. She rocked a little and crooned softly to herself. Then she moved a gnarled hand forward and rested the long talonlike nail of her forefinger on the One Cup.

"Thou art impelled by the conviction that all may be united." She hugged herself and cackled. "Thy cup runneth over. Even the rules of time cannot contain thee. From this chalice, love shines forth in every direction."

Begg's eyebrows twitched. He felt gooseflesh rise on his arms.

"What a great vision, O man. What wonderful and peaceful empires might grow in such radiance."

Her cackle was a mockery.

She said, in her own language, *"Si khohaimo may pachivalo sar o chachimo."*

There are lies more believable than truth.

"Lies, ma'am?" he asked.

"In order for discontent to be eliminated. A truth greater than any lie. That serenity may come when every desire finds false gratification."

"And the truth?"

She touched the Five Coins. "Thou art on a journey toward it, O man. Thee and thy four companions."

Begg frowned. "Four?"

"The albino sorcerer, who dreams us all into being from worlds away and through vast cycles of time. The emissary Sans-Serif, who plays his part blindly, though he has the second sight. The fated von Bek, who does the Devil's work. The woman—so singular—who recalls as little as thee, and is filled with as much as thee."

Violet Damm?

"The Devil's work, ma'am? Do you warn of betrayal from von Bek?"

She made the sign of the horns with her right hand and waved it in the air to ward off evil.

"Dost thou judge Shaitan, O man? Hast thou sanction to do so?"

"I think not."

"Thou hast nought to fear from von Bek—but much to fear

from"—she placed a finger on the One Sword—"a decision made in the midst of conflict."

She moved the finger to the Six Coins. Begg saw tears well into her eyes.

"Ah! Horror! Will six become five, O man? All depends on the fall of the sword."

Now, Begg went cold.

The sixth must be Doctor Taffy Sinclair.

Was Ancient Lilith suggesting that a wrong decision might result in his friend's death?

Whose decision?

Who would wield the sword?

CHAPTER 24
The *Rom Baro*

With harness bells jingling, and pots and pans clinking and clanking, the caravan wended its way across the Wallachian steppe. The black soil was firm, the trails wide, and the tributaries easy to ford. There were no forests—no trees at all—just an endless expanse of flat arable land.

The weather remained fine. Scudding through the blue sky, clouds cast shadows which, as they slid over the ground, made it appear liquid and unstable.

Begg, seated beside Gideon Lakatos on the lead wagon, felt uneasy. Empires had washed back and forth over this territory, leaving corpses as tidemarks. The caravan was riding over the unconsecrated bones of the undiscovered dead. Here lay the countless victims of invading Persians, Macedonians, Celts, Romans, Goths, Huns, Slavs, Mongols, Byzantines, Hapsburgs, and Ottomans.

Here, too, the victims of Vlad the Impaler.

No wonder the soil was so dark.

Begg sighed. How many, taken away "for questioning" by the Iron Guard, might also have ended up here? It was not his way to generalise when on a case of this kind, but for a moment, he was overwhelmed by this stark image of mankind's bloody history.

Will it never stop? he wondered. *Is every plane of the multiverse stricken by this same curse? Will people always rationalise—with religion or politics—their basest animal instincts?* The more absurd their beliefs, the more fiercely they defended them—even to the point of denying naysayers their basic rights to be housed, to eat, to be educated, to enjoy peace, to have hope, or, indeed, to live.

Begg was not a religious man, but he valued common decency, generosity, empathy, and tolerance. The *Salut Christi* was emblematic of those qualities. That it attributed them to an opal containing a drop of Christ's blood was incidental and did not matter. The effect was more important than the cause.

His mission revolved around an illusion. If world leaders could harness it, use the *Salut Christi* properly, might it calm the hideous tides that had deposited so many bones here? Might it quell the present insanity of Nazism?

He did not know.

It was a matter of faith, and he had none. He was a detective. Rational. Religion might provide a motive but deductive reasoning proscribed any reliance on it. He did, nonetheless, recognise that human nature demanded the comforts of ritual, and human history was proof of the terrifying power of superstition and corrupted belief.

Therefore, the chalice must not be contaminated by spilled blood.

Blood for Arioch.

Taffy Sinclair's blood!

Begg's austere characteristics hardened. Staring out across that featureless plain, he became grim and withdrawn.

By midafternoon, the crops had given way to thistles and scrub.

The Tziganes did not trouble to scout ahead. Now that they were on the move, there was no need. From their *vardos*, they could see for miles.

To the east, halfway to the horizon, amid a patch of cultivated fields, a small village broke the unending flatness—wooden houses, with barns and outlying farmsteads. Peasants could be seen moving back and forth, going about their business.

To the west, so distant they resembled ants, men herded cattle. "On their way to a livestock auction," Lakatos observed.

Zenith, hatless and riding one of the mares, came alongside.

Irritated, Begg snapped at him, "You are inviting trouble. Your white hair is like a beacon. If the Iron Guard should see—"

Insouciant as ever, the albino lifted his shoulders.

"Would you not welcome the excitement?" he drawled. "This is limbo made manifest. The most unforgiving region in the whole of Europe. Be thankful it is spring, my friend. In the winter, the blizzards are constant. In the summer, the heat is unbearable. The chief advantage of the route, of course, is that Vera Pym is unlikely to have anticipated us choosing it."

"Tomorrow is May Day," Begg observed. "Is she trying for Lamaneagra by then? Are the rites of Arioch tied to the seasons?"

The sky reflected in the albino's circular, dark spectacles.

"No. Seasons, calendars, the phases of the moon, they are far too regular for a god of Chaos. Besides, if La Pym wanted to be there by tomorrow, she has taken the wrong route. Even in vehicles designed for rough terrain, she has two days of travel ahead. As do we. It is a neck and neck race."

He looked into the distance.

"I bear a message. The *rom baro* invites you to take wine with him. Perhaps it will improve your mood."

This was an honour the detective had been expecting. He nodded, hopped down from the *vardo*, and waited for the fourth, in the middle of the line, to come trundling past. Zenith rode on with Gideon Lakatos.

The king's caravan was the only one not hung with pots and pans. It had the finest and freshest paintwork and was decorated with the most colourful ribbons. Begg hoisted himself onto its tailboard.

"Rom Baro?"

He heard the voice of a boy call in French, *"Veuillez entrer, Sir Seaton Begg, détective Anglais!"*

Pushing aside a light curtain, Begg ducked into the interior. It was surprisingly spacious, despite overloaded bookshelves running down one side and, at the far end, an occupant of immense physical stature.

Arcan Maljodi resembled a brown-skinned barbarian. He was broad-shouldered, meaty-armed, and barrel-chested. His greying black hair was thick, long, and curly. His beard coiled in waves down to his waist. His black eyes glared. He looked ferocious.

He smiled, revealing dazzling white, perfectly formed teeth. When he spoke, it was with the child's voice Begg had already heard. The high pitch didn't match the body at all.

"Sit, my most welcome guest!" The king indicated the bench opposite the shelves. The multitude of rings on his fingers glittered, the bangles on his wrist clattered. He was wearing a wide belt of leather and brass, a blue shirt open down to his hard stomach, white Arabian *shalwar* trousers, and soft deer hide slippers.

"I am honoured to meet you, Rom Baro," Begg said, settling. "My goodness, you have an impressive library. I mean no offence, but it is not what I expected to find in a Tzigane wagon."

Maljodi handed him a skin of wine. "Literature is my greatest passion, O raj Begg. You see here classics in French, English, German, and Russian. This—" He leaned forward and extracted a small volume. "This edition of *Notre-Dame de Paris* cost me two horses and my fifth daughter's hand in marriage. I was robbed. Look closely, and you will see that the rear half is bound in from an entirely different edition. You cannot trust anyone these days. Especially rascally book dealers. Yet, these volumes of *Middlemarch*, this George Eliot, I exchanged for only a Turkish rug. A bargain, you'll agree?" He returned the books to the packed shelves, sat back, and sighed. "I have devoted my life, my family, all my wealth to the pursuit of literature, and in your eyes I see—what?—scepticism?"

Begg took a sip of wine. It was excellent.

"Scepticism? No, not that. Perhaps fascination. It strikes me that you are an extraordinary man, Rom Baro."

The king laughed. It sounded like the giggle of a twelve-year-old. "Then there are two of us present."

Begg acknowledged the compliment with a smile.

The big man went on, "For all that I enthuse over the most acclaimed literature, the men who scratch around in dusty old bookshops on my behalf know to keep their eyes peeled for such as this." Maljodi pulled a slim periodical from one end of a shelf and passed it to the detective. "Those who bring them to me are paid generously."

Begg found himself holding an edition of *The Septimus Blane Library*, a fourpenny dreadful. The story was entitled "The Lethal

Shadow Device: Septimus Blane vs Doctor Morton Kitchener." It was attributed to James Colvin but Begg knew this to be pseudonym. The author was, in fact, his own scapegrace brother, Warwick.

He said, "Um—"

"Wonderful stories!" Maljodi cried out. "Based on your investigations, yes?"

"Inspired by them, perhaps," Begg said. "They are about as factual as the adventures of Dick Turpin, Claude Duval, or Buffalo Bill."

Maljodi smacked a hand onto his knee. "But your boy assistant, the inimitable Topper. He is real, surely? I would be delighted to meet him. Where is he?"

Begg felt his face tighten. "His name is Taffy Sinclair, and his boyhood is long past. He is currently a prisoner at Lamaneagra. If we do not reach him in time, he will be murdered."

"What?" the king squeaked, his dark eyes widening. "This is a rescue mission? The English princess did not say so. You will need to fight?"

"I think it likely."

"Then, by the gods, we will stand with you. I shall redden the earth with my blood to prevent the death of that marvellous boy! Let me think a moment—" He paused and knocked his knuckles together. "Yes, I will have Ancient Lilith contact others of the Caldararii. They will meet us on the way—with weapons!"

Begg rubbed his unshaven chin. "Contact? How will she do that?"

The king grinned. He tapped the side of his head. "She is *drabarni*. She can communicate with others of her kind by thought alone."

The detective kept his expression neutral.

"We shall not set camp," said Maljodi. "We will take turns sleeping and keep moving. In a little less than a day, we will reach Bazău. Do you know it?"

"I do," Begg confirmed.

The Carpathian Mountains bisected Roumania, the range shaped like the letter J. Bazău was in the southeastern part of it, on the outermost curve of the foothills. It was at the crossroads of the country's three principal regions, Wallachia, Transylvania, and Moldavia.

"An industrial city, is it not?"

The king nodded. "We must go around it carefully, and by night, for it is the hub of many railway lines, and the Iron Guard will be watching it closely. The English princess mentioned that the demon, Klosterheim, commands those who would stop you."

"You know him?"

"Bengesko niamso!" Arcan Maljodi hissed the words, then added in French: "Cursed German!" He slowly shook his head. "The times change. Even monsters aren't what they used to be. Once the Carpathians were crawling with *strigoi* and *pricolici*—vampyres and werewolves—but now we have the Iron Guard and Major Johannes Klosterheim. Much worse!" The king raised his wine and drank deeply. He wiped the back of his hand across his lips. "Do you know what he calls us, O raj Begg? Not Tziganes, not Roma, not Gypsies. To Klosterheim and his hounds, we are *zigeuner*. It means *untouchable*. It is a word they use for all people they deem inferior."

He patted his bookshelves.

"You were surprised by this little library, eh? Maybe surprised that I can read. Not what you expect of a mere *zigeuner*."

"I do not call you that, Rom Baro, and would never do so."

Maljodi waved away the objection. Then, he clapped his hands, a report like a gunshot.

"Ha! I shall tell you a truth. The albino with whom you ride, he is the last *voivode* of Lamaneagra, the last High Priest of Arioch. Oh yes, I know! Yet, for all that, he is no more nor less unique than you or me, or any other person in this world. We are all singular, and we do ourselves a disservice every time we state our race or our nation or our religion, or refer to others by those tribal names."

Begg took two Havanas from his pocket and passed one to the king. He lit a match and, as he offered its flame, said, "Even as I received the invitation to visit you, my thoughts ran along similar lines. My companions and I are not only on a rescue mission. We also seek a stolen relic believed to possess the mystical power to stabilise empires, that they might coexist in peace, to the benefit of all their people."

Maljodi snorted his contempt. "All their people? *Byah!* Empires are suppression, massacres, and genocide. An empire defines itself not by who its people are—but by what they are not. Your adopted Mr. Joseph Conrad says as much."

Begg exhaled a fragrant plume.

"I don't disagree, but this relic symbolises the finer qualities of our species. It is said to influence the behaviour of—"

"But does it?"

"Powerful men in my country's government think so, and are acting accordingly—ergo, it has influence."

The king grunted. "I remain unconvinced."

"Frankly," Begg said, "so do I."

"Yet you risk your life to retrieve it?"

"Given the current state of affairs in Europe, perhaps any chance is worth taking."

Arcan Maljodi reached out his hand. "The wise man makes his judgment with his ears, not with his eyes. I have read many accounts of your adventures, and you—albeit in the guise of Septimus Blane—are usually portrayed as a man who stands for the British Empire, come what may. In listening to your words, I have learned that you are rather more of—what?—an internationalist? There is ambiguity in you. As if many versions of you exist. You possess a healthy scepticism, and you can change your mind if events warrant it. That is good. So, I say it again: My people and I stand with you."

Briefly they shook hands.

Then they smoked their cigars. For a little while, as the swaying Gypsy vans cast lengthening shadows, the two talked of other matters: of books and bookshops; of the many countries that Begg had visited; of the Appleby horse fair in the Yorkshire Dales; of the famous Gypsy congregations; and of Tzigane songs and superstitions.

The caravan rolled through the unchanging landscape. The sun went down. The stars and half moon lit the way. In the distance, a night-crake called.

"Sleep," the king ordered. "By dawn we shall be past Bazău. The mountains are not high, but it will take a day to cross them. There are many villages. You and your friends must be disguised. You will be made Tzigane."

"Monsieur Zenith might object to that," Begg observed.

Maljodi gave a fierce smile, and in his childish voice said, "On this occasion, His Excellency will do as we tell him. His death would bring *prikaza*—bad luck—to my people."

Begg made a sound of agreement. "If he died, I should rather regret it."

Maljodi looked surprised. "Ancient Lilith must read your cards again, O raj Begg! Of this, I am certain: She will predict that if Zenith dies, you will have a better chance of living!"

The metatemporal detective thought this was probably true. His truce with the albino could not last. The feud—*a la morte!*—must resume.

It was simply a question of when.

CHAPTER 25

Greenshirts

The caravan's progress was better than anticipated. When Sir Seaton Begg awoke at dawn and joined Ulric von Bek on the chief's *vardo*, Lakatos said, "We are well past Bazău."

The trail threaded from village to village between thickly forested slopes, deep into the mountains. The inhabitants of these tiny, isolated communities resembled peasants in some Balkan opera, as if time had stopped five hundred years ago. Begg vaguely recalled having pursued more than one case here in other versions of the past, and was struck by a haunting sense of déjà vu.

The villagers pushed their children indoors as soon as the wagons approached, but otherwise expressed no overt suspicion or hostility. They were eager to replace old ironware and baskets, and the Tziganes did brisk business, carried out "on the run," the travellers not stopping even for a minute.

When the caravan neared the famous little city resort of Sinaia, Lakatos guided it onto a narrow side trail, ascending the forested slope. It was hard going, the horses straining, branches thrashing the wagons' sides and tops, frequently knocking off the pots and pans, and with thick undergrowth tangling the wheels.

"The Iron Guard are unlikely to have penetrated this far into the mountains," the chief told Begg, "but I think it wise to go around Sinaia rather than through it."

The detective, now fully disguised as a Tzigane, pulled a rug around himself. At this altitude, it was cold, with patches of winter snow remaining.

"You appear to know every path," he observed.

"Yes," came the simple response.

For the next three hours, there was nothing to see but trees, everywhere coming into leaf. Then they returned to the main path and resumed the trek from settlement to settlement. Now, however, they were suddenly less welcome. Villagers spat on the ground, slammed their window shutters, hurried inside, and bolted their doors.

"Move on!" someone shouted. "Gypsy thieves and sorcerers are not welcome in Christian homes!"

Lakatos smiled sadly at Begg and von Bek. "You see how persuasive and pervasive the Iron Guard can be? These villagers would rather go without cooking utensils than deal with a people they are told to hate. Yet, we are fellow Christians. Our churches may be the wild glades, of which we are all God's stewards, but Jesus Christ is our saviour, and we carry crucifixes." He showed his silver cross, which hung on a chain around his neck. "And rosaries." He clicked his tongue. "Where is it written: Love thy neighbour, but hate every stranger? What do we threaten?"

"These are troubled times," Begg responded, "and simple folk focus their fear of an uncertain future on whatever is unfamiliar. You represent the fear itself."

He lit a massive meerschaum, which the *rom baro* had given him after the detective mentioned that he missed his battered old pipe.

The three men were seated at the front of the lead wagon. Zenith rode beside them. He had finally accepted the need for disguise and was wearing knee-high boots, baggy trousers, an enormous fur coat, and a wide-brimmed black Bohemian hat. With his tinted glasses, he resembled a wild but romantic mountain bandit.

They had seen little of Sans-Serif. The special agent was currently drinking wine with Arcan Maljodi and the man's daughter. The king had already confessed to von Bek that she was impossible to marry off due to her opinionated nature and walleye, which was considered bad luck. Maljodi was, therefore, delighted when the Turk displayed every sign of infatuation.

"I shall get the hunchback drunk, and he'll propose before this journey is over."

"It might not take much," von Bek observed. "What's her name?"

"Esmeralda."

The Wäldensteinian made an excuse and left.

The shadows lengthened, the sky turned purple, and the drawn-out, quavering songs of wolves chorused from the deep mountain forests. Passing the Sita Buzăului monastery, they emerged into a cultivated basin. To the west, just visible in the twilight, the medieval Saxon walls, bastions, and towering Black Church of Brașov.

Lakatos pointed at distant activity. "More Tzigane. They are packing after a May Day fair. It used to be a profitable time of year for us, but fewer people come to the fairs now."

"They are your *familia*, Vodja?" Begg asked.

"No, not Caldararii. They are Laetzi. We shall avoid them."

By midnight, the wagons had crossed the basin, navigated a long, narrow valley, and left the Carpathian Mountains.

They were now on the Transylvanian plateau. In two days, they had travelled more than two hundred miles. Zenith estimated two-hundred and fifty more to Lamaneagra.

Begg was concerned about the horses. There had been stops along the way to rest, feed, and water them, but the detective could see they were dead on their feet. He was about to mention this when Lakatos jerked his chin to the right.

"Alexandru," he murmured. "My brother."

Peering through the moonlight, Begg spotted a single *vardo* standing beside a stream beneath a hill. Tethered nearby, a small herd of dray horses.

"Your actual brother?" he asked.

"Yes, he is two years my junior. Ancient Lilith has summoned him. He has weapons and replacement horses for us."

"Truly," murmured Begg, "the ways of the Tzigane are mysterious. You have a powerful *drabarni*."

"We do," the *vodja* agreed.

Begg decided not to mention that, yesterday afternoon, he had noticed one mare and one man missing from the caravan.

Lakatos ordered the wagons to a halt. Rapidly, men unharnessed the exhausted drays and replaced them with fresh animals. A wooden crate, taken from Alexandru's *vardo*, was loaded into the king's.

The chief and his sibling embraced and slapped each other's backs. They exchanged murmured words for a few minutes, then Lakatos returned to his wagon.

Alexandru mounted his van and led the tired horses into the night.

The chief said to Begg, "We have fifteen rifles and ten pistols, with ammunition, all dating from the Great War but in good working order."

"I hope they won't be needed," Begg responded.

"Alexandru reports that small groups have been spotted entering the pass that leads to Lamaneagra. If they are armed—"

There was no need to finish the sentence.

The race against Vera Pym resumed.

The country was all glacial drumlins now, gentle rolling hills. There were no forests, only grassy slopes, snaking valleys, and fast-flowing streams. To the right, the silver-topped Carpathians loomed. What villages they passed were dark. Everyone was asleep—or pretending to be.

Another man took the reins so Lakatos could rest. Begg and von Bek joined him in the wagon, nine men crammed like sardines in a tin, but too weary to complain. They slept solidly.

Up before the sun, the Tziganes and their passengers washed in an icy, frothing brook. They ate a breakfast of *preste*, a savoury breadstick dipped in flavoured yogurt. The horses grazed. Those men and women who had been up all night got into the wagons.

In the first rays of dawn, Begg spotted a mounted figure on a distant hilltop. The rider was wearing a black cloak and a wide-brimmed hat. The horse, also black, was magnificent—by its compact build and elegant lines, an Andalusian.

Sunlight reflected from binoculars, then the horse reared, pirouetted, and plunged over the brow of the hill and out of sight.

The din of approaching hoofs caused Begg a moment of disorientation. How could the rider have covered the distance so quickly? Then Zenith came thundering into camp on a wild-eyed mare. He had been scouting, and brought bad news.

"Iron Guard. A dozen men. Five minutes away. Troopers and a captain."

Arcan Maljodi was bathing his feet in the stream. He picked up his slippers and strode over. In his little boy's voice, he barked, "Off your horse, Excellency. Into my *vardo*. Lift the rug, open the trapdoor, and get into the space beneath with the rifles. I'll be along presently."

Zenith obeyed without hesitation.

"Sir Seaton, Sans-Serif, look busy, say nothing. Von Bek, cover your head with a scarf, that dye was useless, your blond hair is obvious even with a hat. You look like an autumn stoat. Get in a *vardo* and go to sleep. Vodja Lakatos, you do the talking."

The king disappeared into his van. Begg understood why. His great size would be seen as a challenge. The Iron Guard would go at him like a bull to a red rag. Petty men, given authority, love to demonstrate it.

The metatemporal detective crossed to a dray, led it to the front wagon, and set about harnessing it.

Minutes later, an *Echipa Morţii—Death Squad*—of the Iron Guard rode in, twelve unsavoury men in green shirts and black riding breeches, polished jack boots, and vicious spurs. Some sported dirty *shakos* or braided jackets on their shoulders to appear like old hussars. Heavily armed with a variety of sabres, carbines, and German small arms, they each wore an armband bearing a triple cross.

Without dismounting, their wolfish leader snapped, "Who speaks for you people?" He was a narrow-eyed, thin-faced man, slightly disfigured by a harelip and heavily pocked cheeks. Five crucifixes hung from his neck, plus a small leather bag. Members of the Legion of the Archangel Michael carried Roumanian soil in this fashion. They were fervent nationalists. The man had spoken in the Roumanian language and was no doubt violently opposed to the use of French, the favoured tongue of the country's elite.

Lakatos recognised this, and when he stepped forward, he answered in Roumanian. "I do. We stopped to water our horses, Commander, and are preparing to move on. We are doing no harm."

"On to where?"

"North to the Hungarian border."

"For what purpose?"

"For no particular purpose. It is our tradition."

The legionnaire sneered. He turned to his men. "You see, they are like filthy migrating animals, driven by instinct alone." He put a hand to his holstered pistol. "Are you transporting Jews, *zigeuner*?"

"No. We are good Christians."

"Are you certain? What will I find if I search your vans?"

"Nothing of consequence."

"And that one?" The commander nodded toward the king's wagon, so obviously different from the other four.

Lakatos shifted his weight uneasily.

"Well?" the commander prompted, drawing his pistol and holding it loosely, as if unaware of it.

"It is the *rom baro*'s."

The commander dismounted and signalled his men to do the same. He passed the reins of his horse to a lieutenant. Then he stepped close to Lakatos, his chest out, his chin up, his eyes fixed on the chieftain's. "Get your king out here."

Lakatos returned the stare. "It is not my place to tell the *rom baro* what to do."

Without breaking his cold gaze, the commander extended his arm sideways and put a bullet through the wagon's wood panelled side.

The report echoed away over hills. The horses snorted and shied.

He raised his voice. "If I missed you, Your Majesty, I advise you to come out before I shoot again."

A moment passed; then Arcan Maljodi heaved his great bulk down and approached, waving a book in the air.

"Le Père Goriot!" he cried out. "There is no better villain in all literature than Vautrin—and you just put a bullet in him!"

With an astonished expression, the Roumanian turned to face the king. Then, in a comically high-pitched and mocking voice, the legionnaire mimicked him. "No better villain in all literature!" He put his head back and laughed. His men did the same.

"Stop."

Instant silence.

Sir Seaton Begg had spoken the word quietly but with unmistakable authority. The detective stepped away from the horse he had been tending. "What is your name, Captain?"

The Roumanian swung round and aimed his pistol at the Englishman, but he looked puzzled.

"It is I who ask the questions, *zigeuner*." He paused, and narrowed his eyes. "I am Captain Ion Bacaloglu, commander of the *Echipa Morții*, Fifth Brigade of the Iron Guard, representing the Legion of the Archangel Michael. You are—?"

"Sir Seaton Begg, an emissary at large of His Britannic Majesty. Your organisation is illegal, Captain. The Vaida-Voevod government outlawed it two years ago."

"Yet here we stand. I see now that you are not of these people. What are you, a godless, Jew-loving, Britisher spy?"

Begg ignored the question. "Go on your way, please, Captain. You have absolutely no jurisdiction in this province."

"To the contrary," said Bacaloglu. "I have this much."

He swivelled and shot the king. The report sounded louder than before.

Horses scattered.

Arcan Maljodi reeled backward and hit the ground. At the same moment, Bacaloglu's chest exploded, and he also dropped, to die without a twitch.

Monsieur Zenith spoke languidly into a shocked silence.

"I would strongly advise you all to stand perfectly still."

He stood firmly astride the tailgate of the king's wagon, a smoking Martini repeating rifle at his shoulder.

He and Bacaloglu had fired simultaneously.

Sir Seaton Begg said, "Rom Baro?"

Arcan Maljodi sat up. "Straight through *Père Goriot* and into my shoulder."

"Are you badly hurt?"

"Hurt? I am dismayed! It was a first edition. Two bullet holes. It is rendered unreadable."

Begg knelt beside him. "Allow me to examine your wound."

"I would be grateful." The king nodded toward Bacaloglu. "Him?"

"Dead. Zenith never misses."

They both started as another rifle shot rang out.

"Over your heads that time, brutes," Zenith declared, addressing the eleven remaining Greenshirts. "If I see another of you reach for a gun—"

They all showed their hands.

Sabahattin Sans-Serif, who had been down by the stream pretending to clean pans, moved among them and removed their pistols. He did not speak Roumanian but had heard the word *"evreu,"* knew what it meant, and had noted the disdain with which it was uttered.

"You do not like Jews?" he murmured in French to one man.

Responding in the same language, as if it were a foul taste in his mouth, the guard said, "Roumanians cannot find jobs because the Jews have taken them. They bring foreign notions. They corrupt our honest peasantry with talk of education and opportunities they cannot hope to achieve."

"You have my sympathy," Sans-Serif replied, admiring a confiscated Luger. "We have made immense advances in Turkey thanks to Jewish ingenuity. We even survived the depression unscathed, which was due solely to their commercial acumen. We could have suffered like everyone else, but, oh no, the Jew forced us to be secure and economically stable. Can you imagine anything more humiliating than being prosperous on the Bosphorus?"

"Ach!" the Greenshirt agreed, wide-eyed as the Turkish agent slowly polished the pistol barrel with the man's own shirt tails.

Ulric von Bek delivered clean neckerchiefs to Begg, for use as bandages. After the detective had sterilised the king's knife over a cigar lighter, he proceeded to dig the bullet out of Maljodi's shoulder. His jaw clamped, the *rom baro* did not make a sound, though perspiration beaded his forehead. Begg cleaned the wound, bound it, and fashioned a sling. Ancient Lilith provided soporific drugs and pain-killing herbs.

"Thank you," said Maljodi. With assistance, he rose to his feet, then addressed one of his men. "Go find their horses. We shall claim them. Recompense for trouble caused." Turning his eyes to the eleven Greenshirts, he murmured to Begg, "They will come after us now. We should kill them."

"But won't."

"Of course not. Do you take us for savages?"

"Far from it."

"We Tziganes have a talent for knots. We will tie them in a chain to that tree by the creek. By the time they have freed themselves, they will be hungry, and we shall be far away."

"Their captain?"

"If I left them a shovel, they would not use it. They'll carry the corpse to a church. Those unsavoury thugs are Orthodox Christian fanatics. They use the cross of Christ as a weapon and as justification for cruelty and murder."

The Gypsies rounded up the horses and secured the still-frightened Greenshirts. As an afterthought, they removed the Fifth Brigade's riding boots, exposing shredded socks and filthy feet. The disgusting footwear, they threw into a pile and set alight.

"Take a much-needed bath," admonished Sans-Serif, flinging the final piece of fouled leather into the flames. "And let us hope that no one downstream drinks from the water today."

Soon the caravan was on its way again. Once it had reached a safe distance, one of the legionnaires found a coward's courage and screamed after them, his voice echoing across the hilltops.

"You will not escape us! Klosterheim will ferret you out. *Zigeuners!* Jews! Foreigners! You are destroying the country we spilled Christian blood to defend for centuries. The Executioner of Kravonia will dig you up like spring worms. Do you hear me? Major Klosterheim already posts a reward for you. You will stand trial as living proof of the foreign infiltrators sneaking into our country. You are riding through the gates of Hell—where Klosterheim rules a principality! He will take your soul, Mr. Jew-Loving Britisher! Mr. Humpback! Mr. White Wolf! Mark my words: He will take your souls!"

CHAPTER 26

Major Johannes Klosterheim

They could sense Johannes Klosterheim closing in on them. Already, they were travelling as rapidly as they possibly could. At every crossroads, haunted by impending evil, they expected him to swoop.

Transylvania boasted some good roads. For the past day and night, the caravan had taken advantage of them, crossing from one highway to another but never deviating far from its course. The motor traffic was light, mainly haulage lorries trailing clouds of dust.

Twice, they encountered other Tzigane caravans, both belonging to the Familia Laetzi. They exchanged curt, unsmiling nods and brief, inscrutable hand signals.

The time passed uneventfully. The landscape was repetitive. Villagers were coldly hostile and purchased not a single pot or pan.

A day, a night, and the next morning, a change. The air became humid. In the north, the sky darkened. A storm was coming.

Sabahattin Sans-Serif provided the only excitement as they crossed the plateau.

The Tziganes rarely married outside their race. Arcan Maljodi's group, however, was clearly delighted by a prospective union between the Turk and their "unlucky charm." While Esmeralda's walleye was a curse, Sans-Serif's mismatched pair, and his hunched shoulder and generally disordered physique, were the opposite—they promised good fortune! The balance achieved through the couple's match would give the tribe enviable new respect. The Turkish special agent had brought a powerful wyrd to Esmeralda's family.

Hugely popular with them all, he valued their enthusiasm with admirable gravitas.

The magical aspect of their relationship made little sense to Sir Seaton Begg—but neither did the notion that a silver chalice could propagate love and stability until it was filled with blood, after which it would disseminate Chaos.

"The Turk is a powerful *drabarno*," Gideon Lakatos explained. "Though he knows it not. Esmeralda may be the one to unlock his talent. It would serve us well to be affiliated with him. Ancient Lilith foresees that he will influence powerful men. Perhaps he will make it easier for us to continue our traditions in these tumultuous times."

The little community of fifteen men, eight women, and their *rom baro*, conspired to give Sans-Serif and Esmeralda plenty of time to themselves.

Whispered gossip accompanied the caravan across Transylvania.

"He makes her laugh. I have never heard her so constantly amused."

"See how he glances at her all the time?"

"She has promised to cook him *salmaia*!"

"He told her she is as beautiful as any woman of old Constantinople."

"She is wearing flowers in her hair!"

That storm-threatening morning, the special agent was riding with the king's daughter a little distance to the west of the caravan. They were now just twenty miles from Lamaneagra.

Zenith trotted his mare alongside the lead wagon, speaking with Sir Seaton Begg, Ulric von Bek, and the *vodja*, Lakatos.

"This is a fast animal," Zenith said, patting his mount, "but by the time she reached the hill, your black rider was long gone, Begg."

They were discussing the mysterious cloaked figure on the Andalusian horse. It had been spotted on four occasions since Begg first saw it. Following them. Watching them.

"Klosterheim?" Lakatos asked.

Von Bek shook his head. "In a hat and cloak? No. He is a man for uniforms, sabres, and swagger sticks."

A strong gust of wind slapped at them. They smelled rain.

"We must hurry," Lakatos announced. "If the downpour is heavy, it could cut off the pass." He pointed to a village nestled in a steep-sided valley to the northeast. The Carpathians towered behind it, stark and black, the most massive of them white-crested. "That is Dragomireşti, a Jewish stronghold. The people despise the Iron Guard and are friendly toward the Tzigane." He addressed Zenith. "And to your people, too, Excellency."

The albino gave a single nod. "That is so."

The chieftain continued, "We shall leave the caravan with them. The entrance to the pass is not far from the village. The final stretch of the journey will be on foot."

The wagons trundled toward the mouth of the valley. The air

became damp and electrified. Begg felt his skin prickling and pressure in his skull. He saw lightning flicker in the north.

Incessantly, he fretted about Taffy Sinclair, abducted exactly one week ago.

"Gentlemen," murmured Zenith. "Where are Sans-Serif and the woman Esmeralda?"

They looked to the left, scanned the hills, saw nothing.

The albino dug his heels into his steed's flanks and galloped off. He breasted the closest hill, dropped out of sight, and rode over the next. Ten minutes passed with no sign of him.

Lakatos uttered an exclamation. A medium-sized lorry was entering the village.

"Unusual," he said. "I have not before seen motor traffic in Dragomirești."

Zenith returned leading two horses.

"There were signs of a struggle. A splash of blood. Boot prints. The Iron Guard has them."

He rode to inform the king, taking the two mares with him.

"Von Bek," said Begg, drawing his automatic. "Check your weapon."

They neared Dragomirești, a village of small wooden dwellings with high thatched roofs, a little synagogue, and a handful of bigger whitewashed buildings.

The lorry had stopped in front of a square, brick-built structure.

"In such a village," von Bek observed, "I would expect to see people in the streets and working the fields. Yet, there is no one but him." He indicated a sole figure, standing in the middle of the main road, apparently awaiting their arrival.

Zenith, having left the retrieved horses with one of the Tziganes, drew alongside. The caravan rolled into the village. Lakatos slowed it as they came abreast the lorry and neared the waiting man, who was holding a bugle, trembling, fear flashing in his eyes.

"Good morning!" the *vodja* called. "We are Caldararii. We have fine pans, tools, and baskets. They are yours if you will allow us to set up camp on the outskirts of the village. We will cause no trouble."

The man shouted back, "I am sorry. I have no choice. They threaten my family." He raised the bugle to his lips and blew a single blast. Then he took to his heels, disappearing around a corner.

Surrounding doors everywhere crashed open. Uniformed men piled out, levelling rifles and machine guns.

"You are surrounded," a Prussian voice declared. "Anyone with a weapon should throw it down immediately. If you fail to do so, you will be shot dead on the spot."

Begg, von Bek, and Zenith slowly held out their pistols and let them fall.

Four legionnaires dragged Sans-Serif and Esmeralda out from the back of the lorry.

A thin man marched into view. His uniform was perfectly tailored, and emphasised his height.

Major Johannes Klosterheim.

"Down off your horses and out of your wagons. Now! *Raus! Raus!*"

In the distance, thunder grumbled.

The Tziganes gathered beside their vans.

"Which one of you is Sir Seaton Begg?"

The metatemporal detective jumped to the ground and stepped forward. "I am."

Klosterheim strode over and stopped in front of him, eye to eye. The German was as tall as Begg but almost skeletal, with hard grey eyes in a pale, cadaverous face. He was wearing a long black coat over a charcoal uniform, a peaked cap, knee-high boots, and leather gloves. He removed the latter and said, "I am Major Klosterheim, and I am pleased to finally meet you, Herr Begg. I bear a message from Madame Vera Pym."

"I have also keenly anticipated this meeting," replied Begg. "The message?"

"Simply this."

Klosterheim struck Begg savagely across the face with a leather glove. The loud crack split the air, then faded into a loaded silence.

Again, thunder muttered over the mountains.

Begg drawled, "I look forward to giving her my response . . . in person."

Klosterheim's eyes held Begg's for a moment, then slipped to the left, to where Ulric von Bek was standing.

"Oh!" The German grinned, revealing slightly overlong canines. "The end of a good chase, is it not, von Bek? *Es ist gut.* I bring you news."

Von Bek's gaze was steady and scornful. "I am uninterested in anything a Nazi has to say."

"*Ach, ist das so?* You do not, then, wish to know how I tortured then executed the man who printed your pamphlets? You have no curiosity to hear how I burned to ash every scurrilous word you wrote about Chancellor Hitler? Or that an internment camp is to be built in Sachsenburg, with a place reserved in it for you, and special instructions issued pertaining to your treatment there? It seems to me that you are carelessly overlooking matters that will much influence your future—what little remains of it."

Von Bek laughed in his enemy's narrow face. "Go to Hell, you pathetic upstart."

Klosterheim quivered with ill-suppressed rage. "There to caper in your ancestors' playground? I think not."

He wheeled, paced away, then turned back.

"Lieutenant," he said to one of his men. "Select three of the *zigeuner* men and one of their women. Stand them against that wall. It is a little school, I think, *nein*?"

"Major—" Begg began.

In a blur, Klosterheim's pistol came out of its holster and its muzzle centred on the detective's forehead.

"Not one word, Herr Begg, or I shall add another woman."

Four Tziganes were dragged to the school and pushed against it. Begg had spoken with each of them during the trek: Mihai, barely out of childhood, a talented musician; Andrei, in his fifties, a great and amusing storyteller; Marius, father of three, metalworker; and young Ana-Maria, with the sweetest singing voice.

"Shoot them," said Klosterheim.

Machine guns flashed and chattered. An electric detonation rent the heavens. The wagons creaked and shook in a sudden gust of hot wind.

Four corpses crumpled to the ground.

The school bore a glistening red stain.

Arcan Maljodi emitted a sob and stumbled forward.

"Why?" he cried out, his little boy's voice agonised, full of despair. "Why did you do that?"

"To demonstrate that I can," said Klosterheim. "Who are you?"

"I am Arcan Maljodi, the *rom baro*, the king. Please, I implore you, there is—"

Klosterheim tilted his head inquisitively. "What happened to your arm, Your Majesty?"

"I do not . . . this? One of your people, an Iron Guard, put a bullet in my shoulder. There was no need then, and there is no need now. Surely, we can—"

"He was negligent," Klosterheim observed. "His aim was off."

He raised his pistol again, and shot Maljodi in the head.

The gentle giant, the lover of literature, dropped to his knees and pitched forward onto his face. His blood pooled into the compacted earth of the village street.

His daughter Esmeralda screamed. A low moan rippled through the gathered Tziganes.

"There are two options," the major announced. "You will all do exactly as I instruct, or I will very happily kill you, one by one, here and now. Which shall it be?"

No one spoke.

A raindrop hit Begg's cheek.

"You *zigeuners* will enter the school, you will sit down, and you will neither talk nor move. Any that do will be immediately shot. *Verstanden?* Now, move!"

The Caldararii reluctantly obeyed.

Klosterheim turned to the two Greenshirts holding Esmeralda. "Her, as well."

They hauled her into the school.

Sans-Serif struggled in the grip of his guards. The fury on his face was incandescent. If looks could kill, Klosterheim would by now be windblown ash.

The German pointed his gun at the Turk.

"Your name?"

Sans-Serif tried to speak but was overcome by emotion, and simply ground his teeth.

Zenith interrupted, his voice calm, its tone blithe, as if he were participating in a game.

"His name is Sabahattin Sans-Serif. He is a special agent of the Millî Emniyet Hizmeti. If you shoot him, my dear Klosterheim, you will incite an incident with the Turkish government. As things currently stand for Germany, it is unlikely to be a development that your exalted leader would welcome."

The major hesitated, then lowered his weapon. He moistened his lips with his tongue, then addressed the albino.

"Take off your hat and those spectacles."

Zenith complied.

"Gott im Himmel!" Klosterheim exclaimed. "I have won two von Beks in a single throw. And one of the accursed albino breed, no less."

Zenith put a little brown cigarette to his lips and drew on it. He puffed fragrant smoke out through his nostrils and regarded the major as if he were a vaguely interesting plant. His stance relaxed, his attitude insouciant, he appeared utterly unconcerned.

Finally, after a pause so unnaturally long that Klosterheim's men had started to cast glances at each another, the albino drawled, "Not merely a von Bek, my dear Klosterheim. If you wish to address me, you may call me Zenith."

Klosterheim blinked. "And," he said quietly, "who or what is Zenith?"

The albino shrugged.

"Who, just that. As to what—in some countries, I am called a thief."

Klosterheim narrowed his eyes. "A thief in company with Sir Seaton Begg? Then you are his prisoner?"

Zenith offered a very slight smile. "That, I think, would be the most obvious explanation."

A flash of lightning turned the albino's pink eyes ruby red. In that split second, he seemed a supernatural being, and Klosterheim flinched back a step.

Then, as thunder roared, the rain suddenly came down in a solid sheet, swept to a steep angle by screaming wind.

Klosterheim gestured toward the small, Romanesque building by the lorry.

"In there, the four of you, quick march!"

They obeyed, glad to get out of the storm, which in the time it took to duck inside, had already soaked them to the skin.

To Begg's surprise, the premises turned out to be a former county police station and gaol. Places like this served villages for miles around, and were used to hold offenders from the region before their subsequent removal to the nearest city. This one, however, was now superseded by more recent constructions in bigger and less-isolated settlements. He could see at a glance that its stone walls were ancient and that it lacked plumbing and electricity.

Currently, it was used as a storage shed, with boxes and buckets of grain stacked to one side. The old holding cell was empty, separated from the main room by thick floor-to-ceiling iron bars, with an inset door.

A single paraffin lamp provided the only illumination.

Klosterheim stood back as five Greenshirts pushed Begg, Zenith, von Bek, and Sans-Serif into the cell. The door clanged shut. The lock clicked.

"I have twenty men of the Iron Guard in this village," he declared. "You cannot escape. Soon, Fräulein Pym will restore the Temple of Arioch. She will then decide what is to be done with you. I predict that your blood will redden its altar." He faced Ulric von Bek. "But not yours. You are mine, von Bek, and will be held in custody until the Sachsenburg camp is completed. There, you will serve as an example to any who think to oppose Chancellor Hitler."

He gestured for his men to precede him out of the station. At the door, he turned back and added, "When this storm has passed, I shall fill the silence that follows with gunfire. The *zigeuner* filth that brought you here? You shall listen to every last one of them executed."

He departed.

Sans-Serif staggered forward, clutched the bars, and shrieked, "Klosterheim!"

Thunder vibrated the walls.

The Turk moaned and slid down to his knees.

Begg tested the lock. Had it been well-oiled, he might have picked it, but it was old, stiff, and resistant.

He kicked at the walls. Rotten stone!

"I shouldn't waste your strength, my friend," Zenith murmured. "We might scrape through it, but it would take too much time."

The detective ignored the advice. He crossed to the small, high barred window, took out his pipe tampering tool, and with its little blade, began to hack away.

Hours later, he had made barely any progress at all.

He was thirsty, hungry, and filled with despair.

The rain stopped.

The thunder ceased.

At sunset, the shooting began.

CHAPTER 27

The Pass

The first loud report was accompanied by a shouted protest and an engine coughing into life. More shots cracked and echoed. A vehicle accelerated and, amid increasing gunfire, was driven around the old police station to the back.

The village erupted with the clamour of battle.

Ulric von Bek cried out, "What the blazes is happening?"

"Nothing that Klosterheim has planned, I'll venture," answered Sir Seaton Begg. He turned, hearing a clang at the window, and saw black-gloved hands threading a chain through the bars. Beyond them, a broad-brimmed hat and a black domino mask. A horse's quiet snicker explained the individual's elevation.

A whisper. "Stand well back."

The detective motioned for his companions to squeeze into the corners where the bars joined the walls. Zenith met his eyes, his own glinting red. The albino loved nothing more than the promise of action, of imminent danger. Only then did his ennui abate, only then were the opium cigarettes left untouched.

Outside, the din increased. The engine roared. With startling abruptness, the window and the ancient stone wall around it jerked outward with a deafening crash. Part of the roof fell in. Stone thudded and rattled, and for a moment, the entire scene vanished beneath a cloud of dust. Then, out of the thinning haze, made orange by the light of the paraffin lamp, a pile of rubble materialised.

"Come on!" Begg commanded.

The four prisoners clambered to freedom.

The rain had abated, but low storm clouds still concealed the moon and stars. In the gloom, Klosterheim's lorry was visible just ahead, the chain trailing. The black cloaked figure jumped down from its cabin, ran across to a magnificent Andalusian stallion, and swung up into the saddle. All the while, from the street at the front of the half-wrecked station, gunfire continued to pop and crackle.

The rider cantered over, took four rifles from a sling, and handed them down.

"Nicely done, Miss Damm," said Begg.

Violet Damm's gapped teeth gleamed beneath her mask. An exhilarated grin, for like Zenith, she loved to be in the thick of it.

"I've been keeping an eye on you." She passed down a box of ammunition. "I thought it wise to hold myself in reserve until reinforcements were required."

"Splendid!" Begg declared.

She turned her head a little and offered a nod to the albino. "We meet again, Count Zodiac."

"Monsieur Zenith today, Miss Damm," he returned graciously. "I am surprised but delighted to renew our acquaintance. Not since Petrograd, I think? The February Revolution?"

"Petrograd?" she responded. "Ah, you remember?"

"Not very well. I know only that we were introduced there. I do not recall the circumstances."

"That does not surprise me. Yes, it is true. We met for the first time in that city and at that time, but I'll confess, since then, I have not been wholly absent from your affairs. There was the occasion when you stole the blueprints for the Whittle Turbocompressor."

"They turned out to be a forgery."

"And the Ripley diamonds."

"Which I subsequently discovered to be paste."

"And your abduction of Prince Matabusi."

"I kidnapped a mannequin."

"Those failures, and others, were my doing, dear friend."

He bowed. "Marvellous! I congratulate you. You have been an invisible but keenly felt thorn in my side."

She gave an acknowledging bob. "The Sisterhood of Solitude is always fascinated by your various—shall we say—*exploits*."

The albino regarded her, his expression inscrutable.

Von Bek cleared his throat. "We are all glad to see you, Miss Damm, but might we save the exchange of pleasantries until later? The raging battle behind us is hardly conducive. What is the state of play?"

"All fire and fury, gentlemen! Under cover of the storm, I unloaded the rifles hidden in the king's wagon, then incapacitated the men guarding the school, and distributed the weapons among the Gypsies. The enemy is engaged, as you can hear."

Begg gave a single, decisive clap. "Then we must join the fray."

"No," she countered. "I shall assist Lakatos and his people. We will keep Klosterheim occupied while you forge ahead. You must hurry."

"But—"

She cut him short, speaking urgently. "No! Listen! The pattern in time must be properly arranged. I insist that you get going immediately. It is vital. And for pity's sake, do not forget that poor Taffy Sinclair's life is in your hands."

With that, she lifted her rifle, kicked her heels, and sent her charger careening around the corner into the main street.

"Sisterhood of Solitude?" Zenith murmured. "I take it all is more than it appears?"

Begg made no reply.

"Forgive me," Sans-Serif announced. "But I must also remain here to fight. This may come as a surprise, but there is a woman—"

Ulric von Bek grinned. "Go and defend your Esmeralda, friend."

"You know of our—?"

"I know."

"And I," said Begg.

"All Transylvania, I should wager," added Zenith.

"Sans-Serif," said Begg. "Stay safe. I would not like to lose you."

The special agent hesitated, then extended a hand. "It is a shame you are not a Turk."

"Indeed so," agreed Begg. He gripped the hand, patted the back of it, and muttered, "Get to work!"

Sans-Serif nodded to von Bek and Zenith, then slipped away.

Begg turned to the albino. "You can lead us, even in this darkness?"

"I can," Zenith replied. "Follow."

Keeping low, the three men sidled along the rear of the street-facing buildings. Twice, stray bullets whistled past, perilously close.

The rifle-fire receded behind them. They came to the last of the village's outlying houses and followed the road. It soon became little more than a dirt track. Zenith, in front of Begg, was barely discernible, despite his white hair and skin.

The wind tugged at their clothes. Thunder continued to grumble. The clouds, so low they seemed only just out of arm's reach, occasionally flared with nearby lightning.

For half an hour, they trekked up an increasingly steep incline. Listening to the echoing shots, Begg supposed the combatants had hunkered down in the houses. He imagined terrified homeowners pressed into corners, shielding their children, unable to comprehend these terrible events in their isolated little community.

"Here," said Zenith, indicating a fang-shaped rock towering twenty feet into the air beside the path. "Keep the wind off me, will you? I have to light a match."

He moved to the side of the rock. Begg stood to shield him. The albino struck a flame and thrust it quickly into an opening.

"Good!" he exclaimed. "There's a supply."

He pulled out a brand, a three-foot-long cut branch with an oil-soaked cloth wrapped around one end. He handed it to the detective, drew out another, which he gave to von Bek, then a third for himself.

When the brands were all burning, sputtering and sparking with every gust, he lowered his own to illuminate a barely discernible trail that diverged from the path at right angles, snaking steeply upward.

"This is the way," he said. "Sir Seaton, I must remind you that you have sworn to never speak of—"

Crack!

A bullet smacked against the rock, inches from his head, and shrieked away in ricochet.

"Don't you move!" a familiar voice yelled. "I have the woman."

A little way down the slope, a battery torch snapped on. By its light, they saw Violet Damm, her hat and mask gone, her hands bound behind her, her arms gripped by two legionnaires.

Major Johannes Klosterheim held a pistol to her head.

"I'm sorry," she called. "They shot my horse from under me. My foot got trapped when the animal fell."

"Herr Begg," the German called. "I made a deal with Fräulein Pym. I would hamper your progress, and in return, she would give me von Bek. My interest is in him, not in you or in her primitive ritual. I have much work to do in Germany. I cannot waste any more time in this godforsaken country. So, I propose a simple exchange. Violet Damm for the man who stands beside you."

After a brief silence, Begg responded.

"Major, Miss Damm works for the British Secret Service. Like all agents, she understands that circumstances may arise wherein her life is forfeit, and that there are certain principles for which she must be prepared to die. Am I correct, Miss Damm?"

"You are," she responded. "When this dog Klosterheim kills me, it will be the three of you against the three of them. You hold the higher ground, and I have seen you in action. I know these men will die. Farewell, my dear Sir Seaton Begg! It has been enormous fun!" She pressed the side of her head against the muzzle of Klosterheim's pistol and murmured to him, "I am ready, you devil. Pull your damned trigger."

He snarled, "You are bluffing."

"Don't be a fool. Get on with it."

Von Bek took one pace forward. "Wait!"

"Von Bek—" Begg snapped.

The man from Wäldenstein silenced him with a raised hand. "What are your terms, Klosterheim?"

"The Britisher is a man of his word, *nein*?"

"I am," Begg answered.

"And the albino?"

"If I give it," Zenith called, "you may depend on it."

"Then I say this. Von Bek will walk to me, the woman will walk to you. If you make any unexpected move, we shall open fire. When we have von Bek, you will allow us to leave unmolested. You will not follow. When we reach the village, I will call for my men to cease fire and retreat. We will depart in the truck with our prisoner. Whatever of your *zigeuner* friends remain will be allowed to go on living. In the meantime, if you are foolish enough to do so, you can continue to the Temple of Arioch and meet your deaths there."

"What will become of von Bek?" Begg asked.

"He will be detained until the Sachsenburg camp is built, then incarcerated there."

"Not executed?"

"And made a martyr? That would not suit me at all."

Von Bek said, "I agree to the terms."

"Don't be an idiot!" Violet Damm shouted.

Zenith placed a hand on his cousin's arm. "Ulric, this will not go well for you. Would it not be better to—"

Von Bek wheeled to face him. "You know the von Beks. You know we are fated to do the Devil's work. This is a part of it. I cannot tell you how, but I have a certainty that—" He pointed at the Germans. "That my destiny lies in that direction. I must go, Monsieur Zenith. I cannot allow Miss Damm to die in the hope that I might live. What kind of man would do such a thing?"

In the flickering light of the windblown brands, Zenith's ruby eyes expressed a great internal struggle.

Von Bek added, "There is no time for debate. Mr. Begg's assistant, Sinclair, is in dire peril. Allow me to give myself, that a life might be saved."

Zenith's jaw muscles flexed, then he nodded, gripped von Bek's hand, and took a step back.

He shouted, "Klosterheim, my word is given."

In a low voice, Begg said, "There is still a chance. When you reach the village, Sans-Serif and Lakatos might—"

Von Bek smiled. "Perhaps, Mr. Begg, but I have a feeling that providence will deem it otherwise. Now, please, your mission—"

They shook hands.

The detective called to the major, "You have mine, too, but we shall keep you covered. If you intend any trickery, know that you will be the first to fall. Release her."

Von Bek handed his rifle and brand to Zenith and started down the slope. Violet Damm came toward him.

As they passed each other, she said, "You are being extraordinarily reckless. Do not for an instant trust Klosterheim to honour the deal. At the first opportunity, kill him."

"I know him better than anyone, Miss Damm," he said, "and I shall."

She continued up the slope to Begg and Zenith.

Klosterheim called out, "I would meet you again, Herr Begg. However, I am afraid it will be impossible. The pleasure of taking your life goes to Vera Pym. Spare me a thought when she plunges a sacrificial dagger into your heart."

With that, the major backed away, his men dragging von Bek. They descended along the track and were swallowed into the gloom.

Zenith, noting the expression on her face, said, "Do not feel bad, Miss Damm. The story of the von Beks and the Klosterheims began three hundred years ago and will probably continue for three hundred more. You will be at best a short footnote in that long saga."

Begg got to work on her bonds. "Where Klosterheim is concerned, Monsieur Zenith, you and von Bek appear peculiarly fatalistic."

The albino shrugged. "That family is driven by a greater-than-human destiny. They are bound to it and can never be free."

Begg hissed through his teeth. "This entire affair is far too replete with superstition for my taste."

Damm's bonds fell away. She picked up von Bek's abandoned brand and rifle. Begg gestured for Zenith, then the woman, to precede him along the precipitous path. As they climbed, he mused, "The major seemed sincere in his intention to imprison our friend. That gives us some cause for hope. Once we have dealt with La Pym, I shall embark on an undercover mission into Germany. Come what may, I mean to rescue Herr—"

"You will not get the opportunity," Zenith interrupted. "Circumstances will work against you."[*]

"Then, I shall work against circumstances."

"You will fail."

Sucking at the thin mountain air, their leg muscles straining, they ascended.

Begg felt wretched. They had lost von Bek without a struggle. Should he have whipped up his rifle and tried for a headshot? Angrily, he pushed the notion aside. There was every chance, in such darkness, that he would have hit Damm instead of Klosterheim.

---

[*] Ulric von Bek's story is continued in *The Dragon in the Sword* by Michael Moorcock (1986).

The wind began to shred the clouds, so that every few minutes the stars and moon shone through, making the landscape suddenly bright. Their brands' flames spluttered, near horizontal. Black shadows writhed around outcrops and boulders. Patches of snow glittered. It was bitterly cold.

Zenith led the way into a high and tightly narrow mountain pass, with sheer walls of naked rock to either side. The wind moaned, whistled, and howled through it.

The trio trudged on. Begg put his arm around Damm and walked with her hugged close, giving her his body heat. He could feel her trembling violently. She was strong, but she could not endure such conditions for much longer. At any moment, she could collapse. So might he.

Then, below the clamorous wind, they heard another sound.

"An avalanche?" Damm suggested, through chattering teeth.

"No," the detective responded. "That's a waterfall."

Zenith guided them around a sharp angle, and there it was, a fantastic column of water, sparkling silver in the moonlight, appearing to fall all the way from Heaven to Hell.

They found it impossible to see from where it originated. It poured directly out of mountain-clinging cloud. To what depth it descended could not be ascertained. It apparently cascaded straight through solid rock.

It roared relentlessly down, wall to wall, preventing any further progress. From here, Begg saw nowhere to go except back.

Then, he looked again.

Something was wrong. It was difficult to make out in the shifting gloom, but parts of the water appeared somehow static, hanging in midair while the torrent flowed around them.

He stepped away from Violet Damm, raised his brand, and

moved closer to the cataract. She accompanied him, frowning, puzzled. Zenith hung back, watching them, a slight smile playing on his lips.

Abruptly, in a single step, the illusion broke. Begg and Damm had reached a position where perception and reality clicked into agreement.

The narrow pass twisted to the right, and there, just beyond the turn, was the waterfall, dropping into a well, eroded over the course of millennia.

In front of them, what they had initially taken for the deluge was, in fact, a tremendously wide, flat, and polished vein of pure, shimmering silver.

From the ground it rose vertically as far as could be seen, a vast, unlikely mirror, with just a few irregularities here and there. It was these that had caught Begg's analytical eye, for while the greater part of the vein's surface was precisely angled to reflect the fall, making it appear to block the pass, the inconsistencies in its surface were not.

"It's phenomenal!" Damm shouted over the din of the water and the wind.

"Even more so," Zenith responded, "in being entirely natural."

"Geologists would be beside themselves!" Begg exclaimed.

"Much as, from where you are currently standing, the waterfall appears to flow beside itself, eh, Sir Seaton?" Zenith quipped. "Do you see how the metal has luminescence? This type of silver is known as 'Argint Lunar' and can be found nowhere else in the world. It is said to add the light of other realms to whatever it reflects."

"It is extraordinary. This is the only path to Lamaneagra? No wonder the province is virtually unheard of. The moment one sees the reflection, the natural inclination is to give up and turn back."

"We do not have far to go now. The path runs behind the fall. Tread carefully. If you slip, you'll be swept into the netherworld."

Begg and Damm followed the albino. Such was the cacophony, that further conversation, even shouted, was impossible.

Their backs pressed against the wet rock, they inched along, with the water racing past the end of their noses. The brands held by the men went out. Violet Damm's was knocked from her hand. To their almost childlike wonder, they were not immediately plunged into darkness. A further marvel revealed! As they emerged beyond the fall, they found that the silver-veined passage, now no wider than an Istanbul alleyway, glinted with the metal's uncanny luminescence.

Displaying her gappy grin, Damm put her lips to Zenith's ear. "I now know your secret, m'sieu. This is Fairy Land and you are King Oberon."

Soaked through and freezing, they pushed on.

The waterfall became a steady, diminishing roar behind them. The wind, however, screeched and buffeted, tearing along the rocky corridor at near hurricane speed.

Damm walked with her rifle slung over her shoulder by its strap, her hands pressed to her ears.

Abruptly, they stumbled out onto a wide shelf of rock overlooking a great, mountain-bordered basin. The clouds were by now in tatters, nearly all swept southward, exposing a dense river of dazzling stars—the Milky Way—bisected the dome of night, the half moon set in it like a jewel in a belt.

Threads of light adorned the sides of the snowcapped mountains. Begg peered at them, perplexed, before it registered that they were streams in which the starlight reflected. Around them, on the lower gradients, the vague shapes of a once-cultivated land could be discerned, the rough lines of long-overgrown fields, the near washed away ribbons of dirt roads.

From the middle of the bowl and ascending the southern slopes, a medium-sized town sprawled, most of its buildings in ruins, the marks of fire blackening its highest reaches. And, above the topmost houses, a castle, such as Begg and Damm had never imagined, let alone seen.

Though fire had marred its walls, and parts of it had collapsed, it was an edifice of staggering, ethereal beauty. Its many slender towers soared into the air, ragged banners still fluttering above them. The many crenelations were tall and narrow, the arrow-loops high slits with cloverlike openings at their tops. There were ramps and bridges and walkways. Begg had the impression of many vivid colours, though these were all robbed of vibrancy by the quality of the light.

Delicate and otherworldly, the stronghold did not resemble anything built by human hands.

"Castle Arioch," said Zenith. "In the oldest legends of my people, sometimes called Kaneloon."

He added, so quietly that it was lost in the wind, "Home."

CHAPTER 28

Lamaneagra

They picked their way carefully down toward the town. Begg noted that the air grew noticeably warmer.

Zenith pointed toward the middle of the circular valley. "Hot springs and bubbling mud, plenty of geothermal activity. The Ciomadul volcano is not many miles distant. Our land, well served by the rocks beneath it, is a part of that mostly dormant chain."

They followed an overgrown road past a decrepit wooden farmhouse, its thatched roof sagging over rotting planks. A weed-tangled path led from the road to the front door. Stark in the moonlight, a human ribcage lay amid the tendrils and leaves.

They saw many more bones as they drew closer to the town. The remains told the story of true genocide. Not a human soul had survived to bury the dead. Empty eye sockets declared outrage at all they had witnessed. Naked teeth grinned their last moments of terror.

Now, the terrible retribution meted out to the traitorous Tzigane, Black Djordji, felt just.

What resistance had these peasants and artisans offered their killers? There were no signs of fighting, only of the indiscriminate and wholesale slaughter of innocents.

Begg had envisaged hundreds killed. He was wrong. Thousands had died. He breathed the dust of the wronged, the entire population of this peaceful principality, which had done nothing save trade amicably with the Tziganes and preserve a chosen way of life.

The depth of Colonel Simeon Vassilionu's crime was inconceivable. Even with the evidence all around him, and despite the cruelties and horrors he had witnessed in his long career, Begg struggled with the idea that one man could order a massacre of such horrifying scale.

They reached the town's outskirts and moved along the cobbled north–south road, visible beneath invasive vegetation. To either side, houses were burnt-out shells. Those that still stood were riddled with bullet holes. Furniture and belongings had been dragged into the street and smashed. Everywhere was littered with rubble and wood fragments. Among the debris, items of solid, shimmering, Argint Lunar. Candlesticks, brooches, bracelets, belt buckles, cups, bowls—a treasure trove, scattered on the ground.

For a decade and a half, time and the elements had gnawed at the ruins and remains. Yet to the metatemporal detective, so proficient at building a clear picture of events from the clues left behind, the death and destruction might have occurred yesterday. Begg observed how this was the skull of a man battered to death with a rifle butt; that of a woman shot through the head; here, the ribs of a bayoneted child.

He fought his nausea, his desire to turn away from all this and accept any account of it but the truth. It was too blatant, with no vestige of shame, no attempt to cover the crime.

They navigated past wrecked carts and wagons, finding it impossible to take more than three or four steps without their boots crunching down onto shards of bone or kicking against spent cartridges.

Though the distant wind still soughed, they had an overwhelming sense of silence, an almost supernatural suspension of sound, as if existence itself held its breath.

Their presence, simply because they were living, was profane.

"I can't bear it," Damm whispered huskily. She glanced at a child's skull. Her eyes brimmed with tears. "My heart will break."

"This atrocity," Zenith said quietly, "was committed by just twenty-five men."

"Twenty-five!" Begg exclaimed. "How is that possible? Twenty-five men could not have—"

"In the winter of 1921, one of those twenty-five soldiers, Corporal Laurentiu Barbu, approached me and asked for protection."

Begg stumbled to a halt and gaped at the albino. "He—?"

Zenith gave a grim smile. "The creature had no idea who I was—who I am."

"Protection from—?" asked Damm.

"By then," said Zenith, "only ten of the twenty-five remained. The rest, murdered, assassinated, one by one, by their former commander."

"He was covering his tracks?" Damm folded her arms as if against a sudden chill.

"More than that, Miss Damm."

Begg murmured, "The silver."

"Quite so," agreed Zenith. "This is what Barbu told me—"

As they turned right, taking a road winding up through the dreadful necropolis to the ethereal castle, the albino gave his account.

"Guided by the traitorous Black Djordji, Vassilionu led his men through the pass. His orders were straightforward. He was to inform the *voivode* that this province now lay within Roumanian borders and would be subject to Roumanian law. Djordji, however, had already told the colonel of the mirror in the pass, and of the mines"—Zenith pointed to the north—"which, in daylight, are visible from here, at the base of the tallest of the northern mountains."

"Stop!" Begg hissed. "I hear something!"

For a minute, they stood and listened. From afar, as if from deep underground, a strange music throbbed and sobbed and pounded. It sounded like agony, like vocal cords forcibly stretched to reach notes of which no human should be capable. Not one pain-racked soul, but a hundred, singing all the sorrow and loss of centuries.

"The Choir of Arioch," Zenith murmured.

"They are being tortured!" Damm exclaimed.

Zenith raised a pale hand. "There is no *they*, Miss Damm. The choir is an arrangement of natural shafts and tunnels leading from the mountainside down to the temple, itself a cave. When the wind blows in a certain direction, it enters those rock passages and causes the music you hear. A strange and remarkable phenomenon. It very rarely occurs, and is said to augur Arioch's increased interest in the mortal realm."

A large, ruined building blocked their way. For some unidentifiable reason, its rubble crawled with small black beetles. In the moonlight, it seemed the shadows themselves were writhing, the pile of shattered stone a living, shapeless mass.

They picked their way around it and continued on.

"Vassilionu came here seeking to enrich himself, I suppose?" suggested Begg.

"Avaricious to the point of insanity," Zenith confirmed. "He armed his men with Maxim guns, repeating rifles, pistols, hand grenades, and canisters of chlorine gas. They marched out of the pass and descended onto the town. All wore gas masks. To the Lamaneagrans, they must have resembled hellish demons. That is what they were! The breeze was in their favour. The yellow gas billowed ahead of them through the streets. People dropped dead by the hundreds before they even realised they were under attack. Then came the bullets, bayonets, and bombs. They had no chance."

"Monsieur Zenith," Violet Damm whispered. "I am so sorry. It is awful beyond words. That any man could be responsible for all this!"

"Oh," the albino answered in a brittle tone. "Vassilionu's iniquities didn't stop here. When he and his men thought everyone dead—"

"Your father?" Begg interjected. "The *voivode*?"

"Vassilionu had torn the *Sigiliul Tutorelui*—the Guardian's Seal—from Sadric's finger, shot him, and left him to die. My father crawled into the secret Chamber of the Sword and was still living, guarding the *Salut Christi* to his last breath. I was at that hour approaching through the pass. By the time I reached the waterfall, the colonel and his men were looting as much silver as they could carry."

"How did you get past them?" Damm asked.

"By keeping my distance. Rather than descending, I skirted around the edge of the basin, remaining high on the mountain slopes. I reached the castle and was inside it when the Roumanians departed."

The bizarre music of Arioch's tormented choir was clearer now.

"As you know, I delivered the *Salut Christi* to the von Beks in Wäldenstein, then pursued Vassilionu to England. I was singularly unsuccessful in finding him."

"But, eventually, this corporal, Laurentiu Barbu, came forward," said Begg.

"Yes."

They were by now halfway up to the castle, bones, flattened bullets, and shell casings everywhere. The detective imagined the panic, a stampede as people fled the invaders, seeking the safety of the stronghold.

"All twenty-five men had made small fortunes from their looted silver," the albino continued. "In return for their silence, Vassilionu promised more. He spoke of establishing a mining company, each man with an equal share in it. Instead, he murdered them. Corporal Barbu had, through his own criminal involvements, heard of me. He made contact, sought an interview, and I granted it. He asked me to save him from the colonel."

Damm said, "Your response, m'sieu?"

"I regret to say that I lost control and shot him through the heart." Zenith sighed. "I had learned sufficient, however, to lead me to Vassilionu. I killed him the following year, and regained, as you know, the *Sigiliul Tutorelui*. There were then just eight of the men remaining. Six months later, none."

"You killed them, too?" asked Begg.

He received no answer.

"There are legal means by which—"

"Say nothing of that, Sir Seaton Begg!" Zenith snapped. "Look around you. No word of the law you keep was ever written for this. There can never be justice, only cold, merciless vengeance. I shall never—*down*!"

Something tugged hard at Begg's collar. Zenith crashed into him and sent him to the ground. Violet Damm fell on top, dragged by the albino.

The crack of a shot echoed.

"Sniper!" Zenith hauled his companions into the shelter of a low wall. "I saw movement on a tower—the second from the right."

Begg raised his head for a second. He ducked back. A bullet whined past, splintering the rotten wood of an overturned wagon.

"La Pym has a sharpshooter with her," he said. "A dwarf. 'Sureshot' Orville Thott. He is clearly on sentry duty."

Zenith turned to the woman. "Miss Damm, to rescue Doctor Sinclair, there are things that Sir Seaton must see. He already knows that, to protect those secrets, I shall later have to kill him. We are currently under truce." He addressed the detective: "Until we are both back in England?"

"Agreed," Begg responded.

"I have no taste for killing women, even those as dangerous to me as you have proven to be. Therefore, Sir Seaton and I must proceed alone. You will, I hope, provide a distraction." He nodded toward the north. "I suggest you move slowly and cautiously in that direction, taking frequent potshots at our friend on the tower. At best, you will hit him. At worst, he will hit you. Fervently, I hope for the first and not the second."

He handed her his spare ammunition. Begg did likewise.

If Violet Damm could help save Taffy by accepting a death sentence from Zenith, she would have taken it without hesitation. However, she was experienced enough to see the sense of the albino's plan, and was compelled to simply murmur, "Good luck."

She crawled away.

A minute later, they heard her rifle bark. The answering crack came immediately.

"Missed!" she called, for their benefit.

Her next shot sounded from a little farther off.

They waited for five more reports, by which time she was exchanging fire a good distance away. Then, staying low, they zigzagged along the road from wrecked cart to wrecked cart, doorway to doorway, wall to wall.

The human remains lay in even greater profusion. Zenith's face could not possibly be any whiter in the moonlight.

An avenging spirit, eyes ruby fire, he flitted through the shadows, Begg on his heels.

The entrance to the castle came into view. Huge wooden doors, set between a barbican of thick granite, had once secured it. Only one remained, half-shattered and hanging from a single hinge. Four of Arioch's eight arrows, worked in iron, held it together.

They passed from Sureshot Thott's line of sight, and cautiously crossed the bailey. From far above, the sniper's Enfield cracked again and again. Violet Damm was keeping him distracted.

The gunfire, together with the discordant tones of Arioch's choir, did much to cover their crunching footsteps. They found it impossible to walk quietly, treading a carpet of bones, leaving deep footprints in the dust.

They reached the keep. Cautiously, the two men passed under a doorless arch. Faint light streamed through high slit windows, but did little to illuminate the vast interior.

Zenith knew where he was going. Blindly, Begg followed. Vaguely aware of a high ceiling, he could just make out a multitude of slender columns and the toppled ruins of marble statues. Mainly, he could see only what passed within arm's reach—smashed furniture and the ubiquitous dead.

When they reached a much smaller arch, Zenith struck a match. The flame illuminated the top of a spiral stone staircase. They descended.

The choir now sang a throbbing, primordial dirge. Begg could barely credit that wind blowing through flues, conduits, and ancient lava tubes could be responsible for such notes. Some resembled the high-pitched night song of wolves. Others reverberated, a deep bass vibrating through the floor. Now, too, he could discern a rhythmic distant chanting. That, surely, was human!

The match burned out. Zenith struck another.

He used up four more before they stepped out onto flat flagstones. The albino uttered a quiet exclamation and crossed to a wall where a lamp hung from a bracket. He lifted it down and lit the wick within. It gave surprisingly strong light.

"It is unlikely that she will have posted guards in this part of the castle," he said. "We are safe enough."

Begg gave an affirmative grunt. He was disturbed by the ghastly expression on his companion's chalk-white features. Zenith's skin glittered with perspiration. His eyes appeared fixed, as if they could no longer move in their sockets. His lips, drawn tight, made his mouth a bloodless gash. He moved stiffly and breathed rapidly.

"M'sieu," Begg said softly. "If you tell me the way, I can proceed alone."

The responding dry chuckle might have been a death rattle.

"I have an obligation."

"I will be your agent."

Zenith looked at him. Begg saw abject horror.

"No," the albino rasped. "It must be me. I must end it."

End what? Begg wondered. *The long quest for vengeance?* He sensed his companion meant something else.

"Come," Zenith said. "It is not far."

He led the way to a room, once a spectacular library, now black with soot and ankle-deep in ash, not even ransacked, just utterly despoiled.

Through a doorway, along a corridor of vandalised friezes, they found a medium-sized chamber containing a broken printing press of medieval design. Through to another, in which what appeared to be ceremonial robes had once hung, now on the floor, rat-chewed and rotted.

Zenith stopped by a naked wall.

"There is a door," he said. "Can you see it?"

Begg frowned, moved closer, and scrutinised the stone.

"No."

"Yet it is there. It opens onto the Chamber of the Sword. On the other side of that room, another secret door gives access to a corridor, which leads from a different part of the castle to the Temple of Arioch."

"That is the way Vera Pym and her gang went?"

"It is the only route she could have found. There will be sentries, but by going through the Chamber of the Sword, we should emerge a good distance behind them."

"Very well." Begg waited, then added, "Shall we proceed?"

Zenith didn't respond. He was staring at the wall. Sweat was dripping from his face.

"My friend," said Begg. "I understand that this is difficult for you, but Doctor Sinclair is—"

Zenith turned to him. Half his face glowed yellow in the trembling lamplight, the other half in black shadow. His crimson eyes were unnaturally wide.

"Begg—" he whispered. "The chamber. *My father is still in there!*"

CHAPTER 29
The Temple of Arioch

"Open the door," said Begg. "I shall go in alone." He crossed to a pile of ceremonial robes and picked them up. Of rich silk, samite, and jewelled inlays, they were now stiff, dusty, and crumbling.

A grisly stain on the floor, black in the lamplight, spoke of blood splattering, then smearing over the flagstones. The course of that frightful trail vanished into a dark opening in the wall. Zenith had quietly employed a hidden lever and caused the concealed door to silently swing open.

Begg read the floor. Colonel Vassilionu bayoneted Zenith's father out here. After he departed—there, the bloody footprints—his victim, bleeding to death, dragged himself into the secret chamber containing the *Salut Christi*, to die with it in his hands.

Now, Zenith stood with his back to that room. With a shaking hand, he passed the lamp to Begg. "I . . . cannot."

"Wait here," said the detective.

He stepped through the cleverly disguised door, entering one end of a long, narrow, arched space. It was unfurnished. Halfway along its length, engraved in the stone wall to his right, the Eight Arrows of Arioch. Opposite them, a deep alcove. On the floor beneath it, a corpse.

Begg moved forward.

Over the years, animals and the elements had disturbed the dead in the town and accessible parts of the castle. In this sealed chamber, however, with its cold, dry atmosphere, nothing had touched the body, and it was complete. It had mummified.

Zenith's father, Voivode Sadric of Lamaneagra, High Priest of Arioch and Guardian of the *Salut Christi*, died in a pool of blood.

From the chest down, blackened gore caked his yellowed robes. Clawed over his chest, his hands tightly clutched something that was no longer there. Begg did not doubt that the *Salut Christi* would fit perfectly into that stiff grasp.

The broken forefinger of the right hand stuck out at a horrible angle. Colonel Vassilionu's doing. He had brutally wrenched the Guardian's Seal from it.

On the sticklike wrists, bangles of Argint Lunar silver. Fallen beside the wizened head, a circlet of the same precious metal. Symbols of an office scorned, of a faith kept for thousands of years, and obliterated in a vicious instant.

"I see you, Simeon Vassilionu," Begg hissed in ill-restrained fury.

He examined the clear, full prints of someone who had knelt in the dying man's blood, remaining there for some time before walking unsteadily away. The size of the feet and shape of the stride matched Zenith's. They repeated the albino's account—how his father had died in his arms, how he had wrested the chalice from that protective grasp.

Begg leaned over the cadaver and scrutinised its desiccated features. Though the eyes had fallen in, and the skin stretched tightly over the skull, the face had apparently been a handsome one in life. Even in its current state, he could detect Zenith in the same exquisitely tapered features, the same strong jawline.

The expression, though, was one of terrible suffering and profound despair.

Silently, Begg made a vow. "If we survive this night, father of thy people, father of my enemy, father of my friend, we shall create for thee a place to rest."

He draped the rotting robes of office over the corpse, arranging them to conceal it completely. Then he looked toward the doorway and called softly, "Monsieur."

After a moment, Zenith entered. He glanced at the mound of cloth, swallowed, then directed his gaze at Begg.

"Is he—?"

"Nothing has disturbed the corpse."

For a second, it appeared that Zenith's legs would buckle. Then he straightened, pulled his shoulders back, smoothed his milk-white hair, and lifted his chin a little.

The detective rose from his crouch. Zenith took the lamp from him and, in its light, studied his face.

Despite Begg's acute powers of observation and deduction, he could not tell what the albino was thinking, could see only that immense emotions were at play.

Then Zenith moved the lamp to direct its light past him, and said, "Behold, Sir Seaton Begg, the black sword, the name of which must never be spoken."

Begg wheeled, uttered a cry of amazement, and staggered back a step.

He faced an enormous unsheathed Zweihänder broadsword, hanging point downward in the alcove, its straight crosspieces resting on a bracket. From the red gemstone in its hilt to the lethal point, it was about five feet long, and forged from a black iron. However, as Begg examined it more closely, he became uncertain. There was a peculiar quality about the metal. It was so intensely black that it appeared to suck the lamplight from the air, darkening the surrounding atmosphere in a manner that felt wholly alien and uncanny.

There were grotesque runes carved along the length of the enormous blade. They vaguely resembled Brythonic script, but appeared much older. When he moved his head, inky hues glimmered in their carved recesses, but were gone before he could name them. Bloodreds and purples, perhaps.

These observations came after the first overpowering impression, so intense, it had caused his initial recoil, the instinct to step away.

The sword was alive.

"Ridiculous!" he muttered to himself.

"Yes," Zenith agreed, "but palpable, isn't it?"

"You feel it, too?" Begg asked. "A living—"

"Malevolence? A sense of atavistic, unhuman malice? Yes, my friend, I feel it. So has everyone who has ever seen the blade. A strange phenomenon, no?"

"Very."

"There is a legend, of course. A demon inhabits the blade. My sorcerous ancestor, known as the Kinslayer, brought the weapon to this world. Only the albinos in our family line have ever been able to carry it with any measure of safety—and even that illusory."

Begg raised an eyebrow.

Zenith gave a quick, wolfish smile. "All nonsense, of course. I believe it was forged from the metal of a fallen meteorite and that the evil emanating from it is simply a form of radiation to which, perhaps, albino blood is somehow immune." He shrugged. "It's as good an explanation as any. Scientific rather than supernatural."

He turned from the alcove. "We are wasting time. The ceremony might have already begun."

Keeping his eyes averted from the corpse, Zenith moved around it, striding to the far end of the chamber. Putting his back to Begg to conceal what he was doing with his hands, he gave attention to a particular area of the wall. Beside him, stonework silently swung inward. The "choir music" boomed out, so loud they both winced. Howls and roars, whines and deep rumbles. *Whale song,* Begg thought. *If the whales are experiencing intolerable anguish.*

The sounds came on a breeze laden with a mélange of powerful odours—opium predominating. The moment Begg breathed it in, his senses reeled.

"Grief!" he exclaimed, nearly stumbling. "The stench!"

They moved into a corridor, its floor, ceiling, and walls of blue-veined marble. Zenith put down the lamp. It was no longer required. There were glowing lanterns hanging from wall brackets along the length of the passage.

He unslung his rifle and held it ready. Begg did the same.

"The ancient rituals of Arioch," the albino said quietly, "involved the burning of hallucinogenic powders. My—er—proclivities—will have given me a measure of resistance. You, on the other hand, would be well advised to keep your respiration shallow."

He gestured to the left and led the way. The corridor sloped downward and, rather than being straight, twisted this way and that, so they could never see very far ahead. Begg surmised that it was originally a natural tunnel through the mountain.

There were no bones, no debris, no sign that Vassilionu's men had penetrated this far.

As they descended, the chanting voices gained clarity.

Zenith said, "Those are Vera Pym's followers."

The metatemporal detective could make out words now, though the language, if it were one, was unfamiliar.

"Arioch kaa-shadaal! He shinaa! Arioch shaa-tanaa! Grow inaz! Arioch draal-kodaa!"

Two men with two rifles against—how many?

His mouth was dry. He felt unsteady on his feet. The fumes were overpowering. When he looked at the veins in the marble, they pulsed. He was walking through an artery—into the heart of a monstrous beast.

He blinked.

The marble was just marble.

A bend to the left, another to the right, then the corridor was straight, about a hundred yards long, open at the far end. Open to what? Begg could not quite see. Beyond an ogee arch, there was only streaming smoke illuminated by reddish-orange light. The gateway to Hell.

The noise was tremendous. The atmosphere pungent.

He staggered, his shoulder bumping the wall. He could feel the fumes behind his eyes, the Choir of Arioch throbbing through the marrow of his bones.

Zenith turned. "Begg?"

"I'm all right."

"Your eyes have dilated."

"I'm all right, I tell you!"

The albino stared at him for a moment, shrugged, and continued on.

Begg fought the temptation to take a deep, bracing breath. He was acutely aware that when they reached the arch ahead, he would look through and probably discover Taffy Sinclair—alive or dead.

As if to herald his arrival, the wind gusted through the cave system, releasing a single, deep, booming note, like a foghorn on the Bosphorus magnified ten times over.

It occurred to Begg that he was still in the water. That Suleyman the Strangler had dragged him under. That he was entangled in the weeds and drowning. These were his final seconds, everything from waking in the hospital onward, an illusion.

Zenith's hand hooked under his elbow and hauled him up. It was only then he realised he had fallen.

The floor shook. The chanting took on a note of hysteria.

"Arioch kaa-shadaal! Arioch draal-kodaa!"

Zenith moved ahead and reached the arch. He stopped at the threshold. Staggering to his side, Begg stood, swaying slightly, his vision subtly distorting, his spatial awareness awry, distances flexing around him.

He struggled to separate his drug-addled senses, to take in the scene one piece at a time, rather than as a single, overwhelming impression.

From his feet, a long, shallow stairway of white marble swept down to the base of a vast cavern. The bottom step abutted a marble floor, a great, flat, white disc set into the irregular rock. It was circled by eight equidistant columns. They soared impossibly high, up to the cavern's shadowed, smoke-veiled roof.

In the centre of the floor, an altar. Radiating from it, eight arrows in black marble, each point touching the base of a column.

Around all this, stalagmites and stalactites of every size, some merging to form natural pillars. On the far side of the enormous cave, a pool of dark mud bubbled and steamed, adding its vapours to an already dense atmosphere.

The air was dangerous, thick with consciousness-altering smoke, rising from numerous censers, caught by the stiff wind and whirled around the cavern. The marble centrepiece appeared to be at the heart of a raging storm, the Choir of Arioch providing the thunder.

This was the stage, hot and infernal, illuminated by brands with flames driven near horizontal. The scene enacted upon it captured and held Zenith's and Begg's attention.

A black-robed crowd, perhaps 150 strong, circled the altar, standing just within the ring of columns, hands raised, their heads thrown back, their faces ecstatic.

"*Arioch kaa-shadaal! He shinaa! Arioch shaa-tanaa! Grow inaz! Arioch draall-kodaa!*"

At each end of the altar stood a tall hooded figure. Begg recognised Vera Pym's erstwhile female companions.

La Pym wore her Red King robes and golden mask. Her arms were outstretched, and in her right hand she held a big jewelled kris of a kind Begg had only previously seen in ancient Etruscan reliefs.

A silver chalice—the *Salut Christi*—glinted brightly on the altar. Suspended by his ankles above it—Taffy Sinclair! He was unconscious, arms hanging down, his fingers just inches from the precious artefact.

"Alive!" Begg exclaimed. The utterance was almost a sob.

He raised his rifle and aimed at the woman. She warped and shimmered. Suddenly, Sinclair was in his sights.

"By heaven!" he said, his voice slurring. He lowered his

weapon. "I can't see straight to shoot. What are we to do? Two against—"

Zenith put a hand to the middle of the detective's back.

"Two?" he questioned. "No, Sir Seaton. That would be most unwise."

"Then what—?"

Zenith uttered a melancholy laugh. "My dear friend, I am afraid you must meet your fate alone."

He gave a forceful shove.

Begg, propelled violently forward, lost his footing and went tumbling down the stairs.

CHAPTER 30

The Kinslayer

Begg thudded to the bottom of the stairs and rolled into the crowd, his smoke-fuddled wits violently displaced by the fall. His rifle, knocked from his grasp, clattered away. He was unarmed and vastly outnumbered.

The chanting abruptly halted. Someone shouted an order. A figure approached, signed to another, and they took Begg under the arms and jerked him upright. He recognised Max Dragan. The other man was Chinese.

They dragged him to the altar and roughly thrust him to his knees.

A small part of his mind, compartmentalised and detached, calm and rational, watched as if from a great distance. The rest, hallucinating, struggled to make sense of the beautiful golden face that loomed close, its enigmatic smile swelling to fill his vision.

From behind it, Vera Pym said, "Here, the indestructible Sir Seaton Begg." Her sarcastic tone cut through the cacophony of whistling wind, the booms, groans, and screeches of Arioch's choir. "I should have known that Klosterheim would fail to stop you. The man is little better than a beast. A killer without compunction, yes, but—pah! He has no imagination. Well, it matters little. You are too late. As you see, the Cult of Arioch is gathered. The ceremony is complete aside from the culminating act. Can you not feel the potency in the air? The thinning of the membrane that separates this realm from the next?" She raised her hands as if in victory, the blade glinting, the light catching the Guardian's Seal on her middle finger. "We have Arioch's attention! He waits only for us to wash the foul Nazarene out of the chalice, then its power will be ours, and he will manifest!"

In unison, her followers murmured, *"Arioch kaa-shadaal!"*

"Perhaps it is well that you are here," Pym went on. "A representative of law. A tasty morsel with which to welcome the Knight of the Swords."

"Arioch shaa-tanaa!"

Begg ran his tongue around his teeth, gauging the shape of his mouth, uncertain whether it would function to speak.

"You, madame," he slurred, "are hopelessly insane."

He chuckled, tried to stop, but could not. His body shook with laughter. Vivid colours played at the periphery of his vision. He started lose cohesion, melting into the sensory bedlam.

She struck him. Not a slap, as he might have expected, but a solid punch to the nose. It jolted his head back. Blood spilled onto his chin.

"Much obliged," he mumbled, and meant it.

"I am sick of you, Begg. I am sick of your self-righteousness, of your legend, which you worked so assiduously to establish and in which you so heartily believe. What arrogance! What narcissism! Believing yourself an eternal champion—of what? Of the scum that populates the world with its worthless offspring?" Her masked face tipped back, and she gave a peal of laughter.

"Where—" he said, struggling to form words. "Where . . . have you been these years past? Where did you go after you fled England?"

She leaned closer. The golden face, full of moving reflections, dispersing at its edges and streaming into infinity. In the empty sockets, her eyes, widely dilated, were black as the depths of Hell.

"Where? Home, Begg, back to the Cult of Arioch, into which I had been born. My people had been shunned for generations, exiled and isolated, scratching the soil for survival on Russia's Kamchatka Peninsula. But I had high expectations of Lenin! He was secretly one of us. Did you know that Christian zealots burned his great-grandmother as a witch?"

Begg tried to get to his feet, fell back, the cavern spinning around him.

"Russia!" Pym went on. "I returned to Russia. And Lenin? What a disappointment. He was too busy playing the political game to give attention to our plight. Then, that devil Stalin killed him with poison—that is the truth!—and the purges began. We would be exterminated. It was inevitable unless I did something. You see now why I became the Red King, Mr. Detective? If I could make it appear that the Bolsheviks were attempting to destabilise the Turkish project, if I could draw the Soviet Union into war with Europe, that would be the end for Stalin."

She touched her forefinger to his forehead and prodded hard.

"Do you doubt that Arioch, though long banished from this realm, can yet influence it? Do you think it happenstance that the spy chief commissioned by Britain to hunt the Red King was himself intent on fomenting war over the Bosphorus? That, rather than opposing me, Sir Vivian Clarke hired me? That he also revealed to me the presence in Istanbul of the object I had for so long sought—

the *Salut Christi*?" She again jabbed at Begg's head. "That is the power of Arioch!"

"*Arioch draall-kodaa Arioch!*" her followers intoned.

She turned her hand in front of Begg's eyes to display the *Sigiliul Tutorelui*. It swelled into his mind, filling it. The black opal on a gold setting. The eight arrows.

Ring. Chalice. Sword.

Mere objects, he told himself. *It is the human mind that invests them with power.*

Then, he recalled the malignancy emanating from the black blade, and he felt less certain.

"I am the Guardian," Pym said. "The favoured child of the Lord of the Seven Darks. With his hand to guide me, I shall use the power of the chalice to overturn the world order. In a few moments, you and your assistant will die. Your blood will usher in the Age of Disruption and Unfettered Possibility. No rules. No laws. The end of the great deception of universal morals and ethics!"

Begg heard someone say, "An age without meaning," and recognised the voice as his own.

The drugs carried by the smoke coursed through him. He was disassociated, drifting, dissipating into a swirling kaleidoscope of scintillating colours, multilayered odours, and the pulsating drones, squeals, and reverberations of the mountain.

He was no longer Sir Seaton Begg; he was merely a figment of someone else's dream.

Taffy Sinclair's upside-down eyes cut through the visual maelstrom. They were glazed and dilated, but immutably fixed on him. Was there recognition? A glimmer of hope? Any expression at all? As he coalesced back into himself, Begg could see no sign of intelligence—except that when he swayed to one side, the pathologist's eyes followed.

Vera Pym pressed the blade of the kris against Sinclair's throat.

Abruptly, the wind dropped to a stiff breeze and the Choir of Arioch fell silent.

She announced, "It is time."

A susurration ran through the crowd. *"Arioch kaa-shadaal! He shinaa!"*

The air crackled with expectation.

From a small pocket of rationality, Begg assessed his position.

He was on his knees. Max Dragan was on his right, the Chinese man to the left. Both had fingers dug into his shoulders—but not hard. His obvious intoxication had made them careless.

Pym was beside the altar, about three long paces away.

The gathered adherents massed around the edge of the circular floor.

The Red King's voice rang out, echoing in the vast space.

"To thee Arioch, Lord of the Seven Darks!"

"Arioch kaa-shadaal!" the crowd chanted.

"To thee, Arioch, Earl of Entropy!"

"He shinaa! Arioch shaa-tanaa!"

"To thee Arioch, Knight of the Swords!"

"Grow inaz! Arioch draall-kodaa!"

"To thee Arioch, Lord of the Higher Hell!"

"Arioch yan taa kee, Arioch!"

"To thee Arioch, I give this soul that thy will may be—"

Sir Seaton Begg shot upright, the tremendous force of his leg, back, and arm muscles behind his right fist. His knuckles caught the point of Max Dragan's chin, snapping his head back with such violence that his neck broke with a horrific pop. The corpse, lifted off its feet, somersaulted backward and crashed to the floor.

As his arm came down, Begg twisted, slicing it horizontally. The other man was turning. The detective's hand chopped into his larynx, crushing it. The recipient reeled, clawing at his throat, unable to draw a breath.

Begg pounced onto Pym, knocked her knife hand aside, grabbed a handful of her robes, and hauled her away from Taffy Sinclair. She fell, sliding across the marble.

He made a grab for the *Salut Christi*, intending to throw it far across the cavern. He only managed to get his fingertips to it, sliding it from beneath Sinclair, before the crowd was upon him.

Hands grabbed, pushed, punched, and clawed. His clothes tore. He was lifted and slammed to the ground, kicked and stamped on.

He heard Vera Pym shouting, was hoisted to his feet, then propelled through the furious mob back to the altar.

Begg could muster no further resistance. He was clinging to consciousness.

A man and a woman pushed him backward onto the stone altar. The man—Viktor Bolotnikov!—growled, "For the bullet you put in my leg!" and struck Begg hard on the side of the head. The other was one of the two tall women. Her companion was standing nearby. These, and the gunman Thott—out on the castle turret—were, with a single exception, the sole remaining members of the Istanbul-based Red King gang. Only Madam Melody was missing. Whether she was here or not, Begg was in no fit state to determine.

Taffy Sinclair looked down at him. A flicker of recognition. A hissed exhalation. Faintly, a single word. "Begg."

"Now, Sir Seaton," said Vera Pym, stepping forward. "Die!"

Holding the kris point downward with both hands, she raised it high to plunge into his heart.

"For Arioch!" she screamed.

"NO!" bellowed a deep, resonant voice.

The word echoed. NO! ... No! ... no! ... o ...

As if in response, the wind gave a final strong gust, and sounded its last note through the flues and lava tubes, the tremendous blast of a heralding trumpet. Then—

Silence.

Begg, Pym, everyone—even Taffy Sinclair—turned their eyes to the stairs.

Descending, a figure of alabaster white!

He was in black trousers and boots, but stripped above the waist, gripping a great black broadsword, holding it horizontally over his head. His long white hair whipped about in the breeze. His eyes were like fire.

The crowd whispered, "Kinslayer!"

One after another, they dropped to their knees and fell forward in supplication.

Bolotnikov and the tall woman stood gaping, their hands falling away from Begg. A belt held the woman's robes and, in the back of it, a Webley pistol. Brazenly, Begg bent forward and plucked it out. The woman felt nothing. She was too enraptured by the descending apparition.

The albino glared at Vera Pym. "Dost thou dare declare thyself the child of Arioch?"

In the cistern beneath the Istanbul hammam, Begg had thought the albino's face thinner than it used to be. Now the drugs in him accentuated the difference. The eyes were more angled, the ears a little pointed, the skull long and narrow. In stature, he appeared taller, though the rangy build was the same. The musculature was extraordinary, slim rather than bulky, the muscle fibres pressing through the skin, like bunched piano wire.

In the hazy atmosphere and fiery illumination, he glowed like a supernatural being.

Pym stammered, "I . . . I mean only to . . . White Wolf . . . please . . . if . . . if I may serve—"

Begg blinked, astounded. So that was it! Zenith had used his heritage and the warped ambitions of a madwoman to style himself a sorcerer reborn!

Audacious beyond belief.

How would he employ such power?

Begg would never find out. There was this single opportunity and no other option. At the optimum moment, he must raise the Webley and shoot the albino through the heart.

As Zenith, holding his pose, reached the bottom of the stairs, Bolotnikov and the tall woman dropped to their knees. Only Vera Pym remained on her feet. The kris fell from her numb fingers as the sword-bearing apparition approached.

"Remove that mask," Zenith commanded.

Slowly, as if in a trance, she raised her hand, slid the strap from the back of her head, and pulled away the golden face. Her features, thus revealed, were frozen in an expression of shocked bewilderment, as if she were looking upon a thing she knew to be impossible, unable to mentally process it.

Zenith lowered the point of the sword sideways until it was directed at Sir Seaton Begg. "What is this?"

Pym moistened her lips with her tongue. "For thee, my . . . my lord. A soul . . . upon which to feast."

Turning, Zenith took a step toward the detective.

Now!

Begg slid off the altar, down to his knees, raised the gun, and fired, almost point-blank.

A loud crack preceded the report by the merest fraction of a second as the flat of the sword's blade smacked hard against his hand. The bullet whistled past the albino's ear and into the depths of the cavern. The gun skittered across the floor.

Begg clutched his hand to his chest, grimacing, his knuckles burning.

Zenith looked into his eyes.

"After all these years," he said, "it ends."

He swung the sword high.

"I am sorry, Sir Seaton Begg, but for Arioch—this!"

The weapon came sweeping down.

CHAPTER 31
Stealer of Souls

The blade missed Seaton Begg's left ear by a hair's breadth and slammed onto the *Salut Christi*. The clang sounded like the striking of a great cosmic gong, resonating through Begg's cranium, into the secret depths of his mind, and to the core of the eternally flowering multiverse. Through plane after plane of existence, across vast cycles of time, the impact altered realities, causing in some a call to arms; in others, a conclusive cataclysm; in many, merely an instant of insight, or a consequential coincidence, or a spontaneous touch or word that forever changed a relationship or a destiny.

This, Begg sensed as the sword rested for a second just an inch from his ear. The skin on that side of his face prickled and blistered, and he imagined a wicked and lascivious moan issuing from the blade.

Vera Pym uttered a quavering, despairing wail.

Zenith withdrew the weapon and turned to face her.

"Madame, the Cult of Arioch is finished. Our long history ends this hour."

Pym's eyes widened. Recognition at last counteracted her shock—and delivered an even greater one!

"You!" she whispered. "It is you! Monsieur Zenith. How . . . how?"

Softly, he said, "Vera, my dearest Vera, you should have told me. Back then, when we were—" He sighed. "Had I known you commanded the exiles—"

"Do not address me by that name! Don't you say it." Her eyes, horribly wide, were those of a fanatic whose long-held plans, at the brink of fulfilment, had crumbled to dust. Her mouth was contorting, white foam gathering at its corners, lips curled inward, thinned to nothing against her teeth. "I am as my mother was and as my daughter shall be: Constanta Elisabeta Anna Lacusta, of the immortal Family Lacusta, which refused the imposition of insipid Christianity upon our faith. The Lacustas, who did not betray Arioch, as did your accursed family!"

Zenith shook his head sorrowfully. He lowered his sword's point to the floor.

"You are the only woman to have ever professed romantic love for me," he said. "And I believed that lie. You were using me when you should have been confiding in me."

She clasped hands to her stomach, gripped by the intense sorrow in his voice, and blinked over and over, as if she might wash him from her sight.

He continued. "You learned from my nightmares of the catastrophe that had befallen Lamaneagra, yet still you withheld the incredible truth that the exiles still existed. Survivors! Colonel Vassilionu's genocide was incomplete! Do you not think I would have—"

She snarled scornfully. "Joined us? You would not have been welcome!"

Begg saw where the Webley had fallen. Very slowly, careful to not attract notice, he inched toward it.

All around, the cultists were raising their faces, looking with puzzlement and curiosity at the albino. Some rose to their feet.

Zenith uttered a slow, sad laugh.

"Join you? No, madame, not that. The ancient beliefs are too rancid a dish for me. I would not be so poisoned. But, to honour our forebears, I would have offered material support. I imagine the Soviet Union is not currently conducive to—*No! Don't do that!*"

She had squatted to retrieve the kris.

His sword point came up.

"Imposter!" she shrieked. "You dare to defy Lord Arioch? He will flay that loathsome white skin from your weeping flesh! He will shatter your bones to a thousand fragments while you beg for death! He will lap your foul blood while your soul hangs forever in limbo, doomed to relive its final moment for eternity!"

She threw the knife. Zenith deflected it with his blade. It went spinning away.

"Kill him!" she screeched at her followers. "Kill him! Kill him! Kill him!"

Producing guns, knives, and coshes, the circling crowd pressed inward.

Behind Zenith, Viktor Bolotnikov pulled a pistol from his belt, took a pace forward, and put its muzzle to the back of the albino's head. His finger whitened on the trigger.

Begg raised the Webley and fired, taking the Russian through the neck.

The report signalled pandemonium.

The cavern thundered with echoing gunshots and bellowing voices. Leaping to his feet, Begg moved, ducking this way and that, drawing a bead on those who held firearms, and shooting them down with a sudden, icy proficiency. His gun emptied in a matter of moments. He dived for another, dropped by one of the fallen, and kept up the assault.

Zenith swung his blade with such rapidity, it appeared as insubstantial as black mist. A bullet ricocheted from it, showering sparks, and whined into the heart of one of the tall women. As her knees buckled, the sword hissed through the air and into the side of a charging knifeman. The metal paused inside him, and the man's face expressed utter dismay, a strange realisation; then his eyes rolled up, and he crumpled to the marble floor. The razor-sharp edge slipped out, whipped sideways, spattering gore, and severed a spine. It jerked back, the jewelled pommel crunching between murderous eyes. The blade rose and descended onto an eggshell cranium. It slashed through a shoulder to the breastbone, sliced knee tendons, stabbed a pulsing heart, cut an artery, and took two heads in a single arc.

Zenith howled. Possessed by the blade, his vocal cords took on an alien, metallic vibrato.

Though adrenaline was nullifying the insidious effects of the hallucinogens, Sir Seaton Begg was still seeing through a warped lens. It was clear and sharp at the centre, where lay the sights of his gun, but at the peripheries the world twisted, shifted, and became malformed and surreal. Every distorted perception, had he given it attention, might have held him in a state of paralysed fascination.

He breathed the odours of sulphur and rust, felt every scream as a scratch, every gunshot as a slap, saw multicoloured light flare and scatter like departing souls, tasted vinegar and iron.

And he heard the black sword howl and groan with lewd craving.

The albino gripped the weapon in his bone-white hands and appeared to have no control over it. The blade directed the albino! And it did so without mercy, without regard for how Zenith might feel about the carnage inflicted.

Begg vaguely understood this impression to be no more real than the others. In his exertions, he was gulping lungfuls of air still contaminated by strong opium and other less readily recognisable drugs. But awareness of intoxication did not reduce the insidiousness of the conception. It was so powerful that, if he survived this battle, he knew he would always remember the black sword as sentient and depraved. It would haunt his nightmares for the rest of his life.

If he survived this battle!

Two against a hundred and fifty!

Back-to-back, Zenith swinging and thrusting, and Begg with empty pistols reversed in each hand, clubbing, punching, and kicking.

Bullets tore past them, occasionally ploughing shallow furrows through their skin but, by some miracle, never making fatal or disabling contact.

Dripping from head to foot with gore, the old adversaries became a single, savage, and monstrous entity. Black-robed figures jostled around the frightful creature. They collapsed dead or agonised or unconscious at its four feet; they dropped, screaming, as the blade thrust and sucked at ghastly wounds; they tripped over one another, accidentally falling onto their own knives, succumbing to bullets fired by other cultists.

Begg and Zenith felt they were fighting for hours. In truth, only a few minutes passed before panic gripped the opposition. Shouts of fury and vicious intent turned to cries of alarm and helplessness.

Individuals broke from the crowd and ran up the marble stairs, frantic for escape, desiring only to avoid the terrifying black sword.

Begg slipped on the blood-slicked floor, thumped down, and knocked his head hard against the marble. One of the guns flew from his fingers. Dazed, he pushed himself up. A booted foot thudded into his face, rocking him back. His vision blurred, then refocussed, and he was looking down a gun barrel. With his empty hand, he slapped it aside, grabbed the wrist, and hauled his assailant down. She fell on top of him—the other tall woman—and squirmed to get her gun against his body. He still held a clubbed pistol, smashed it against her ear, and she went limp.

Pushing out from beneath her into a rapidly emptying battleground, he staggered to his feet and was immediately challenged by a short but heavily built man. He dodged a slashing knife, closed the distance, and delivered a sleep-inducing uppercut. His assailant, out cold, toppled with his back and legs straight, like a felled tree.

The stairs were crowded. Fleeing cultists shoved and clawed to get past each other.

Begg flinched as the black sword plunged into the base of a chin and out from the top of the cranium. He turned away, sickened.

Unsteadily, he stepped over the dead and the wounded and approached the altar. Vera Pym was standing close to it. Her arms were at her sides. She had retrieved the kris and was holding it loosely in her right hand. In the grip of psychosis, her face was blank, eyes wide and glazed, mouth open, drooling.

The detective took a knife from the ground and clambered up to Taffy Sinclair. His colleague was suspended from a short rope affixed to steel cables stretched between the pillars.

Begg cut him down, lowered him awkwardly, then squatted and sawed through the ankle bindings.

"My God," Sinclair whispered.

"You are all right now, old chap." Begg's voice was a dry rasp. "We'll be out of here soon."

He jumped down to the floor.

The temple had emptied. Zenith stood, panting, his dripping blade's point on the ground. He was leaning heavily on the crosspiece, confused, as if uncertain of his identity.

Begg surveyed the dead and wounded. He ground his teeth and pushed his fingers through his hair. He and Zenith had defended themselves, fighting for their own and Sinclair's lives. But to be responsible for all this! Another bloody massacre in this land of bloody massacres.

He employed what remained of a sleeve to smear blood from his mouth.

Stepping toward Pym, he winced, halted, looked down, and saw that his left thigh had received a nasty gash. His jacket had at some point been torn from him. His shirt was hanging loose and ragged. He ripped a strip from it and bound the leg.

When he looked up, it was to find Zenith standing before him. He scrutinised the albino and muttered, "I cannot tell what of that blood is yours, or even if it's really you beneath it."

"A measure of it is mine," Zenith replied. "But I have no serious injury. You?"

"Cuts and bruises."

Zenith cleared his throat. "Sir Seaton, I . . . I do not know what . . . I became someone . . . something—" He faltered.

"You need say nothing. I experienced it all. I have no questions, no comments, no requirement for discussion. Do you understand?"

After a hesitation, the albino gave a curt but grateful nod. "I understand." He looked at the sword, held by his side, and an expression the detective had never seen in him before passed across his face.

It was fear.

"Only I can hold this loathsome blade. I do not want to. The sooner it is returned to its alcove, the better. Let us get—"

"Monsieur Zenith!"

They wheeled.

Vera Pym stood facing them, the kris in her right hand, her left raised, a ring held between the forefinger and thumb.

"The *Sigiliul Tutorelui*," she said. "The Guardian's Seal."

Her face was fixed in a rictus grin. Whatever sanity had kept her functional was gone. A string of spittle swung from her chin.

She had once been beautiful. She was now tragic and repellent.

"It signifies all you were born to be, all you were meant to inherit from your illustrious family, who could trace their forebears back to before the sheepherder despoiled the earth with his meek, submissive tread."

Zenith's eyes reflected the fire of a nearby brand.

"That is correct," he said.

"It first belonged to the Kinslayer, whom you have this night impersonated—unless the legend be true."

He raised an inquisitive eyebrow.

"Ah!" She giggled, a cold, foreboding sound, like pebbles rattling down a mountainside in advance of a deadly avalanche. "Unless it be true. In which case, thou art truly the White Wolf, dreaming he is Zenith. Is that so?"

He shrugged. "How could I possibly say, if I am the dream rather than the dreamer?"

"How, indeed? But this ring," Pym continued, "not only connects you to your family, and your people, and your country, and to the ancient faith, it may also be a conduit to the core of who and what you are, is that not so? It might be said that your very identity resides in this gem with its eight engraved arrows and its gold setting."

Zenith was silent for a moment. Then he lowered his face a little and regarded her through hooded eyes.

"Maybe so."

"You lost it to Colonel Simeon Vassilionu."

He said nothing.

"You lost it again in a poker game."

Still, he did not respond.

"And now, my dear Monsieur Zenith, my *amoureux*, destroyer of all I have fought for, you lose it once more. To me. Forever."

She palmed the ring, drew back her arm, and with all her strength flung the precious relic across the cavern and into the bubbling mud pool. Instantly, the viscous sludge folded over it and swallowed it into subterranean depths.

Zenith stood absolutely motionless.

"Now," she said in a mocking tone, "you have nothing. Nothing but that cursed sword."

She raised the kris, and with a demented shriek, launched herself at him. One stride, and her heel landed on the red opal, knocked out of the *Salut Christi* and said to contain a drop of Christ's blood. Her foot slithered across it and out from beneath her. She lost her balance and toppled, arms windmilling, toward Zenith. As if by its own motive power, the black sword came up and met her, point to midriff. She slid along the full length of the blade, bumping the crosspiece, her contorted face stopping an inch from Zenith's, their lips almost touching.

"Non, ma chère femme," he murmured. "I do not have the sword. The sword has you."

She gave a tinkling laugh, almost of merriment, panted, sobbed, then raised her face, leaned forward, and kissed him.

She drew back.

"I am my own daughter," she whispered. "Immortal Vera Pym of the endless Lacustas. We shall meet again, m'sieu. *C'est inévitable.*"

She whimpered, and her eyes filled with horror.

"Oh, but it is cold. So very cold."

He put an arm around her shoulder, eased the corpse to the ground, and spoke softly in a language the detective did not recognise.

Tears shone like drops of blood in crimson eyes.

CHAPTER 32
Aftermath

"Forgive me, my dear detective, but I could see no other option."

"You might have discussed it with me first. I could have playacted a fall down the stairs."

Zenith shook his head. "I doubt you would have convinced. Besides, you were in no fit state to discuss anything. The drugs had taken rapid effect. It was a potent brew. I daresay Monteith the Chemist concocted it before his untimely demise."

"Ah yes. Monteith." Begg stared into the distance. "Murdered at the fancy dress ball—by you."

"Let us not entangle ourselves in the details."

The detective inhaled the pure mountain air. The oxygen enriched his blood and drove out the remaining hallucinogens. He relished the clear blue morning sky, the absolute silence that hung over Lamaneagra, the ambient clarity.

"You wish me to believe myself a decoy rather than a sacrifice?"

"Quite so. Something to keep them occupied while I went to fetch the sword. A distraction to delay Doctor Sinclair's death."

"We could have attacked together."

Zenith dismissed the notion with an elegant flick of his hand. "Against such numbers? They would have rapidly overwhelmed us. A manifestation was required. An unexpected flash of superstitious dread to paralyse them. Only then could we gain the upper hand."

They sat on a slope above the ruined town. Castle Arioch was some distance to their left. Both men were wrapped in black robes against a descending chill, which defied Lamaneagra's volcanic warmth and the brightness of the spring sun.

On their way out of the temple, Zenith had returned the black sword to its secret room. Begg carried the battered parts of the *Salut Christi*.

Violet Damm was waiting for them. Last night, at her eleventh shot, Orville Thott's homicidal career terminated with a bullet taken between the eyes.

Most of the cultists had fled to the pass, desperate to get away before Zenith's vengeful blade claimed their souls. The supposed reality of supernatural evil was too much for their silly, romantic minds, and most had reached the waterfall and were long gone. Nine lingered, held at gunpoint by Damm.

"We want to bury our dead," ventured their spokesman.

"Very well," Begg had said, "but first, two of you will guide Miss Damm down to the temple. She will keep you covered while you gather all the weapons and throw them into the mud pit. She is a formidable sharpshooter. I advise against defiance or sudden moves."

When the sullen cultists later reemerged from the castle at pistol point, they carried provision-filled hampers, meant for the post-sacrifice celebration. Taffy Sinclair, the intended offering, tucked in like a starved schoolboy. Begg, Zenith, and Damm were also ravenous. They ate a breakfast of bread, cheese, cured meats, and fruit. On a campfire, coffee brewed.

Sinclair's hearing had recovered from Madam Melody's assault. "When they strung me up," he told Begg, "I was turned upside down, and my ears popped. It was awful. The first thing I heard was their infernal chanting."

Of his journey to Lamaneagra, he had little to tell. "Bound, gagged, and bumped about in a box for most of it."

The cultists carried corpses from the temple into the valley. They dug with tools discovered amid the town's debris, and buried Vera Pym—Constanta Elisabeta Anna Lacusta—with the rest, in a mass unmarked grave.

Of the ten injured, two died from their wounds. It left seventeen in total. Once the burials were complete, they were permitted to depart. Except one. The surviving tall woman remained, hands bound behind her back, Begg's prisoner.

Speaking of her fellows, in French with a thick Russian accent, she said, "I swear by Arioch that none will ever reveal the location of this place. Though we were exiled generations ago, it remains sacred to us. We cannot bear the thought of nonbelievers"—she turned her head and glared at Begg and Damm—"like you filthy pigs, contaminating it."

"She speaks the truth," said Zenith. "The surviving cultists will not speak of it."

"What is your name?" Begg asked her.

"I am Sophia Anya Gorbanevskaya Zhigulenko, Priestess of Arioch."

"I am going to hand you over to the Turkish National Security Service, Sophia Anya Gorbanevskaya Zhigulenko. You will reveal to them every detail of the Red King's murder campaign."

She straightened and raised her chin. "Never. Arioch will prevent it."

Later, Begg and Zenith constructed a makeshift stretcher and reentered the castle. They brought out a mummified corpse and carried it high up the slope above the town.

They collected rocks and made a cairn.

The funeral rites were unfamiliar to Begg. Zenith spoke ancient words from a lost religion. They would never be uttered again, for he was the last of his family's line.

He recited those thrilling, musical, mysteriously potent and profound words, and Begg, hearing grief and respect, was deeply moved.

They stood silently for a minute; then the detective reached out and squeezed the albino's arm. "I shall wait a little way down the hill."

Thirty minutes later, Zenith joined him.

Now they sat side by side. Zenith lit one of Begg's proffered cigarettes. Together, like old comrades in the battle's pause, they smoked and surveyed the ruins.

Begg said, "There was a moment, when they called you Kinslayer and White Wolf, that I thought you had planned all along to make yourself a deity."

Zenith uttered a low laugh.

"And have that pathetic cult at my beck and call? I will confess that, when I held the sword over you, I did for an instant imagine this land restored and repopulated—"

"With you as its prince?"

"Naturally. But what would I do as leader of such carrion? Fanatics cannot be relied upon. Give them what they want, and they soon become dissatisfied. They gain their sense of power from believing what others decry. Should their convictions be confirmed, they would feel themselves identical to everyone else, and search for another hopeless cause—another mark of their supposed superiority to the rest of us. It is why the Nazis can never win. They have gained power, but self-destruction is intrinsic to their nature."

"So, you sliced the chalice instead of my skull."

"The truce holds. My word is good."

"It was only for a fleeting instant that I doubted it."

Zenith drew on Begg's cigarette. He had no desire for his own opium-soaked tobacco. The loaded atmosphere of the temple had been too much even for him. The hallucinations he suffered while wielding the black blade had terrified him.

Minutes passed, then the albino murmured, "In her final moments she said, 'I am my own daughter.' What did she mean by that?"

Begg flicked away his cigarette butt. "I cannot be certain, but it is rumoured—or perhaps merely theorised—that a rare breed of female metatemporal exists who has the ability of parthenogenesis. That is to say, she can become pregnant without need of fertilisation. It is also hypothesised that the offspring of such a female is in every respect identical to the mother, and that when the latter dies, the child receives all the memories and personality traits of the parent."

Zenith sighed and closed his eyes. "Do you mean to tell me that, somewhere, a young Vera Pym has just awoken?"

"Yes."

After a long pause, the albino muttered, "If I am truly a dream, the dreamer must have chosen his supper unwisely, for he is prone to nightmares."

Begg turned his head and gazed at his companion. "Monsieur

Zenith. Count Zodiac. White Wolf. Those names and more. I have often wondered at your mercurial nature, strange view of life, and at the manner in which you defy consistency. It is, indeed, dreamlike in its lack of logic. However, having shared with you what we have recently experienced, I believe I understand you a little better."

Zenith gazed across the valley at the opposite peaks.

"But I suppose," Begg added, "that when I traverse time and the multiverse, I shall forget, as I so often do, and you will once again become unfathomable and dangerous. Nevertheless, a trace of friendship and trust may remain. I can but hope so."

Zenith made no response. He stood, stretched, rubbed a sore arm, and changed the subject. "When we return to Istanbul, I shall not linger. And you?"

"I have matters to attend to." The metatemporal detective resigned himself to Zenith's compulsive secrecy. Begg had learned as much about him as was ever likely. "There is a silversmith named Gulvenkian Ogg. I shall take the *Salut Christi* to him to see if it can be repaired."

"Then?"

"It is to be given to President Kemal, a symbol of trust from Britain and France and their allies."

"In the hope that, should there be war, Germany will be opposed on multiple fronts?"

"That is so."

The albino was silent for another stretch. Then, "I must accompany you."

"It is not necessary."

"It is. The *Sigiliul Tutorelui* may be gone, but I was born to be Guardian of the Chalice whether I wear the sign of that office or not. I will remain with it until it is handed to Kemal."

Begg acquiesced. "Very well, I have no objection."

He stared at the vapour from the hot springs, curling across the lowlands like the great grey ghosts of ancient saurians. Forgotten lives and anonymous deaths haunted the valley, stretching all the way from the Mesozoic era to the present. Begg could sense them in the soil, feel them in the air.

As if reading the detective's thoughts, Zenith murmured, "This is the last time I shall stand in this valley. Perhaps I will be fortunate enough to forget it. Memories gain no foothold here. Little of the place has ever been recorded. It is a land of the lost, of ancient cruelties, ancient lore, of forbidden wisdom banished to a tiny mountain-bound theocracy by all the People of the Book as they carried Jehovah—and only Jehovah—forward."

"Even your forefathers fell before them," Begg commented. "Allowing the eight arrows of compassion to overwrite the eight arrows of Chaos. An entire system of belief obscured."

"They were a tiny community surrounded by mighty empires. It was a case of do or die."

Begg understood why those rival empires had chosen to hide the chalice in Lamaneagra. But what would history have been without it? What of Europe, if the chalice had not exerted its balancing influence?

That was the crux of the matter, for of course, there was no balancing influence. Begg still maintained that—in this reality, at least—the silver bowl possessed no supernatural power whatever.

President Mustafa Kemal, however, might think differently.

So the *Salut Christi* would be returned to the city of its birth.

Begg and Zenith descended to the town and prepared for departure.

"There is something I must do," the albino announced. "Will you wait for me in Dragomireşti? I shall join you this evening."

Begg gave him a sidelong glance.

"M'sieu?"

"It is a personal matter. Will you indulge me?"

Begg shrugged and called to the others. "Time to go."

He, Sinclair, Violet Damm, and Sophia Anya Gorbanevskaya Zhigulenko, Priestess of Arioch, ascended the long incline toward the rocky shelf and the mouth of the pass.

Begg limped along, his gashed thigh stiff and painful.

"What is Zenith up to, old man?" asked Sinclair.

The detective stopped and turned to gaze at the ruined town. The albino was on his way back to the castle.

"Probably, Taffy, he is moving the black sword to a different hiding place. It is all that remains of his heritage, but he has no desire to keep the hideous thing. Equally, he will not want anyone else to have it." Shielding his eyes against the midday sun, he pointed at the crags above the stronghold. "If you squint, you'll make out what looks to be a monastery up there. I see other such buildings dotted around the mountainsides. For certain, there are hiding places more secure than the castle's hidden sword room."

They moved on.

Today, there was no wind in the pass. The air was motionless, as if yesterday's storm had left absolute exhaustion in its wake.

They heard the waterfall long before they came to the great frothing column, which fell out of cloud into subterranean infinity. Again, they pressed their backs against the rock, and one by one risked the narrow, wet shelf behind the thundering cascade. Begg went first, immediately soaked by the spray. Violet Damm followed. The Russian woman next. She was halfway across when the shelf gave way beneath her. With a scream, so shrill it could be heard even over the roaring water, she plummeted into pitch darkness.

Begg, Sinclair, and Damm stared at the gap in dismay. It was four feet wide. Not far to jump—but sideways?

The detective signalled for Sinclair to wait. He took off his black robe and proceeded to tear it into strips. These he knotted together to make a sufficient length, adding a big knot to weight one end.

Sidling out onto the shelf, he threw the heavy end to the pathologist, while keeping hold of the other. Sinclair caught it and wound the ribbon around his wrist until it stretched taut across the fissure.

He braced himself, then hopped crabwise, landed, tottered on the edge, and was rocked by water hitting his flailing arm.

Begg hauled him to safety.

"Phew!" Sinclair gasped, his face drained of colour.

They continued on, rounding the sharp turn, not stopping until they could look back at the great mirror of Argint Lunar silver to see a waterfall that wasn't where it appeared to be.

"Arioch is without mercy," Begg commented. "I shall have to remain here to help Zenith across."

"No," countered Damm. "You tore up your robe, you have no jacket, and your shirt is in tatters. You will freeze to death. I shall stay."

"I can—" Sinclair started.

"I shall stay," she reiterated. There was no arguing with her.

Begg handed over the makeshift rope. "We'll send someone up from the village to relieve you."

With obvious reluctance, the detective and his friend departed. They moved along the narrow ravine, both exhausted, saying little.

Soon, they were out in the open, stumbling down a steep

incline, along a goat trail to the fang-shaped rock, following the path to the village.

It was well past midday. They found Dragomireşti subdued and battle-scarred.

Bullet holes pocked the houses. Two residences had burned down. The five Tzigane *vardos* were parked at the lower end of the village. Campfires burned. Gunpowder, ash, and the rich aromas of cooking food flavoured the air.

Sabahattin Sans-Serif came forward to greet them, his bald head, left forearm, and hands bandaged. He gazed at Begg askance, his bulging eye directed at the detective's shredded attire.

"You foreigners," he commented, "have no dress sense." He cocked a thumb toward the wagons. "Shall we find you some warm clothes?"

"Please," said Begg.

As they made their way along the main street, the detective noted that the lorry was gone.

"That devil Klosterheim took it," said Sans-Serif. "He climbed in with a gun to von Bek's head. Then they drove off."

"Did he order his Iron Guards to retreat?"

"No. He left them here to die."

The Turk indicated the uncultivated, rock-strewn fields to the west, where a pile of uniformed corpses lay beneath a fluttering black mantle. Crows. Strutting from body to body, their sharp beaks tore at blood-soaked fabric and exposed skin. Nature's efficient undertakers.

Begg and Sinclair averted their eyes.

They reached the wagons and were greeted by Gideon Lakatos.

"I am pleased to see you, O raj Begg," he said. "This is your friend, whom we came to rescue?"

"It is."

Lakatos shook Sinclair's hand. "I welcome you. Come, sit by a fire. There is food if you wish it. The villagers have supplied us with wines and beers. The Iron Guard treated them badly. They are grateful that we came."

"You have lost many," Begg murmured.

"Yes. There are only nine of us left."

The detective put his palm to his forehead. "Vodja, this is . . . I would not have—"

"No," Lakatos said, raising a protesting hand. "The Iron Guard would wipe us from existence. You did not put us in danger's way. We were already there."

"But—"

"Those who fell are now buried beside our *rom baro*. They are honoured in death." He signalled for them to sit. "Rest. Eat. I will fetch clothes for you."

Begg told him about the incident at the waterfall. The Tzigane chief dispatched two men, one to wait for Zenith, the other to escort Violet Damm back to the village.

Begg and Sinclair ate a little, washed, changed their clothes, then took to a wagon and slept.

Five hours later, a horse whinnied, and the vehicle jerked into motion.

They woke and moved onto the tailgate, sitting under the light of other worlds, the night sky crystal clear and bright.

A man came alongside, riding one of the mares.

"O raj Begg," he said. "Miss Damm returned. And a little later, His Excellency. They are both sleeping. We are crossing the Carpathians. We will journey through Moldavia back to Constanţa. It will take longer, but is much safer. There are fewer of the Iron Guard in the east."

Begg nodded his thanks.

The Tzigane spurred away.

After a long, contemplative silence, the detective said, "Taffy, the woman, Sophia Anya Gorbanevskaya Zhigulenko, could have revealed much about the cult and the Red King assassinations. Both matters are to some extent resolved, but such cases cannot be considered closed until we have thoroughly understood the background."

"Just our luck, Begg. Our best source falling into a watery grave."

"No, not our best source," the metatemporal detective responded. "There is another, possibly of higher rank. Someone notably absent from that dreadful ceremony." He paused, then added, "We must locate and capture Madam Melody!"

CHAPTER 33
Back to Istanbul

Esmeralda's father was dead. She had nowhere to go. Ancient Lilith informed her that her destiny lay "beyond the clan." Esmeralda knew that none of her seven brothers, all leaders of other caravans, would accept her. She was bad luck. When they learned what had occurred at Dragomirești, they would say she should, shortly after birth, have been left in the woods.

Sabahattin Sans-Serif seized the opportunity. He hated all religion. All superstition. For that which made her an illness, he was the cure. He married her on the third day of the return trek to Constanța.

A rapid romance, the Turk observed, but, "Right is always right, and waiting for it to be wrong is always wrong."

The Familia Caldararii held the wedding ceremony in a beautiful meadow, on the bank of the Milcov River. The setting was perfect. The river flowed down from distant foothills a little north of Focsani, on the Moldavian-Wallachian border. The caravans came from all corners of the compass in response to Ancient Lilith's summons.

Begg noticed how the old woman's amazing telepathy had once again been accompanied by the mysterious absence of a man and a horse.

By noon, the encampment had swollen to twenty-one wagons.

All morning, pigs, calves, rabbits, venison, chickens, and wild ducks roasted over open fires, and hedgehogs baked in clay. With big wooden spoons that resembled broom handles, women stirred massive iron cauldrons bubbling with soups and stews. The smoky fragrance of paprika and garlic filled the air.

While the women prepared the feast, the men drank wine and with much gusto and laughter told tall tales of the bride's father, the *rom baro*, Arcan Maljodi, celebrated rather than mourned. The story of his life, his heroism, his poetry, his library, and his extraordinary literacy would be passed from generation to generation far into the future, throughout the wide borderless world of the Tzigane clans. He was being immortalised.

One of the king's grinning sons introduced Begg to a squirming, wide-eyed tatterdemalion. "This is Pyramus. He is the *rom baro*'s fourteenth grandson. Eleven years old—and special! Tell our honoured guest why, Pyramus."

Shyly, the boy said, *"Je peux lire."*

"It is true, O raj Begg! He can read! He inherits all his grandfather's books, excepting those we buried with the *rom baro*—the Balzacs and editions of *The Septimus Blane Library*—for him to enjoy in the afterlife. And, since there is nowhere else to put all the remaining books, Pyramus will have the king's *vardo*, too."

Begg patted the lad's shoulder. "Pyramus, I envy you. You have page after page of adventures ahead."

At midday, Sans-Serif and Esmeralda exchanged lumps of

salted bread. A woman knotted a *diklo*, a headscarf, around the bride's head.

Nothing more was required.

"It is done," Gideon Lakatos announced. "Now, we fill our bellies, drink, and dance until we are hungry and thirsty again."

Before anyone could respond, an earth tremor rocked the encampment, setting pots and pans clinking and clanking like a metallic round of applause.

"Aieee! A wonderful omen!" Ancient Lilith cackled. "Esmeralda and her *gadjo* will move mountains!"

The celebration commenced, boisterous and unrestrained.

In the midst of it, Sans-Serif took Begg aside and said, "I am grateful for that *diklo*. It covers her bald patches. She was feeling self-conscious."

"I noticed them," Begg said. "On the other women, too. Surely, they didn't engage in hand-to-hand combat with Klosterheim's thugs?"

Sans-Serif threw up his hands. "No, they did it to themselves. On the morning after we defeated the Iron Guard, while you were still in the mountains, the Tziganes mourned their dead. It was noisy. A lot of wailing and calling on the saints. The women ululated like wolves, slapped themselves, and pulled out clumps of hair. Then they all washed in the stream, tore up some clothes, and did something with knots on a length of rope. It was a strange and complicated ritual. I did not understand it. I am a Turk. Traditions in my country make sense."

"Such as the carrying of talismans to ward off the evil eye?" suggested Begg.

"Exactly!" Sans-Serif dug his fingers into his beard and gave it a tug. "Ay! Ay! But what a mess she made of that beautiful hair!"

"It will grow back. I am glad she has this happiness after the loss of her father. You make a fine couple."

Sans-Serif grinned, showing his long, unsightly teeth. "An unusual one, too. The Tziganes do not normally allow their women to marry a *gadjo*. I have Ancient Lilith to thank. She has declared me a *ray baro*."

"A great lord?"

The Turk rolled his bulging eye. If the other eye rolled, too, the squint hid it. "She has attributed to me far more power than I actually possess. She believes I am destined to improve the fortune of Tziganes throughout Eastern Europe."

Begg recalled his tarot reading.

All depends on the fall of the sword.

"I advise you to keep an open mind," he said. "Ancient Lilith has remarkable insight."

"Ridiculous!" Sans-Serif snorted. "I am just an intelligence officer. I have no political influence." He peered down. "Oof! Will you look at that? The music is making my legs twitch. I think I had better indulge them. Will you come and twirl around with my bride? She would find it amusing, I am certain. You foreigners dance like clowns."

"I had every intention of requesting the honour," Begg responded.

They joined the throng and danced a wild jig to the music of guitars, tambourines, drums, and fiddles. It would have been memorable even in Zenith's absence, but when the albino took up a violin and began to play, the Tziganes threw themselves into a frenzy of joy.

Sir Seaton Begg had rarely heard Zenith play anything but adagios, the most plaintive compositions. To discover he could also evoke such unbridled gaiety was astounding.

Spontaneously, the Tziganes formed a circle around Dancing Tabitha, and while Zenith played a slower tune, that beautiful young woman demonstrated why she was so named. An exquisite fusion of profoundly eloquent sound and motion.

From that enthralling interlude, Zenith launched into a passionate flamenco, but he could not maintain it. Halfway through, it grew excessive, the notes becoming subtly discordant, the rhythm imprecise and increasingly frantic. Begg knew his modern composers, and this was no Schöenberg or Ives—this was the brink of madness.

He grew alarmed for the albino. Uneasily, he studied the fixed expression on the alabaster face, the reckless glint in the crimson eyes.

Abruptly, Zenith put down the violin and plunged into the crowd. He shouldered through the revellers, with Begg following, though keeping his distance.

Violet Damm danced past, laughing in the arms of a delighted Gideon Lakatos. As she was whirled backward by the *vodja*, she stared after Zenith, and when Begg came alongside, threw him a glance of bemused concern. His mouth close to her ear, he murmured above the noise, "I don't know. Stay here."

Zenith moved between the wagons, out of the camp, and toward the river. He did not glance back.

Begg watched him settle on a short, goat-cropped natural lawn sloping down to the water. The detective hung back, loitering in the shade of an age-blackened oak.

Casually, the albino took his platinum case from a pocket, extracted a brown, opium-saturated cigarette, lit it on the flame of his silver Calibri, and started to smoke. He performed the actions in an abstracted manner, while he gazed at the swirling current.

Begg shuddered, suddenly frozen to his bones.

Zenith had not paid attention when selecting his cigarette. One of them differed from the rest. There was a little red band around it. Its tobacco was soaked in curare. It was the "death cigarette," intended for any situation from which escape was impossible.

Death rather than prison.

It might be in his hand now.

Begg hurried forward. Then he stopped. There was nothing he could do. Zenith had already drawn deeply, three times exhaling smoke. If it was toxic, he was already a dead man. Begg would not be able to save him.

The detective hesitated, then turned and strode back to the wedding party. If Zenith was going to collapse and convulse and spit foam, he would suffer those paroxysms with his privacy intact. No witnesses. That is how he would want it.

Ah! What that man had endured! Revisiting the scene of his peoples' massacre. Destroying the relic he was born to protect. Losing the ring that symbolised his authority. Abandoning the sword that connected him to his cultural history. Burying his father. Killing a woman he had once loved.

Begg sighed, and over the course of the next hour, had anyone looked into his eyes, they would have seen only anxiety and sadness.

Later, however, he spotted Zenith sitting by a fire, and though the albino had oft been an implacable enemy and would be again, the detective felt relieved. Such was the strangeness of their friendly, deadly compact.

The wedding celebrations lasted well into the night. The caravan, led by Gideon Lakatos, decamped at dawn, its depleted numbers bolstered by the addition of two *vardos*, nine men, and five women.

The little convoy travelled southwest without interruption. The Iron Guard was operating deep in the hinterland, where thinly dispersed government forces could not easily find them. Rather than pursue the more mobile Tziganes, they were focussing their despicable attentions on settled Jews.

Two days later, in the late afternoon, the wagons stopped on the outskirts of Constanța.

"We will continue south, following the coast," Lakatos told Begg and Sans-Serif. "In maybe a week, we shall be camped at the edge of Istanbul. Esmeralda will want to visit us." He addressed the Turk, "And you, Ray Baro, will surely want to bring us many nice things from the city."

Sans-Serif cleared his throat. "Um . . . yes, perhaps a bottle of raki?"

"Yes, a bottle each would be nice," said the *vadjo*. "I would also like a gramophone and some jazz music to play on it."

"Oh."

"And Ancient Lilith would certainly be grateful for a comfortable upholstered chair, to go in her wagon."

"Ah."

"Some other things. I have given Esmeralda a list."

Sans-Serif paled. He muttered an assurance and moved to join his wife, and Zenith, Violet Damm, and Sinclair, all saying their goodbyes.

Alone with Lakatos, Begg said, "On the day we joined you, Ancient Lilith told my fortune. I crossed her palm, but in retrospect, I feel the offering was insufficient. Take this, please, my friend, or I shall feel embarrassed." He handed the Tzigane a wad of high-denomination notes.

Without so much as a glance at them, Lakatos gave a nod and

slipped them into a pocket. He shook Begg's hand. "We will see you at Istanbul."

"No," the detective said. "I shall be gone by then."

Lakatos smiled. "I do not think so." He slapped Begg's shoulder and walked away.

Two hours later, the detective and his companions booked night passage to Istanbul. They had only four hours to wait, much of which they spent in an excellent restaurant.

After they had eaten, Zenith wandered off on his own, his manner introspective, wreathed in solitude.

"Keep your guard up," Damm said to Begg and Sinclair. "Your truce will not hold for much longer. You have both seen and learned too much. He wants to kill you. It is in his eyes."

"He will make no attempt until England," Begg said.

"Do not be so sure."

The albino rejoined them at the port but, after they boarded the steamer, took to his cabin. He did not emerge for the entirety of the eight-hour voyage.

The vessel docked at dawn.

The morning *adhan* echoed across the city: *"Hayya 'ala-s-Salah! Hayya 'ala-l-Falah! Assalatu khairum-minan-naum!"*

Rise up for prayer! Rise up for Salvation! Prayer is better than sleep!

"Take me back to the London muezzins, Begg," muttered Sinclair in a plaintive tone. "Rag and bone! Penny pies! *Evenin' Standard*! And not forgetting the Sally Army band on Sundays." After a moment of reflection, he added, "Of course, there's also the bloomin' bells of Saint Mary's. Maybe it's not so bad here."

"Everything's an intrusive noise until you get used to it," observed the detective.

Sinclair frowned, absorbing this.

They walked from the dock and made for a line of taxis waiting to serve the disembarking passengers.

"Your intentions, Begg?" Zenith asked.

"I still have a suite at the Shangri-La Hotel," the detective responded. "Will you join us there for breakfast?" He addressed the others. "The rest of you, too?"

They went in two taxis, Zenith with Sans-Serif and Esmeralda, Begg with Sinclair and Violet Damm.

"Here's a how-to-do," said the pathologist. "Aside from it obviously not being Sunday, I have not the foggiest idea of where we are in the week. Is it Wednesday? Monday? Christmas?"

"Don't ask me," Begg exclaimed. "I'm in the same boat. Keep your eyes peeled for a newspaper."

Damm clapped her hands. "How wonderful it is to live the life of a Gypsy, where time has no dominion."

At the Shangri-La Hotel, the manager sighed. "I didn't think you were coming back." His tone implied that he wished it were the case.

"I believe the rooms remain in my name for a day or two more?" said Begg.

"Three more. Your belongings have not been disturbed."

"Then my guests and I will take breakfast. Have it sent up, please."

"Six of you?"

"That is our number."

With the merest suggestion of a shrug, the manager acquiesced. As he took their order, he eyed Zenith's chalk-white skin, hair, eyebrows, and lashes. Roseate irises met the inspection with imperious disdain. The hotelier flinched and picked up the phone for the kitchen.

"After we have eaten," said Damm as the adventurers settled in Begg's lounge, "I must contact Temporal headquarters." She looked down at herself with a rueful expression. "I shall also need to tidy myself up."

"But you look perfectly marvellous, Miss Damm!" Sinclair exclaimed. He reddened. "That is to say . . . er . . ."

She laughed and blew him a kiss. "*Au contraire, mon chérie*, I look like a scarecrow."

"I must also report to my superiors," said Sans-Serif. "They know I have been travelling with foreigners. They probably think something dreadful has happened to me." He gave a lopsided smile and placed a hand on Esmeralda's arm. "I must also take my wife to see her new home."

Begg glanced at Zenith, who said nothing, his face inscrutable.

"Doctor Sinclair and I will attempt to find a silversmith named Gulvenkian Ogg." The detective opened a satchel and extracted an opal and the two dented halves of the *Salut Christi*. He placed them on a table. "We shall commission him to repair the chalice, if that is possible. Then, providing he is in a fit condition to do so, Major Nye will present it to President Kemal. Sans-Serif, I shall suggest that, when he does so, you accompany him."

The Turk gasped, his bulging eye opening wide. "Me? The president? But I . . . Why?"

"Because you are a good and loyal Turk, a credit to your country, and the most appropriate representative of our little band."

"Agreed," they all murmured, Zenith included.

"I . . . I . . . then, of course, I . . ." Sans-Serif turned helplessly to his wife. She grinned and clutched his hand.

Begg picked up the opal and held it to the light. "Undamaged. The black sword missed it." He clicked his tongue. "It is not a valuable stone in a lapidary sense. Nor geological. Only the dark spot—the inclusion—is of any interest. Do you see how it contains hints of unusual colours? How they alter when I move the stone?" He paused and frowned. "Odd. There is a slight mesmeric effect. Something . . ." His words tailed off.

"Begg?" asked Sinclair.

"Hmm? I don't know, Taffy. Probably nothing." The detective snapped out of what seemed a momentary trance. "Plenty of gemstones have an inclusion, of course, so it is not the presence of it that matters but, rather, what is claimed of it. The blood of Christ? How? It is nonsense. Yet, empires have haggled over it because they thought it true. Not only that, they believed it had some magical influence—one that Vera Pym meant to pervert with Sinclair's blood. Perhaps it is the peculiar effect of these colours that—"

A knock at the door interrupted. Breakfast arriving. The kitchen had been efficient. Esmeralda stood to grant entry.

Sinclair shuddered and raised fingers to his unsliced neck. "I suppose I should feel honoured that La Pym considered my type O sufficiently powerful."

Begg grunted. "The power was in the sacrilegious act rather than in your—" His mouth snapped shut.

Esmeralda had opened the door wide, stepping back to allow a trolley to be wheeled in by the waiter.

There was no trolley. There was no waiter.

Madam Melody stood on the threshold.

She opened her mouth to sing.

CHAPTER 34

The End of the Chalice

Begg acted without thinking. He threw the gemstone.

There came a second of a brain-liquefying tone before, as the windows webbed with cracks, the jewel shot across the room straight into Madam Melody's mouth.

She said, "Gump!"

Clawing at her throat with one hand, she staggered forward and raised an automatic with the other.

Esmeralda took a single step. Her fist came up in a perfect uppercut, straight to the point of Melody's jaw. A loud clack, the head rocked back, the knees gave way, and the singer fell flat on the floor.

The violent jangling in their ears faded to a stunned, transfixed silence.

Sans-Serif broke it. "My darling wife! Did you hurt your hand?"

"Yes, but I hurt her jaw more," Esmeralda said. "Is she a witch?"

"Yes, I think so."

"Definitely," Sinclair stated with conviction.

Begg crossed the room and squatted beside the fallen woman.

He felt her pulse, lifted her eyelids, and muttered, "Out for the count." He forced open her mouth and looked inside, pressed his fingers around her throat. "Good Lord! She swallowed the stone."

Zenith uttered a deep laugh.

Begg cast him an enquiring glance.

"I am wondering," said the laconic albino, "which is the most efficacious method of spiritual cleansing, dousing in sacrificial blood, or passing through an unwilling intestinal tract."

"Careful, she's coming around," Damm noted.

Begg said to Sinclair, "Find me something to secure her wrists. We must gag her, too. My ears are still hurting."

A few minutes later, Madam Melody was in a chair, hands tied behind her back, mouth secured, eyes glaring.

"Presumably," said Begg, looking down at her, "you had this hotel watched and were alerted as soon as we returned. Were you La Pym's reserve? Waiting in Istanbul to assassinate us, in the event that we escaped her?"

The platinum blond's nose wrinkled in an aggressive snarl.

Begg turned to Sinclair. "You'll have to take her to Doctor Matossian. Ask him to keep her under observation until the opal . . . um . . ."

"Reappears," the pathologist supplied.

Begg addressed Sans-Serif. "Might I call on you to accompany them? An official presence will be required to insist on the gag."

"I shall also organise a police guard," answered the Turk. "My wife can wait here?"

"Of course."

"And you, Begg," asked Zenith. "Will you now seek Gulvenkian Ogg?"

"Yes."

The albino pulled his tinted spectacles from his pocket and put them on. "Then I shall accompany you. Miss Damm, would you do me a very great service by coming along, too?"

"Me? Why?" she asked with raised eyebrows.

"You, like Sir Seaton, have been an enemy of mine for a very long time. I have it in mind that, when you and I next meet, we shall be in opposition once again. For the past few days, however, we have travelled, if not as friends, then at least as colleagues. You have assisted me through exceedingly taxing circumstances. I would have both you and Begg at my side as we bring the matter to its conclusion."

"You are sentimental, Monsieur Zenith?"

"Maybe so. It is an emotion with which I am unaccustomed. I find it . . . difficult. Your support would be—"

"You have it. I shall come."

As she turned away, she met Begg's eyes for an instant. A flicker. A signal passed:

Danger!

They departed the hotel, leaving Esmeralda to await their return. Begg did not tell the manager the windows in his suite were cracked. He would do so when he checked out. There would be further money to pay, another entry on his expense account for the Temporal Service to query.

Sans-Serif and Sinclair, with Melody between them, hailed a taxi and set course for the Surp Pirgiç Hospital.

Meanwhile, Begg, Damm, and Zenith purchased a bottle of raki from a shop across the street, then flagged down a vehicle and directed its driver to the Mevlanakapi neighbourhood. That, Begg recalled, was the location of the clubhouse which Gulvenkian Ogg frequented.

The journey was uneasy. The albino barely spoke, darkly brooding. Tension radiated from him. Begg imagined he could hear a clock ticking, counting down to the end of their truce.

At the Knights of Silver and Gold clubhouse, they were informed that Mr. Ogg was in his workshop, just two streets distant. They walked there in the shadow of the ancient Theodosian Walls. It was a warm, clear day, a promise of a hot summer to come.

The silversmith's was a long, low brick structure behind a row of shops on a fairly quiet street. The air warped and shimmered around a furnace in its yard. They saw Ogg as they approached. He was at a workbench, a little, wizened old man, not much taller than a child, with long white hair and a beaklike nose. He wore spectacles with lenses as thick as pebbles.

Entering the yard, Begg hailed him and made introductions.

"How might I help you, Sir Seaton?" Ogg enquired, glancing curiously at Zenith. "Are you a client? An old one, if so. I recognise you, and your name seems familiar, but cannot place you. When did you last draw on the talent of the remarkable Gulvenkian Ogg?"

"I have never done so, sir," said Begg. "You have mistaken me for another."

"But you?" Ogg asked the albino. "Surely—?" He put a hand to his neck as if it pained him.

"No," said Zenith.

"That is strange. Very strange. But I am old and full of memories. They are a jumble and often become confused."

Begg put the bottle of raki on the smith's workbench. "We would like to consult with you, if we may. Will you accept this gift in lieu of a few minutes of your time?"

"Ah! Most generous. I rarely touch the stuff but I shall not refuse it. I regret that I am not much of a conversationalist, but if there is information you require concerning silver, then I shall surely know it, for I am Ogg, and I am considered the finest artisan of the age. In what are you interested?"

"In an artefact known as the *Salut Christi*. Have you heard of it?"

"Yes, I have," said Ogg after a moment's thought. "An object of obscure legend. A silver chalice. It was supposedly crafted by a guild of alchemists here in Constantinople more than a thousand years ago. There is no credible evidence that either the guild or the chalice ever existed."

Begg drew the two semicircular pieces from his satchel. "I possess some such evidence." He placed them on the bench.

Ogg moved a portable wooden step into position, hopped onto it like a bird onto its perch, and leaned over the bent metal. He lifted one half and put it close to his face, examining every inch. He did the same with the other. For nearly five minutes he was absorbed and said nothing. They watched in silence.

Finally, he peered at Begg. "By the Prophet's beard! This is astonishing! It appears genuine. I have not seen such silver since I lived in Petrograd many years ago. Where on earth did you find it?"

"That," said Begg, "is a very long story. There is a more important consideration. Namely, can it be repaired?"

"No, not to pristine condition. Not even by I, the remarkable Ogg. You see this broken housing in the middle of the bowl? Once, it held—"

"We have the opal," Begg interrupted. "We can supply it in a day or so."

Ogg's eyes, made enormous by his lenses, widened dramatically. "Well, then . . . yes, I could repair it. But—"

"Sir Seaton," interrupted Violet Damm softly. "The von Beks are developing a regrettable habit."

The detective turned.

Zenith was behind the young woman, his left arm clamped around her neck, his right hand pressing an automatic to her temple.

Begg froze and exhaled.

"Monsieur—" he began.

"My word holds true." The albino's usually mellifluous voice was harsh. "Our truce is not broken. However, I have no such agreement with Miss Damm. I now give my word again. If you do not do exactly as I tell you, I will put a bullet through her head."

"No better than Klosterheim, then," said Begg, his tone derisive. "To think, I held you in some little regard."

Damm murmured, "Don't worry, Sir Seaton. I doubt he will hit anything vital. That I took my eyes off him long enough to allow this suggests a woefully empty skull."

"Gentlemen!" Ogg cried out. "This is my place of work, not a theatre. Leave the chalice with me. Certainly, I shall be delighted to repair it, and will do a better job than any other could offer. And due to its historical significance, I will happily waive any fee, for I long ago lost my desire for riches. But I must insist that you take your melodramatics to a more appropriate venue—"

"Mr. Ogg," Zenith interjected. "Attend to your furnace. Ensure its temperature is such that silver will be melted."

The old man straightened and put his fists to his hips. "I certainly will not be ordered about in my own—"

"Do you wish a corpse on your premises?"

"Do as he says, please, Mr. Ogg," murmured Begg.

Ogg scowled obstinately, then sniffed, sighed, and lowered himself from his step. "It seems that wherever I go, I must deal with barbarians. You are as bad as the Bolsheviks who ran me out of Russia many years ago." He crossed to the furnace and got to work.

Zenith addressed Begg. "When he tells us the furnace is ready, you will place both halves of the *Salut Christi* into it."

"Why?"

"Because it must end, Sir Seaton. This absurd reliance on the imagined significance of certain objects. Are we infants, that we disavow any culpability for the state of our lives? That we must credit—or blame—inanimate matter for our successes and failures?"

Begg gave a near imperceptible nod. "I understand and, indeed, share the sentiment, but this is not the time. If Herr Hitler's ambitions get out of hand, we need Turkey to stand with us, to oppose him, and put Germany at a tactical disadvantage. With the *Salut Christi*, we can gain President Kemal's trust. Without it, in the advent of war, this country may remain neutral—or worse."

"That is my point. To place reliance on—*Yes, Miss Damm! Reach for your gun, by all means!* Slowly, if you please. Draw it out with your fingertips. That's it. Now throw it aside. Good! Thank you. I strongly advise you to refrain from any further efforts. I am in no mood for games. I must see the chalice destroyed and will do so, even at the cost of your life."

Begg could see by his strained expression that the albino was committed to his course. Zenith was responsible for many murders, but he had no taste for killing women. Indeed, he liked and admired Violet Damm. There was no doubting, however, that he would now shoot her dead if provoked.

"Begg," said Zenith. "The Nazis have imbued the swastika with all their foul prejudices and twisted ambitions. With those horrible notions thus solidified, they feel no requirement to give them any further thought, no need to question them. They simply gaze fanatically upon the symbol, their minds in abeyance, and follow their insane leader blindly into Hell. The swastika! Which had previously represented auspiciousness and good luck. Which India reveres as a token of spirituality and divinity. What is it really? Simply an arrangement of straight lines! And you would resist it with what? A different arrangement? Do you not perceive the utter absurdity of it all?"

"I do," said Begg. "But when millions of innocent lives may be at stake—"

"Innocent lives have been at stake throughout history. Ever do they fall to some asinine and arbitrary conception. My people! Slaughtered because another line—an imaginary one of demarcation—shifted across their land. Because a certain component of rock that glistens attractively is assigned great value!"

Begg opened his arms, palms outward. "Again, I am in broad agreement. I do not think, however, that the destruction of the chalice will make any—"

"Change must start somewhere. Here, now, today!" Zenith's lips pulled back over his teeth. He appeared to struggle with fierce emotion, gained control of it, then in a less overwrought tone, continued, "My . . . my valued friend. Though I stand here with a gun to Miss Damm's head and a promise that she will die unless you destroy the chalice, I call upon the curious bond between us. I would ask a kindness of you."

A bark of laughter from the detective. "You really are quite extraordinary! Even to consider in these circumstances that I would—"

"Hear me out. Please."

Begg narrowed his eyes, his face grim, his fisted hands white at the knuckles. A moment, then he gave a curt nod.

"Shortly, our truce will end," the albino said. "We shall return to London and, inevitably, one of us will finish the other. Before that deadly battle begins, I ask that you write a detailed account of this affair. Istanbul, Roumania, Lamaneagra—all of it. And I request a guarantee. When I am no more—whether it be before or after your own regrettable demise—the story will be made public."

"That you be remembered?" Begg's voice held a faint trace of scorn.

"As a person? No, I do not care to be immortalised. I am but a fleeting thought, my personality, my existence, merely a figment of some other's imagination. But, if dreams have meaning, then so do my actions. That is what I would have recorded. Not what I am, but what I have done—what happened to my people, how I suffered, and how I responded. The truth of us is not in who we think we are. It is in what we do. I would have future generations know that I destroyed the *Salut Christi*. I would have them know that it is time to grow up and take responsibility."

For nearly two minutes, the detective said nothing. He stared at the albino. He saw the automatic press a little harder into Violet Damm's head. He felt Istanbul living and pulsating around him, built on the ruins of Byzantium, a mighty empire that destroyed and was in turn destroyed.

Gulvenkian Ogg broke the tense silence. "The furnace is at the required temperature, gentlemen. But please, the relic is of immense historical significance. I am a great silversmith. An artisan of unsurpassed talent. I beg you not to deprive me of this—"

Begg jerked up a palm to stop him.

To Zenith, he said, "I will do as you say, and pass my notes to my brother, Warwick. He will see to it that your actions are portrayed accurately albeit in fictionalised form in *The Septimus Blane*

Library. You realise, however, that his stories, while frequently based on my real cases, are generally derided as cheap fiction?"

Zenith gave a nod. "It does not matter. The account will survive into the future, and perhaps one day, when the world and its cultures are considered a little differently, the yarn will be reassessed. Do I have your word?"

"You do."

"Then you have my sincere gratitude." The albino paused, before adding, "I believe, Begg, that you may have helped me to . . . to gain something resembling a soul."

The metatemporal detective lifted both halves of the silver chalice and carried them to the furnace. As he threw them inside, Ogg wailed in anguish.

When Begg turned back, Violet Damm was standing alone. Monsieur Zenith the albino was gone.

CHAPTER 35
A Final Atrocity

The following morning, while Violet Damm communicated with London headquarters and Sabahattin Sans-Serif settled Esmeralda into her new home, Begg and Sinclair visited Major Nye at the Surp Pirgiç Hospital.

"Great heavens!" exclaimed Doctor Matossian, as they stepped into his office. "You both appear to be in good shape. Is something wrong? Would you like me to smack you over the head with a hard object?"

"We intend to forgo further injuries if we can manage it," said Begg with a rueful smile. "I must confess, I am surprised to find you in good humour. The attack on the nursing home was—"

"An outrage. I assign no blame to you. If anything, you came to the rescue. By God, Sir Seaton! When they catch the Red King, I hope he hangs!"

"He was a she, Doctor, and she got what she deserved. There will be no further assassinations in Istanbul."

"A woman? Good Lord! Dead?"

"Dead. How are the patients?"

"Major Nye will make a full recovery. As for your prisoner, she is, if you will pardon the indelicacy, probably feeling somewhat relieved. I was informed five minutes ago that the gemstone has passed out of her system. What would you like me to do with it?"

"Throw the damned thing in the Bosphorus," said Begg. "It is worthless and nothing but trouble."

Matossian reacted with surprise. "Then why was she brought here? There was no medical issue. The stone is not large. She could have—"

"A change of circumstances. We thought we would require the gem. Now, we do not. After we visit the major, we will take her off your hands."

"Very well. Nye remains bedbound, but you can see him. I shall treat Madam Melody to a final examination and have her made ready for you."

They found Nye in ill temper.

"They refuse me my cigarettes," he grumbled. "And I have nothing to read. I am bored rigid. So—report! Have you recovered the chalice? What of the Red King?"

Pulling up chairs, Begg and Sinclair sat beside the bed. The detective gave a concise account, with occasional interjections from his friend, of all that had occurred since the attack on the hospital. When he finished, Nye glared at him, plainly furious.

"Worse than a failure. I should have you shot."

"There were no options. Had I tried anything, Zenith would have killed Violet Damm. The Sisterhood of Solitude would not respond well to such a loss."

"For God's sake! The Sisterhood? It's a bloody myth!"

"You know that's not true."

Nye's fingers dug into his bedsheets. "Besides, she was working for the Temporal Service and is perfectly aware of the code. So are you. Agents must always be prepared to lose their lives. You should have jumped the albino. He is a common thief and a traitor."

"There has never been anything common about his thefts, Major, and you cannot accuse him of treason, for he is not English and no longer has a country of his own to betray."

"Pah! You fool! You have lost us an opportunity to ally with Turkey. Your blundering could cost us the war."

"There is no war."

"There will be."

"And you seriously think that a small silver bowl could have averted it?"

"It does not matter what I think. It matters what the Turks believe, whether it be true or not." Nye put his hands together and cracked his knuckles. "Leave it with me. I shall have this Ogg fellow make us a copy."

"And deceive the president? What if Kemal later learns the truth?"

"He won't. Only Ogg will know. He's very old, you say? Easy enough to remove."

Begg recoiled. "You would have an elderly man murdered?"

"For security."

"No, Major. I cannot allow that. There have been quite enough deceptions and assassinations in Istanbul. I shall have the National Security Service arrange for Mr. Sans-Serif and I to meet with the president. We will tell him the whole sorry story."

"Absolutely not. I forbid it. You are removed from the case with immediate effect. Go home. Find yourself a common robbery to investigate."

Begg rose and smoothed the creases out of his jacket. "You

are not on active duty, sir. You cannot issue orders. As a matter of fact, I am currently acting head of the Turkish Bureau. My decision stands."

"Begg—"

"Good day. I wish you a speedy recovery."

"Begg! Come back here. At once! Begg, if you—"

His voice faded behind as Begg and Sinclair exited the room and passed along the corridor.

Sinclair pushed back his thinning hair. "He could cause you a lot of trouble with the Temporal Service."

"In this time and realm, perhaps, but in others—?" He shrugged. "Besides, it rather depends on Kemal and how he responds to our account."

They crossed the hospital to the wing where Madam Melody was held. Yesterday, she had been left with a four-man police guard. The constables had strict instructions to keep her gagged except at meal times, when they must be ready to knock her on the head with a truncheon should she attempt to sing.

Now, as Begg and Sinclair pushed through double swing doors, it was immediately apparent that something had gone wrong. Farther along, by another set of identical doors, nurses were milling about, some in an obvious state of disorientation. The square windows in the doors were shattered, glass granules scattered all over the floor.

"Oh no," Begg muttered, and hurried forward. He grabbed a porter by the arm. "When did it happen?" The man pointed to his bleeding ear and shook his head.

The detective opened the doors, and with Sinclair at his heels, entered a scene of destruction. A trolley of medical equipment had overturned, someone having fallen against it. Amid the scattered tools and metal bedpans, three nurses slumped, gasping in agony, hands pressed against their ears, blood seeping between their fingers. Beyond them, beside the open door to another room, two policemen lay dead, gore running from every facial orifice.

In the room, much worse. Two more policemen, two nurses, and a doctor, all dead.

The doctor was Matossian.

Begg hissed through his teeth and bent over the corpse. He used his thumbs to close the eyelids, then gazed miserably at the familiar, good-natured face. "I am so sorry, old fellow. You exemplified everything for which Turkey is striving. This should not have happened."

"Begg," Sinclair said quietly. "It only just did. The trail is fresh. We might catch her."

Begg straightened and nodded. "Do you have your weapon?"

"Yes."

They exited the room. Since Madam Melody had not passed them, they knew she had gone the other way along the corridor. They hurried down it, and as they went, Begg rapidly questioned the confused-looking hospital staff. Some had seen the fleeing woman. A picture emerged. Melody had run along here, turned that way, raced to the doors, gone through, slowed to a walk so as to not attract attention, made for that exit, and stepped out into the grounds.

Fewer witnesses there, but a couple of footmarks, and the trail led to a gate and out onto a street.

From there, not a trace.

Madam Melody, the only surviving member of the Red King gang, had made a murderous escape.

"She will leave Istanbul by the fastest possible means," said

Begg. "We will go at once to Sans-Serif. He can have the ports, roads, and airport watched. I fear it will be useless."

It was. Three days passed with no sign of her.

"She is out of the country, I am convinced of it," the Turk concluded when he, Esmeralda, and Violet Damm joined Begg and Sinclair for dinner at the Pera Palas Hotel. The detective and his assistant had moved back there after being unceremoniously ejected from the Shangri-La—the cracked windows, the final straw. Begg paid well over the odds for repairs, but the manager stood firm, predicting that the establishment would collapse to rubble if they remained.

"I have alerted headquarters," said Damm. "She has been added to the Most Wanted list. I will instruct our agents in this part of the world to keep their eyes peeled. Or do I mean ears?"

"*You* will?" queried Begg.

She displayed the gap between her upper incisors with a wide grin. "I forgot to tell you. You are relieved of duty. They have made me the new Six A. I am Sir Vivian Clarke's successor."

Begg exclaimed, "That's marvellous!"

Sinclair wagged a finger at her. "When you move into your new office, have that confounded radio equipment removed. It's not reliable."

"Don't worry, Taffy. I shall soon have the place shipshape."

She winked and touched the red rose tattoo on her inner wrist. Begg and Sinclair understood. Metatemporals were not inclined to maintain permanent postings. The Sisterhood of Solitude would soon find her bigger fish to fry. Six A was strictly for the short term.

"Congratulations, Miss Damm," said Sans-Serif. "I am delighted. We shall continue to work together. I have always enjoyed contact with foreigners. They make a wonderful contribution to the life and soul of this great city."

Begg and Sinclair gaped.

The Turk turned to the detective. "I also have news, Sir Seaton. The Millî Emniyet Hizmeti requested an emergency meeting with the president. He has granted us an hour of his time the day after tomorrow."

"What is it," muttered Sinclair, "that politicians fail to comprehend about the word 'emergency'?"

Sans-Serif angled his bulging eye at the pathologist. "He will be in Istanbul on that day. The alternative is ten hours on a train to Ankara, arriving there just as he departs for here."

"Ah! I keep forgetting that Istanbul is no longer the capital."

Begg said, "Very well. We will cool our heels in the city for a little longer."

"My wife and I would also like to extend an invitation. Her family is now encamped to the west of the city. Since our wedding celebrations were cut short, we intend to visit them—"

"Cut short?" Sinclair interjected. "We were eating, drinking and dancing from dawn until long past midnight!"

Esmeralda, sitting next to him, prodded his arm. "Silly man! It should have lasted a week!"

Begg, having already said goodbye to Gideon Lakatos and his band was disinclined to repeat the experience. However, it would be impolite to refuse. Besides, here was a chance for mischief.

"We gladly accept," he said. "I expect you will need us to help carry all the gifts you have for them."

The Turk grabbed his full glass of wine and emptied it in a single swallow.

Turning to Violet Damm, Esmeralda said, "You will come, too, of course?"

"I regret that I cannot," Damm answered. "I must travel to

London, there to brief and be briefed. I have a berth on the *SS Winchester*. It sails tonight. In fact, I should say goodbye now. I have to pack."

"For how long will you be in Blighty?" Sinclair enquired.

"Hours rather than days."

"Then we won't see you on our return?"

"No, dear friend, we shall not meet again." She quirked an eyebrow. "Until the next adventure."

"Guns loaded, Miss Damm."

"Always!"

The next day, Gideon Lakatos gleefully accepted fifteen bottles of raki; a wind-up gramophone; records by Gershwin, Rodgers and Hart, Duke Ellington, Louis Armstrong, Count Basie, and Benny Goodman; an upholstered chair; bag after bag of brand-new clothes selected by Esmeralda; and, from Begg, a large box of Cuban cigars.

To get it all to the camp, Sans-Serif had rented a small truck.

"I need a promotion," he complained. "Only days married and already I am—what is the expression?"

"Stony broke," Sinclair supplied.

If the Turk's woes were real, they were soon swept away, for the next hours were filled with merriment.

The meeting with the president occurred late the following afternoon, which was fortunate, as it gave them the morning to recover.

It was two very smartly dressed men who were ushered into the presence of Mustafa Kemal. One was tall, rangy in build, with steely blue-grey eyes. The other possessed mismatched limbs, a hunched back, a bald head, a big beard, and a bulging eye. They were received with equal politeness and charm, gestured into chairs, served with drinks, and listened to with rapt attention.

Sir Seaton Begg recounted the history of the chalice, ancient and very recent. He described Lamaneagra and its terrible fate. He cleverly obscured the role played by Zenith, for he had promised to keep it concealed until the albino was dead.

Sabahattin Sans-Serif told the story of the Red King and her assassination campaign.

Together, though unrehearsed, they wove a spellbinding tale of fanaticism, greed, cruelty, murder, and faith. President Kemal did not interrupt. Frequently, his eyes widened, and it seemed he might ask a question or even utter an exclamation of horror, but always he restrained himself and allowed them to continue.

When they were done, he asked them to explain again the supposed nature of the *Salut Christi*'s influence. He knew some of it, of course, for he had months ago been informed what it was, what power was attributed to it, and that Britain and France and their allies intended for it to be returned to Istanbul.

Now, he frowned. "I am a man of a practical nature, messieurs. I see what must be done and I work to achieve it. I have no time for the supernatural. Conversely, I recognise the persuasiveness of symbols. The *Alti Ok*—six arrows—of the Republican People's Party, for example. Curious, is it not, that everything I intend for my country is represented by those six arrows—and you meant to offer me eight." He smiled. "The *Salut Christi* is, or was, more than we need."

After a pause, he said, "I am interested to hear your thoughts concerning Chancellor Hitler and events in Germany, Sir Seaton."

The detective shared them.

After some further questions, Kemal said, "You have given me much to think about. I thank you. Now, if you will excuse me, I would like to speak in private with Mr. Sans-Serif. My secretary will see you to a lounge and provide you with whatever refreshments you prefer."

Begg stood, bowed, murmured, "It has been an honour, sir," and departed.

An hour later, Sans-Serif joined him. The Turk looked shocked. He was trembling. His mouth worked but he was unable to articulate.

"What is it?" Begg asked, stepping forward to offer a steadying hand. "What has happened?"

Sans-Serif gulped and stammered, "He has . . . he has just . . . just made me his chief advisor to the minister of foreign affairs."

Begg laughed so hard that tears came to his eyes. He took his friend's hand and pumped it vigorously. "I cannot think of a better man for the job!"

Later, on their way back to the hotel, the Turk said, "This in confidence. If war comes, Kemal will seek to keep Turkey neutral. However, he also told me that, should a situation arise where neutrality becomes problematical for this country, it is highly likely that he will declare against Germany."

"That," said Begg, "is at least something."

Twenty-four hours later, Sir Seaton Begg and Sinclair stood at the stern of a large passenger steamer and watched the spires and minarets of Istanbul fade into the distance.

"Taffy, I am not convinced that we have achieved anything."

"We know a lot more about Monsieur Zenith than we did before."

"Which has only made him more determined to kill me. Our duel has, in the past, been almost playful. Now, there will be no quarter given."

Sinclair nodded toward the receding city. "Also, we have left Turkey in a better state than we found it. The Red King's reign of terror is finished. Foreign workers can assist in modernisation without fearing for their lives. And we have given the president food for thought."

"Yes, there is that. I believe he may be one of the most important leaders of our times. If he takes to heart what I said concerning the power of symbols, much of which, I freely admit, I borrowed from Zenith, then perhaps he will have a positive influence not just in Turkey but upon the world's stage." The detective looked to the east, where the sun was flaring red as it nestled into the horizon. "He may be just the man to persuade other leaders to leave history in the past, where it belongs. Ah! What a world we would have if they all took up his slogan and modelled the future upon it."

"His slogan?"

"Yurtta sulh, cihanda sulh."

Peace at home, peace in the world.

Epilogue

Typical of the London midsummer season, the weather was hot and humid. With characteristic recklessness, Monsieur Zenith the albino now resided in an apartment overlooking Dorset Square, a few minutes' walk from Sir Seaton Begg's Sporting Club Square premises. He had, however, seldom emerged from it since his return to London.

Reclining on a divan, he smoked one of his opium cigarettes and raised to the light the glittering fire opal from the *Salut Christi*. Everyone concerned with its retrieval was either dead or had dismissed it as worthless. It had been easily, though surreptitiously, acquired during an unannounced and undetected nocturnal visit to the Surp Pirgiç Hospital.

He gazed into its dark core and allowed drug-induced visions to envelop him.

The strangely formed, vividly coloured, and impossibly tall towers of a bizarre city spiralled into an alien sky. He rode on the back of a dragon, lifted by a fragrant wind, and soared above an endless sea, his long white hair whipping around his face. He trod shimmering paths from world to world, each realm a slight variation of the other. He reclined on a divan in a sorcerous realm and dreamed of Zenith reclining on a divan in a London apartment.

"This object has no meaning," he whispered. "It is a crude gemstone with no power or value. It is merely . . . a memento."

A soft knock at the door.

Frank Oyani entered and bowed.

"Excellency, a package has been delivered. I found it on the doorstep."

Zenith made a nonchalant, dismissive gesture, only vaguely aware of his faithful retainer.

"Wrong address," he slurred. "Hand it in at the post office next time you go. And Oyani, you know better than to bother me with such trivialities."

"It is addressed specifically to you, Excellency."

With a frown, Zenith sat up. "What did you say?"

Oyani repeated himself.

"Armagnac," said the albino, grinding his cigarette into an ashtray. "To the brim."

A filled tumbler was handed over. Zenith gulped the liquor.

"Show me."

Oyani placed a little parcel on a low table. The package was not much bigger than a matchbox, wrapped in brown paper. A label bore the words MONSIEUR ZENITH and the address.

"If it is a bomb," the albino drawled, "it is a very tiny one."

He set down the gemstone, lifted the parcel, and unwrapped a small black jeweller's box. Snapping it open, he saw a card upon which was written:

THAT YOU MAY CARRY IT ALWAYS, AS FATE DICTATES. S. B.

Zenith removed the card to reveal beneath, mounted on white velvet, a black zirconium tie clip. It was fashioned in the shape of a broadsword with runes engraved along its blade. Set into the pommel, a tiny ruby.

Zenith murmured, "Pack our things, Oyani. We are discovered. We must relocate."

His servant bowed and left the room.

The albino put down the box.

For almost two minutes, he stared into space, his alabaster features unreadable. Then he crossed the room and lifted his violin from its case.

After a moment of contemplation, he put the instrument to his chin and began to play the initial melancholy bars of Enuscu's first composition, "Poème Roumain."

A romantic might imagine the glint of tears in his dreaming red eyes.

The End

RAISING READERS
Books Build Bright Futures

Dear Reader,

We'd love your attention for one more page to tell you about the crisis in children's reading, and what we can all do.

Studies have shown that reading for fun is the **single biggest predictor of a child's future life chances** – more than family circumstance, parents' educational background or income. It improves academic results, mental health, wealth, communication skills, ambition and happiness.[1]

The number of children reading for fun is in rapid decline. Young people have a lot of competition for their time. In 2024, 1 in 10 children and young people in the UK aged 5 to 18 did not own a single book at home.[2]

Hachette works extensively with schools, libraries and literacy charities, but here are some ways we can all raise more readers:

- Reading to children for just 10 minutes a day makes a difference
- Don't give up if children aren't regular readers – there will be books for them!
- Visit bookshops and libraries to get recommendations
- Encourage them to listen to audiobooks
- Support school libraries
- Give books as gifts

There's a lot more information about how to encourage children to read on our website: **www.RaisingReaders.co.uk**

Thank you for reading.

---

[1] National Literacy Trust, Book Ownership in 2024, November 2024
https://nlt.cdn.ngo/media/documents/Book_ownership_in_2024

[2] OECD. 2021. 21st-century readers: developing literacy skills in a digital world. Paris, France: OECD Publishing.
https://www.oecd.org/en/publications/21st-century-readers_a83d84cb-en.html

BRINGING NEWS FROM OUR WORLDS TO YOURS...

Want hot-off-the-press info about the latest and greatest SFF releases?

Look no further than the Gollancz newsletter! Your one-stop shop for news, updates, discounts and exclusive giveaways.

Sign up now:

@gollancz